She blinked, and the wounded air was gone. The rattle of the train, the babble of voices, felt like silence. The day had gone unsteady though, even here.

"A wind's coming, I think. A bad one." Philippa knew it was worse than that, but the whirlwind was what mattered now.

"Kid get spells like this often?" a guy sitting just forward of the door asked.

"Weather witch," Chick told him flatly. "A good one." Karl nodded confirmation.

On her knees now, Philippa searched the passing fields for any forerunners of the wind. Her spine ached and crawled from trying to read the chaos.

A light breeze curled across the fields, and a flock of the blackbirds scattered at the bending of the weeds. "Feel that?" Philippa said. "Smell it?" She glanced around at her friends and the skeptical faces beyond them. "Kinda stale?"

"Don't smell nothing. Don't see nothing," the doubting guy said. He cocked his head to one side. "I hear another train coming. But this stretch is all double track."

Now that the fellow had pointed it out Philippa could hear it rumbling to meet them. Something odd about the sound, though, a whine that set her teeth on edge.

Chick went white. "Hellfire! Ain't y'all never heard a twister?"

A Wind
Out of Canaan

Book One
of
Away Yonder

Sally Gwylan

A portion of this book was published in shorter form in the March 2003 edition of *Asimov's Science Fiction* under the title "In the Icehouse."

ISBN: 978-0-9853682-1-0

Published by
Bird's Nest Press
Correo, NM

In memory of Iva Lucas Turner of
Havana, Arkansas,
1898-1981,
a tough, generous soul

On Jordan's stormy banks I stand,
And cast a wishful eye,
To Canaan's fair and happy land
Where my possessions lie.
Oh, the transporting rapt'rous scene
That rises to my sight;
Sweet fields arrayed in living green
And rivers of delight.

—"Sweet Prospect"
words by Samuel Stennett, 1787

Part One

1

An icy gust smacked into her a couple of steps beyond the shelter of the trees. Philippa cringed from its bite, wrapping the stolen jacket tighter around her ribs. A hiss and yammer of wind filled her ears beneath her watch cap, gnawing at her nerves—a wrong wind, almost an angry wind though, cold as she was, she couldn't settle on what made her feel so.

Below on the lake's near shore a weathered building was hunkered down, half-dug into the slope, its tin roof streaked with the glittering, smoking snow. Philippa ducked her head and started kicking her way downhill towards it. Christ Jesus let it be the ice house the jungle was hid away inside of, she thought in dull misery, like that older kid had told her about before he'd jumped down to wait on a rattler heading south.

Where she could've been heading too, but there'd seemed no call then to swap trains. That morning in the Duluth rail yards the air had been no more than October-brisk, on the warmish side if anything. Clear sky, and none of the grumbling ache along her bones that generally told her a storm was due. Mile on clicking mile had gone by, and just when a body'd figure the day would be at its warmest she'd started seeing a dusting of white over the stump-jagged countryside.

Maybe that or the growing cold had led the handful of other boes to drop off at Shugan—all but the old man she hadn't paid much attention to, sleeping off a drunk on the car's dirty floor.

But he'd roused. Soon as they'd left Shugan's empty dairy barns behind the old stew bum'd sidled up to her with his stink and his whiskery grin and the want dark as a coal pit in his yellowed eyes. When the freight stopped to take on water, she'd slipped under the guy's arm and hit the snowy ground running, and never mind the place looked like the backside of nowhere.

First water tower west of Shugan, she'd been told. Follow the path through the band of woods to the ice house, and you'd be set. But if there was woodsmoke rising from the place the wind snatched it away before her watering eyes could note it.

The train's hoarse whistle cut through the hissing wind: once; twice. Philippa jerked at the sound, but kept going. The rumble of the freight pulling out reached her through her numbing feet. At least it was taking the old man with it; gone in the way of trains, and thank Jesus for that.

Unless he'd got off and followed her. Dizzy from the new pulse of fear, she half-turned to look behind her and fell, up to her elbows in powdery stuff. Nothing but trees and blowing snow. Philippa gulped cold air, shivering hard as she got again to her feet. It was only the strange wind spooking her.

At last the double doors of the ice house loomed overhead, wide enough for a flatbed Ford truck. There'd been a covered loading shed here once, but all the boards and roofing were gone, the bare framework offering no shelter at all, nor any sign anybody'd been here in years. Maybe, she thought as the cold bit down all the worse now she was stopped, the whole thing about a jungle for kids where there was always food was nothing but a campfire yarn, like the exploits of One-Hand Jack or that song about hens laying soft-boiled eggs and such.

Philippa drew in a sobbing breath. This was the place; it had to be. Even if it wasn't, if she could only get inside she'd manage until tomorrow. An upper corner of one of the doors leaned out a little, loose from its hinge. She scraped a little snow away and kicked hard at the door, hoping to rotate it enough to scramble inside. The only thing the blow did was knock snow further down into the roomy depths of her rubber boot. She had a distant feeling that her toes ought to hurt from it.

Dropping to her knees she put her right shoulder to the door, straining against the planks. Her boots scrabbled for purchase in the snow; found enough to keep pushing. The door yielded no more than the building's stone foundation might have. Panting, head leaned up against the wood, her eyes strayed up to the heavy bar above her head, finding the metal fixtures that held it in place: solid brackets, two to each door and one on either side. A padlock too, rusty but intact, secured the bar. Understanding sank in slowly. Whatever had put this ice farmer and his dairyman neighbors out of business, the lousy post-War farm prices she'd heard about her whole life or the Crash itself, his doors still held.

Philippa's strength ran out of her like the sweat from a breaking fever; she crouched in the snow and lashing wind, shivering, gasping in lungfuls of burning air. She should've stuck it out on the train, stew bum or no. A panicky nausea swept through her at the memory of the man's grabbing hands, followed by shame and despair.

You had to be tough to get by on the road, to be able to do whatever you had to. All the kids knew that. Get wise, the older girls said, and whoring seemed to work fine for them. But she couldn't. The thought made her sick, or blind angry, or worse. There'd been a few times a fellow had cornered her, and then the world would go away for awhile. She'd come back to herself on some main stem miles away, walking the cracked pavement like she had someplace to get to.

This time the world might really go away. The wind that sucked warmth from her, that hunted along the building's edge and mumbled constantly in her ears, gave no sign that it would die down with the night. Folks said freezing was an easy way to go, but so far it didn't feel easy at all.

"Chump. Stupid frill," Philippa muttered, her voice slurred by cold-stiffened lips. "Get up! Get moving!" The words didn't unlock her muscles. Being huddled low to the ground at least made her a smaller target. Rage tightened her throat. "Coward. Goddamn gutless coward," she whispered, shivering.

Thunder cracked and rolled away across the sky. Shocked to her feet by the sound, Philippa looked wildly around. What was it they said about thunder in a snowstorm? Something bad, but she couldn't recollect just what it was.

At least she was up and moving. Defiant, she faced into the teeth of the wind, to work her way lakeward along the wall.

The ice chute hatch, halfway along the side of the building that faced the lake, was pretty near buried by a snowdrift. Both hinges were torn out of the wall, and the small door sat a little crooked in its opening. On her knees again, Philippa dug frantically, trying to protect her numb hands with the long sleeves of the chore jacket. When she had a space clear in front of it, she rocked the door up and to the side.

Ducking through the low doorway, she stood cautiously, her head rising into the still darkness. Used to the snow glare outside, she couldn't see a thing beyond the rectangle of light at her feet. People were here, though; she could smell woodsmoke laced with a hint of coffee and stew—food, just like she'd been told. Dizzy with relief and sudden hunger, Philippa braced herself against the rough wood of the wall.

"Come in, brother, and get warm," a voice rang out, echoing in the huge space, a girl's voice with a rolling, musical accent Philippa couldn't place. The sound of it, the welcome, brought new tears to her eyes.

"Yeah," a rougher voice added. "Welcome, brother, and shut the goddamn door!"

Wearily Philippa turned to crouch on the wooden planks of the ice chute, wrestling the hatch into place. With some effort she got it settled so no more than a light breeze whistled around its edges. Just being out of the wind was a great relief. It was funny, though, how the feel of the unseasonable storm stayed with her, like it had got down inside her, humming in her chest. Like she was in the center of the storm.

Thunder cracked again, and she jumped. Still she waited until she could see the faint outlines of the chute running down to an uneven floor. Somebody below said something, words she couldn't catch, and somebody else laughed. Fear froze her in place a moment longer; but she was used to that. Nothing so familiar would keep her from the fire.

She shuffled down the steep chute to the center of the space, her numb feet as clumsy as lumps of mud. Slowly her eyes adjusted to the light that filtered in through small vents up under the eaves.

The ice house was cave-like and shadowy, big as a dry goods warehouse and a good two stories high now she was down inside it. Sawdust was everywhere, packed beneath her feet into a cushioned aisle, piled randomly on every side. The space showed signs of having been divided into walled bays but, like the loading shed outside, most of the partitions had got stripped away. One at the back of the ice house had been built up to make a good-sized shanty; a short length of stovepipe stuck out above it, spilling smoke into the upper reaches of the building. A rough ceiling rested on what looked to be the beams of the old loading platform, though she couldn't see a sign of the doors she'd tried to enter—boarded over, must've been. Otherwise daylight would show where that one door hung loose.

A shudder took her. She could've died no more than fifty feet from safety.

Determinedly she set off down the aisle. Down here the air smelt mostly of pine resin and mold and something unfamiliar that tickled her nose like old axle grease, something that was more a feel to the air than a regular smell. Off to her left was a shadowy heap of busted-up old machinery and stuff, piled halfway to the roof in places. It wasn't until she passed it that she saw a smaller shanty had been cobbled together practically in the middle of the junk pile. Or maybe the junk had got piled up later? Funny thing to do anyways. Neither smoke nor voices marked the place as occupied, so she went on.

A flicker caught the corner of her eye from near the odd shanty's further wall, gone before she could swing around to spot what made it. A scurrying rat, maybe, though her mind had tagged it more as light than movement.

Philippa shrugged. Whatever it'd been was nothing for her to fret about now. Drawn by the promise of warmth and stew, she pushed aside the ragged blanket that shrouded the door into camp, and stepped through.

2

*S*quinting, Chick examined the sleeping dog he'd been whittling. Something about how the head tucked into the body made the poor thing look like its back was busted, or so it seemed in what light made it through the temporary gaps in the ceiling. Disgusted, he snapped shut his jackknife and stuck both dog and knife deep in his coat pocket. He lay back on the sawdust piled up against the stone foundation of the ice house. Come tomorrow morning he could take a better look. If the carving was as lousy as he thought, he'd toss it in the oil drum that served the camp as a stove. Wasn't nothing but a chunk of firewood to start with, anyhow.

He looked around camp for the newcomer that Mara, the bossy, foreign-talking cook, had yelled a welcome to some minutes back. All he saw was the same faces he'd been looking at all day, a few younger than him and none much older, excepting Zeno, of course. Zeno was thirty-one, and his clown's sad-eyed face showed every bit of it. Given that gangs of road kids generally didn't feel too kindly towards jockers, the two of them wouldn't have stopped here at all, only that freak blizzard had blown up out of nowhere this morning. It'd been take their chances in this out-of-the way road-kid jungle or turn into icicles in the boxcar. Oklahoma got some humdinger snowstorms on occasion, but not like this one. If this was winter in Minnesota, as far as he was concerned you could keep it and the whole upper Midwest as well.

Trouble was, Zeno had his mouth set for spending the winter in Chicago. He had cousins there he swore would put them up. Dubious, Chick eyed his jocker across the dim space.

The Greek was bent thoughtfully over the makeshift checkerboard, his balding head nodding close to that of the kid he was playing.

Chick's gut twisted. Karl, the kid was called. Green-eyed as a cat and good-looking with it, in spite of a haircut so short he must've just suffered a delousing at some mission. The guy had a frill he was paired up with—Betts, the blondie with the bad cold—and so was an unlikely punk. Knowing that didn't help Chick's feelings any.

Looking around, Chick saw he wasn't the only one watching. Junkyard Johnny, the tough kid from Joliet, had his eyes on them as well, or at least on Zeno. Nothing friendly in that look at all, at all.

Sooner they hightailed it out of here, the better.

Zeno's hand darted out, moving a bottle cap. He looked up, catching Chick's eye just for a moment but the sudden heat of it burned down into Chick. Restlessly he shifted, leaning forward to rest his elbows on his knees and incidentally covering the evidence of his response, should anybody—that Junkyard guy, for instance—be looking.

Motion at the blanket-hung doorway caught his eye. No surprise: the newcomer was another kid, awful young to be traveling on his own. If he was, but nobody else followed him into camp. A snow-dusted watch cap was pulled down tight over his ears, but his back was straight and his chin stuck out defiantly.

Her chin. Maybe. Chick studied the reddened, pug-nosed face, trying to figure it out. Whichever it was, the kid had guts.

"Yuns got room for another body in here?" The drawn-out Southern vowels fell easy on Chick's ears, familiar as home, though the accent was more mountain folk than hill country. And still Chick wasn't sure whether the kid was a girl, or a boy whose voice hadn't got around to changing.

"Sure," said the runty kid who was Junkyard Johnny's sidekick. He yawned and waved a negligent hand at the camp. Nip, they called him. He was even younger than the newcomer. "Pull up some sawdust."

The cook's pal, redheaded Lukas, propped himself up on one elbow. "Here is room for everyone." Bohunks, Zeno had said he thought they was, Hungarians or maybe Czechs. All relaxed this fellow acted, but he'd been watching the door the whole afternoon, just like Mara had. Waiting for someone.

"Appreciate it," the new kid muttered, stumping frozen-footed across the packed floor to the stove. He—no, it was definitely she—must have felt Chick's stare, because she turned her head to face him, the dark eyes defiant once more.

Black as hell those eyes were, with a spark like a drowning child somewhere way far down inside them. Chick found he was on his feet without knowing how he'd come to get up. He was a good head taller than the girl, who couldn't be much more than twelve. Feeling foolish, he asked, "Hey, bo, whereabouts you from?"

"Mansfield, Arkansas," she answered him warily, sniffling. She wiped her nose on a sleeve. "South of Fort Smith. You heard of it?"

He had to shake his head. "Nope. I come from over to Davis, in Oklahoma, as much as I'm from anywhere. But mostly I claim Chickasha." It was an old joke, but without his name attached, it didn't mean much.

She nodded, acknowledgment but nothing more. When he didn't say anything further, she walked on.

Slowly Chick sat again on the piled sawdust. Her eyes weren't black, of course, but a deep brown like those of his Momma's people, which was maybe why they'd affected him so strong. She was just another girl, even if she was more self-possessed than most. He sighed, still feeling like a fool.

Mara the cook had paused in her onion-chopping to talk to her. The girl dumped potatoes from her jacket pockets onto the floor by the crate that served as a table, a pathetically small pile of them, but you always brought something to a jungle if you could. Nobody liked a freeloader.

A body settled on the sawdust close beside him.

Zeno, Chick found to his startlement. The Greek was bent over, fiddling with his shoelaces. "You out of the running already? How'd you manage to lose to that chump?" Chick asked.

Zeno shrugged. "*Hyesse*, I let the kid win. Only one here who's any good is little Nipio there." He nodded toward the runt, and then grinned at Chick, but there was a curl to his lip and doubt in his eyes. "I just got lonely, hey?"

He'd seen all that stuff with the new kid; of course he had. Though he had a rough tongue when he got riled, Zeno was a good jocker. He never raised a hand to Chick even when he went on a bender as he did from time to time, but he did have a jealous streak. Well, hell, who didn't, Chick thought bleakly, wondering if Junkyard Johnny was watching this as well.

Let him. In the shadow cast by their thighs Chick covered Zeno's broad hand with his own, squeezing hard before he let go. "Let's get the hell out of here tomorrow," he said. "I'm fed up with sitting around."

Zeno's smile got more real. "Chicago. My cousins'll give us a hand. Maybe I can find work in the shipyards."

Fat chance, Chick thought. Even for welders there were no jobs. And he was getting tired of hearing about those cousins. "Sure thing," he said, trying to smile as a shiver went through him at the thought of that dirty, frigid city.

Heat from the nearby stove licked at Philippa's cheeks. Her pinched stomach rumbled at the pungent smell of the onions the dark-haired girl was chopping. With stiff hands she dug deep in her overalls pockets for the last potatoes, glad to be shet of them. They'd come out of the same barn where she'd snagged the chore jacket and rubber boots, in a little farm town she'd never learned the name of, on the ride up to Duluth. Two days ago it'd been, but without a fire to roast them on they'd done her no good. People had been known to eat them raw, or so she'd heard, but she had no stomach for it. Nor for stealing, for that matter, but at the time it had seemed another case of doing what you had to.

The cook had laid aside her knife to stir the meat-smelling stew that simmered on top of the stove. She smiled at Philippa and stuck out her free hand. A sort of bracelet that looked to be intricately knotted from thick red cord clung to her wrist under the cuff of her sweater. "I am Mara," the older girl said, a singsong rhythm adding a lilt to the words. "I apologize! Most who come are male, so always I say brother."

Coming in here would've been a sight easier if she *was* a boy, or leastways could pass for one. "It's OK," Philippa stammered. Tears started again in the corners of her eyes, and embarrassment heated her face. Awkwardly she shook the outstretched hand, the palm warm and dampish against her cold skin, impossible to defend herself from.

Lightheaded, she let go too soon. "Call me Arlie," she said, impulsively grabbing for a name. After a bit she added, "Guess some folks'd make that out to be 'Arkie'."

Well, other boes took road names. Though she'd always liked her name well enough, she'd got teased about it back home in Mansfield. Back when she still had a home; when Meemaw was alive. Her grandmother had been the only one who got away with calling her Filly.

Mara threw her head back and laughed. Her black hair was cropped short as a boy's. On her it looked swell. "A far way from home, too, I think maybe. In Arkansas is weather like this?"

Philippa tried to be nonchalant. She pulled off her cap, freeing her long, untidy braid to hang heavy against her back. She shook melting snow from the wool. "Sure," she said, though it wasn't true. Bad storms, yes, but not ever one felt wrong like this one did. Other boes were watching and listening, that black-haired Oklahoma kid who'd stopped her among them. "Only not so early, is all."

"Ain't right, cold like this so soon. Whoever heard of a blizzard way up in October? And thunder in a snowstorm's dreadful unlucky," proclaimed the lanky youth who'd taken the place of the old balding guy at the checkerboard. Two sizeable brick-red birthmarks marred what was otherwise a decent if longish face. He frowned, then flicked an Orange Nehi bottle cap one square over. "Weather's goin' to hell."

"How many times you gonna say that?" said another fellow, a tough guy to judge by his scarred knuckles, though he didn't look to be more than fourteen. Without another word he got up and stomped out. Cabin fever, Philippa hoped, and not a feud.

"Everything's going to hell, Deucey." The stubble-haired kid playing opposite eyed the layout thoughtfully. "Give me one good reason why the weather oughta be any different."

Deucey, Philippa thought with another glance at the lanky kid's birthmarks. There's a guy whose moniker was written on his face. She wondered where the name she'd given Mara had come from. But that didn't matter. It had a good ring to it.

Mara touched her arm, claiming her attention. "Coffee is in that pot. And so you are knowing, we have a privy for when is needed." The cook waved a hand toward the camp's doorway. "Out there, against far wall. And a flashlight for finding hangs by the door." Mara's smile grew crooked, and not very convincing. "Night is much dark."

Philippa was astonished. That explained the odd shanty she'd passed, but jungles didn't tend to run to anything as fancy as an actual built privy. Or flashlights, for that matter, never mind fancy Coleman lamps like the one that was hanging overhead from the rafters, unlit. She managed a nod.

The stubble-haired boy spoke up again, grinning slyly. "Let me finish walloping Deucey here, and I'll show you where it is."

Philippa froze, a grey fear washed down through her. Jesus knew she didn't need no more trouble like that.

"No, you won't, Karl," a girl's hoarse, muffled voice answered him promptly. Some of the other kids laughed.

After a moment, Karl laughed too. "All right, Betts. Have it your way."

Relieved, Philippa turned to look for the girl. It had to be the kid stretched out full-length on the sawdust with a brown plaid coat pulled over its—her—head. Sometimes girls treated you mean when their guys showed you any attention, no matter that you didn't want it.

She could live with that. "Think I saw it on the way in, anyways," Philippa said, not to be rude. She saw that Mara had gone back to her chopping, big, scrubbed parsnips this time. "You need help?"

Mara shook her head. "Flo helps me tonight." She nodded towards a beanpole of a girl, seventeen at least, whose hands glistened pinkly from the juice of the canned tomatoes she was cutting into chunks. The dark-haired girl gave her a cool, summing look before fishing another limp tomato out of the can. "Is enough," Mara said. "Supper is some later."

The reminder knotted Philippa's stomach up with hunger. She moved off, to be out of the way as well as a bit further from the enticing smells. Coffee would help, she told herself, and bent to take off her rubber boots.

Zeno snorted in disgust. Curious, Chick glanced at him, and then to see what he was looking at.

It was the new kid, sitting on the ground now, struggling out of the patched and floppy boots she wore. Shreds of damp newspaper came spilling out of their depths along with her tennis shoe-clad feet.

Chick looked a question at Zeno.

His lover shrugged. "Girl that young belongs at home."

Chick's mouth tightened. She wasn't likely to have had much choice about hitting the road, which Zeno ought to know perfectly well. Most road kids didn't. Chick himself sure hadn't, not with his father going crazy mad after catching him out back of the house with Paddy. More than a year later Chick's collarbone still ached sometimes from the one blow Pa had landed on him. "That kid Nip's younger than her."

Zeno studied him impatiently. "He's got the bulldog to watch over him. The road'll eat her alive if she doesn't find herself a daddy." He scowled again at the girl, who was standing uncertain and barefoot, holding a pair of ragged socks in one hand and her soggy jacket in the other, looking for somewhere to hang them. "Which is not so likely, as homely as she is." After a moment he shrugged. "Females on the road are trouble."

Chick stared at him, trying for patience. He had an urge to call her over, to point out the line of nails sticking out of one of the overhead beams, but lucky for him it looked like the sick girl, Betts, was already doing that. "What do you care?" was what he found himself saying instead.

Zeno grinned at him then, slow and warm as the sun coming out of the clouds. "I don't, much."

After a couple of flat-footed tries Philippa managed to stretch tall enough to hook the collar of her jacket on one of the nails. Damp as they were, she put the socks and tennis shoes back on. Might be they'd dry faster that way, and anyways she didn't care for the sight of her blotchy, swollen feet.

"I'm Betts," the girl croaked as Philippa straightened. A livid crease on one cheek marked where she'd pillowed her head on her arm. "I heard your name already."

Philippa nodded. "That's a bad cold you got there." Bits of sawdust clung to Betts' blond, chin-length hair. Washed and fixed up to bring out the curl, it'd be pretty. Her sister had wanted to cut her hair that way when Philippa had first gone to live with them. Philippa, heartsick over losing Meemaw, wouldn't agree, and never mind that braids were years out of fashion. That had been her and Corinna's first fight, but not nearly their last.

Betts rubbed her forehead fretfully. "And how! That damned wind don't help, either." After a moment she looked up, squinting through puffy eyes. "Say, listen, kid. Don't take what Karl says to heart. He don't mean nothing by it."

Philippa tried to smile. "Didn't figure he did." She turned away to hide the lie. "You want me to fetch you some coffee?"

"You wouldn't have a smoke on you, would you?" Betts asked wistfully.

Philippa shook her head. "Got some papers, but that's all." She'd spotted the packet lying on the planks of a Duluth wharf and had tucked it away against future need—not that she cared much for smoking, even if it did help kill the hunger pangs.

"Too bad." Betts sighed. The sigh turned into another round of coughing, deep as the honking of a goose. She waved an unsteady hand at the washtub that sat near the stove. "Water," she managed to wheeze.

Philippa dipped her a cupful with one of the tin cans that sat next to the tub, then poured herself coffee from the pot on the stove, wrapping her can up in the cuff of her sweater. The heat soaked into her fingers, making her wish she could hold the makeshift cup with her feet instead.

Scooping out a seat for herself in the slope of the bulwark Philippa lay back, tired but too hungry to doze off. A sip of the coffee made her sigh in appreciation. The stuff was real, not chicory and rye, and from the first boiling of the grounds too. The bitter drink felt warm all the way down. She drank it slowly, beginning to relax. She had a place for the night, and soon she'd have food, which was about as much as a body could hope for anymore.

Idly she scanned the room, meeting the scrawny kid's intense gaze, the one who'd talked to her first. Nip, she'd heard him called. The kid didn't look away, so Philippa did, uneasy at the attention. Leastways he was too young to cause her much grief.

The wind still battered the planks that sheathed the ice house's upper walls, seeming to come from every which way at once. Thunder cracked again. She started, spilling coffee on her hand. Uneasily she wiped it away.

Truth was, the wind bothered her more than the unlikely snow and thunder. It wasn't just unseasonably cold, but—the word kept coming to her—somehow wrong, like it carried despair and fury. Almost that, only wind didn't have feelings. Wind had notes, and this one was sharp as a busted shard of glass. Wind tied everything together, but this one had been ripped loose some way. Philippa shivered, cold coming over her once more.

Corinna would mock her for that. Her older sister was about as weather-wise as a chunk of Arkansas stone, unlike Philippa, who took after their daddy's side of the family.

Corinna was also about as sensitive to a body's feelings as a rock. Philippa's mouth tightened as she recalled her sitting at the supper table in their raggedy old farmhouse, telling Hank in a mincing voice all about his sister-in-law's latest 'fancy'.

And Hank's burning eyes on her, watching her be shamed. Drinking it in for later.

Dizzy, dry-mouthed, Philippa sat back up. Her heart beat fast and thin and her new breasts ached. She gripped handfuls of the sawdust, forcing herself to breathe slow.

In a lull of the wind the redheaded guy laughed long and hard at something somebody had said—Flo, or maybe Karl, because they was all sitting together. The sound helped settle her back into this particular jungle, this particular evening.

Most of the kids were leaning back on the sawdust bulwark, jawing, though the guy who'd gone out earlier hadn't come back. Philippa thought she could hear him poking around outside, though with the shrill racket the storm was making it was hard to be sure.

Mara wasn't doing much of anything for the moment but watching the doorway while she absently wiped her hands with a rag. The Okie boy and the old guy sat off by themselves, nearer to her, their heads close together. The black-haired kid looked up, his expression defiant. When he noticed her a rueful sort of smile tugged up one side of his mouth.

The old guy looked up too, scowling until she looked away.

3

*H*ead held high, sweating in the heavy, alien garments, Simon stood waiting before the two pillars of the slipgate, his arm and shoulder beginning to ache from the weight of the sack of dried beans he held. Still there was no brightening of the air between the pillars, no sign that the Jaguar's Eye was opening for him. The other stations in the Hall of Crossings seemed to be having no trouble returning his fellow *dugrilat* to their interrupted missions, which did not help his resentful state of mind.

Neither he nor the others should have been called back here in the first place. Council delegates had demanded interviews with field missioners, as though they would learn anything the reports would not tell them. It was plain that the Great Council had become rotten with Haan-style 'benevolent ministers', drunk on their own importance. They were jealous of the honors earned by the Dugri, whose missions had spread the Five Principles throughout the world for almost three cycles of years. Now new-made dugrilat such as he carried word to a benighted sister world across the great void, and the arrogant delegates could not bear it.

Uneasily Simon shifted the sack to his other arm. Too well he knew that either Lukas or Mara would have done a better job withstanding the delegates' questions than he had. Instead they had been left to cover for his absence—no more than a few hours there, it should be, though he'd returned here at midday yesterday to wait on the Council's pleasure. Time ran much slower on Kahgomadri, the Night World, than it did here, no matter that it felt the same wherever you were.

"Patience," Conrad, his mentor, counseled from behind him. "You need not keep the coat fastened, you know."

Setting the sack on the speckled tile by his feet, Simon fumbled with the coat's fastenings. Buttons, he reminded himself. There were so many Night World words to remember.

Opening the coat helped a little. He blew out a calming breath before turning. "Is adjustment needed, do you think?" he asked as politely as he could manage. Vaitnu, the gate technician, had also been his teacher. But if opening the slipgate was going to take awhile, perhaps he could go sit for a time by the fountain in the atrium at the center of the Crossings branch. The hushed music of its flow might help take the taste of this afternoon's bullying from his mouth.

"It may be only that one of your wanderers is in the gate area, keeping it from opening," Conrad said. The old man squatted comfortably near the console, the hem of his work smock draped over his knobby knees. He'd earned his honor name the hard way, alone, passing as a native of the Night World for a year of their time, only to endure prolonged quarantine when he returned home, enforced by senior dugrilat who claimed his thought had been contaminated.

Bullying existed within the Dugri, as well as without, Simon reminded himself, letting go another long breath. He'd had plenty of reason to know it his first year as a cadet. Next to that, the worst of the councilors was no more than a blustering gasbag.

Caught up in the console displays, Vaitnu greeted Conrad's suggestion with a dismissive flick of her hand. "The mirror tell hasn't flashed. I begin to think the problem may be some deep imbalance in the anchor frequencies, unlikely as that seems. But if so, it is stubborn…" Vaitnu's words trailed off as her fingers stroked the surface of the display for another long moment. She made a face and muttered something. Her hands sped up. "Yes. Yes. There."

The blaze of light that edged the opening slipgate caught the corner of Simon's eye, brought him around to face what lay now between the pillars, a shape like a huge cat's eye opening wide on darkness. Cold excitement clutched at his belly as he snatched up the sack of beans and stepped forward. He'd crossed over more than a dozen times by now, but he hadn't yet gotten used to it.

"Check the anchor settings, Simon! Remember what I taught you of deep field adjustments!" the technician called after him, her words echoing strangely as he entered the humming unspace of the slipgate.

His first whirling step seemed to take him nowhere. Uncertainly he stepped again, the motion endless. This isn't right, Simon thought, with a mounting sense of dread that was worse for being bodiless.

And then he was falling, pitching forward into darkness, though for less time than it took him to catch a startled breath. The wrist of his ladened arm and then the side of his face collided, hard, with a splintery, cold surface, knocking what air he'd managed to gain out of him again.

Icy air, it was, smelling of dusty pine resin and urine, as was his next breath. Simon staggered upright, a trickle of relief easing his disorientation.

The privy in the ice house. He was here, and safe; his thudding heart proved that. But darkness pressed heavily on him, and that was wrong. Although the time correlation between the two worlds was never certain, he should have returned here somewhere in the middle of the afternoon.

Around and above him the building's timbers creaked, wind hissing through the high vents. A storm, he realized in despair. How was he to explain coming back at night, dry and unruffled from out of such weather?

Find your way across the lightless ice house floor, he told himself. Go out into the night. It need only be for a moment.

The fine trembling that had started up in the muscles of his arms and back was just from the cold. Hesitating would not help him. Simon forced his free hand from its refuge in a pocket and began to feel his way along the board wall. The door should be no more than a step or two to his left. The enclosure the setup crew had built was only three paces wide and just deep enough to allow for the framed privy trench with the support boards across it, plus room to walk in front. Some of the reactions they'd gotten to this arrangement had let them know this wasn't quite the usual way of doing things here, but none of the *ihaaztbinit*, the young wanderers, had objected, and it served its dual purpose well.

After the first step Simon found he'd shut his eyes; he found it easier to move that way. Back when they'd been settling in they had practiced the night-blind crossing of the ice house, he and Mara and Lukas, egging each other on. Always Lukas moved more surely than either he or Mara, insisting that if you kept your eyes open and waited for it, there was light of a sort. Simon had never found it so. But then Lukas had been born here, one of Kahgomadri's uncounted abandoned infants. His coloring—cotton-pale skin and hair like fine copper wire—was the proof of that, though he'd been raised deep in the children's branch of a settlement warren, like any other Cultivator.

Some practices of this world were astoundingly barbarous.

Simon's hand brushed the prickly wool of the blanket that curtained the door. He grasped it in relief, then froze as it was yanked from his hand. His eyes flew open, to be blinded by the full glare of a flashlight beam.

"Holy Mary Mother of God!" a girl cried. The light swung crazily as the flashlight dropped from her hand and rolled away, coming to a rest with the bright end inches from the base of the left-hand wall. Still there was enough light for Simon to recognize a tall young woman who'd come to the ice house with a couple of guys. Fior, he thought her name was, though as she didn't talk a great deal she hadn't made a clear impression on him. Several days ago that had been—no, only two in this world's time. Unless, Simon thought, discovering another fear, there'd been a really serious fluctuation in the correlations. He might have been gone for days.

"Simon? You near to give me a heart attack!" A hand clutched the front of her dingy yellow sweater. It was her only wrap, which was why she was still here when her companions had moved on. She frowned at him, regaining her composure. "I thought you scrammed this morning!"

Ah, that at least was some reassurance. Simon let the bag of dried beans slip from his shoulder down into both hands. He held it clutched to his chest like a shield. "I went to town only. See? I brought us beans."

"You trying to tell me you walked ten miles in this weather to bring us a bag of beans?" Disdain edged her words. "Geez. You're nutty as a fruitcake. Lucky you didn't curl up and freeze out there." Bending, she swiped at the fallen camp flashlight, retrieving it. "You done in here? 'Cause I gotta pee and I don't care for an audience."

Simon edged his way out the door. She could think him as crazy as she wanted if she didn't ask awkward questions. "Be my guest," he said, pleased with himself for remembering the phrase, though the shivering that had settled into his bones made his voice shake.

Alone again in the darkness, Simon paused to find his bearings. Contrary to his fears there was some light here, reflected upward from the gaps in the camp ceiling, but it dazed his eyes. He could see generally where he needed to go, but not the path that would take him there. Gritting his teeth, Simon shifted the heavy bag back onto his shoulder and set off slowly, feeling his way with his feet. At least he no longer needed to go outside. The girl had already seen him as he was. He would simply have to make the best explanation of it that he could find.

Philippa glanced up, roused from a near doze by a draft from the doorway. An older boy stood there with the curtain falling shut behind him, an uncertain look sitting oddly on his swarthy hawk's face. He had a twenty-pound croker sack of something balanced on one shoulder and was bundled up in his coat like made sense for a body'd just come in from that terrible blow outside.

Only he couldn't have just come in. She frowned in confusion. There wasn't a bit of snow on him, nor any damp for that matter, but she was sure she hadn't seen him in camp before. The white gas Coleman lantern that hung near the door lit the space much too well for her to be mistaken.

"Simon!" Mara cried, jumping up. "We worry for you."

"What happened?" demanded the kid who'd stomped off earlier. "Change your mind?" He'd stayed out in the shadowy ice house for a good half hour before coming back in with an armload of wood, his face pinched with cold. Philippa already had him tagged as somebody to steer clear of.

"I went to town only," the new guy said placatingly. "Walked in. A ride I find to come back."

He was another one of them, Philippa realized, foreign like Mara and the redhead, his deep voice a little singsong and his c's having that little extra kick to them, like Mara's when she'd said 'coffee'. He smiled stiffly. "Night come too soon."

He was a rotten liar, though why he'd bother in the first place was a sure enough mystery. The tough kid snorted in derision, but let it drop. Nobody else commented, though a few faces looked as puzzled as Philippa felt.

Mara took the guy's arm and led him to the stove. "Warm yourself, Simon," she told him, handing him a rag-wrapped can of coffee. "You shiver." He did, too. Philippa could see it, a deep shuddering that threatened to spill the drink. Holding the can in both hands he sipped at it, making a wry face at the taste.

Flo came in then, her sweater wrapped tight around her. Fumbling, she hung the flashlight up on its nail by the door and hurried to the stove, shivering as bad as—what had Mara called him? Simon. As she went she shot him a scornful look that he didn't see. The guy didn't lift his head or turn around, even when Flo stood, shoulders hunched and hands held out to the curve of the rusty barrel, no more than two feet from him.

Well, that'd explain there being no snow on his coat, Philippa thought caustically, rubbing both arms against a sudden chill. They'd been out there somewhere, argufying or loving it up, or more than likely both. It was like a guy to leave her to wait out in the cold just so they wouldn't be seen coming back in together.

Though that didn't make sense neither. She hadn't paid much mind, but seemed like Flo had left not more than ten minutes ago.

Keeping his head down, Simon took a sip of the steaming coffee, hoping the tall girl would say nothing here where everyone could hear. It seemed no one else would question him, though the stubborn hush that followed his tale made it clear he hadn't been believed.

There were new ihaaztbinit here this evening, a boy and a man of about thirty who sat against the far wall talking with their heads close together, as well as the younger one he'd passed coming in, still with the single braid of a boy not yet into puberty. Three more to doubt him. Such incidents were not good for their mission, which depended on building trust as least as much as it did on logical argument. Another fault that had branched from the Council delegates' arrogance.

As well there was their slipgate to worry about. Now that light and warmth surrounded him, an uneasy memory of his overlong crossing flickered in him, souring his stomach. Vaitnu hadn't seemed very worried, but even if the problem with the anchor frequencies was minor, he never wanted to have to endure another crossing like that one.

Across the stove from him, Mara absently stirred the pot of stew. When he moved she glanced his way, questions crowding her eyes.

Before he could speak the girl who'd mocked him spoke through chattering teeth. "You want me to do that, Mara?"

Simon let his mouth snap shut, wishing the girl would warm enough to go sit down. Anything he said she would hear too. Not that she'd understand, but to make it seem they had secrets wasn't good. Talking in their own tongue bred yet more suspicion, though this world had uncounted languages, and theirs had been accepted without question as one of these.

Mara answered her easily, "No, thank you, Flo. Nothing is to do until I cook the bread." She laughed. "I stir only to smell the stew, yes?"

Flo. He'd have to make a point to remember that. Night World names were awkward. Even his own honor name had taken practice.

Out of the corner of his eye Simon saw Flo grin even as another convulsive shiver went through her. She said, "Yeah, I get you."

He cursed himself. Of course the Kahgomadri girl was still cold in that inadequate sweater. He could have brought back a coat for her from the shelves of them kept for missioners in the storage chamber off the Hall of Crossings, but, tangled in his own bruised feelings, he hadn't thought of it; had taken the sack Conrad had handed him without question.

Simon frowned down at the contents of the makeshift cup. The metal these people used so much of made anything taste terrible, but the coffee sat badly in his uneasy stomach. What he needed was the soothing bitterness of *kaklotl*, whipped up with some fine-ground maize meal for body and only a little dried chili to heat the tongue.

They had kaklotl in this world, he'd been told, but they made it horribly sweet. "Take this," he told Flo, holding out his coffee. "Warm you."

She eyed him warily. "Something wrong with it?"

He put an expressive hand over his belly. "Belly hurt, is all." He tried a smile.

Flo wrapped her hands around the swaddled can. "Yeah, that's jake. Don't mind if I do." She took a cautious sip. "Thanks. Geez, but this stuff is good."

Simon worked the buttons on his coat so that it fell open, then wriggled his arms out of it. "Take this also, to borrow."

Her dark eyes narrowed. "Hey, you guys want me to shove off, you can just say so." She set the cup down on the crowded stove barrel top, pushed it in between the pots of cooking food, and stalked away.

Mara sighed. "What bad news must you tell us, Simon? Why did they call you back?"

Simon watched Flo as she went to sit by the pale-haired girl Betts, feeling helpless. "I didn't mean so."

"You did. And I did," Mara said. "Should I bring Lukas?"

Rattled, not thinking, Simon flicked his fingers in negation.

"A day home and you forget our training," Mara chided, though she smiled a little at his slip. "No one is near. Talk, Simon."

Heat rose to his cheeks at her reminder. "Delegates from the Great Council came. Many dugrilat were called back, not me only."

Mara's mouth twisted as though she tasted something sour. "The *dzinsit* faction?"

He nodded slowly, watching her. She understood the internal struggles of the councils much better than he. "So it looked to me. I report as they asked. They didn't like how I told them."

At that she laughed. "Simon, you always tell them they are wrong."

Stung, Simon answered her. "Yes, when they are. I am Ngorvisla, a Cultivator, not the hand-servant of a posturing delegate. Not a, a"—he searched for a stronger English word— "not a bootlicker."

Mara patted his arm affectionately. "And for that Conrad chose you."

He flushed again, though he didn't doubt her instincts. "They tell me nothing but insults, so I have nothing else to tell you." Here he was, giving another report, he thought, a little resentful, a feeling that faded as he recalled his other news. Bits of the ceiling rattled overhead at a particularly strong gust of wind. Simon glanced up it uneasily. "Only that the slipgate works badly. It would not open at first. And my return was…" He searched for English words, but found none that told how frightened he had been in that crossing. "Was long. *Much* long. Vaitnu says we must check deep settings."

4

Anchors. Philippa frowned, trying to make sense of what the new guy was gabbing about, so serious all of a sudden. She couldn't hear it all in the first place, and some of it had been foreign words. Finnish, maybe; she'd heard there was a lot of Finns here in Minnesota, all tightfisted as hell. Or might be it was Hungarian or some other lingo; road kids came from a tinker's lot of backgrounds.

But anchors was a funny thing to talk about out here in the middle of nowhere. Unless they had themselves a boat, pulled up on the shore of that lake outside? Or maybe Simon had stole one to get back here, and that's how come he'd lied earlier.

Absently she rubbed at her feet through the canvas shoes. They'd thawed enough to start up itching, and her big toe was throbbing as well.

Maybe they was bootleggers, hiding cases of gin under the junk pile out there. Sure, and they rowed the stuff into town to all the speakeasies lining the streets of that dead-and-alive little burg. The pure foolishness of the notion made her grin.

Mara was talking now, low and reassuring, answering the guy's worry, whatever it was. The tuneful rise and fall of the voice distracted Philippa, woke the same hum in the center of her chest as she'd felt earlier, when Mara had called out her welcome, a warmth that both pulled her in and scared her.

Setting the lid back on the stew pot with a clang, Mara came around the stove to wrap an arm around Simon's waist, leaning into him. The guy smiled faintly down at her and ruffled her short cap of hair. He had a braided cord around his wrist too, Philippa saw; black and glittery instead of red like Mara's was. Some kind of boy-girl thing, she decided, turning away, the spark of humor and the music draining out of her.

About then Betts flopped down beside her, wheezing like walking ten feet had wore her out. "That food's not gonna run off, kid. You don't need to keep such a close eye on it."

Shoulders hunched, her face heating, Philippa didn't look up right away. To top it off her stomach gave a rumble at the mention of food. She cast about for something to say. "You guys must've had you some awful good luck before the storm hit." The smell off that stew hinted of meat, a rich sausage maybe, as well as tomatoes. It'd been weeks since she'd tasted meat.

"Around here?" Betts scoffed. "Not likely. We all brought something in, but Mara and them got a big stash of grub. I dunno where they get their mitts on stuff like that, or how they hauled it out here, for that matter. Maybe Simon walks it in from town." She snickered a little, and ended up coughing. A sip of water eased the spell, and she went on. "Anyhow, Mara sure knows how to cook it up."

A jungle that always had grub, just like that kid had told her. Philippa risked a glance stove-wards. The redhead had joined Mara and Simon. Philippa watched as the cook pulled him in close too.

As the hug ended, the redhead glanced up and found Philippa watching them. He flushed to the tips of his ears, then smiled uncertainly at her, one reddish eyebrow cocked.

Caught staring again. Biting her lip, Philippa looked down at her hands, balled up in her lap. She asked, her voice careful, "They boss this jungle then?"

"Yeah, kind of. Mostly Mara does. They were here first, see. Nobody kicks about it. She's generally reasonable for a bohunk."

Questions bubbled up inside Philippa, almost as insistent as the hunger. Something was different about the cook and the two guys she was with, something more than the bracelets and the accent. Eastern European, if Betts was right about that. Though Philippa had always thought those folks tended to be blond and pale-skinned. Which Lukas was, though she'd have pegged him for Irish from looks alone.

A new idea occurred to her. "She and those two guys ain't Christers, are they?"

Betts spit out the water she'd been swallowing, an involuntary action that set off another coughing fit. When she regained her breath she wheezed, "That's the funniest damn thing I heard today, kid. They're some kind of Reds. Karl says they sound like the Wobs he used to hear in Bughouse Square, but they say they belong to some outfit called Cultivators, or something like that. More to my taste than Christers, if you know what I mean. You'll hear more about it tonight, I expect."

Philippa shrugged. Both Christians and Wobblies tended to preach at you, though the Christians she'd run into on the road seemed more likely to do it while your belly was empty. On the other hand her Meemaw had been a stout and cheerful Baptist, taking her along to camp meetings and sings as well as Sunday church. Philippa had sung right along with her grandmother, getting lost in the vast, scratchy harmony of the hymns.

But Meemaw was two years gone, and Philippa didn't want to think about that anymore. That and a lot of other things.

Anyway, it made sense about Mara and them being Wobs or whatever, though it didn't quite explain the calm assurance she felt from them. Well, Mara and Lukas, anyways. "Blessed assurance, Jesus is mine…" Except that whatever assurance they had wasn't Jesus, apparently.

A movement by the door caught her eye, the redhead reaching up to take the flashlight from its nail. His wrist slipped bare for a moment; he wore one of those bracelets too.

Philippa blinked at that. She watched, puzzling over it as the guy pulled his cap down so far that it hid most of his rust-red hair, and ducked out past the curtain.

Well, Jesus knew she'd seen stranger arrangements on the road than two guys to one girl.

Awhile later, quiet-footed in his dirty socks, Karl came, squatting down easily in front of Betts, and catching hold of her hand. After a minute of him and Betts making eyes at each other, Philippa scooted uneasily away.

Karl turned a grin on her. "Say, Arlie, I heard you talking papers a while ago." He fished a Bull Durham bag out of an inside pocket with his free hand and held it up. "Just so happens I got some makings."

Betts' eyes lit up. "You been sitting on that all this time, Karl? That's no way to treat a girl!"

Karl turned his attention to her, teasing. "Wasn't much good without papers, now was it?"

"Yeah, well, we could have used newspaper or something," she shot back. "But if we got it, let's not just gab about it."

Philippa emptied out the one good pocket left in the thin wool dress pants she wore as an underlayer, retrieving the cigarette papers along with her penknife, a pencil stub, a nickel, and her lucky penny. She picked the packet out of the scant handful and tossed it to him, eager to get herself out of the way. "Here, Karl. They's all yours."

He caught it casually, flashing her another grin. He and Betts each slipped a paper loose, trading gibes as they settled down to rolling.

Philippa eased a little further away from them; it wasn't a cig she wanted, but food. And she was just as happy to have Karl's attention focused elsewhere, no matter if Betts was right about him.

The scrawny kid sat down on the far side of her, blocking her in and a sight too close for her comfort.

"Looks like a good thing to get in on," he said awkwardly, hunched over, his restless hands tucked between his knees. He tried to smile at her, but only managed to look anxious. "They call me Nip."

Philippa's empty stomach clenched. Not again; why couldn't guys just leave her alone? Casually, lightheaded, she got to her feet. The big toe on her right foot jerked with pain when she shifted weight onto it. She drew in a deep breath, checking an impulse to snap at the younger boy. "How about you take my spot? I gotta go take me a little walk before the grub's ready."

Nip's mouth opened in the beginnings of a protest. He thought better of it before he spoke, and after a few seconds of casting about asked, "Well, hey then, Arlie, want me to roll one for you?"

Philippa hesitated, not wanting to hurt his feelings further. Other people's hurt feelings came back to haunt you. "Well, yeah. If you want to. I might smoke one later."

His pinched expression brightened. "Swell. After supper, maybe."

Feeling trapped, she nodded, and turned to find her way out.

There was no flashlight on the nail to the right of the doorway. The redhead must still be out there, an awful long trip to the privy. Philippa hesitated, then pulled aside the curtain anyway.

An unsteady beam of light shone some ten or fifteen yards off, enough to show her the plank wall of the privy though the light was to one side of it. The beam swung up and caught her in the eyes, blinding her before it moved aside.

"I am sorry!" Lukas' voice came to her across the gulf of frigid air. "I am too long."

Philippa blinked the afterimages from her eyes. "Got the trots?" she asked politely, walking out to meet him. Heck, it was his business if he wanted to risk his neck poking around that junk in the dark and cold.

The redhead looked puzzled. "Trots? I don't know this." As he reached her he held out the flashlight, pointed now at the ground between them. "You take. I see enough." Beneath the sprinkle of freckles his face looked very pale.

She took the flashlight, the metal warm from his hand. "Thanks."

He smiled, but there wasn't much heart in it. Maybe he did have the trots, after all. Wondering, she turned to watch him hurry back to camp.

Two of the wanderers lay tangled together, passing a lit tobacco stick from hand to hand. Simon watched, brows drawn down, as the boy—Karl?—stroked the side of the pale-haired girl's breast. That was yet another thing about this world that he found unsettling. They seemed to make no decent division between work and home behaviors, between right hand and left.

You are unfair, he told himself, shifting uneasily as he looked away. This was home to these wanderers while they were here. It was only for Mara and Lukas and himself that this mission was a workplace. And, as they'd been warned in training, it was much harder here to maintain the genderless discipline of work, the right-handed path.

Simon smiled a little bitterly. If he was truthful, jealousy was also part of his reaction. He should have sought out a Sharing while he was back in Ebvili. There had been time, but no girl had invited him. He felt awkward going on his own.

"It is uncovered!" Lukas' voice hissed in Simon's ear, in their own tongue.

Startled, Simon turned to look at him. Caught in his own thoughts as he'd been, he hadn't noticed Lukas come in. "What is…" he began to ask when he caught sight of his *bvarit*'s ashen face. That gave him half his answer. The team that had prepared this place had piled many things around the slipgate anchors to hide them, heavy things, discards they'd found in the ice house or in the—what was it called?—the dump out on the edge of the woods. They could identify very few of them, but it hadn't seemed to matter. "Both?" he asked, a note of panic in his voice in spite his effort to keep it calm and level.

Lukas hugged his knees. "The left-hand anchor only." He scowled. With an effort he shifted to the Night World language. "Junkyard Johnny was out a long time. I will take bets he was the one."

Mind racing, Simon considered what must be done. The camp flashlight was not hung by the door. Someone was already out there.

Seeing him glance that way, Lukas said, "Arlie has the light."

That was a name Simon didn't remember hearing before; one of the newcomers, he supposed, but it made no difference.

For now he must use his mind and Lukas' memory rather than his eyes. "The front dial was set right?"

The anchors had been installed inside the emptied casings of two massive Night World devices for joining metal—welding, they called the process. As a convenience the technologists had rigged the clumsy dial mechanism on the face of the disguised anchor so that it could fine-tune the slipgate harmonics, while deeper adjustments had to be made on the control slate hidden behind a plate on the back. That surely no one could have tampered with. Yet even a slightly altered harmonic could cause problems—such, perhaps, as his difficult crossing?

Lukas hesitated. "I look but cannot tell. Simon, you know these things more than I."

"When Junkyard was out—was before I come back?"

Lukas nodded. "Oh, yes. Just before night."

Simon smiled, relieved. Vaitnu had thought the problem deeper, but she was not here to make a direct assessment. He was, and unlike the painstaking tuning needed for the deep frequencies, readjusting the front dial was not hard. Why look for a complicated answer when a simple one would serve?

"I will go when the flashlight comes back," he told Lukas. He tapped his teeth with a forefinger, thinking. Once he was done he would need to send word to Vaitnu, so she wouldn't worry further. That, however, could go in their daily report.

There was also the issue of keeping the wanderers from tampering with the anchor again, now that it was within their reach. Perhaps he could disable the front dial functioning from the main control slate?

One way or another they could solve that. Relaxing for the first time in hours, Simon settled down to wait.

5

"*P*eaches," one of the kids groaned reverently.

Chick opened one eye. Somebody had turned down Mara's white gas lamp a little, but it was still bright enough to whittle by, had he cared to. A few feet away sat Zeno, tamping tobacco down into his pipe, making a big production of it. Chick watched him affectionately. That was just about the last of the pouch of fancy pipe tobacco Chick had swapped six of his best carvings for a couple of weeks back, as a birthday present. Zeno didn't smoke the stuff above twice a day, to make it last.

"I picked a heap of 'em in Missouri last year," the horse-faced guy said, the one who'd taken Zeno's place at the checkerboard earlier in the evening. Deucey. "Peaches, I mean. Heck, I might have picked these ones we just ate."

Not much interested, Chick shifted a little to ease his full belly. That Mara might be bossy, but she sure as hell was a good cook. She'd dished up stew, oddly spicy and thick with tomatoes and onions and sausage. Crisp hush puppies had gone along with it, as much of both as anybody could eat. And then when Chick had stuffed himself with those, the foreign girl had lifted dessert from the other pot: a steamed pudding laced with sweet canned peaches.

It wasn't pie, but by God it would do. As a general thing
Chick did what cooking him and Zeno managed, having learned
to do a passable job of it traveling around from wellhead to
wellhead with his Pa. Stew wasn't hard and neither was hush
puppies, but doing them well was another thing entirely.

He looked around for Mara, thinking he might tell her so,
but she must've gone out to the privy.

"Leastways I picked 'em for a couple of days," the guy was
saying. "Until a bunch of niggers gets together and run us
tramps out. Said we was taking food from their kids." He
sighed.

Chick frowned. By his accent the guy was from someplace
like Kentucky or Tennessee, and backwoods to boot, so maybe
this was just how he was raised to talk. But Chick was half
Chickasaw, no matter that the government said there wasn't any
such tribe any more. And some Chickasaw looked more black
than Indian. His Uncle Hiram had told him they'd come from
slaves the tribe had back in Civil War days, but nowadays wasn't
much to choose between being called nigger or Indian, at least
in Oklahoma. "Yeah, well," he said, trying to hold onto his
temper, "you probably was."

The guy glanced at him uneasily. He waited a beat before he
answered. "We all got to eat, brother. Them and their kids and
me and you. What you gonna do when there ain't enough to go
around?" He paused again, then added, "Anyways, it ain't gonna
happen again, not there. Rode past that self-same orchard a
month later and the whole durn place was nothing but a heap
of splinters. Tornado hit it."

Karl frowned thoughtfully, his hand pausing mid-stroke on
the blonde's hair. She'd dozed off with her head in his lap. "Lot
of those this year."

Nip piped up. Even a heavy meal didn't seem to slow him
down. "Yeah, but there is enough food to go around! There's
plenty! I read in the paper about how they set a whole mountain
of oranges on fire out in California and then shot a guy tried to
grab just one of them." He kicked at the sawdust.

"Got that right, runt," the Chicago kid said. "And meanwhile
we get nothing but beans and misery in the damn missions,

while old man Hoover sits on his fat behind up in the White House doing jack-all."

"Not for much longer, he's not," Zeno muttered around his pipe, old rage smoldering in his eyes. "Us vets are going to vote that whore's bastard out."

Chick winced, fearing for the pipe stem and even more that Zeno'd shoot his mouth off and get them too much notice. Zeno had spent the first part of the summer jungled up in D.C. with his old Army pals, pushing for early payment of the promised veterans' bonus. Until the Senate had killed the Patman bill, when, as he'd said, his itchy feet got the best of him. It hadn't been much more than two weeks after Chick and Zeno first got together that news of the Bonus Army being driven off the Anacostia Flats with gas and bayonets had hit all the newspapers. Chick had tried to ease his jocker's shame and rage that night, but it'd been like jumping in front of a truck. That had been the only time Zeno—crying and cursing and already half-plastered—had been rough enough in sex to really hurt him. Afterward he'd staggered off and hadn't shown up again at the jungle for two whole days.

Steeling himself, Chick risked gripping Zeno's shoulder for a moment. Without looking at him, the Greek took the pipe from his mouth and drew a deep breath, muscles easing just a little under Chick's hand.

Grumpily Betts rolled away from Karl and sat up. "Hell, Nip, at least the missions'll give you guys beans. Us girls they hand straight over to the cops. We get jailed for whores, or a one-way ticket back to whatever hellholes we came from." Her face was flushed from fever. Flo nodded her support, her thin mouth twisted up sour, but Chick saw that Arlie was taking all the talk in, those black eyes of hers wary as a jackrabbit's.

Lukas spoke up for the first time. "Nip says so, and it is true. In the fields is plenty and with much work for us. Together we can make this land a paradise." Conviction sang in his reedy voice.

But conviction of what? Chick studied him, confused. He'd heard versions of this pitch plenty of times, but generally you could tell right off what the guy was selling, whether revolution or the Second Coming.

"Yeah, brother, they's work one place, but ain't no money to pay anybody to do it," Deucey grumbled. "And someplace else they's food aplenty, but no work to trade for it, and no money. It's money's the problem. Them bankers is sitting on all of it."

Lukas turned to look at him, his hazel eyes shining. "Think, Deucey! What is money? Only paper, bits of metal you cannot eat. Let the bankers keep money! What we make together is from work and belief and, and agreements. Money is nothing."

That Simon guy leaned forward, both his hands held out. He hadn't said much since claiming he'd walked back from town through the storm, though he'd relaxed after awhile. Now he looked confident and serious as a preacher launching into the meat of his sermon. "What do we need? He gestured at the makeshift ceiling overhead. "Food and shelter. Clothes. Other people. Once we have, for what is money?"

Karl sniggered. "For smokes?" he suggested, but not very loudly.

Though he didn't care to buy whatever they were selling, Simon's words had moved Chick. "A roof over our heads that don't leak, and grub on the table; decent clothes to wear and decent work to do and folks to do it with—that's family. That's home." Weariness that was more than the end of the day weighed him down. Home had been the farm outside Davis, had been Grammy and Chick's cousin Victor who were for sure dead, and Uncle Hiram who'd likely drunk himself down to join them; had been Uncle Joe, whose last letter had sounded so defeated. It sure as hell wasn't wherever his Pa had moved on to by now. "We ain't got any of that, Simon. If we ever had it, it's long gone." Roughness crept into the words, causing heat to rise in his cheeks. "You saying you can take us home again?"

In the silence that followed, Chick searched the others' faces. Lukas looked frustrated, but Simon frowned in concentration. Betts had stretched out again, not so close to Karl. Most of the other kids just looked restless. Not the Arkansas kid though. She wouldn't meet his gaze, but her eyes had the shine that came from unshed tears.

Zeno was huddled around his pipe, his jaw still set, giving nothing but his back and a little of his side to Chick.

Chick shrunk into himself, wishing he'd just kept his mouth shut.

"Take you home?" Simon said then, slowly. "No. We *make* home."

"Bull!" Junkyard barked. "I've had enough of this crap you Wobs keep dishing out. Beginning to feel like I'm flopping in a goddamn mission."

"He does not say the work is easy, Junkyard," Mara said, switching off the flashlight as the door curtain fell shut behind her. Her round cheeks were reddened from the cold beyond the jungle's walls, her expression stubbornly serene. "You must hold the idea and hope in you, and share it between until enough work to make the home." Chick watched her cross to where Simon was sitting and kneel down to whisper in his ear. Her calm front slipped a little; worry showed in the tense curve of her back. Fumbling gingerly in her coat pocket, she pulled out a little kid's striped rubber ball, dropping it in his hand like it meant something.

"Nuts," Junkyard muttered, looking bitter. "No use trying to talk to you. You guys got ya heads up in the clouds somewheres. Me, I just wanna get by."

Betts raised her head. "Oh, put it on the low needle for tonight," she pleaded hoarsely. "I've got an awful headache."

Standing once more, the cook looked Betts over. "She is right. Quiet talk now." Watching her as she went to kneel by Betts, Chick thought she was just as glad for the chance to calm things down.

But maybe that wasn't the whole picture. Of a sudden Simon looked like he'd bit down on bad news, and Lukas had gone skim-milk white under the freckles. Seemed all three of them had a worry Chick couldn't guess at.

The rubber-shelled sphere lay cupped in Simon's hands, an accusation. The Jaguar's Eye had opened for Mara, but the report Simon had impressed into the sphere's activated ceramic core, whispering out in the frigid dark after he'd finished a quick reset and testing of the anchors, hadn't gone through. Mara said the ball had come sailing back out of the slipgate a few breaths after she'd thrown it. She'd caught it by instinct, scorching her fingers. Heat had crazed the sphere's surface with tiny cracks and muddied its bright colors.

Which wouldn't have affected the message it held, of course, but how had it gotten so hot? Simon tightened his fingers around the sphere, now cooled to skin temperature, then tucked it into a pocket.

What if it had been Mara herself trying to cross, or Lukas? He looked up. Lukas avoided his gaze, though Simon had felt the weight of those greenish-brown eyes. His bvariti had trusted him to fix technical problems. Somehow he'd made this one a lot worse.

Smothering the burn of shame inside him, Simon began to tell over every step he'd taken, looking for the flaw.

Philippa drew a ragged breath, glad Mara'd put a stop to her pals' soapbox speechifying. Not that she had any real objection to what they'd had to say—other than that silliness about money not mattering—but the ghosts of home had been too much on her mind already this evening.

The talking didn't stop altogether, but it quieted down to a tense sort of murmur. Careful of her throbbing toe, she stretched, trying to ease the knots that had built up in her back and shoulders. Moving didn't help much. She was wound tight as a dog with its hackles up.

But that wasn't just her. There was an odd, nose-wrinkling smell in the air, she realized then, and a tight, electric edge to things that didn't come from that argument. It was something like what she'd felt when she first came into the ice house, but a lot stronger. Like thunder building up again, though there hadn't been any for a couple of hours now. Didn't make any more sense than the blizzard itself did.

Beyond the ice house walls the wind was up again. She wrapped her arms close around her knees, feeling how the battering gusts were pulling the heat out of the place. Hope to

Jesus my clothes has got dry, she thought, eyeing them from across the room. She was going to need them tonight.

"Karl!" Mara sang out. The cook was squatted down by the tub of meltwater, a striped rag hanging limp from her hand.

The good-looking kid's head jerked up. "Huh?"

"As not-winners of the checkers games, you and, and— Zeno is your name?" Mara said, swiveling to take in the older balding guy as well. "You and Zeno are washers tonight. Water is hot on the stove."

"Cripes," muttered the kid. He stubbed out his cigarette on his boot sole, and stowed the butt in a pocket before he got to his feet. He and the other kids must've gone through half the papers in the packet she'd given them. "OK." He managed a grin. "Guess that grub was worth it."

The balding man got up too, dusting his trousers off. "Let's get to it, then." The Okie boy scowled, more at Karl than Mara or anybody else.

"Good. Dishpan is in that box." Mara pointed with her chin to the crate she'd used as a table. The chores settled, she dunked the rag she held in the meltwater and wrung it out. When she laid it across Betts' forehead, the sick girl twitched irritably away from the trail of wet that dribbled down her cheek, but then let Mara smooth the cloth into place.

Mara asked Betts something. Philippa couldn't hear the question or Betts' mumbled answer, or the reassurance that followed; nothing but the tones of voice. She was glad someone was helping the sick girl, she told herself, unable to bear sitting still any longer.

Favoring the banged-up toe, she went to check on her clothes. The overalls felt pretty near dry, all but the pockets. The jacket, once she snagged it down from the nail it hung from, proved to have a dampish collar. She shrugged it on anyways and limped towards the doorway. Not that she needed the privy, not yet, and anyways there was something about that place she just didn't care for. But she needed to move around out where nobody'd stare at her.

The runty kid called after her. "Hey! Wait up!"

Philippa set her teeth and kept going, but Nip caught up to her within a few steps. "Hey, Arlie, you want that smoke now?" he asked eagerly. He fumbled a hand down inside his ragged green-and-black striped sweater, searching for his shirt pocket. "Got it!" He held up a skinny cigarette in triumph.

Philippa looked at it and then at Nip's face. Her braid had fallen forward when she turned, irritating her cheek. Impatiently she shoved it back. A sound like distant buzz saws started up between her ears, and there was a sour taste on the back of her tongue. "Lemme be, Nip. I don't want the damn smoke."

The boy gaped at her, then his mouth snapped shut. Anger smoldered behind his dark eyes. Without a word, he stalked back to where he'd been sitting. That's torn it, a small voice in Philippa's head commented, but she didn't care. She turned again to the doorway.

A broad hand caught her shoulder and spun her around. She banged the damned toe against something, and bit her tongue in order to not cry out.

Nip's pal Junkyard glared down at her. "Hey, no need to be rude to the kid! He was doing you a favor!"

The bad taste seemed to run all the way down to her belly, a mingling of fear and nausea. Her shoulder burned where the bully had grabbed hold. With relief she felt rage sink through her, the sour sickness turning bitter and icy as the wind outside. "Keep your goddamn hands off me, jackroller," she hissed, leaning in toward his face, hardly able to hear her own words for the howling in her mind. Up close, his breath stank more of rot than of the supper's onions.

The first blow caught her on the side of the head; a second clipped her jaw. She reeled backwards into one of the support posts, but used it as a launching pad, charging headfirst for the knot in the rope that held up Junkyard's canvas trousers. Arms caught her short of her target, and held her tight, no matter how she twisted. "Lemme go!" Philippa yelled.

Other voices were shouting as well now. Someone grabbed her braid and yanked her head back to look at him. It was the Okie kid. "Shut up and settle down, willya?" he was saying, his face screwed up more with worry than anger. Beyond him

Philippa could see Junkyard, his arms pinioned by Karl and the long-faced guy. Water darkened Junkyard's shirt where Karl gripped him; Karl still held the tin plate he'd been washing.

Mara stalked in between the two groups, her face rigid. She looked at Junkyard and then back to Philippa. Philippa shrunk into herself.

Mara spoke very clearly. "You want to fight, that is—what do you call it—is jake. Get your things and go out. No fighting here." Her sweeping gesture took in the frozen night beyond the ice house walls. "Fight outside all you want. Not coming back until morning." With that pronouncement she swept back to where Betts lay wide-eyed.

Sick and shamed and hurting, Philippa didn't want to fight anymore. "Lemme go," she said again, but this time she whispered it.

Lukas and the Okie kid stepped away from her, letting her slip to her knees. Simon caught her gaze and held it for a moment, his hawk's eyes summing her up pretty small. "Foolish boy," he told her before he turned away.

Confused, Philippa watched him go. Had he somehow mistook her for a guy? She reached back to touch her braid, but her shoulder seized up, bruised somehow, stopping her. She could feel the weight of the hair anyways, dragging at her aching neck.

The guy was a foreigner, him and Mara and the redhead. He must've just got his words confused.

Chick kept a wary eye on Junkyard as Karl and the other guy let him go. Wiping the back of his hand across his mouth, the troublemaker glared a moment at Arlie, though she didn't see it. The look held a promise of further trouble down the road, when the consequences weren't so drastic. Foolish, Chick thought he'd just heard somebody call the guy, but snake-mean was more like it.

Junkyard shook out the tension from his arms and shoulders, and turned back to the stove where his pal stood, the pipsqueak's black eyes gleaming with excitement. Junkyard whacked the younger boy on the side of the head, then let his arm hang around the kid's neck as they walked back to where they'd been sitting before.

Chick felt his lip curling at that. Just pals, they were. No funny business there; none of that pansy stuff. Chick looked to Zeno to share the unspoken thought, but, flour sack in hand, the Greek was scowling down at the can he was drying. More than anything he looked disgusted by the whole thing—or by Chick getting himself involved, maybe.

Movement in the corner of his eye brought Chick around. Wincing, the girl was pushing herself upright. She didn't look at anybody, or say anything, but just started unsteadily again for the doorway. Telling himself to let her go, that maybe she just needed to take a leak, Chick found he'd followed her out.

The kid was tough. That louse had socked her really hard, twice, and instead of screaming like most girls, she'd gone for him. But he might've done her some serious damage, busted some teeth or even her jaw.

"Hold it, kid! Let me look at what he did to your face," he said, stretching his legs to get around in front of her.

"In a minute, OK?" The words sounded thick, like talking hurt her, but at least her jaw was working. He peered at her in the dim light that came through the curtain, but she turned her face away.

She spoke again, desperation forcing the words out. "Just lemme be!"

Chick hesitated. "You oughta take the flashlight with you, at least."

"I don' need it!"

The defiant wail, familiar from a hundred childhood scrapes, got through to him. With a wry smile he stood aside and let her go. "You come see me later, kid, you hear?" he called after her.

Philippa stumbled through the deep sawdust alongside the ramp until her groping hands came up short against the wall. She needed something to lean on and the large stones of the foundation would do. They smelt of dust and felt like ice against her skin. She pressed first one side of her face and then the other against the grainy surface, easing the throbbing of her bruises. Her scalp ached too, and the damned toe. Jesus, but she was a mess.

Philippa shook, standing there. Junkyard could've hurt her, real bad; why did she do these things? And now Mara figured her for a troublemaker.

Sometimes she just couldn't take being scared of people any more, doing what they wanted her to, or running away. She thought of the pounding she would've liked to have given that stuck-up bully, felt the blows in her arms and knotted fists. A vision of what she'd do to him, given half a chance, filled her mind, unclear on details but very bloody. The sour, choking taste returned as bile rose in her throat, and then she was on her knees, retching.

Afterward she rested her forehead once more on the stones and breathed carefully, trying to steady her mind. Cold air curled around her, slid by in a fitful stream, stirred up by the unabated wind on the other side of the walls. She found she was shuddering as the cold soaked deeper into her. Anyways, it was time for her to go and do what she had to do keep Junkyard off her back while she was here. Waiting didn't make it easier.

Limping back across the sawdust, she smelt again that peppery, axle-grease odor mixed in with the tang of the pine resin. A high squeal stabbed at her ears, ending abruptly with a hollow pop. Yellow sparks flew up from about where the jumble of broken machinery was, next to the privy. They traced a shower of arcs halfway across the ice house.

And then the smell was gone, and the sparks, and the tension in the air. The wind seemed to have quieted for the moment as well. Eyes wide in the darkness, Philippa stared around her. Had she imagined it, her senses playing tricks on her? Just to be sure she poked at what she could see of the woodpile by the jungle, the closest place the sparks seemed to have come down.

Nothing. After a moment of shivering indecision she headed for the doorway and the warmth of the stove.

6

Simon's head snapped up at the inhuman screech from beyond the camp walls.

"What the heck was that?" the youth called Deucey said, letting fall the pipe they used to prop the stove door shut. The black length of it clattered on the stones of the makeshift hearth.

"Betcha that storm's ripped away some roofing tin!" Karl answered him, piling the last of the dried dishes inside the pot where they were kept.

Simon stood, straining his ears, wishing they would all be still. And then they were, all of them standing and listening as he was. Even the wind had died down some, long enough for him to be sure the noise was gone now.

Roofing tin. The people here knew the sounds of their world far better than he did, but what if Karl's guess was wrong?

Karl slung the dishtowel on the line hung above the stove, next to a motley collection of socks, then wiped his hands on his pants. "Let's go take a look."

"Aw, forget about it," Junkyard Johnny said. "Too goddamn cold out there."

The dishwasher ignored him. Moving quickly, Simon stepped to block his path. "I will go," he said, thankful that no one else seemed driven to investigate.

Karl scowled at him, chin out.

Simon met the youth's gaze squarely. "I. Will. Go," he repeated, letting emphasis take the place of the argument he didn't have.

"That is right, Simon," Mara said. Her voice was calm, but there was dread in her wide black eyes. "We fix this place. To go is our responsibility."

Karl rolled his eyes, giving up. "Well, geez, go on then if you're so damned hot about it."

"For Pete's sake, quit yakking and go, or I'm gonna." somebody said from behind Simon. "That kid Arlie's still out there." It was the older of the two new youths, Simon saw as he turned.

"Yes," Simon said, pushing past him, not really listening.

They were talking about her, or leastways she heard her name. Philippa reached for the curtain anyways, and then stumbled aside when someone barged through it. That Simon guy, she thought, pausing a bit to let the pain in her jostled toe ease. He'd been in a god-awful hurry.

The Okie kid was standing almost in her way. Relief eased the lines of his face as he stepped back to let her by. "We lose some roofing out there?"

Puzzled at the question, Philippa answered him over her shoulder. "Not that I saw."

Karl called out to ask what the racket had been then.

"No idea. Didn't see nothing." Except sparks, but that had likely just been her eyes acting up. Nothing else made sense.

Other people asked her stuff but, shivering, she ignored them. What she wanted was to be left alone to go stand over the stove for a spell until she got the cold out of her bones, but even that'd have to wait.

Nip wasn't going to look up at her. Both him and the older guy seemed like they was working hard at acting bored. But it wasn't for either of them she was doing this. Drawing breath, she launched into her apology. "I didn't aim to snap at you that way, Nip. It was decent of you to save me the smoke," she said, and tried to sound like she meant it. Talking made the side of her mouth ache.

Nip looked off to the side, scowling, and then, finally, up at her. He shrugged. "OK." It was a grudging acceptance. At least it was unlikely he'd bother her much any more.

Philippa turned to Junkyard then; that was harder. Without the armor of rage she was scared stiff of him. "And I'm right sorry for calling you a jackroller." This at least was true. The older boy had the makings of a bully, and was dangerous with it, but jackrollers—bums who robbed their own kind for what little they had—were the scum of hobo society. "See, I was just mad."

Junkyard, laying back on the sawdust of the bulwark, his hands laced behind his head, nodded without enthusiasm. If she hadn't apologized to his sidekick first, she wouldn't have got even that. For now it'd do.

Shaky but relieved to have the ordeal over, Philippa hobbled toward the warmth of the stove.

Chick reached out and snagged the girl's sleeve as she limped past. "OK, kiddo," he said, keeping his voice low, aware of Zeno's disapproving eyes on him. "I said I was gonna take a look at that jaw, and I mean to do it. And the foot too—what the heck did you do to that?"

She pulled her arm free but without much energy. He wasn't hanging on hard. "Ain't nothing wrong with me," she muttered.

Chick sighed. The kid was just about as exasperating as his cousin Virge's little brother, Duwayne, had used to be. "Then there ain't no harm in me taking a look, is there?" He tried to keep his voice reasonable, even as he wondered why he was bothering. Somehow it just seemed the thing to do.

She eyed him with a weary distrust. After a minute she looked away, shrugging a little.

"So why don't you come sit down by the stove?" he went on, herding her along. "Here, where the lamp'll shine on you."

Stone-faced, she sat on the edge of the rough platform, half curled into herself like a wary puppy.

"There you go." Chick gave her his best grin, the one that generally disarmed housewives. It didn't seem to have much effect on her, though. She held still as he felt the side of her face, but tensely, her chin up like it was all she could do not to bolt.

The cheek near the mouth was swollen some, about like you'd expect. He probed the line of her jawbone and had her open and shut her mouth. The joints felt OK. "You bleeding?" Gingerly he hooked two fingers in her cheek to peer inside.

Panic flashed in the dark eyes and was gone; the feeling no more than stomped on, he was pretty sure.

"Nuh-uh," she said around his fingers, lying. He let go. Turning away, she reached up to cup the side of her face.

"Bit your cheek, looks like," Chick told her, looking at the pinkish spit on his fingers. "And you'll be lots of pretty colors by morning. Lucky kid." He slapped her lightly on the upper arm, the way he would've Duwayne. She looked surprised by that, but the tightness of her shoulders eased. "Okay, let's see the kicker."

Obedient this time, the kid bent to her holey canvas shoe. "Just so you know," he said, watching while she struggled with the laces, "my moniker's Chick O'Shea, though most folks just call me Chick."

The kid's fingers slowed a moment as she thought that over. A bit of a smile curled the unbruised corner of her mouth, though it didn't last. "Chickasha, like where you come from."

"That's the one," he agreed, pleased she'd made the connection. Uncovered, her big toe showed swollen and discolored. Chick cradled the end of the foot in his hand; ice cold, all but the toe. The kid looked a little sick at the sight of it.

"Zeno is getting snow," Mara the cook said at his elbow, as she folded herself easily to her knees.

Breath caught in his throat, Chick quick scanned the camp. No Zeno. But even if Zeno was mad, he wouldn't have just taken off, not at night and in this weather.

The kid's foot twitched. Loosening his hold, he asked, "Did I bump it?" though he didn't think he had. She shook her head, but tears had gathered in the corners of her eyes.

Mara had moved in closer, crowding him. She reached up to feel the kid's face. "Not bad damage, Arlie," she concluded, the same as he had. "But snow helps. How is your toe hurt?"

"Looks bust to me," Chick commented, but neither of them looked at him. The girl's gaze stayed fixed on Mara's face as she moved and talked. He had a suspicion that the tears had more to do with the cook being there than anything he'd done.

Arlie spared a glance for her toe. She swallowed. "Kicked a door," she said faintly.

Mara nodded. "Snow helps this also." She glanced over at Chick with a mischievous smile. "Here we have very much. In the south you are neighbors, yes? Arkansas and Oklahoma are beside each other? Perhaps together you should go find better weather there, bring back to us."

Chick frowned, unsure of what the cook meant, only that there was flirtation in it somewhere. Before he could try to figure it out the kid pulled her foot free of his hold.

"I ain't going nowhere with him or nobody," she said, her voice shrill. "I go my own way."

"A joke only," Mara responded, looking in surprise from Arlie to him and back again. Uncertainly she smiled. "Forget, please. We settle you for the night, over to our other sick one, yes?"

Head down, Arlie nodded. Chick, feeling slighted, was distant and careful as he helped her hop over to an unoccupied stretch of sawdust near Betts. Behind them the cook paused to turn down the light from the Coleman.

When she rejoined them Mara had Arlie's overalls in hand. As the kid wriggled into them, Zeno came back in. "That crazy wind is not so bad," he reported, not meeting Chick's gaze. He thumped the can of snow down beside them. "But it's cold as the heart of a damned whore out there. Glad it's not me getting iced up." Shivering, he went off to warm himself at the fire.

Drawn in spite of his misgivings, Chick went to join him.

Snow packed around Philippa's toe eased the throbbing pretty much right off, though the cold from it and the pack Mara'd handed her for her cheek sent waves of shudders through her whole body.

"No blankets," Mara said, watching her. "I am sorry. After I wrap the toe we will pile up sawdust over you. Good warmth for sleeping." She'd settled herself cross-legged near Philippa's head. "Now say why you made angry those boys."

Philippa's fit of the shudders got worse, went deep as the bone. Her mind had gone blank white on top like the skin of ice on a pond, and none of the words underneath could break through.

Mara waited. At last she said, shrugging in that one-sided way she had, "You don't want to talk, that is jake. I have other things to worry. Later I come back for wrapping the toe."

Her being mad again was more than Philippa could take. She grabbed for Mara's sleeve with her free hand as the older girl started to get up. "No," she whispered. The soggy, rag-wrapped snow pack slipped to one side.

Mara paused, balanced on one knee, her dark eyes neutral.

"It's just, it's just there's too much. I can't get it to…" Philippa drew in a deep breath and tried again. "About that Junkyard guy and all, see, sometimes I just get so mad. Nuts, kinda. Guys want me to do stuff with 'em, and when I can't they… they push at me. Sometimes I run away, but sometimes I get crazy."

Mara settled back down on her heels, but warily. "What 'stuff'?"

Philippa could see the older girl didn't have any notion of what she was talking about. She shut her eyes for a moment, fighting panic. "They want me to go with 'em, guys do," she whispered. "You know. Like you with Simon and your other pal. And like how Karl does with Betts. Nip wants that, wants to be like the older guys, see. Everybody tells me 'get wise,' but I can't. I don't want to. I want them to let me be."

Mara's forehead wrinkled. "But I am not with Simon and Lukas, not so, not here! Does everyone think this? We are comrades in the work, not man or woman to each other. In the work that is wrong!" She paused. Philippa, confused and shamed at having gotten things bollixed up again, hoped desperately she'd come out with something clearer.

The older girl drew a thoughtful breath and blew it out again. "See, it would be like you copulate with your brother, yes?"

A ghost explosion flashed behind Philippa's eyes, almost like what she'd seen when Junkyard socked her. Funny how words could do that about as well as a fist. Mara's comment hadn't been a direct hit, but close enough. Hank had used to call her Sister, though he didn't have no right to it.

Long practice allowed Philippa to slide such blows away, out of sight, hiding most of the effects. She forced herself to let her breath out slowly. "Sorry, Mara."

Mara nodded. "Better to understand," she answered, matter-of-fact. She was silent a moment, distracted, listening to the wind, it looked like. It had build up to a howl again. She turned to Philippa again and spoke decisively. "If you don't want to copulate with a boy, Arlie, nothing is wrong. Say this without insult and he goes away if he is… taught well. If not, you must fight, but to insult first is asking for hitting." Her face creased in a sudden, warm grin. "Sharing sex is good like nothing else, but you must want. Someday soon you know this.

"Hold the snow on your face, Arlie. I will come back." Setting the can down, Mara left at a deliberate pace, stepping around the kids who were already bunked down for the night on her way to the door out into the cold.

Dazed, Philippa watched her go. As the older girl disappeared through the curtain, she realized that Simon hadn't never come back in. Looking around, she couldn't make out Lukas either. He might be one of the figures bundled up on the floor, though, with their caps pulled down and sawdust heaped up over their feet.

It wasn't enough, what Mara'd said. She hadn't really understood, but then Philippa hadn't told her all of it.

But could it really be true that the other girls were wrong, maybe not for them, but for her? Was it possible to go ahead and be friends with guys without them pushing at you for sex and attention and all the other stuff that got mixed up with it? It was the pushing she couldn't bear.

Would they stop if you told them to, like Mara said?

She didn't want to have to tell them. It wouldn't be an issue if they thought she was just another boy, like it seemed Simon had mistook her for. Philippa yanked her braid out from under her shoulder, out where she could look at it. The brown hair was dulled and greasy, a lot of it coming loose from the plait. Still, sometimes when she had it tucked up inside a cap she had less trouble.

Meemaw had used to brush her hair every evening she got a chance. Philippa recalled the comforting pull against her scalp, and the occasional twinge of pain when the brush got caught. Meemaw's full voice saying, "Hold still, Filly. Lord a'mighty, but you're restless tonight!" The feel of her grandmother's fingers braiding the strands again, a lot faster than she could do it herself back then.

Blinking against the stinging in her eyes, Philippa let the braid slip from her grasp. Best not to think about that either.

7

Simon coughed; drew a prickly sleeve across his forehead. Cold as it was out here, he was sweating inside his coat. The clammy layer of cotton next to his skin made him even colder, but still the sweat came.

The readings made no sense. His first panicked look at the control slate had seemed to show nothing wrong. The frequencies were in balance and the slipgate on minimum, ready to open, in spite of the severe heat damage he'd found on the front panel of the dummy welder that held the anchor. Even the standard test had come out fine, like the ones he'd done after resetting the anchors. But scrolling back through the record on this anchor—the one the wanderers had uncovered—he was finding instances where a peculiar instability blurred the frequency mandala, or even wrenched it out of shape.

His bare hands clumsy with the cold, Simon separated the petals of the mandala, letting the images of each component flow past him, reading the patterns they made rather than the specific details. Harmonics. Power consumption. Power transmission…

With a stroke of a fingertip he stopped the flow; set it spiraling forward again. What should have showed as a steady stream of energy, the golden rope that tied the worlds together, as Conrad had termed it during their training, had snarled dramatically, then thinned to a fraying thread. It was as though the power was somehow being drained away. And this could be no more than one part of the problem, he was sure.

Swallowing, Simon drew back from the anchor, as though simply touching the display slate could cause the entire system to collapse. Just the lack of energy flow would cause them serious difficulties, not immediately, but once they'd drawn down what was stored in the thermal layer the technologists had added to the depths of the lake outside. Opening a slipgate took as much power as that consumed by a square *li* of a Night World city, even if only for a brief moment. If they were going to call for help—if it was even possible, given what had happened earlier—they'd need to do it soon.

If he could only figure out what was causing all this, he perhaps might fix it himself. That would save Ebvili the trouble of sending someone to repair it at the only time they could, in the darkest hour of this world's dark night, while all the wanderers in the jungle slept. Shifting to a more comfortable position—his calves had begun to burn from the strain of squatting beside the massive welder—Simon reached hesitantly for the glazed surface of the slate. The key had to be somewhere in the record of the past day.

Yes, certainly, a voice from inside him mocked; he could fix it as he had the imbalance from the wanderers' tampering. A simple job, that had been.

The faint squeak of wood on wood brought his head up. The access hatch, which had been built to seem no more than a section of the privy's left-hand wall, slid free. Lukas' shadowy face appeared, furrowed with concentration as he set the hatch carefully aside. Beyond him Simon could see a portion of the privy interior, and another dark opening on the far wall where the twin anchor sat.

"What did you find?" Simon demanded, though he kept his voice low. Sound carried oddly in here, sometimes echoing from one side of the wide space to the other, and at other times damped down by the sawdust.

Lukas didn't answer; he only gaped at the anchor's face. Simon peered over the top, examining it again in the yellow light of Lukas' flashlight. The dial was gone, melted away, and the orange paint of the metal showed a spider's web of scorch marks. The top edge of the case sagged a little, as though it had been on the edge of melting. Knowing what he did now, the sight wasn't quite as shocking.

"Wh-what did this?" Lukas stuttered, something he rarely did anymore. "It is destroyed!"

"It isn't." Simon gripped his bvarit's shoulder to steady him. "At least I hope it is not. Though we have some power problems, I found the immediate test results were normal."

"As they seem to be on the other. Yes." Lukas glanced at Simon for the first time, hope in his eyes. "That wouldn't be possible if either was not functioning, would it?"

"If an anchor ceased functioning," Simon told him grimly, "we would have worse problems than we do. But something is still wrong here, something that intermittently throws the entire harmonic field off-balance. And that…"

"Simon!"

Starting, they both turned at the piercing whisper. It had been Mara's voice, though Simon couldn't see her out in the heavy darkness of the ice house. He swept the flashlight across the uneven, debris-scattered floor, the beam low so as not to blind her.

There she was, half the way across the floor to them but looking stranded, as though her courage had given out. Irritated, Simon lighted her path.

Reaching them, Mara squatted down beside the anchor, arms wrapped tight around herself against the cold.

"I thought you would come out earlier," Simon said, turning away. She was better with the technical aspects of slipgates than Lukas was, to begin with. And they had to decide what to do next, all three of them together.

Mara's chin came up. "I left as soon as I could, Simon. It isn't good for us all to go at once, so I helped tend Arlie's hurts, from the fighting."

That new wanderer, Simon thought, scowling; the youngest of them. He kept his mouth closed down tight on the frustration that bubbled up inside him. Even the children here fought like animals, and more often than not over nothing, as though they didn't suffer enough pain in this frigid, barbarian world of theirs.

Lukas spoke hastily. "He is only worried, Mara. There is some instability in the slipgate."

Mara turned to him. "Can you fix that?"

No details for her, Simon thought bitterly. She speared to the heart of any matter. "Not without knowing what causes it."

She gave him a faint bow of approval for his honesty. "Then one of us will need to go call for help, tomorrow when the storm calms."

Walk the fifteen li to town in truth, not just a story told to explain an absence. In this world you needed protective clothing only against the cold; sunlight would not overwhelm you. Simon drew a deep breath, coughing again as the frigid air caught in his throat. Perhaps he would volunteer to go if it should come to that.

But they were not yet to that point. "We may be able to use it, Mara, for a message at least. You might have only been unlucky before. Come see." Simon woke the control slate by tapping it, and showed her what he'd found.

Lukas came around to peer over her shoulder. He gave this up soon enough, however, muttering, "I will get a new message sphere," as he left.

"Yes, I see it!" Mara said. "That is strange. Will it be safe for a repair technologist to cross here?"

Simon thought. "I wouldn't choose to take such a risk. Still I'll mirror all the data from both anchors in the new report for Vaitnu to assess, along with my warning." He smiled wryly. "If someone must travel here from St. Paul or a farther mission, the sooner they get our message, the better for us."

"So, you fancy that skinny bit of jailbait, hey?" Zeno asked, propped up on his elbows, his fedora tipped back on his head as though Chick's answer wouldn't matter to him one way or the other. It was the first thing he'd said since Chick had followed him back over to the corner they'd staked out.

Chick hugged his knees. "Hell, Zeno. She ain't nothing but a little kid." Try to help somebody and see where it got you, he thought bitterly. He wished Zeno would just go ahead and blow his stack. He wouldn't, though, not here in the jungle.

Zeno nodded like he was being polite. "Not so smart, either, judging by how she took on the Bulldog. But like they say, there's no accounting for tastes."

"From what I hear," Chick answered him—the anger that was rising in him thick in his voice, and it was all he could do to keep it low—"brains ain't what guys want a girl for. But you know as well as I do that I ain't interested in messing with girls. You know it! So how come you keep poking at me about it?" Zeno was looking at him now, at least. "Kid just seems like she needs some looking after. That's all it is."

Zeno's dark eyes held his. "I met a kid like that a few months back. Late June, I think it was."

Chick looked away; rubbed his face. He was very tired, and a headache had started up behind his eyes. With the scavenged metal signs that formed the movable ceiling panels shoved back into place to help hold in the heat, it seemed like the air in the jungle was getting kind of thick. "It ain't like it was with us, Zeno. I swear it ain't. And the kid don't want my help anyway."

Zeno's broad jaw tightened.

I ought to just keep my trap shut, Chick told himself, scared now. "It's you I want to be with," he whispered. "Please, Zeno."

Zeno's nostrils flared, though the angry hurt hadn't left his eyes. Lips barely moving, he said, "Go on out. Wait."

Shaky, breathless, Chick obeyed. As he got to his feet he scanned the jungle for potential trouble. He thought the cook and at least one of her pals were still gone. Him and Zeno would have to watch their step. At least with the wind howling like it was, a little noise wouldn't matter. Most everybody else looked to be sleeping, curled up under their coats if they had them, or huddled close to somebody who did. The horse-faced guy Deucey was sitting up next to Flo, though, both of them as near the stove as they could get without risking getting scorched. First turn at fire watch.

He tried strolling out easy like all he had on his mind was a piss, but his leg muscles twitched at odd moments. Watching him, Flo let her lip curl. Bitch, he muttered, pulling up his collar. What was it to her what he did?

At the doorway, Chick grabbed hold of the curtain. He hesitated, then pulled it back to step out into the darkness. The sweat on his upper lip chilled to ice as the draft hit him.

A flash of light caught his eye from across the ice house; to one side of the privy, not in it. Still as a rabbit, Chick squinted at the figures moving before and behind the light. A murmur of voices came to his ears, but, try as he might, he couldn't make sense of any of it.

It had to be foreign kids, though what could keep them over there next to that mountain of junk in this cold? Sure wasn't no love nest.

He faded back into the deeper shadow of the woodpile. Maybe they had themselves a radio transmitter hid out there. The cockeyed notion made him grin in spite of the roil his feelings were in. Sure, they were Comintern agents who'd snuck over the Canadian border to organize the masses, and now they were off giving their daily report to their bosses.

Well, that was about what they'd sounded like after supper, but who'd bother spending time on road kids like him and the others? Regretfully Chick let the idea go.

Close at hand the curtain stirred. Stiffening, Chick reached out, taking hold of Zeno's arm as it appeared, to warn him, to draw the man near.

Between desire and the sick dread that still crawled in his guts, he thought he might just puke.

When Simon began the preparation of his report, Mara went back to the jungle to divert any of the wanderers who might feel a need to visit the privy. Transferring the anchor data to the new sphere was simple and quick, as the mirroring process was designed to be. Simon took a little more time with his verbal report. Flashlights off, he and Lukas sat huddled together against the privy wall fartherest from the waste pit. He found he had to speak through clenched teeth to keep them from chattering. There wasn't much added warmth in Lukas' shoulder pressed against his, but it gave him comfort in the darkness.

"Have I forgotten anything?" Simon asked at last, his big hand covering the ceramic core in its voice cradle, to muffle their discussion enough to pause the recording.

"The storm," Lukas said, after thought. "Just in case." Minor weather disturbances were not uncommon in the vicinity of even perfectly functioning slipgates. "You weren't here when it began. I will report on it." His groping hand found Simon's, and took the cradle and sphere.

The report done, Simon sent Lukas back to the jungle to wait. There was no need for more than one of them to be at risk, though the quick test he did of the anchors showed them functioning normally for the moment. Nervous in spite of this, his left hand damp on the newly sealed rubber casing of the sphere, he woke the slipgate.

For a long moment nothing at all happened, and Simon's stomach and hand both clenched tighter. Then a light-filled crack appeared in the space between the two hidden anchors, and slowly the Jaguar's Eye opened, brilliant and golden, though it lit nothing in the small space of the privy.

Brilliant and golden and somehow billowing lopsidedly, as though the wind outside blew across it. Still, it was open. Not hesitating, Simon tossed the sphere underhanded into the light's center, which swallowed it without a trace.

He stepped to one side, by the doorway, and waited. If his report was going to come back to him, he wanted to know it.

Nothing happened but a growing distortion of the Eye. The bottom curve seemed too high, as though it floated free a handspan above the sawdust floor, and Simon had a sudden understanding of his stumbling arrival hours earlier. He'd never noticed a slipgate doing that before.

Belatedly remembering the choked-down energy transmission, Simon let the slipgate shut. A shortage of power might cause such an effect. Maybe.

To be shivering again in the frigid darkness was almost a relief. Still he waited awhile, leaning on the doorpost.

The slipgate did not reopen on its own; nothing came hurling out of the void between worlds. Simon felt a smile stretch his numbed lips as he pushed through the heavy curtain, flicking on his flashlight. One way or another, help would come.

Philippa woke when Mara tried to slip off her shoe. Without thinking about it she jerked her foot away; folks who messed with your shoes while you slept generally meant to steal them.

Mara smiled at her. She looked tired and more than usually foreign in the dim light, and the smile didn't lighten her eyes. "Shh, Arlie. I try not to wake you."

"Umm." Philippa tried to make sense out of things. The air seemed somehow heavy. She'd been dreaming, she realized: the wind driving a secret fire that ate across paradise, which looked like she used to imagine Canaan Land in the hymns. "It late?" she asked, and started to yawn. Her sore jaw protested. She cupped a hand to it, to soothe it.

"No."

Still holding her jaw, Philippa looked around at the jungle, blinking away the grit in her eyes. Sitting up nearby, Betts coughed fitfully. Karl knelt before the stove poking at the fire, face reddened by its light. It was another whole fire watch later, anyways. Chick and the old guy were curled together spoon-fashion for warmth, the old guy's stained brown fedora resting on the side of his head, keeping that ear from the chill air. Across the camp Junkyard and Deucey slept with Nip between them, snug under a share of the older boys' coats.

Guys could do that, huddle up with their pals on cold nights, and nobody'd try to take advantage.

Mara had got the shoe off and had placed a fold of cloth between the broken toe and its neighbor. Being touched made the damn thing throb again. Using an odd hook-bladed little knife to start the process, Mara tore off a long strip off her shirttail. She wrapped it carefully around and around the two toes.

Philippa watched the older girl. The look of concentration on her face did not alter the anxious lines around her mouth. "Mara, what's going on? Something's wrong, ain't it?" Philippa stopped breathing for a second when she heard her own words. She hadn't meant to say them.

Mara's mouth tightened. She stared off over Philippa's shoulder. "Nothing wrong, Arlie."

"Can I help?"

Mara met her gaze, a hard look. "Go to sleep."

Philippa tried again, taking an indirect tack, drawing on a confused memory of her dream. "Lukas talked about this land could be a paradise. You guys really believe that?"

The older girl scowled. "I *know* that."

"And we all gotta work together somehow to make it that way?"

"Yes." Mara sighed. "Listen, Arlie, tomorrow we talk of this." She bent again to help ease the rubber boot over Philippa's canvas-shod foot.

Philippa hissed at the pain. After she got her breath back she whispered, "Call me Philippa. That's my born name."

Mara nodded, trying to smile.

Philippa wasn't done yet. "So if we all gotta work together, and if what's going on has to do with that someways, tell me what the score is."

The older girl shook her head in exasperation. She was smiling, however, a real smile. "Go to sleep, Philippa." She stretched up far enough to lay a kiss on Philippa's forehead, a brush of dry lips.

Meemaw had used to do that. Philippa lay still and hugged the feeling close.

"I know," Mara said softly, almost like she was talking to herself, "that here could be paradise because where I come from —the world I come from, Philippa—is so now, is paradise. No night is there, and no hunger. All have work and each other. Still is the same earth and plants and people. So we come here to teach, to share the ways of making your world what it can be.

"Dream well."

Philippa lay rigid and trembling, her thoughts spinning wildly as she watched Mara go. Tears squeezed hot out of the corners of her eyes. She felt like a big scab had been ripped away, leaving her as exposed as flesh scraped clean of skin. That guy Chick had said it: the place where your needs were met and your people were, that was home. She needed to be there.

Another world?

Hope was terrifying.

Eventually she slept.

8

The shriek of a train braking roused Philippa, though she was confused not to feel the slowing sway of a boxcar beneath her. The cold, stale air carried a solvent reek like a leaky tank car was somewheres close by. Had she fallen asleep beside the tracks? There were other sounds too, a roaring that was both inside her head and outside it all at once, and dry clickings like hobnailed boots on stones. Somebody coughing, and voices.

Took a long while for that to spark panic in her groggy mind, but when it did she struggled to sit up, to drag open her eyes so she could figure out where to run to get out of sight.

Rough walls; a dimly lit roof overhead. Philippa gaped at them. The ruddy glow that leaked from the rust pinholes in the oil drum stove showed huddled sleepers all around her. It was Betts who was coughing, low and steady in her sleep. This was the ice house jungle, and a long walk from any tracks, let alone a rail yard. The roaring and clicks continued, though, and the air still stank of solvent. This was wrong; she knew it, but the suppressed thunder in the air, the wind's pounding, filled her head like a balloon and made it hard to think.

But hadn't that tension gone away earlier, back when she'd seen the sparks?

No one seemed to be standing watch. Philippa fixed her cloudy thoughts on that notion, which at least was something she could understand. With nobody watching the fire would go out. Crawling to the stove because it was easier than trying to stand, she nudged the metal plate far enough aside to peek in.

Sullen flames flickered low over the coals. Cripes, she grumbled to herself, why couldn't people just do what they were supposed to, instead of shoving their jobs off on other folks? She was going to have to fetch more wood from the pile.

Unsteadily she pulled herself up, using Mara's wooden crate to help. It took a couple of tries. She wasn't dizzy, exactly, but the floor didn't seem to be in the right place.

She limped in the general direction of the door. Karl was sitting up, she saw then. "Help me get some wood," she told him, or thought she did.

He didn't look at her at all. He muttered something she couldn't make out through the racket in her head. He tried to stand as she reached him, but couldn't manage it.

Red face; watery, unfocused eyes; sloppy movements. Didn't make sense out here in the middle of nowhere, but looked like he was drunk as a polecat. Disgusted, Philippa staggered on past him.

Simon sagged against the privy's doorframe. The freezing air out here had cleared his thoughts somewhat, but still his temples pounded. With one hand he pushed aside the curtain.

Lukas and Mara both turned slowly to look at him, their faces bewildered in the dull beam of the flashlight. "No one is here!" Mara said. "But the slipgate opened, did it not? You felt it too?"

Simon nodded, puzzled. His *iyar pukko* had pulsed like a second heartbeat against his wrist, a passive alarm dragging him from heavy dreams. Though in fact a pall of drowsiness still clung to him, as if the dreams would not release him. "Perhaps they hid when they heard us." He turned to look out into the darkness; too quickly, for his head swam and he lurched sideways, clutching at the curtain to save himself.

His weight was too much for the fabric. It tore loose from the nails that had held it, and followed him down.

Dazed, Simon pushed himself up to his knees, spitting bits of sawdust. His body felt heavy as earth. Could he be ill, in spite of the protection that was the primary function of his iyar pukko? He felt very odd.

"Look what you've done, Simon!" Holding onto the doorframe, Mara gazed down at him, looking so appalled he felt a spurt of laughter. The impulse died, though, before it reached his mouth. Clumsily he untangled his hand from the folds of dusty cloth and got again to his feet.

"No one came through," Lukas said tonelessly, out of sight behind the wooden wall. "They have only sent us back a message."

Pulled by sudden hope, Simon followed Mara back into the privy. Perhaps Vaitnu believed them capable of rebalancing the system on their own, and so had sent them advice.

Hesitant, Lukas held the sphere out. "It is damaged."

The rubber casing was shredded and blackened, worse than the one Mara had brought him. Simon took it; felt the trace of heat in it still. He turned the sphere beneath the orange beam of the flashlight. Hope withered as he saw the remains of the stripes. "This was my report," he whispered.

Mara reached for it. "Are you sure?" As she did so, a golden sun rose behind them.

Turning, Simon saw the blaze of an open slipgate, the shape of the Eye billowing madly as though it would tear free of the anchors. Adrenaline cleared his mind and gave him the energy to act. Dropping the sphere, he threw himself at the right-hand wall. Lukas was already scrabbling at the other access hatch. "Shut it down, Lukas!" Simon hissed. "Help me ease it down!"

Philippa found the woodpile by falling over it. "Cripes," she muttered, scrabbling to free herself from the icy tangle of branches. Somebody had the durn flashlight. She'd seen dim flashes of its light over by the privy as soon as she'd got out here, and heard voices too. Tried to yell at whoever it was to come help her, but seemed all she could do was croak.

She pulled weakly on a branch to free it, then felt along its length. Frustrated, she let it fall again. This stuff was too long to go in the stove. She groped her way around the pile on her knees, trying to recollect which way the heap of cut wood lay. Her thoughts kept chasing their tails, though. No blessed help at all.

A sudden brightness snagged the corner of her eye; brought her around. Philippa's mouth fell open. A tall, golden rectangle had opened in the darkness like the door to paradise.

No, wait a minute, Philippa told herself, blinking to try and clear her eyes. It had to be the privy's doorway, but then what was the light? Had the storm knocked a hole in the wall beyond, and let the rising sun in?

Couldn't be. Confused as everything was, Philippa was dead certain it was hours yet until dawn. She squatted where she was, gripping her aching head as though that might help her understand.

A bulky figure stepped in front of the light, outlined there, bent a little forward as though reaching out for something. Sweater-and-coat-bulky, short-haired, not very tall. Mara. Philippa breathed the name.

This *was* the door to paradise, the one Mara had told her about. It had to be.

"Mara!" she cried, staggering to her feet. "Let me go with you!" She ran out of breath before she finished.

But Mara had heard her, all right; the girl jerked around to peer blind into the darkness. A god's voice boomed out a question, rolling like thunder up in the rafters, though the words were some foreign gabble, other than Lukas' name.

She didn't care what it said, Philippa told herself, and started struggling toward the light across the soft, uneven floor. After a moment it came to her that the godlike voice sounded a bit like Simon.

"Go! Is, is danger!" Mara yelled at her. The older girl was switching back and forth in the doorway like she couldn't decide which way to head. Her voice sounded OK though, only panicky and out of breath.

If they were going off to paradise she didn't aim to be left behind. Philippa hurried as well as she could. Three steps later her foot came down in a hollow, and she fell again, wailing in frustration. Her outstretched hands broke her fall, sinking up to the wrist in soft, warm sawdust.

Warm. Almost hot. For a long moment Philippa left her hands where they were, soaking up the warmth, but then she started coughing. This close to the ground, a scorched smell joined the chemical stink she'd begun to get used to. She peered around her, but staring at that golden light had blown her night vision. At first she couldn't make out a thing, and coughing didn't help.

She shut her eyes and then opened them again. Dark patches marked the sawdust here and there; shadows? But a little ways off there was a faint wisp of blue that danced away before she could focus on it.

Danced like low flames over one of the dark patches. She *had* seen sparks earlier.

"Fire!" Philippa bawled, scrambling back from it. "Fire! Everybody out!"

After slightly too long a pause, she heard Simon's god-voice exclaiming, "Fire?" The end of the word twisted into normalcy.

Lukas shrieked, "Simon!" Mara's silhouette raised a hand, stepped towards the light and seemed to stumble; was gone. Philippa gasped, choking on the fumes she drew in.

And the light bloomed golden. A new, unearthly wind howled through the ice house, inside it, not out, a blinding chaos of whirling sawdust.

Darkness clamped down, sudden as death. The doorway was gone, and Mara, and the wind too, though dust still hung thick in the air. If Mara's pals were still around, she didn't hear them; nothing but a dead silence. Despairing, Philippa covered her nose and mouth with one hand, and struggled back toward the jungle. Whatever had happened just now, she still had to wake everybody up and get them out.

A pop, felt more than heard, was her only warning as the patches of burning sawdust ignited the dusty air. Fire, the air itself burning, roared up behind her. Philippa dove forward; swam forward gasping through fire; breathed fire.

The light left her beached in its wake, but fire stayed in her lungs.

Chick came awake on his feet, thunder like he'd never heard before crashing inside his head. When he tried to move he found stuff was leaning on him, poking him, splintered planks, he thought, and maybe sheets of metal.

His heart was pounding like he'd run a mile. Confused, he blinked to clear the haze from his eyes. Red light danced on the stones of the wall in front of him, and smoke stung his throat when he drew breath. Was there a fire?

A girl shrieked. Chick jerked around to try and find her. Something heavy slipped from his shoulder off to one side, but it smacked something else that swung up, jabbing him hard in the belly, knocking the wind out of him.

Jackknifed over, coughing, he tried to get a hold on himself as the screaming faded to a pitiful, breathless whimper. He had to get free first, before he could do a thing else.

Like get the hell out of here! he thought, panic knotted in his guts.

But where was Zeno?

Get free. Find Zeno. Find the girl; was it the Arkie kid? He clawed and slithered his way upward, until he was more on top of the tangle than down in it, enough to move, to look around.

Fire was eating its way up the remains of the one standing jungle partition, and starting on bits of the fallen ceiling. Half the eastern ice house wall was gone, blown out, not to mention a good bit of the roof, but all that was too high up to do anybody any good getting out.

At least he wasn't the only one up and moving about, thank Christ. And one of them was Zeno, hatless, kneeling and digging bare-handed in the sawdust like a terrier after a rat. Chick clambered across to him; grabbed him by the shoulder. "You OK? For Pete's sake, Zeno, are you OK?"

Zeno's face when he turned it up was that of a man looking straight into hell, his eyes spread wide as banty eggs. "Arnie's under here, Dink!" he gasped, pulling at Chick's sleeve. "Trench wall came down on him when that last whizbang hit. Get a shovel!"

Arnie? Dink? Shocked, Chick jerked loose. "You nuts?" Then understanding flashed in him. Zeno thought he was back in France, in the war. Chick took hold of both his shoulders, meaning to give him a shake, but the mad desperation in Zeno's eyes stopped him. No time to try to bring him out of it.

Hastily Chick glanced around. Karl and Deucey weren't far off, trying clumsily between them to work free a sizeable panel of wood. "Betts!" Karl yelled, coughing, reaching down into the dark space below with his free hand. Fire, yellow and roaring, licked closer to them.

"Over there!" Chick said, pulling Zeno around. "You got turned around, see. Arnie's under there." He gave Zeno a push, praying he'd go.

He did, at a stumbling run and not looking back.

But it had been from somewheres else Chick had heard that scream—over there, where the jungle wall had collapsed. A hoarse yell came from there now, and a hand groping out of the mess. Not a girl's this time, but Chick threw himself at the treacherous tangle of wood, crawling on all fours to reach it.

There was nothing. No sight, no smells, no sound but the unending echo of Lukas shouting inside his mind.

"Siimonnn!"

It had taken what had seemed an eternity for him to recognize the nothingness, torn as he was by the scream, by his failure. Now they seemed one thing; the only thing there was.

Nothing. And the knifepoint of failure.

Again.

"Come on, wake up!"

Philippa opened her eyes. Someone was slapping her back. She breathed in, and tried to scream. Her throat and lungs felt flayed. She curled up into a ball, struggling to find a balance between pain and her need for air.

"C'mon now, kid! You gotta move!" the voice begged her. "I can't haul you 'cause I got Betts." It was Karl. His skin and clothes were charred in places, his eyes dazed. Betts lay sprawled next to Philippa, set down or dropped there, her face bruised and slack.

"OK, OK, I'm moving," Philippa whispered. "Go on." She raised her head and gazed stupidly around.

The ice house was a scene out of her Meemaw's Baptist hell. No more than fifteen feet from her flame shot up from what must've been the woodpile, the heat of it beating against her face. Beyond it the wall above the stonework foundation had caught. Small fires were scattered everywhere. A few figures, unrecognizable in the flickering glare and drifts of smoke, worked frantically at a pile of junk near the wall.

A pile that was all that was left of their camp.

Already Karl was halfway to the ice chute, Betts dangling head-down over his shoulder. Philippa crawled after him. Her hair hung down into her face, ragged, getting in the way of her seeing where she was going. She shoved it back but it wouldn't stay put.

Ahead of her, part way up the chute, Karl choked and stumbled as he reached a layer of smoke that hung thick and billowing above them. Unbalanced by Betts' limp weight, he fell flat on the steep slope. His worn boots kicked frantically, trying to find enough purchase to boost himself and Betts to the top. Scrambling up behind him, Philippa grabbed one of his flailing boots and jammed it against the chute's raised edge. She held it in place while Karl got his other knee beneath him. Then the weight was off her straining arm and shoulder as Karl shuffled upward once again.

A little further up the endless ramp she hit the smoke layer herself. Philippa's scorched throat and chest clamped up. She pulled herself another foot higher as vision blacked out, then rolled over the chute's edge, back down to the sawdust floor. She landed more or less on her feet, but let herself slide all the way down. There she dragged dirty air into her lungs regardless of the pain.

Uneven footsteps sounded on the ramp above. She opened her eyes: Deucey, half-dragging somebody.

That was… How many? Four. Not enough. There was still the Okie kid Chick, and, and… She couldn't think anymore.

Above her the roof had caught in three places. She stared, fascinated, at the way the bright flames outlined the rafters— until a length of planking broke free and spun downward.

Lord a'mercy, but she had to get out of here! Philippa rolled to her knees and pulled herself painfully to the base of the chute. The old balding guy staggered past just as she got there, Flo hanging limp in his arms. Dead, something deep in Philippa's mind told her. She winced away from the clammy feel of it.

Climbing was harder this time. Mountain of glass, she thought wearily, a vague image from some book of tales floating up in her mind.

The chute shook under heavy footsteps. Forearms trembling, Philippa tried to scoot over as far as she could. If I roll off again, she told herself clearly, I'll never get out.

"Thank Christ! I thought… we'd lost you too," Chick panted from behind. "Hold on. Be back." He plodded past her, a smaller kid dangling from his shoulders in a fireman's carry. Dirty striped sweater. The scrawny kid with the cigarette, but she couldn't bring his name to mind.

The layer of smoke swallowed them both.

Philippa laid her head down on the planks. She could make it up on her own, if she just had a moment to rest.

Something big whomped down behind her, and she jerked up again, scuttling upwards without the need to think about it. Then a hand grabbed her jacket collar; hauled her blind and wheezing through the smoke and whirling dust, out into the snow and the still night air.

9

*O*ut in the ruins something snapped like a charred stick might under the pressure of a boot. Chick's drooping head jerked up. "Zeno?" he called, ignoring the glances he got. "That you?" He scrambled to his feet and turned away from the light of the campfire they'd built down inside the foundation wall, peering out into the wavering shadows.

Nothing. Likely it had been no more than a shifting of the treacherous jumble of beams in the southwest corner.

"You sure he made it out?" Junkyard was staring down at his filthy hands, opening and closing them like he wasn't sure they worked anymore. "Maybe he's buried under all that crap with the Wobs."

"I seen him go up," Arlie whispered.

But Chick had already rounded on Junkyard. "Sure I'm sure! He was hauling Flo out while you was still cross-eyed and no use to anybody!"

Junkyard's hands curled into fists. "Didn't do her much good," he muttered.

On the edge of snapping back at him, Chick saw that the guy still looked pretty pasty underneath the soot. Truth was they all felt like hell warmed over, exhausted and burned and bruised, not to mention sick to their stomachs if how he felt was anything to go by.

"Can it, fellas," Deucey said, hoarse from the smoke. "Ain't fittin' to talk that way about the dead."

Wearily Chick squatted down, rubbing at his forehead with one sleeve. At the moment it wasn't the dead that worried him most. Zeno was out there somewheres, and maybe not thinking straight. It had seemed like he'd snapped out of his funk helping to free Betts. But then when he'd hauled Flo out, had laid her down in the snow and seen she was dead, with the blood from her all sticky down the front of his coat, he'd up and walked off into the trees without another word.

"Mara and them ain't… under that stuff neither." Arlie breathed like talking hurt. Chick looked down at her. The kid had lost her eyebrows and lashes, he saw, along with most of her hair. Scorched patches showed around her nose and mouth.

"Yeah? Did you see 'em come out?" Hope rose in Chick. The kid had been out in the ice house when whatever it was had blown up and set the fire going. Could be she'd seen what nobody else had. And if the Wobs had got out, Zeno might be holed up with them, wherever they'd ended up. Out among the trees, maybe.

Arlie opened her mouth to answer, but Junkyard drowned her out, a keyed-up edge to his voice. "Wasn't talking about no dead people, Deuce. I was talking about Zeno. Whaddya think, Nip?" He poked the dozing boy beside him with an elbow. "You guys figure that old wolf just decided to take a hike, leave Lambie here on his own?"

Rage and fear washed through Chick like a tide of cold, cold light. He was going to have to fight the lousy son of a bitch. "Take it back, Junkyard!" he said through gritted teeth.

Junkyard curled his lip. "For cri-yi-yi! Can't you take a damn joke?" He shrugged Nip's head off his shoulder and got to his feet. "All right then, you ain't nobody's little lamb. And I'm the damn queen of Romania." He bent to snatch the unburnt end of a stick from the fire. "Gonna have a look around." Sitting up now but still dazed, Nip watched him go.

Chick watched after the guy too, the fear ebbing, leaving his rage to smolder on its own.

"Watch how you go!" Deucey called after Junkyard. "Ain't nobody looking to go rescue you again."

Junkyard only grunted.

Chick looked around at the remaining faces at the fire, trying to judge what they were thinking. Nip only curled miserably up in the space Junkyard had left, and shut his eyes once more.

Deucey met Chick's gaze squarely. "Oughtn't to take that fella so serious. From what I've seen he picks at folks when he don't know what else to do with himself."

Chick nodded. Deucey was probably right. On the other hand there were things a guy had no choice but to take serious.

Across the fire Karl sat as he had since they'd settled back down inside the ruins: rocking back and forth, cradling Betts' head in his lap. He sure enough had something to worry about other than who Chick lay down with. Each breath rattled in Betts' throat, and heat radiated from her skin like it did from the foundation stones. She'd come halfway around earlier, when Karl had stuck a piece of ice in her mouth. Without even a tin can they had no way to melt snow or even carry water, and anyway the lake was frozen solid.

Which was a funny thing in itself. He'd dipped up a couple of cans of water out of the lake yesterday afternoon. It'd felt warmish on his skin, at least until the air had hit it. Just now, though, it'd taken him and Junkyard pounding at it with rocks to break loose enough ice to ease their raw throats.

"I seen Mara leave," Arlie whispered at his elbow. Chick turned to her, confused until he recollected that he'd asked her about that, back before Junkyard had started ragging on him. The kid was staring into the flames, a hand tugging aimlessly at her burned hair. "Right before everything blew," she went on. Chick had to bend close to hear her. "Heard the other two yelling."

Chick frowned. "They left before?"

Junkyard, his makeshift torch no more than a flicker out in the darkness, made a choked sort of yell. Then he called out, "C'mere, you guys! And somebody bring more light!"

He wasn't going to listen, Philippa thought wearily as Chick turned at Junkyard's call. And she needed to tell somebody what she'd seen, crazy as it was. She let her hand fall to her lap as Deucey got up. He picked his way across to Junkyard, a bony hand shielding the flame from a pine knot to keep it going.

"Holy Jesus." The two guys stood staring down for a long minute. "Looks like we found one of 'em," Deucey called back at last.

"Zeno?" she asked uneasily, glancing at Chick, feeling the charred ends of her hair scrape the back of her neck under her turned-up collar. Maybe he'd gone back in, and she hadn't seen it?

Chick glared at her and everybody else. "I told y'all already he got out!" He scrambled to his feet and stalked over to see what they'd found. Unsteadily Nip followed him. Karl, his hands full with Betts, stayed put. Maybe it was the firelight, but Philippa thought she saw the gleam of tears in his eyes.

Panting with the effort, she struggled up to join the others, though she hung back out of a clear line of sight, wanting to know while being scared to at the same time.

Junkyard had knelt and was scraping ash away with the end of one of his boards. A sweetish smell like that from overdone pork wafted past Philippa's nose, mixed in with the charcoal reek of the fire.

Nausea twisted her belly into a knot of stone, made it harder for her to breathe. It couldn't be Mara. She'd seen her fall into that doorway. But if Chick was right wasn't nobody else missing here. One of them hadn't made it home. She stared at the flaky ash that covered the ground.

"Jeez, it looks like one of those Egyptian mummies," Nip breathed, awestruck.

"It's a guy. Simon or Lukas," Junkyard said flatly, wiping his hands roughly on his trousers. Getting up, he pushed his way past them.

"Not much we can do about him now," Chick said after an uneasy pause, his voice thin and pitched too high. A painful gagging interrupted. Philippa turned to look. A few yards away Junkyard leaned one-handed against a fallen beam, his back jerking as he heaved into the charred shadows. The other guys all looked away. Chick went on like he hadn't heard. "Pile rocks over him come morning, him and Flo too, I guess." He backed carefully away, not entirely steady.

"Pile rocks over who?" a guy asked from behind them. Not Karl.

The Okie kid whirled. Relief showed raw on his face in the firelight. "Zeno! Where the *hell* have you been?"

The man's broad-nosed face tightened. After a little too long a pause he said, "I heard the ruckus and came to see what was doing." He was shivering, Philippa saw, and no wonder. The front of his coat hung wet and heavy.

There was another pause between him and Chick, and Philippa's attention wandered. Something white caught her eye among the fine ashes, a strap of some kind. She bent to pick it up, though doing so squeezed the breath out of her. She stood for a moment clutching the thing until her lungs eased and her vision cleared again.

A few flakes of blackened cloth clung between the strap's many braided strands, but the material itself seemed unmarked by fire. Cool when she first touched it, the strap warmed quickly where it lay draped across her palm.

The guys went back to the campfire, taking their makeshift torches with them, but also the barrier their bodies had made between her and the dead boy. Starlight was enough to sketch the huddled body, to pick out bared teeth as bone white as the curious bit of strap.

Lukas, she thought, reeling back. The teeth grinned horribly at her. How she knew it was him she wasn't sure, but she had no doubts at all.

Cautiously she picked her way across the rubble back to the warmth of the flames. Not long after Junkyard came as well. No one said a thing about weak stomachs—a stomach like a girl's was what she'd heard boys jeer at each other. But not tonight.

Simon grunted in surprise and pain as something smashed into him. Gravity spun and settled; he was lying face down on a mushy surface, icy cold biting his skin. Letting his head rest where it lay, Simon cried, weak with relief. He was back in the world again.

A very cold and dark world. His cheeks and hands were quickly numbing. He raised his head, the stuff beneath him squeaking a little at the movement. "*Tlapal ab tze!*" he called, I greet you! praying someone would answer. No one and nothing did; only the faint creak of branches stirring in the breeze.

A bit of understanding fell into place. Here in the dark those were the wrong words. His thoughts skittered chaotically from one thing to another, but at last he found a word.

"Hello?"

Still there was no answer, though he listened a long time. Beginning to shudder from the cold, he rolled onto his back; sat up. He could see a little: vague slopes and hollows of white stuff like loose, light sand; the tall shadows leaning over him on one hand and two pairs of straight, gleaming lines on the other. There was a name for those…

"Tra—" he found himself whispering, but the word wouldn't come. Above, wide-flung, were thousands of tiny lights in the black dome of night. They drew his eyes in spite of his attempts to turn away.

He'd been told some tale about them. He felt a moment of relief when that at least came to him. Suns; every one of them was a tiny, distant sun.

Impossible. None of the many parallel worlds had more than the one sun. And both sun and world should be wrapped in the red-gold embrace of Nir nev, the very soul of light, of which the sun was only a reflection.

But not here. This was that other place he couldn't quite recall.

He was alone.

He was… He was…

Sümonnn! The memory of Lukas' despairing cry dragged him down into a deeper darkness.

Philippa had dozed uneasily on and off, head resting on her knees. Outside their small camp was utter silence, except when a piece of the building's remaining framing crashed down or a stone cracked. Far, far to the east she sensed the sun's warmth licking at the trailing edge of a night turned clear and calm. There was no trace left at all of the uncanny weather, and this at least comforted her.

Chick cleared his throat and spoke into the quiet. "Come sunup I reckon we'll find them other two."

"Hope so," Deucey answered after a minute. "Hate to think of animals getting at 'em."

Philippa squeezed her eyes shut. They'd never listen. She'd best save her breath, which was still hard come by.

But the words squeezed out of her anyway. "They ain't there. I seen 'em, going home. Leastways I seen Mara, and heard Simon."

"Say what?" Deucey had turned to stare at her.

"And Lukas, you said." Chick's voice was gentle.

Philippa made a face. "Yeah. That's him Junkyard found. About the right place."

Junkyard roused at the sound of his name. Nip, curled up beside him, didn't stir. "What's she on about?" Junkyard demanded.

Chick ignored him. "And this was before the fire? You ain't trying to say they set it, are you?"

Philippa looked up at him, startled. "Huh? No!" A cough racked her for a painful minute or two before she managed to go on. "Sawdust was smoldering, see," she wheezed. "Musta been a fair while... before I found it. Before the wind... inside stirred it up... and everything blew."

"Dust explosion, hey?" Chick's pal Zeno straightened, interest gleaming in his bloodshot eyes. "Could be. That'd explain half the damn roof ending up all the way over by the trees." He frowned. "But how'd it get so windy inside?"

"Mara leave the hatch open when she went out? That what you telling us?" Deucey looked bewildered. Junkyard made a sour face, muttering under his breath.

"I had to kick the hatch out when I carried Betts up the ramp. It was shut then." Karl's voice was rusty. His hand smoothed Betts' tangled hair; the girl turned her head fretfully away.

Philippa sighed. This wasn't getting any easier. "OK. Here's what happened. I wake up, only I'm feeling kinda groggy. Hard to walk."

Zeno was nodding, though he had yet to look at her. "Carbon monoxide." He sounded like he was talking to himself. "From the sawdust."

She stifled a spurt of resentment. But it could be he was right. "See, the stove's burning low, so I go out for wood. Karl's sitting up, but he don't hear me."

Karl met her gaze then, his face screwed up, trying to remember. Doggedly she went on. "Then I see this light in the privy, all gold and bright as day! And Mara was there."

"Likely she had that gas lamp out there with her," Deucey told her kindly. Zeno's eyes had narrowed. Chick was listening, though.

She shook her head. "Lot brighter'n that. I head over. Mara says something, and Simon." She paused, remembering how funny his voice had sounded. "But I trip. Feel the sawdust all warm. Patches of char too. So I holler, Fire! Fire!" The last of her breath was gone. She struggled to fill her lungs again.

"I remember that!" Karl said, intent on her now. "And the wind…"

"Simon and Lukas both yell. And, and Mara falls into the light, like it was a door. She was just gone," Philippa whispered, seeing it again, opening a hand like she'd done a hundred times back home, setting free a lightning bug on a summer's evening. "Gone home, I reckon, whether she meant to or not. And then the light just, just balloons, and wind howls in so I, I can't see for the sawdust." The inside, crazy wind; the wind from somewhere else. It had made her hair all stand on end. "Then snap! Nothing but dark and dust." She panted, her throat and chest burning until she had enough breath to go on.

There'd been two wrong winds, really. This last one and the bitter, torn-loose wind that had hunted around the outside walls since before she'd got here. Both of them were gone now Mara's door had sealed itself back up.

"I headed back to rouse you guys. Didn't make it. Fire blew up."

Zeno was scowling like he'd bit down on a rock in a spoonful of beans. Disgusted, he slapped both hands down on his thighs, and muttered something about seeing things.

"Crap! Ya making it up, you dumb cluck," Junkyard said, a shrill tone to the words.

Dull rage flashed behind Philippa's eyes, making the ache in her head worse. They weren't going to believe her, particularly not Junkyard or Zeno. She was a girl, a frill, a bit of skirt. Skirts were supposed to be nice to the guys and otherwise keep their traps shut. That was just how things were.

There was no point in arguing, but she couldn't let it drop. "It's what I seen. You don't believe me, that's jake."

Chick was looking at her too. She dared a glance at him. The smoky blue eyes met hers for a moment, grave and steady.

Chick looked down, poked with a stick in the ashes. "Pretty strange story, sure enough," he said generally. "But y'all recollect how Simon wouldn't let nobody but him go look after we heard that squeal, and Mara backed him up?"

Zeno looked more sour at that, but Karl nodded. "Geez. I sure as heck do."

"And then they were all over there together not long after." He glanced from one to the other around the circle. "Something funny was going on with them guys. I don't figure it matters now though. They all got to be dead or they'd have showed up by now."

"No," Philippa rasped softly. "Lukas, yeah. Maybe even Simon. But Mara's someplace else. I seen her go. Someplace there weren't no fire."

Someplace without her.

Chick looked over at her, waiting. Zeno watched him.

Philippa's hand found the bit of strap in her overalls pocket and held onto it. It could have been some part of the piled-up junk, but it was strange enough to have come from the Wobs— part of their door of light, maybe. She went on again, without much hope the others would listen. "What Simon was saying. Paradise. Land of milk and honey, like Canaan Land in the songs. Mara told me they was… from there, that they come to help us… make stuff better here." If what had happened to their doorway hadn't killed them, there was no reason they'd be dead. That Mara'd be dead. Philippa tried to think about what Mara's home would look like, this place where everybody had enough and nobody would hound you. Where it was okay to keep yourself to yourself. She hungered to see it, to be part of it.

Nobody said anything, not even Junkyard. Karl looked down, and his arms tightened protectively around Betts. Across the ruins from them a sagging roof beam cracked like a gunshot, but they'd grown used to that. Philippa looked around the circle. It was easier to see faces now. There was more light coming from the sky than from the campfire.

Her neck itched from the stiff hair dragging across it.

Eyes met hers; eyes slid away, and all of them alive and hurting in the soot-smeared faces. All of them hungry with a need that shamed them, because there was no way to fill it. If this paradise, this Canaan, this home existed, the door to it had closed.

Maybe Mara and Simon and Lukas had been right, and you could build that here, but it struck her as a long stretch, and a sight too big a task to think about now, in the snow and ashes. She needed a home now. All of them did.

Grief and a solid determination knotted together inside Philippa, like a band around her aching chest. She fought for breath until the tightness eased up and determination won.

If there'd been a door once, maybe there'd be one again, here or somewhere else. Something Mara had let slip about others of her people coming here made her think there might be other ways through. And maybe, just maybe with a lot of luck the uneasy feel of the wind that seemed to come with such doors might help her find one as she traveled about. Or she'd hear about another jungle for kids, one where there was always food.

But not if she was scared all the time. Not if she was just a dumb girl.

Philippa let go of the strap she'd been holding inside her pocket, and found instead the short, heavy length of her penknife. She wriggled it out and pried the blade free of the cracked yellow casing. Pulling off her watch cap, she began the slow task of sawing through what was left of her hair an inch or so from the scalp, one dark lock at a time. She'd be colder without it, she thought, but losing the weight felt good.

A click sounded nearby. She looked to find Chick holding out an opened jackknife, hilt first. Its blade was worn thin from honing. "Here," he said, "Mine's sharp. It'll go faster."

Part Two

10

*G*roaning, Chick straightened. His back ached from the search and his belly for grub, but he was used to both those things. The stink was the worst part of the job—that, and the fact that they hadn't found a trace of the other two bodies, not in the charred beams that were all that remained of the jungle, nor so far in the heap that'd been the privy.

Overhead a raven circled. Two others watched from high branches at the edge of the shelter belt, he saw when he looked around. Generally Chick liked the sleek cockiness of the big birds. This morning all he could think of was those curved beaks tearing sad, dead flesh.

"How long we gonna keep at this?" he asked, loud enough for the others to hear. "We don't want to be around if Farmer John comes to see what last night's blaze was."

Deucey eyed him, tight-mouthed. "Ain't right to leave 'em so." He waved a hand at the charred ruins.

Chick sighed. "If they're buried deep enough we ain't found 'em, they're safe enough from animals." If they were there at all, which he was beginning to doubt. Not that he'd say it, or even try to sort out what part of the tale Arlie had told he might be willing to buy. He glanced at where she sat by the campfire, doggedly prodding the blaze higher under Zeno's makeshift kettle, a deep-bellied piece of heat-warped tin. Water dripped hissing from a pinhole in the metal.

She'd made a pig's ear of the haircut. Odd bits of it stuck out from under her watch cap.

"Chick's right." Karl leaned wearily on the stick he'd been using to poke with. He'd left Betts to Arlie's care for now, but had made no secret that he was anxious to get moving. "I'm going to go up and help dig," he announced.

The first thing they'd done was to haul the burned body up to lie next to Flo's. Without a word Zeno had got himself a piece of tin and started gouging a shallow grave out of the melting snow and meadow grass. The dirt wasn't frozen at all, though the lake still was.

Chick had thought to stay and help him, but with a hard look Zeno had sent him off after the others. And he'd gone, useless though their search had been.

Croaking, another raven joined the ones in the trees, and the raven that'd been circling settled on a beam across the ruin from them. Junkyard cursed and threw a rock at it. He missed, but by little enough that it opened its jet-black wings and flapped lazily away. "If I had a slingshot, those goddamn crows'd find something to worry about," he growled.

Zeno called down, "Birds want breakfast, the same as anyone."

There was a moment of silence. "That's disgusting!" Nip said.

The sound of Zeno's guffaw drifted down to them, though there wasn't a lot of humor in the sound. "It's the way of the world, nipio."

Chick swallowed. He had to agree with the runt. Zeno had a strange idea of what was funny sometimes; an Army sense of humor, a pal of Zeno's, another vet, had told him once.

"You boys gonna help me haul rocks to cover these two up?" Zeno yelled then.

Chick tossed the board he'd been using on the firewood pile. He turned to see Arlie up and hobbling for the crumbled gap in the foundation.

Chick caught up with her. "What the hell you think you're gonna do?"

She looked at him, her small chin set. "Haul rocks."

Philippa sagged against the nearest tree trunk, grateful for the chance to rest while the older guys swapped out carrying the charred length of siding that Betts lay on. Helping bury their dead had worn her clean out. She hadn't managed to haul more than two good-sized stones before she'd had to sit again.

That was one each. Worth the cost in breath.

Deucey had said a fine set of words over them. Wouldn't think he had it in him to look at him now, gawky and anxious as he heaved up the back end of the makeshift stretcher. Chick had the front this go-round. The bit she could see of his face showed a scowl of concentration.

A plop of snow hit the bare back of her neck. Hair had its uses, but she still wasn't sorry for cutting it. She wiped the wet away. Even here in the midst of the trees the stuff was melting. It'd be a fine, brisk day if she could trust her weather sense,though she was a little less sure of that than she had been yesterday.

In spite of Karl's hollered directions Betts, barely conscious, slid a little on the stretcher before Deucey got his end level. They started off again with Karl in the lead, walking backward to keep an eye on things. It'd be a wonder if he didn't trip. Behind the stretcher Junkyard and his sidekick Nip stepped out wearily.

Reluctantly Philippa pushed off her tree trunk and shambled along the slushy path after them. Behind her Zeno's footsteps started up again. He'd trailed her the whole way, saying nothing. It made her back feel itchy.

The stretcher set a slow pace, but it didn't take long for the boys to pull far ahead of her. She set her hopes on the bright patch of sky she could see a ways down the path.

The shush of Zeno's footsteps on the snowy path got closer. Unable to stand listening to them anymore, Philippa stepped aside into a gap in the underbrush.

Zeno halted, looking down at her. "Worn out?" He wasn't a big man, but broad. He took up a lot of space.

"'M fine," she gasped, waving him on. "I'll catch up."

Scorn curled his upper lip. "Don't be stupid. Come on. Nobody gets left behind—not even you." He grabbed her wrist, slinging her arm over his shoulders before she could twist away, catching her around the waist with his other hand, urging her along. Under the fire stink he smelled too much like Hank. What air was in her lungs went out of her along with the warmth the hike had generated. She doubled up, wheezing, desperate for breath, to get away, her feet dragging.

"Hey, girlie!" he complained. "Don't make me do all the work."

She couldn't think, held so close to him. "Let *go*!" she cried, wrenching free only because he wasn't trying hard to hold her. She fell to her hands and knees in the wet snow.

"Hyesse!" He spat. "Die here if you want to."

For the moment Philippa was too busy pulling herself up and away from him to answer. He stepped closer; bent over her and hissed quietly, "Quit messing Chick up, understand?"

"Get away! Didn't. Ask your help!" Rage gave her energy. "Make it. On my own!" But she was talking to his back.

She stood a moment longer, tempted to stay until all of them cleared out. That was stupid, though. Grimly she followed. She'd said she would make it herself, and by Jesus she would. But what the heck had he meant about Chick? Afraid his pal would believe her about Mara's paradise, maybe?

Fat chance.

Head down, she missed seeing Karl and then Chick walk out into the bright sunshine of the railroad right-of-way. It was Karl's shout that roused her from the trance of putting one foot in front of the other, over and over.

"Cripes!" he cried. "Come see what I found!"

Voices pulled him from the calm of his stupor. Chattering, annoying voices. The light had returned some while ago, pale and cold though it was. Eyes closed, huddled shivering inside his coat, he'd still drunk it in like water in a drought.

"Simon!" they said, "Simon!" and he was being shaken. Why did they have to call him that name? Reluctantly he raised his head, mourning the precious body heat it cost him.

Having his eyes open made him dizzy. Faces swam in and out of focus; three or four. They were familiar, he thought, though dirtier.

The wanderers. The ice house mission, his and Lukas' and Mara's. And the slipgate tearing free; he and Lukas working together to shut it down. But someone had yelled something. Had yelled... He couldn't remember, but he knew he'd turned away from his desperate task. No more than a moment, but Lukas had screamed and... Simon lurched to his numbed feet, grabbing onto whoever was near.

Mara. Mara had fallen in.

And Lukas? Lukas' face wasn't one of those around him. He heard the name croaked out, a question, and only then realized he'd been the one to say it.

Some of them wagged their heads from side to side like they'd been seized with a strange joint tremor. Frustrated, he asked again, his voice rising.

Wheezing, Philippa stumbled to a halt at the edge of the woods, hanging onto a branch for support.

It *was* Simon, like the guys had been saying. Surrounded as he was, she couldn't see much more than his black hair and a sleeve of his camel-colored coat, but that was enough. She felt herself begin to shake. He wasn't supposed to be here! Gone home to that paradise of theirs, him and Mara, and something had just gone wrong for Lukas.

At least she didn't see Mara anywhere around. The foreign girl wasn't very tall, though. Driven to make sure, Philippa hobbled toward the small knot of guys to make sure Mara wasn't standing behind one of them.

"Dead," Junkyard was saying when she got close enough to hear, his voice bored and hard. Talking about Lukas, had to be, but a shock went through Philippa anyways. Maybe Mara'd been burnt up in the fire too, and the guys just hadn't happened to find the body. She'd been dreaming or crazy with what she thought she'd seen.

But no. The memory of that impossible light, of the doorway it had sketched, was still too strong in her mind for her to accept that. Which maybe just meant she hadn't stopped being crazy.

Simon just looked at Junkyard, face greyish beneath its cold-reddened patches.

"At least we found a guy's body," Junkyard continued sarcastically, "and it don't look like it was you." Philippa couldn't help but recall him heaving up his supper beside that tangle of blackened wreckage.

"Yeah," Nip chimed in. "How'd you get out?" He was trembling steadily in his holey sweater, sunlight or no.

Simon's face puckered up like he was finding thinking hard. "Out," he repeated, frowning a little. "Don't know. Was nothing, and then was here. In the dark." He said that last word like it was a place, Philippa thought.

Zeno straightened up from where he'd knelt by the tracks, his ear to the shining rail. "Cheese it! Train's coming."

There was something funny about that guy, Chick thought, hanging back to watch Simon trailing Karl, who had the rear end of the stretcher for the short dash back into the shelter of the trees. Nip's question had been a good one, even though the Wob might have wandered here after he got out of the ice house. A fool could see the fellow wasn't in his right mind just now.

A distant chugging broke through his chain of thought. The engine wasn't in sight yet, but he could see the plume of smoke. No point in letting the crew catch sight of them before the train even pulled up to the water tower. Chick stretched his legs, hurrying if not out-and-out running. Ahead of him Simon faded into the shadow of the trees, the back of his coat visible longer than the rest of him.

His tan overcoat; *that* was what was funny. Chick stumbled to a halt again. Simon's coat had been damp in places, he recalled, and all over twigs and leaf bits, but not a bit scorched. No soot on his face or hands, either. Chick and the others had all scrubbed up in the hot water from the makeshift kettle, using up bits of soap gleaned from various pockets. That had helped, but the soot was ground in, and wasn't nothing could be done about their clothes right now. They'd look like coal miners until they could get a proper boil-up.

All but Simon.

Zeno gestured at him impatiently from the edge of the woods. His mind still chewing on the oddities, Chick broke into a run.

A brakie spotted them scrambling into the empty boxcar, but the man turned and walked away. Philippa felt her shoulders ease some as she waited like a little kid or some swank girl for help up over the metal-shod edge of the boxcar floor—today she didn't have the moxie to make it up on her own. At least it seemed the brakie was going to pretend he hadn't seen them. Too many to face down, maybe, but likely he just took pity. They weren't the only boes riding this freight.

Ahead of her Simon was taking forever, fumbling around trying to figure out what to hold onto until Junkyard, cursing, snagged him by the collar and hauled him up. Laid out on the boxcar floor, Simon still flailed about like a beached fish. Muttering, Junkyard shoved him aside.

"Here," he said, reached down a hand for her. She grabbed hold, doing what she could to help. On her knees on the splintery wood floor, sliding out of the way of the next guy, she thanked him.

"Don't mensh," Junkyard said, turning away. Across from them Simon had found a wall to huddle against. He looked completely bewildered.

There was something damp and sticky on her wrist, where Junkyard had held her. Philippa wiped it off on her overalls, only seeing that it was streaky blood by the reddish stain it left. Junkyard's blood, not hers. Broken blisters from digging and hauling the stretcher, most likely. She glanced after him as Zeno and then Chick pulled themselves up beside her.

"If you'd've waited a minute, me or Deucey could've give you a boost," Chick said quietly. He was eyeing Junkyard too, not in a friendly way, maybe remembering the guy socking her. That seemed a very long time ago.

Of a sudden she felt too tired to hold her head up any longer. "Appreciate the thought," she managed to say, though she wasn't sure he heard her.

Up at the front end of the car Betts was lying, eyes shut, struggling for each slow breath. "Go lie next to her, Arlie," Karl coaxed, his arms full of great swaths of paper he'd pulled down from the walls. "You're all done in, and it'll help keep her from getting chilled."

The thought of lying down made Philippa's exhausted legs tremble. "Don't mind," she said, and started forward with one hand trailing along the wall. She was glad for the support in another step, as steam shrieked from the engine's whistle and the boxcar jerked into motion. Starting was the roughest part, with each car yanked forward in turn as the slack was taken up.

Betts put off heat like a coal furnace. Gingerly Philippa settled herself against the older girl. She didn't care to be crowded in so close to anybody, and the warmth had a sickish feel to it, but still it was welcome.

Karl laid the folded paper over Betts, with the edges partway over Philippa as well. His task done, he swayed over to join the other guys where they sat against the wall, legs out in the patch of cold sunlight. Nip was lying down, curled up next to Junkyard and clearly intent on sleeping. And Chick had stretched out on his back, his head propped up on his pal's thigh.

"We go to St. Paul?" Simon—all by himself at the end of this line-up—asked nobody in particular, his voice raised to be heard over the steady rattle of the car.

There was a pause. "Judging by the shadows, I'd say this drag's headed northwest," Zeno said, his tone implying that any fool would already know that.

"Oh. That is good?" Simon said hesitantly.

Philippa snorted. St. Paul was a lot of miles back southward. Head jiggling rhythmically with the sway of the train, she lay drowsing for a few minutes before it came to her that Simon's folks might have another one of their doors there, and that was how come he'd asked after it. Once thought, the notion settled into her with the warm certainty of a hunch. At least it would be a place to start looking.

But not now. Tiredness dragged at her eyelids.

Beside her the sick girl mumbled something, then fretfully pushed the paper off both of them and onto the dirty floor. Scrambling, Karl helped Philippa straighten it out again. Turning carefully beneath the weight, Philippa snaked a restraining arm over Betts. "Shush," she said. "You got to keep warm now, hear?"

"Too hot," Betts muttered. A minute later her eyes fluttered open, trying to focus. Philippa pulled loose of her, but stayed close, propped on one elbow, waiting.

After a struggle the look in Betts' eyes sharpened as she saw the shadowy boxcar ceiling above her. She stiffened. "How'd I get here?" she whispered, licking dry lips.

The constant click and rattle made her words hard to hear, but they weren't hard to figure out. "Sawdust caught on fire and burnt the ice house down," Philippa told her. "Karl hauled you out, but you got you a bad fever. We're gonna get you a doctor." Jesus let it be so.

Betts' eyes narrowed some, looking at her for the first time. "You ain't Karl."

"Of course I ain't. He's over there." Philippa jerked her head toward the line of sitting boys. Betts shifted to look, but the effort seemed too much for her. "I'm Arlie, remember?"

Betts' gaze wandered back to Philippa. After a bit she announced in a severe whisper, "You oughta wash your face." Her eyes drifted closed.

Philippa scowled, worried and irritated all together. "Ain't no more dirty than you," she muttered, but Betts didn't respond. Seeing that, Philippa settled back down beside her.

She didn't seem quite so hot. That was good, Philippa thought, shivering, putting a cautious arm around the older girl once more.

Behind her Simon cleared his throat. "Where is Lukas?" he asked.

11

As they waited on the tidy back porch, Chick gazed idly at the house across the alley. He muttered a weary curse under his breath. Grand Forks was tough. So far they'd had no luck at all.

The blue-painted door opened, no more than halfway. The housewife peered at him and Arlie around its edge, pale eyes narrowed in suspicion. A thin whiff of pickled cabbage came from her kitchen.

Gah, but he hated that stuff. Hungry as he was, though, he'd eat it and say thanks. Chick put on his best back-door smile, scared and hopeful and wide-eyed honest all at once. "Please, lady, can you spare me'n my brother something to eat?" he asked, his hands bunching up his scorched workman's cap. "Our folks' place burnt down yesterday, and we got nothing left."

The woman scowled. She wiped her floury hands on her apron. "No fires around here that I've heard of."

"Wasn't in town, ma'am. Our place is over near Fisher. Or at least it was." He looked down, rubbing the worn toe of his boot on the floorboards and mumbling the last few words. Anymore he didn't bother to think what he'd say. He just let his mouth run.

When the woman just kept watching them with that tight-mouthed look, Arlie spoke up in her raspy voice. "Chimney

caught fire. Roof was a-burning afore we knowed what hit us."
The kid sounded better than she had that morning, and so far
she'd kept up with him pretty well, not that he was exactly
pouring on the coal.

Nobody would peg her for a girl from her voice, that was
sure. It'd been his idea for her to pass as his little brother, in
part because it was just easier that way, but also because he
thought she'd like it. And she had. Even limping and wore out,
she had a certain cockiness to her walk.

"Fisher's the other side of the state line. Nothing to do with
us," the woman said, a gleam of triumph in her eyes for having
thought up a way to tell them no. Chick could never see why
people bothered with that.

The door shut in their faces. After a moment of digesting
their failure, Chick clattered down the steps behind Arlie.

The afternoon was fall-warm, smelling sweet and dusty from
the yellowing leaves that rustled on the trees. "Guess Fisher's a
washout," Chick said, keeping his tone light. It'd been the last
town their Great Northern empty had rolled through, a good-
sized town that had nonetheless looked near deserted. "Any
Dakota burgs come to mind?" He grinned down at Arlie.

The kid shrugged. "Ain't never been here before."

"Me neither." Zeno, who'd been kicking around the country
since the New Jersey steel mills shut down, would likely know.
Town folks were more likely to gift kids, though, so they'd left
him to set up camp down by the river, and keep an eye on
Simon while he was at it, in case the Wob was to take a notion
to go looking for his dead pal. Minding the goddamn baby was
what Zeno'd called it, but it didn't make sense for anybody to
take Simon with them. In the hours since they'd found him the
guy had showed no more sense than a goose of how to get by.
About the only things he'd talk about was where had Lukas got
to and was this St. Paul.

Junkyard had wanted to leave Arlie at camp as well, but she'd
flat out refused. Thinking of it, Chick sighed. It wasn't only
pigheadedness on her part. She'd picked up on Zeno's sour
attitude towards her. And it was just as well for him that he and
the other guys hadn't split up until they'd got to the main stem.

No need at all for Zeno to know he was tooling ringers with the kid.

The next house they hit Chick tried out saying they lived on a small farm a little ways south of town. The pleasant-faced old woman who'd answered the back door just smiled at them and said, "You boys aren't from around here, are you?"

A man's voice, muffled by the walls and angles of the house, came from behind her. "Who is it, Margit?"

The woman turned toward the voice, pushing the door to as she did so. "Harvest tramps," Chick heard her say before the latch clicked shut.

"I got to sit down," Philippa wheezed. She'd dozed a good bit on the long ride here, rocked by the steady sway of the freight, and had felt better for it. Over the past hour or so of walking, though, a lump had settled in her raw throat until it felt big as a jawbreaker.

She eased herself down on the low sandstone wall that bordered a neglected yard. The stones felt warm through her pants, a comfort what with the light stir of air that had begun to chill her ears and the singed back of her neck, whispering of a hard freeze tonight. At least that was no more than a body would expect this late in the year.

Here in town, with its streets and houses and ordinary life, believing in the unlikely things she'd heard and seen was harder. The sense of calm decision she'd come to in the ashes of the ice house had faded some since morning. But still she felt different, somehow stronger in her mind. And every time Chick called her brother, and nobody blinked, she felt gutsy and clever.

Philippa glanced at the western horizon. The sun was getting low in the hard blue sky, about an hour from setting, and they'd made no touches yet. If the other guys were having as hard a time on the main stem, the whole bunch of them would be chewing air tonight. And she was very hungry. She hadn't got much good out of last night's supper.

Even Chick's good humor was wearing thin. He looked down at her, exhausted, expressionless, as though he didn't really see her. She tugged at his arm. "You sit too. Gonna fall over."

He sat. "Somebody'll call the cops directly, Arlie, they see us decorating their wall."

Philippa looked at the dead leaves and trash that had blown up against the wall, the dried weeds poking up from the overgrown lawn. "Naw. Not this dump," she whispered. Whispering was easier. "Oughta offer to rake the yard. Might fly." She didn't feel like doing any such thing.

"Oh, cripes. You're right," Chick said. Wearily he got to his feet again. "Come on, Arlie, you first. You come up with the idea."

Sheesh. But you did what you had to do. "Show you how it's done," she told him with thin bravado, and stood.

The house had been a nice one not very long ago, a square, comfortable-looking place with a broad, gabled roof and a big yard. But shingles were missing and a broken windowpane had a piece of shirt cardboard pasted over the hole. Grass spread from the joints between the cobbles of the drive, making for uneven footing. Philippa watched where she put her bad foot down, and tried to rehearse what she'd say, tried to find her swagger. Showing brass sometimes worked when nothing else did.

"What do you want?" The voice from behind—a woman's, and ill-tempered—pulled her up short and turned both her and Chick around to face it. Though her face was pinched with fatigue the woman didn't look so terribly old, not much more than thirty. She wore a good suit of heather-green wool with a matching beret, and carried a carton that filled both her arms.

"Work, ma'am," Philippa said, straightening her back and trying to speak loud enough to be heard across the fifteen feet that separated them. Straining made her throat seize up, and her words ended in a strangled wheeze.

Chick came to her rescue. "Rake your yard, lady? For any food or old clothes you can spare?"

The woman—blond like everybody else around here, and rawboned—started up the walk to the front door. "I don't give two pins how the yard looks. And anyway I doubt either of you boys have much hard work in you.

"Well, come on," she continued, glancing over her shoulder. "Don't stand there like sun-struck fools."

Lively again, Chick cut across the lawn and followed close on the woman's heels up onto the wide front porch. Philippa trailed him, watching in wonder as the blond woman handed Chick the cardboard carton like it was the most natural thing in the world. As she groped in her purse for the key, the Okie boy peered down into the box.

Philippa could see him thinking, trying to figure if it was worth a snatch. But if he could run, she couldn't, not well enough to pull a stunt like that. He glanced back at her as she climbed the steps, his eyes wide and questioning. She jerked her head once: No. He smiled angelically, showing his chipped tooth.

The woman pushed open the heavy door with its intricately carved fanlight. "Come on through to the back," she said, her voice echoing. Something in how she talked made Philippa think of schoolteachers back home.

Philippa scraped her rubber boots carefully on the worn doormat. She wasn't used to front doors no more.

The wide hall was bare, as was the parlor and living room to their left and right. Dust drifted in the slanting light from the windows. Had to hock a bunch of furniture, Philippa guessed, staring about as they followed the woman. Pictures, too: light patches showed here and there on the striped wallpaper.

"I'm Mrs. Nestos," the woman said, straight-arming the swinging door that led to the kitchen. "Set that carton over on the counter."

Shifting the box in his arms enough to free a hand, Chick yanked the watch cap off the kid's head as she passed him. Arlie flushed, and took it from his hand. He grinned and followed the lady into the kitchen.

The smell of past breakfasts hit him in the gut: Coffee. Bacon. He tried to quiet the grumbling of his belly as he settled the carton on the linoleum counter. The box itself smelled of bread; he found it hard to let go of it. "I'm Chick O'Shea, ma'am," he said, turning.

"Arlie," the kid croaked. She'd stopped just inside the doorway, sagging against the wall.

"My kid brother," Chick added.

Mrs. Nestos had vivid blue eyes, very sharp. "Sit down, boy," she told Arlie. "You're getting my wall dirty." She looked at Chick. "Does he have the TB?" Head down, Arlie slid onto a chair at the cluttered kitchen table.

"Breathed in smoke or something," Chick assured her. "Our place burnt down night before last. Give him a few days, Arlie'll be jake."

Mrs. Nestos scowled at him. "Arlie'll be jake, and Jake will be dead! If he hasn't got pneumonia already he will soon. What on earth possessed your mother to let you drag him around the streets looking for work? He should be in the hospital!" She pushed her way back into the hall, leaving the door to thump rhythmically behind her.

Chick's mouth hung open with a protest he hadn't had a chance to voice. The door had just settled shut when the lady reappeared, holding a skinny brown bottle. She snatched open a drawer and pulled out a spoon.

"No hospital," the kid managed before the spoon, brimming with a dark, thick liquid, got popped into her mouth. She made an awful face and darted a pleading look in Chick's direction.

"He's seemed okay most of the day, ma'am," he said slowly, trying to figure the best angle on all this. "Just a little out of breath. I got no place to leave him anyhow." He ran his fingers through his hair, still sticky though he'd used soap when he'd washed it that morning. "Our sister's been in and out of the hospital since August, and we can't afford that neither. Dad's off working the harvest to try to pay for it."

"I'll be OK," the kid whispered. "Just got kinda woozy. On account of being hungry, see."

Mrs. Nestos turned a stern face on Arlie. "Hush, boy. You've got a fever."

Chick eyed the kid. The red that showed in her face was from the scorching she'd got, he was pretty sure. The cough syrup or cod liver oil or whatever it was had brought a little more life to her face, from the shock if nothing else. Chick snuck her a little wink, hoping to hearten her to ride this out.

"This is a fine mess," Mrs. Nestos said to no one in particular, her mouth screwed up tight but unsure around its edges. "All right. You—what did you say your name was?"

"Chick, ma'am."

"Chick, then. If you want work, go out back and split me a basket of kindling to start. Hatchet's hanging by the bench on the back porch."

The kid used the table to push herself to her feet, that determined look on her face. "I'll help."

The lady whirled on her. "Sit down! You're going to bed after I get you cleaned up."

Arlie sank slowly back into the chair, wild-eyed. Chick came around the table and squatted by her. "You just settle down and do what the lady says, little brother. I ain't a-going nowhere but out back." He swiveled to face the woman. "See, Arlie ain't used to being done for by women, ma'am. Our Momma passed on when he was little. If you think he's up to it, he can do a pretty good job of washing himself. Or I can help him." He gave Arlie a solemn look, only letting his mouth curl up on the side away from Mrs. Nestos, so she'd know it for a joke.

Arlie didn't pull away from him, but it came to the same thing. Her face went very still and hard. "I can wash myself, Chick," she told him. "Go split the lady's kindling."

Stung, he stood, not looking at her. "I'll do that. Ma'am," he said, ducking his head to Mrs. Nestos. He pulled his cap from the pocket where he'd stuffed it and headed out onto the porch.

Second time that kid had pulled that crap on him, he thought as he jammed the cap down on his head. He didn't like it one little bit. Serve her right if he did go off and leave her. Chick snatched the bushel basket from underneath the bench. After all, she'd got somebody else to take care of her now, didn't she?

There was the hatchet. He took it down from the pair of nails it hung from, and fingered the blade. Dull; he'd be lucky not to take a finger off with it.

Philippa pushed a stack of books aside and laid her cheek against the slick enameled surface of the table once Mrs. Nestos had gone off to get stuff ready. She could check that box on the counter for bread or something quick to eat, she told herself. She could nip out the back door and grab Chick, and they'd both be highballing before the woman got wise.

But Chick was mad at her now. She hadn't needed to be mean to him when he was just trying to help. Didn't seem that she could help doing it, though. Something happened and the cold would just come down inside her.

It took the woman a minute or two longer to get the bathroom ready than it had when she'd fetched the cough syrup, but no more. She herded Philippa back up the hallway to the bathroom, and pointed out the towel and washrag, and the old-fashioned flannel nightshirt that lay folded on the deep windowsill. Her husband's, Philippa guessed, wondering where he was and what he'd think of all this when he got home. A threadbare robe hung from a hook on the back of the door.

"Don't try to take a shower," Mrs. Nestos warned her. "I don't want you getting faint from the heat and cracking your head on the tub."

The door shut behind her. Philippa found her head felt swimmy once more. She'd seen a bathroom with an inside toilet before, at the preacher's house when she'd lived in town with Meemaw, but now it didn't seem like this kind of thing could be real. All that gleaming porcelain! She was afraid to touch any of it with her grimy hands.

She turned her head. Motion reflected caught her gaze. The shiny mirror above the sink held the face of a big-eyed, scared kid, burns and a bruise on the wide cheekbones. Ain't neither scared, she told the face, and saw her mouth set stubborn.

The choppy remains of her hair lay flat against her skull most places, except where pulling off her cap had made a cowlick. Once she was clean she could maybe trim the worst bits, supposing there was scissors in the medicine cabinet.

Did having it short like that make her look like a boy? She stared, trying to believe it. All she could be sure of was that she didn't look like any girl she'd ever seen, or much like any recollection she had of herself.

A few minutes later, all her clothes in a heap on the floor away from the clean rug, Philippa felt vulnerable even though she'd locked the little knob below the door handle. Wheezing from the effort, she climbed into the big tub and turned the hot water handle. She let it run, still cold, over her hands. That didn't do much more for the soot that mapped every crease and nick in her skin than the snowmelt in Zeno's makeshift kettle had. She grabbed the bar of soap, white like most everything in the room, and began to scrub. The water swirled gray and soapy down the drain. When it ran warmer from the spigot, she bent her head and began gratefully to wash her ash-stiffened hair.

12

A rosy gold—almost the color of the light at home, although it had no strength, no heat to it—had begun to tint what sky he could see through the tangled branches of the trees. Simon stood transfixed, hands thrust deep in the pockets of his coat, color filling his hungry eyes like a promise: Now that he was near, Lukas would track him by the iyar pukko he wore. Lukas would come, and together the two of them would find the new training mission on the banks of the big lake...

Confusion clouded his thoughts for a moment. This city was St. Paul, wasn't it? There was a river in St. Paul, as well as lakes; that he remembered. But someone had told him a different name for the place. Unease clutched at his belly until he remembered that beside St. Paul lay yet another city. A strange thing, to settle two such huge places side by side, but this must be that other city; he couldn't recall the name of it.

That meant more miles to walk, then, and the day's fast, with no ritual purpose to it, was harder than usual to bear. Still, there would be food at their mission. He and Lukas would gorge themselves as though at a Singing feast. And then the mission's slipgate, another of the Jaguar's many golden Eyes, would open for them; a step or two would...

"Simon!"

He whirled at the sound of the hated name. "Not call me so!"

The man, sweating in spite of the chill and very dirty, glared at him. "Hyesse! What the crap else should I call you? At least it gets your attention, you stupid bohunk."

Simon stood for a long moment, translating what he could of what the man—Zeno—had said. His name; the man wanted to know what to call him. Anxious, he searched his patchy memory. Then it came to him, and he wondered how he could've forgotten. "I am Faahu," he said at last. A brief panic flickered along his nerves again. That certainly was his name, but somehow it was wrong to say it here.

Zeno's lip curled. "Fa-who? Fathead's more like it. Well, whatever the hell your name is, get over here and lay those branches in place while I tie 'em down."

Scorn again, but at least the man's gestures told him what was wanted. Zeno seemed always angry with him. Such things didn't matter, though, when there was a task to do for the good of the group. Obediently Simon went to him, skirting the unoccupied fire-circle they'd found. There were several others in amongst the trees, but men sat around them, sunk in their own thoughts.

Zeno pointed him at the pile of long, broken-off branches they'd spent a long while collecting. "Lean 'em against the crosspiece, see. No! At as much of an angle as you can manage. We ain't building a fence."

Simon did as he was told, watching as Zeno tied the upper ends to the shoulder-high crosspiece with bits of string. He fumbled for words. "What is we make?"

Though he'd been working as though driven, Zeno paused to stare at Simon. "You're kidding me, right?"

Not wanting to rouse the man's scorn further, Simon only looked at him.

"*Ay Cristos!* It's a lean-to, so we don't freeze our hineys off tonight." Zeno went backing to weaving the string in and out of the branches. "Which it just about is already, so get moving!"

The explanation told him nothing, all but the word 'tonight', which echoed in his bones. Simon turned to pull another branch from the pile. It was indeed harder to see. He glanced at the sky, but the color, all but a streak of bruised-looking purple, had drained away. The branch tangled with others. Hands trembling, he yanked it free, spilling the pile so that it lay in a snarl at his feet.

Zeno muttered something under his breath, but didn't look up. Unsteadily Simon carried the branch he held to lay it next in line. Zeno yanked it into place and tied it down. How could such a flimsy construction shield them from the weight of darkness?

Lukas had better come for him soon.

Firelight greeted Chick, reflecting off sullen faces and the shaggy cave of a new-built lean-to. A No. 10 can simmered above the flames, but there wasn't much smell coming from it.

"Any luck?" Junkyard asked morosely. There was only him and Nip and the Wob by the fire. "All we got was a sack of moldy old turnips." He jerked his thumb towards the can. "What ain't rotten is in there cooking."

"Not much I could carry back," Chick told him, fishing the newspaper-wrapped parcel from his pocket. "Biscuits." He handed them over, with a quick glance at the shadowed depths of the lean-to, to see if maybe Zeno was in there dozing.

If he was, he was damn well hidden. Maybe he was off at one of the other campfires visible through the brush and trees. "But you-all should eat 'em," Chick went on evenly. "I had me a sit-down." The memory of the tough little piece of fried meat Mrs. Nestos had served him, dressed up with gravy and canned green beans and more of the biscuits, had faded on his long walk back here, but it was pure swank next to boiled turnips.

Nip grabbed one of the biscuits, gobbling it in two bites, a few crumbs falling into the rolled-up sleeve of the man's suit coat he'd come by sometime that afternoon.

Junkyard whacked him with his hat. "That's more than your share, runt."

Nip ducked away. "Was not! There's four, and he just said he don't want one."

"You're forgetting Karl and Deucey. And say—" Junkyard squinted up at Chick. "—What happened to that flea-brained kid?"

Chick sighed. It was clear he wasn't going to get a chance to go off and make the rounds of the other fires looking for Zeno right away, not without being obvious about it. He settled on the cold ground beside Simon, who was all huddled up and trembling, rocking himself back and forth. The Wob hadn't so much as looked up since Chick had got here. "This lady we put the touch on decided the kid was feverish and put her to bed. Damnedest thing." Damnedest kid, treating him like he was out to rape her or something, he thought, remembering.

Leaves crackled behind him. It was all Chick could do not to turn around. "She made me promise to go back to fetch her tonight. Afraid of being put in the hospital."

"The hospital is just where she belongs," Karl said from the darkness, sounding worn to the bone. "I said it before."

"You oughta leave her square where she is. We don't need a sick kid hanging on us," Junkyard said as Karl and Deucey came out into the light. "Let the old biddy take care of her."

Deucey sat down cross-legged, pulling a quart bottle of milk from inside his coat. He handed it to Chick. "If you already told her you was gonna fetch her, you gotta show."

Chick pressed his lips together and stared at the bottle. It was a stupid idea, setting off in the middle of the night to haul Arlie out of a warm bed. He flicked the lid off the bottle and took a swig, then poked Simon to get him to take it. The guy looked confusedly from him to the bottle and then back at him again. "Drink some and pass it on," Chick told him, then gestured when it seemed he still didn't understand.

Doubtfully the Wob tasted it. His face twisted up, but he swallowed. Wiping his mouth, he thrust the bottle at Nip.

Chick drew in a nervous breath. "So where's Zeno got to?"

A hard ache in her belly pulled Philippa to wakefulness out of a tangled dream. Mara had been standing in a kitchen out in the middle of the plains, she recalled, with wide storm clouds swallowing half the sky above her, misty and reaching along their front edge. Snow clouds, though what fell from them might be icy rain by the time it reached you. Mara'd been laughing merrily, head thrown back, but a hole had gaped in the board floor just a step behind her. Flo had been in there too someplace. Not poor Lukas, though; he couldn't be in paradise 'cause he'd died here, where he didn't belong to be.

That made no sense at all, Philippa realized, opening her eyes to the dim room. Mrs. Nestos' house, and Chick had swore he'd be back tonight, that they wouldn't leave her stuck here.

Restless, uneasy from the vivid dream, Philippa curled onto her side in the warm, sagging bed. That didn't help her stomachache at all and made it harder to breathe. The hour felt late, but a yellow light showed in the hall beyond the half-open bedroom door. She could hear the faint rattle and ding of a typewriter.

Gotta get up, she thought, unwilling, wishing the woman had already gone to bed. In spite of the fourposter and the heavy dresser, the nightstand with its lace doily that now held the small pile of stuff she'd rescued from her pockets when the woman took her clothes, Philippa was pretty sure nobody slept in here. The sheets were too musty and there was an empty spot along the wall near the window that might've once held a dressing table with a mirror. Still the room, the quiet, unfamiliar house, made her fidgety. Better if it didn't, she thought, sitting up and groping for the robe. Better if Chick and them didn't come and she had someplace like this to be when the storm hit tomorrow.

Philippa stopped with the worn robe half around her. The storm front in her dream would hit by late the next day, sure as sunrise followed night. The feel of it coming rumbled deep in her bones. This one didn't have that wrong edge to it like the one that had blanketed the ice house, but any bad weather was hell and misery when you'd got no shelter. She'd have to warn the guys to prepare whatever way they could.

Not that warning them would do a bit of good. As far as most of them were concerned, she was still a dumb skirt.

Philippa winced when her bare left foot touched the cold floor. Going slow never made it easier, so she put the injured foot down as well, and stood. Dizziness swept away both sight and balance. She held onto the bedpost until it passed. Nothing but hunger. The bowl of chicken soup and the melba toast the woman had given her had tasted swell, though the liquid burned her raw throat. But that was all she'd got, and it left her stomach feeling more hollow than before. "Starve a fever," Mrs. Nestos had said, unsmiling, as she took the licked-clean bowl away.

Somewhere in the house a clock chimed the hour. Philippa counted: ten o'clock. Not so late, then. It'd likely be hours before Chick came.

The hinges on the bedroom door were well-oiled and quiet. The floorboards in the hall weren't quiet at all, and neither was her breathing. The typewriter rattle stopped. Philippa heard the creak of someone shifting in a chair, and then the scuff of slippered feet. Mrs. Nestos, her hair in pin curls, appeared in the doorway across from the bathroom.

Philippa clutched the too-big robe around herself. "Bathroom," she whispered, pointing, afraid to move.

Mrs. Nestos frowned and nodded. "Don't get chilled on me, boy," she said, turning back to her room.

It was just at that moment that Philippa felt a warm trickle down the inside of one thigh. All the heat in her body fled with the shock of it. She pressed her thighs together and scuttled for the bathroom, praying she would leave no blood on the floor.

The door shut behind her, Philippa leaned back against it for a few borrowed seconds, her heart pounding and the breath whistling painfully in and out of her nose. She'd only bled twice in all the months since she'd run away. And only once before that. Hank'd caught her hanging the rags Corinna had given her on the line and said—He'd said—

Groping blindly, Philippa found the light button on the wall beside her, and punched it on.

The hardest part had been slicing her hand with the bone-handled razor she found up in the top shelf of the medicine cabinet. Cuts took so long to heal up, and the sight of the blood welling made her queasy. Her palm was slick with it already. She must've cut deeper than she'd meant to. But if there was blood in the hallway, she'd need to show where it come from.

She'd been in the bathroom too long already. Once she was back in the bedroom she could look for something to use for rags, and some kind of drawers to hold them up.

Philippa turned the fancy glass doorknob.

Mrs. Nestos stood just outside in the hall, her hand out like she'd been fixing to knock, but she was staring back down the way Philippa had come. Drops showed dark and shiny against the pale oak floor, too many to have come from a cut an inch long, however deep; Philippa could see that right off. The woman looked bewildered.

She turned to Philippa, and Philippa opened her mouth to offer her excuse anyway. It didn't come out. Nothing at all came out but the raspy drag of her breathing.

"Why did you pretend to be a boy?" Mrs. Nestos asked, her voice flat. Suspicion and hurt warred around the corners of her eyes; she hadn't settled yet to either.

Philippa, dizzy, looked down. "Safety," she whispered. It was part of an answer.

"From me?" The woman's voice got an edge of outrage.

Yes, Philippa thought. "Everybody," she said, softer than before.

Mrs. Nestos didn't say anything for a minute. Philippa felt a new trickle of blood as she waited. She tensed, even though it shouldn't have mattered now the woman knew. A cramp knotted her belly and her breathing got rougher.

"From your 'brother', too, I suppose," Mrs. Nestos said, but there wasn't much force in her bitterness. "Stay right there. There's things you'll need." She turned away.

Unmoored by a tangled flood of emotions, Philippa couldn't have moved anyway. "He ain't...!" she started to say, but the force of her words brought a coughing fit that left her fighting to draw in enough air. *My brother*, she'd meant to say, thinking Mara and Simon and poor Lukas, thinking Hank who wasn't her brother either.

"Chick ain't bothered me," she finally managed, wheezing.

Mrs. Nestos' hands on her shoulders guided Philippa forcefully back into the bathroom. "I'm glad to hear it. There," the woman told her. "Sit. I'll be back in a minute." Then she paused, taking in the reddish stain that was spreading on the rolled-up cuff of Philippa's robe. Mrs. Nestos seized that hand and turned it palm up, exposing the cut. "Little fool," she hissed. Her hands shook as she grabbed the bottle of iodine solution down from the cabinet.

The hot water bottle helped some, but Philippa was too exhausted to relax. Her mind skipped from one thought to the next, refusing to settle. She was so tired of not being able to breathe right. It made everything harder.

Mrs. Nestos handed her a cup of tea. "Drink this," she said. "It helps the pain."

The cup looked fragile, its curved walls so thin they seemed to glow in the lamplight. Philippa sipped at it, careful of her tongue and throat and her bandaged, stinging hand. The tea was hot and a lot more bitter than sweet, though she could taste honey. It had some kind of booze in it too; not gin, Philippa thought. Bootleg gin she'd tasted, a swallow from a bottle passed around a jungle campfire one night last August. This didn't taste near so bad, but the alcohol in it fizzed in her head just the same.

Mrs. Nestos stood and watched her, frowning like she was puzzling something out. Her eyes looked very tired. Philippa recalled the glimpse of the woman's room she'd gotten as she was helped back to bed: the lamp with the ivory shade next to the cluttered desk; the narrow bed; the armchair crowded in by the radio cabinet.

"How come you don't use this room? It's bigger," she whispered, not thinking that asking might be rude.

"This was my parents' room," Mrs. Nestos told her after a moment. "I didn't feel right moving in here after Pappa died." Her studious expression didn't change at all when she spoke.

Philippa shifted uneasily where she sat propped against the headboard of the soft bed. She tucked her feet up so they didn't rest in the hollows left by years of the same old people sleeping in it. She found the breath to ask another question. "Your husband—he off working somewheres?"

Mrs. Nestos' lips thinned. "I'll take that cup if you're done with it," she said.

Philippa gulped the last few swallows of the bitter, stinging tea and handed over the cup. Must be a widow, she thought, or her husband run off and left her. "Sorry," she wheezed. "Didn't aim to pry."

Mrs. Nestos sighed. "You can stay until your lungs heal up. Sit forward." She pulled out the extra pillow Philippa had been propped up against and switched off the lamp. "I'd appreciate you not doing anything further to injure yourself while you're here."

Philippa stayed hunched forward for a moment, letting the offer sink in. Then she slid down under the covers and curled around the hot water bottle, relief and guilt and anxiety all crowding in on her. Maybe it'd be OK to stay here awhile. Mrs. Nestos knowing she was a girl hadn't done her no harm. And with both Betts and her took care of, the guys could likely find a mission to take them in until the storm passed.

She was so tired. Last night's wonder and terror seemed only another dream, and nothing to chase after.

At the door Mrs. Nestos paused. "Wake me if you need to, but get some rest," she said. "Tomorrow we'll talk about letting your folks know where you are."

Panic flashed white behind Philippa's eyes and trembled through every nerve. "Folks is dead," she managed to say.

Silence. Then Mrs. Nestos answered, her tone strained but reasonable. "Somebody back home is worrying about you. I won't have them worrying while you're in my house."

Not Corinna with her angry eyes and her mouth twisted up small. And Hank never worried about anybody but himself. The trembling in Philippa's arms got worse. "Sister don't want me," she whispered, a new cramp tightening her belly. "Please don't send me back."

Mrs. Nestos eyed her for another long minute, a look with no give to it. "We'll talk about it tomorrow," she said again.

13

*P*anting, Chick surveyed the deserted backyard, the frost in the night air stinging his windpipe. They'd hustled getting here, more to keep warm than from any real hurry, though they'd had to dodge out of their way a couple of times—a beat cop once, and then, a mile or more further on, a gang of townie toughs. That would have been worse trouble.

No lights on in the house, which was good. Ragged laundry hung stiffly from the clothesline in the side yard, beyond the shadow of the big tree. Arlie's stuff. The lady must've washed it all.

But there was no sign of Arlie herself.

This whole thing was a fool's errand. He hadn't needed Deucey's prodding to make him come; he'd promised the kid, after all. But they ought to let her sleep on in that warm bed and then he could get himself back to camp. Be there when Zeno returned, supposing the Greek wasn't there already, worrying at where Chick had gone and what he might be up to, and with who—the kind of questions Chick had been asking himself about Zeno all the way across town.

"Which window's hers?" Deucey hissed beside him, shifting from foot to foot. "I'd as lief not hang around here freezing my tail, waiting on her to wake up on her lonesome."

Chick eyed him. The gangly Kentuckian hadn't had to come at all, neither him or Nip. The runt had just happened to wake up when Chick wriggled out of the nest of dried grass and leaves they'd made of the insides of the lean-to. Coming along was just a lark for Nip, but Chick suspicioned Deucey was riding herd on him keeping his promise. Not that it was any of his damn business to start with.

"Hell," he muttered. "That'n." He pointed to the one closest to the west corner of the house. A tall bush came right up to the windowsill, a lilac if he remembered correctly from the time he'd spent out here earlier, splitting wood and fetching and carrying for the lady.

Deuce bent to scoop up a bit of gravel from the alley. "I'll go roust her."

"Give it here. I'll do it," Chick snapped, hand out.

A wry grin twisting his mouth, Deucey dropped the gravel in Chick's palm. "Shore t'ing, boss."

Nip's whispered "Hold it!" came at almost the same moment as the faint squeal of a window sash being raised. A pale, muffled figure perched for a moment in the black square of the west window, then swung around and let itself down into the bush. Had to be Arlie, though the moonlight confused things. The bush swayed; cloth ripped and a wheezy voice muttered a curse.

It was her, all right. Chick swung himself over the waist-high fence to go fetch her.

Near blind under the dry rustle of the tree, Philippa blundered into something that gave more than an elm trunk would. A hand grabbed her arm. She sucked icy air that stuck in her swollen throat like a stone.

"Shhh," Chick breathed in her ear. "Come on. This way." He led the way along the side of the garage towards the back. Straightening against her cramping belly, Philippa followed. Her feet, bare but for the binding on her broken toe, felt for a way around the poke-y things hiding in the frosted grass.

Maybe Chick had brought shoes for her. She had no notion where hers had got to and there hadn't been none in the closet.

No hanging clothes, neither, only some worn men's underthings and socks in one of the dresser drawers. Thank Jesus Chick had been waiting. She had no more than a hazy notion of how to find the jungle they were camped in, or where else she might hole up out of sight in case Mrs. Nestos was to come looking for her.

Her head felt very strange, cottony and singed around the edges. Out here under the night sky the rumbling energy of the coming storm seemed to press in on her and tangle up her aching thoughts.

"Gotta to tell y'all something," Philippa whispered. Chick put a severe finger to his lips, and she hushed.

In the night shadows between the back shed and the fence Nip was waiting. He slapped a hand over his mouth to muffle giggles when he saw her. "What are you wearing!" he whispered when he had control of himself.

"Two union suits and a nightshirt," Philippa hissed back, flushed and shivering, clutching the remains of the robe. It was lucky she'd put her penknife and stuff—the coins and toothbrush and the length of strap she'd found in the ruins— inside a sock before she'd stuck them in the robe's pocket. Otherwise it'd all be scattered and unfindable in the overgrown grass.

Deucey slid around the corner of the garage, holding up a bundle. "Got your duds down off the line. But some of 'em is kindly stiff." Chick shot him an unreadable look.

Teeth beginning to chatter, she freed the ragged wool trousers from the icy tangle. Even wet, wool would help keep you warm, or so folks claimed. She shoved her good hand down inside each leg, to open them up enough to get into.

"Hold on afore you do that," Chick said.

Philippa didn't even glance up. "Hold on your own self," she wheezed. "I'm freezing!" Leaning back against the shed wall, she wriggled into the pants. The cut across her palm made the whole thing more trouble than it needed to be. She cursed herself for a fool as she struggled with the buttons.

The boys waited on her impatiently, Chick keeping an eye on the house while the other two watched the length of alley on the other side of the back fence. "Now, Arlie, you just listen," Chick said as she was fishing her belongings out of the sock. "Wouldn't you be a sight better off stopping here a day or two more, 'stead of coming with us?"

A flash of panic stopped her. "I ain't staying here! She means to send me home!" Her breath faded out on the last word, but he must've read it on her lips, seen what that meant to her, because he shut his mouth on whatever he'd planned on saying.

Deucey hadn't been looking her way. "You sure, Arlie? Ain't likely she'd send you anywheres right off. We could check on you every day."

"No!" she said, and jammed the fistful of her stuff down into her one good pants pocket. Her hand tore straight through the worn cloth. She spat a cussword.

"Hush!" Chick hissed at her. "All right, then. Wait here. You need your boots. And for chrissake pipe down!"

As he slipped off back into the yard, Philippa let herself slide down the wall, too weary to be properly thankful. She ought to get ready, put the socks on, but her good hand was still occupied, clenched around her things. After a minute she stuck the pencil behind her ear, dumping the rest in a scrap of robe before she bent to pull on the first sock.

Chick jiggered the latch hook up with a piece of wire and eased the screen door open. The house was dark and quiet, but still the back of his neck prickled. The kid's rubber boots were where he'd set them himself, thank Christ, and her knitted cap with them. He cat-footed across the creaky floorboards to the kitchen door, grabbed hold of them, then paused. The hatchet hung where he'd left it, the blade gleaming from the going-over he'd given it. Temptation won. He snatched it down, thrusting the handle through his belt, and got the hell out.

Arlie gave him a grateful look when he handed her the boots and cap. Her black eyes were too big for her pinched, cold-reddened face. "Better get 'em on," he told her. "Cinch them boots up tight. We gotta scram before some dog starts up a-yammering."

She managed the cap OK, pulling it on over hair that had seen a bit more of a trim. But her fingers were shaking and clumsy on the laces of the tennis shoes she fished from the depths of the boots. Chick had to keep himself from bending down to tie them for her, but at last she was done with both the laces and the boot catches, and still the house was as quiet as you could hope.

Deuce and Nip headed out, vaulting the fence and sprinting down the moonlit alley. Chick gave Arlie a hand up, then took off on the same tack. A loud crack and a wheezing cry from behind him stopped him one yard down. The kid lay gasping like a beached fish where she'd fallen, a couple of busted fence-slats under her. Moonlight picked out the casing of a penknife and a couple of coins among the gravel, stuff she must've dropped. Weakly she tried to push herself up.

A light winking on in Mrs. Nestos' house caught the corner of Chick's eye. It was dim like it had filtered through a couple of rooms before it got to a window, but the sight of it sent a flash of panic clear through him. Pivoting on one worn heel, he ran back, yanking her up and hauling her down the alley under his arm.

She tried to run; he had to give her that, but her efforts came near to tripping him up. Winded, he let her slide to the ground next to the trash barrels at the alley's end, where Deucey and Nip were waiting.

Hell, Chick thought, slumping back against the fence. Getting her back to the jungle was going to be a real bitch at this rate. "That lady got herself a telephone?"

Eyes shut, the kid answered him, her breath whistling in and out. "Not that I... saw." One of her thin hands squeezed tight around something pale and dangling. She must've managed to grab some of her things after all.

He eased his way to the end of the fence to check the street. It was empty but for a cat strolling across a block or two down.

When he turned back Deucey was eying Arlie. "Might be we should leave her off at the hospital."

The kid stiffened. "I'm OK!" she whispered, the words almost lost in her labored breathing. She rolled to her knees and started pulling herself up on the trash barrel beside her. That was good, Chick thought, going back to give her a hand. It was sure enough time to go. But before he could reach her the barrel tipped; he saw it happening, but couldn't move fast enough to stop it. Deucey, closer, managed to grab a fistful of Arlie's sweater to keep her from sprawling on her face again. The barrel fell with a bang and a clatter as the lid came off.

Nip dived for it, managing to keep the damned thing from rolling noisily away. "Jiminy Christmas!" he hissed, wrestling the thing upright again. "Stupid girl!"

But Arlie wasn't paying him any mind. Still hanging from Deucey's hand, she was reaching, fingers spread, for a length of something bone-white that lay draped across a clump of pale grass, almost glowing in the deep shadows. "Dropped it," she panted.

"What the hell's wrong with her?" Deucey demanded, bewildered, still trying to pull her up. A few steps away, Nip was dancing from foot to foot with the need to run.

Chick snagged the pale strap from the ground and held it out to her. Still flailing, she grabbed for it and missed. It slapped into her instead, the loose end swinging under and around and over her bare wrist.

The feel of the thing changed in Chick's hand, prickled like sometimes when you'd caught hold of a spark plug wire as the motor was turning over. Alarmed, he dropped the end he held. And watched as it fell *sideways* to drape across itself on Arlie's wristbones, to sink right into itself if the moonlight wasn't fooling his eyes.

"Hellfire," he breathed. "If that don't beat all."

A snake swallowing its own tail was all Philippa could think for a long, staring moment—a hoop snake like the old men down at Nethers' store back home used to josh about. But that was just a tall tale; nothing in her world could do what this thing had. Fear and awe crawled through her. A humming warmth circled her wrist, clinging to it like a second skin.

Maybe she ought to take it back off.

"Lemme see that!" Chick reached for her hand as Deucey finished hauling her to her feet.

She pulled back out of Chick's reach, needing to explore it herself first. Gingerly she felt along the knotted band, trying to find some kind of catch.

Deucey reached out to shake Chick's shoulder. "What's wrong with you, Chick? Let's scram!"

A muffled bang sounded from back the way they'd come; a casement slamming shut, not a door. They all froze, heads up to listen. The open window she'd come through; Philippa saw it plain in her mind. Mrs. Nestos had found it.

A squeak came from closer at hand, and that *was* a door. A sleep-hoarsened voice said, "Maybe it was cats this time, Irene. But if it's that gang of hoodlums breaking into my woodshop again, I'm treating 'em to a load of rock salt." The door slammed shut.

Without a word Chick took one of Philippa's arms and Deucey took the other, hoisting her up between them. Stunned and still weak, it was all she could do to hang on, arms wrapped tight around the boys' necks. All her skin shrank from being pressed so close between them, but their sweaty warmth took the edge off her shivers. Panting and cursing, they careened east down the street under the moonlike globes of a street lamp, Nip leading the way.

The cold, hard streets had seemed to go on forever. Lemme down, she'd told the guys back when they were still tiptoeing down alleys. Her breathing had eased up enough so she managed on her own a ways, very slow. Then Chick and Deuce'd taken turns hurrying her along, more out of impatience than anything other need. Made her feel like the littler kid of a pair in a three-legged race.

Now they stumbled down a moon-spattered trail through even colder woods without her being able to recall when the pavement had ended. Even with trees to every side the sky claimed her here, tired as she was—the sweep and play of moving air, the sweet prickle of moisture rising from the ground, the unheard growl of the storm pressing in from the northwest.

The storm. She'd warn them later, when they got there. All she wanted now was to curl up around her belly in the crackling leaves beside the path and shut her eyes until the sun came. She kept moving though. No one was going to call her a quitter.

To either side of her Chick and Deuce dodged and cursed wearily as they half-guided, half-dragged her through the sharp-twigged thickets. Nip trudged behind them, but mostly Philippa forgot he was there anymore.

The boys stopped.

A whiff of woodsmoke caught at her throat. Philippa looked up: the reddish glow of campfires showed between the black and silvered trees. It was a slow moment before she could pick out the shapes of rough lean-tos among the shadows. Beyond gleamed the braided course of the river with the full moon high above.

"Over here," someone whispered. Deucey and Chick helped Philippa around the back of one of the more sturdy constructions to its open face. Zeno stood unsteadily to greet them beside a bed of glowing coals. Philippa felt the rising warmth of it on her cold-stiffened cheeks. Her legs began to tremble.

"Jiminy Christmas," Nip mumbled as he came up with them, collapsing on a stump by the fire. "That took *hours.*"

"You waited up for us," Chick said to Zeno. Philippa could feel a sudden tension in him. She wished he'd let her down. Deucey had already slipped from beneath her other arm, but she couldn't seem to figure out how to sit on her own, short of falling.

There was something she was supposed to remember to tell them now. It'd been important.

"Somebody had t' keep a fire going," Zeno said. There was a matching tightness in his voice, a blurry sort of hurt and anger. The feel of it jangled Philippa's nerves to caution, but the guy wasn't paying her any mind. It was Chick he was mad at.

The small man crouched again by the fire, poking it up with a stick. A yellow pint can with its lid twisted off sat near his foot. The light from the revived fire wasn't enough to read the label, but Philippa'd seen plenty like it. What they called dehorn —alcohol folks put in their radiators to keep them from freezing, and a cheap drunk if you weren't choosy. Zeno's eyes were squinched up and red-veined from more than tiredness. Philippa wondered how he'd got the stuff without any dough, and if he was quarrelsome when he was likkered up.

Zeno laid a busted-off piece of dry branch on the coals and just squatted there watching the flames lick it. Chick didn't move except for the fine trembling which ran through him; Philippa felt it against her side. She pushed away from him, and he let go, not noticing. She slipped to her knees before the fire.

"Y' gone dopey?" Deucey asked in exasperation, crawling back out of the lean-to. "She'll fall in, and then where'll we be?"

Won't, Philippa thought, though the dry heat made her eyelids droop. Breathing in the whiffs of smoke hurt her scorched throat, but she didn't try to move away. Something she was supposed to tell them… She frowned and fingered the strap where it clung to her wrist. It begun to feel almost a part of her.

"She's all right," Chick said, but he grabbed a fistful of her collar as a precaution. Philippa looked up; he was rubbing a sleeve across his weary face. Above him was black, clear sky.

That's right, she thought wearily. I got to warn them.

"Storm's coming," she rasped. "Tomorrow night."

Zeno grunted. "Wha' I tell you, Chick. You don' listen. We sh' beat it 'for th' storm hits."

"Sure thing," Chick muttered. "Whatever you say."

"'Sufficient unto the day'." Deucey stood, shedding bits of leaves and dry grass from the lean-to's floor. "Let's get the durn kid settled so's we can bunk down ourselves. We squeeze in tight, we can all fit."

The branch caught fire; the light from it filled Philippa's eyes. She huddled in on herself, smelling woodsmoke mixed in with, now she was warmer, a rich blood stink that rose from her, that marked her out as prey like Hank had said. Somehow she'd forgotten Betts wouldn't be at camp, forgotten the older girl was lying sick and alone in a charity ward, and maybe dying.

Last night there'd been Betts and Mara, who nobody would mess with, not to mention Flo, but that seemed an impossible long time ago. "Sleep out here," she rasped, knowing that wasn't possible.

Deuce yelped. "Like hell! We didn't haul you all this way so's we could leave you outside to freeze." He started round the fire toward her, feeling his way through the darkness behind Nip, who'd dozed off with his head on his knees.

"Throttle it!" The hoarse protest came out of the darkness, from a nearby camp. "Folks's trying to sleep!"

Chick shifted his grip to Philippa's shoulder and bent down. "Listen to me, Arlie," he said in her ear, giving her a little shake. "Nobody gonna bother you, hear? And if they do, you just sing out and it's took care of." His eyes, when she forced a glance up at him, were fierce and bloodshot. "You hear me?" he asked, and shook her again, but her mind was etched full up with the words she'd pushed away from her hours back, when her blood had betrayed her to Mrs. Nestos.

What Hank had said, that morning last April with Corinna sick and cranky up at the house, and her with her hands wet and smelling of sour iron from the new-washed rags, 'cause even lye soap wasn't enough or maybe she hadn't scrubbed hard as she ought—he'd said, grinning, "Hanging scent flags out for the boys, Sister? Guess I'll hafta load up with buckshot to keep 'em off my property now you're all grown up." Stupid, shaming words, but his grin when he said them made her insides go weak and chill. "I got lots of buckshot," he'd said, husky-voiced, and took a step towards her. And his eyes burned her, caught and held her pinned like a snake's eyes will a bird. Again. That'd been as bad as his hands on her, later, and worse than the pain she didn't much remember.

Her head started pounding and bile rose to burn her raw throat. Philippa swallowed it back down with the rest of that day—being sick on the far side of Wylie's Ridge, and clinging to a grab iron on the side of a boxcar for the first time—and found she was rubbing the strap again where it circled her wrist, steadying herself with the feel of its intricate patterns.

Whatever she'd hoped for a little while there at Mrs. Nestos' house, there was only one road on this earth she could walk might keep her safe. Unless and until she could find a door that led to Mara and Simon's Canaan Land, and that was like praying for rain in a summer like this last one—it might happen but you couldn't lay trust on it. Simon being with them could make all the difference, at least it could if she could make him see how important it was to her, and to the others too if they'd only believe in it. And if he was in his right mind, which he didn't seem to be.

There was no help for it. And truth to tell, she didn't mind.

She made herself meet Chick's gaze again. "I hear fine," she told him, whispering but level-voiced.

Act a boy, be a boy, and give her blood the lie.

"No need to worry, Chick," she went on, glad for how low the fire had left her voice. "Any trouble, settle it myself."

A corner of Chick's mouth twitched like he figured he understood her. "Attaboy," he told her.

As Deuce pulled her to her feet, Philippa caught sight of Zeno's glare. At her, this time, but why did he care what way she chose? After a long second he looked down, his mouth sullen.

"You too, Zeno," Deucey told him. "You gotta get some shut-eye. We can roust Junk or Karl out to watch the fire for awhile."

"Can't either," a gruff voice mumbled from the shadows inside the lean-to. Junkyard, of course. "Took first watch. Not my turn."

Zeno shrugged sloppily. "Leave 'em lie. Won't sleep anyway."

Chick stayed put. "Guess I'll sit up for a spell as well," he said, his voice gone tight and careful once again.

14

*G*eese honked overhead. Philippa stirred under the heavy weight of covers. Flocks heading south, she thought, drowsing in the warmth and dappled sunlight.

"Wish I had my Uncle Hiram's ten gauge," Chick's voice said longingly from close by. Relief trickled through her at the sound. She blinked at the feeling, then recollected how she'd roused, very late in the night, and seen him and Zeno slipping off together, quiet as mice. Chick had had a dark, intent look on his face she hadn't understood. She'd been afraid they'd took off for good.

Chick went on, "Wouldn't one of them big geese taste swell roasted up nice and crisp over the fire?"

She'd never tasted roast goose, but hunger still curled Philippa's stomach into a tight ball at the thought. She struggled to sit up, but the weight above her made it awkward. Coats and jackets lay spread out on top of her and the curled-up sleeper next to her—Nip, she was pretty sure, though there wasn't much of him visible.

Zeno snorted. "They'd throw you in the clink before you got a chance to eat it. Hunting without a license and Cristos knows what else."

She rolled away from Nip and out from under the coats, catching sight as she did so of the pale strap wrapped tight and easy around her left wrist. Curious, she tried to trace where the ends had been, without luck. The band now seemed one continuous weaving of shiny, braided strands.

A bracelet of her own, like that red one she'd seen Mara wearing. Philippa cocked her head to glance at Simon, who was sitting a little ways off from the campfire, his back to a tree, eyes closed and face turned to the sun. If he still had his bracelet on, she couldn't see it. His hands were burrowed past the wrists in the opposite sleeves of his coat.

Those bracelets meant something important to them, even if she wasn't sure what it was. Likely hers was only some old castoff strap, but still it had to be a little piece of their world. Nothing from here could do what this one had. Mara was gone off home and their door destroyed, but at least she had that much.

She flexed her wrist, turning it from side to side. The strap moved with her like it was part of her skin, and didn't bind at all. Which was a good thing, as she had no notion of how she'd get it off if it did.

Her gaze strayed up to an unfamiliar pink scar that crossed the base of her thumb.

Fully awake now, Philippa stared at her palm. No fresh cut marked it at all. Wonder swelled in her like a cool light.

"Jailbirds get fed," Karl pointed out, out by the fire. "That's more than you can say for us."

Zeno retorted, "Not roast goose."

The scar looked near two weeks old, supposing it hadn't mortified, which wounds had a tendency to do, living in the dirt and dust of the road as they did. To be sure, Philippa checked her other hand. The palm was dirty but unremarkable: no cut; no scar.

More than that, she could breathe as easy as pie. Her toe ached some when she wiggled it, but not like it was broke, not like it had. No cramps low in her belly, neither.

Eager to share the miracle, Philippa sat up. Blue sky showed brilliant through the bare branches of the trees overhead. A fine, still morning, all the better for the far-off pressure of the coming storm she felt in the back of her head.

The guys by the fire—Karl, Chick, and Zeno—turned to look at her. Zeno growled, "Cristos, you're lively this morning." His hangover had left him looking puffy around the eyes.

Philippa stuck out her hand to show them. "Hey, look! My cut—it healed clean up! And my throat and everything!" Her voice cracked halfway through, but it came out strong.

Chick listened, looking puzzled. Karl and Zeno squinted at the proffered hand.

They didn't know, of course. "I cut it last night, see," she told them. "At that lady's house. Bled all over the place."

Zeno's upper lip curled into a sneer.

Karl glanced again at the scar on her palm and then looked up at her face, his expression stuck somewhere between outrage and worry. He didn't say anything though.

She pulled her hand back, closing it around the new scar. They didn't believe her. Again. "Swear to Jesus it's true," she insisted because she had to, with the wonder still broad in her mind. But hadn't none of them seen the cut to start with. "I know it sounds like bunk, but it ain't."

Her voice seemed pitched a little lower than she was used to, except when it squeaked. Smoke damage that hadn't healed up with her lungs, maybe. She cleared her throat.

Chick searched her face. His eyes widened, though she wasn't sure why. He said, "Come on out here where I can see you."

Wary, she crawled out of the shelter and went to him.

Chick put away the jackknife he'd been whittling with and pulled a rag from his pocket instead. He dunked a corner of it in the can which served him as a cup and, catching hold of her chin, he rubbed at her cheek. The wet was warm to start with, but cooled fast as the air hit it.

Philippa twisted out of his grasp, scrubbing her cheek dry on a sleeve. "What're you doing!"

He ignored her protest. "Getting the dirt off so I can see your face," he said flatly, turning away, his eyes showing a little too much white. "That bruise Junkyard gave you is gone, and the burns too. Not to mention you ain't wheezing."

Slowly Philippa squatted down by the fire, out of arm's reach.

Karl shrugged uneasily. He looked worn to a frazzle, like sleep hadn't helped him at all. "If you say so, Chick. I can't say I remember a bruise or nothing. We were soot all over most of yesterday." He busied himself dipping out a portion of whatever it was steaming away in the No. 10 can sitting in the heaped-up remains of the coals.

He thrust the drink at her. She sniffed it: No smell to it at all. Nothing but hot water, she figured, but the warmth felt good soaking through the flannel cuff of her nightshirt.

"Looked like a drowned pup," Zeno said, very cool. His ill-tempered gaze stung her. "Still looks like one, for that matter."

Jesus bless, but the guy had it in for her. Philippa wrapped her arms tight around her knees, careful not to spill the water. Chick's face had screwed up sour at Zeno's words, but he didn't say a thing, only fiddled with a twig while the silence at the fireside stretched out.

Philippa took a cautious sip, then made a face. The stuff tasted like sawdust. "What's this?"

"Coffee," Karl said shortly.

Laying an arm across Chick's shoulders, Zeno bared his teeth at her. "My pal here found us a stash of old grounds."

Grimacing, Chick waved him off. "Nothing but dishwater."

A breeze stirred the dead leaves overhead, but didn't touch them down on the ground. Philippa took another sip. At least the stuff was hot. And it didn't hurt her throat at all, going down.

Sunlight glowed red-gold through Simon's eyelids. At home to sit as he was doing, unprotected in the doubled light of Nir nev and the sun, would rightfully be taken as a sign of madness. Here it gave him a pale comfort.

Duty dragged at him. He should force himself to puzzle out what the wanderers were saying. Much of it—words or phrases —sounded familiar, but meaning floated just out of reach.

The tone of the chatter was clear enough, though. His jaw tightened. He couldn't bear to wait here listening to their bickering. He would go into the city, and find Lukas and the training mission on his own. Abruptly he stood. "I go."

They stared up at him, surprise plain in their faces. "Where is it you planning on going, Simon?" Chick asked him.

Hearing the hated name, Simon winced. "I find lake." He tried to sound confident.

"That's right." The man Zeno spoke to the others, not to him. "He's gotta go soak his head."

Simon frowned, trying without luck to make sense of this. From the man's tone, it was meant as insult. Well, that didn't matter.

"What lake is that?" Chick's question held the kind of patience used with small children and the mad.

Simon's chin lifted. "Is most big lake in St. Paul."

Arlie, the boy with the child's braid, watched him hungrily, the thin body poised as though he would leap up to follow. Simon took an uneasy backward step. Arlie's head tilted quizzically, and Simon saw the young one's braid had been cut away. When had they held Passage for him? Simon felt unmoored, as though the question itself was wrong.

Zeno hooted. "Cristos, that'll be a long hike!" Karl was shaking his head.

"We ain't in St. Paul." Chick's voice had taken on an edge.

Another wave of unease washed through Simon. "The city beside," he suggested, hating the hesitancy in his voice.

Chick looked baffled.

"He means Minneapolis," the boy Arlie said quietly, not taking those clear brown eyes off him.

Breathing hard, Chick stood. "They's both of them a good three hundred miles off! Like we told you before, this here is Grand Forks, North Dakota, so sit down before you go getting yourself even worse lost!"

Simon gaped at him. Three hundred miles was... He couldn't remember the conversion factor, but a mile was several times further than a li. "How... How..." He turned to Zeno. "You say we go there!"

The balding man looked surprised. He raised both hands. "Hey, I never said a thing about that, pal!"

Head spinning, Simon stared at the ground. "But how Lukas find me?"

Chick snatched off his cap and hurled it to the ground, raising a puff of dust. "Lukas ain't gonna find you, Simon! How many times we got to tell you he's dead!"

Dead. *Haatzo*. The words set up painful cross-echoes in his mind as he tried to deny that one meant the other. Breath strangled in his chest, Simon stared unseeing at the tangled trees.

It was no good. Though Lukas' grin shone broad and mischievous as ever in his mind, he knew what the wanderer told him was true. His bvarit was gone. He felt again the warmth and weight of the boy leaning against his shoulder in the freezing, ill-smelling privy as they prepared that last report. Lukas had been his friend and not just a comrade.

It was strange that he'd never thought about that before.

An urgent voice called after him in the Night-cursed, mushy foreign tongue, summoning him back. He shook it off; walked away, stretching the muscles in his legs as though that could ease the fist of pain in his chest. He'd failed. Lukas was dead, burned, they'd told him—oh yes, he remembered that now he had stopped hiding like shadows fleeing the coming of the Great Light.

Mara might have made it across. He'd seen her fall into the slip. A memory of unending nothingness flooded his mind, but, gasping, he pushed it away with the branches blocking his way. She wasn't trapped in that. He wouldn't believe it, not now. Not yet.

Lukas was dead, everything that had been part of him gone. That was grief enough to carry.

Cursing under his breath, Chick started to follow Simon. No telling what trouble the Wob would get into on his own.

"Better let him go," Zeno said, putting out a big hand to stop him. "If he's finally getting it through that thick bohunk head his pal is dead, he'll need time to himself."

"Won't get to town that way, that's for sure," Karl said as though it didn't much matter to him anyway.

Uneasily Chick settled back down on his haunches, watching Simon bull his way deeper into underbrush. "Guess you're right." There'd been an undercurrent in Zeno's words that said he knew a little too well what he was talking about. Chick thought again of how the Greek had acted when the ice house fell in on them—frantic, digging for pals who had to be long dead.

"You bet I am." Zeno grinned with that bitter sense of humor he had. "And if he does manage to fall in the river, that's one less worry for us, eh?"

Scowling, Arlie stumbled to her feet. "I'll fetch him back."

Zeno turned a cold eye on the kid. "Be my guest, girlie. I'm sure he'll appreciate it. Maybe he'll give you a little present out there in the bushes, eh?"

The kid went white.

"He's joking, Arlie," Chick said hastily, though it was clear Zeno had meant that last barb to go home. His lover turned the unfriendly look on him. Cold prickled down Chick's spine, but he kept talking. Zeno didn't know how flat-out mean he sounded sometimes. "It's broad daylight. He ain't so far gone he's likely to drown himself." He wished to Christ Zeno would get over being jealous about the kid.

Still white, Arlie spat. She sat again, jaw and fists clenched.

Simon was almost out of sight among the trees. And the crackling Chick was hearing wasn't from his direction anymore. Someone was coming down the path from town: Junkyard, the grin on his face near as big as the newspaper-wrapped bundle in his arms. He fell on his knees beside Karl, laying his burden out before him and peeling back a couple of the layers. The warm bread smell drenched Chick's senses like honey.

"Rolls. A whole tray of 'em," Junkyard said, chortling. "Bakery driver was jawing with some old cluck in the store." He plucked a couple from the pile and crawled the few steps to the lean-to. Snatching off the hat that shielded Nip's eyes, he whacked the kid with it. "Up and at 'em, tiger," he sang out. "Brought ya a scoffing!"

Chick reached across Karl and helped himself to the rolls. He passed a handful to Zeno and then, his own jaw set, threw a couple across to Arlie. Once the bread was in her hands and under her nose her expression shifted. She tore into the food.

Done with teasing Nip, Junkyard looked around. "Say, where's the Wob?"

Mouth full, Chick started to answer just as Deucey, winded, flopped down next to him. He reached inside his bulging coat. "Cheese," he panted, producing a sizeable wedge of yellow cheddar. "A can of coffee. Makings. And bologna." One by one he pulled the items out, ending by tossing two rings of sausage on the paper beside the rolls.

Chick ducked a boot heel as Junkyard tackled Deucey, knocking him over backwards. "How'd you pull it off?" Junkyard cried, coming out on top.

Deucey rolled away, grinning, though his puckered eyes told a different story. "They took off after you. I did me some shopping. Slipped out the back."

"We need it worse'n they do," Chick told him quietly.

Deucey nodded, not looking at him. He fished a jackknife out of his pocket and scooted back over to the piled food.

"Think you fellers could spare us some of that?" A tall old man stood over them, with a younger guy looming behind him.

"Hey, Bad Eye, Slick," Zeno said, leaning back to look up at them. Maybe it was them he'd been with last night, Chick thought, suddenly wary.

Deucey studied the men for a moment. "Just the two of you?" he asked. "That's OK then." He paused and looked at Junkyard. "'Course I got no say about the bread."

Junkyard looked stubborn.

That wasn't right. Grabbing the big can off the fire, Chick said firmly, "We'll share what we got." He pushed to his feet. Reluctant, Junkyard shrugged.

Chick flipped the contents of the big can into the bushes. "I'll boil us up some fresh." More than grateful for a moment to himself, he headed down to the riverbank to refill the can.

Eyes burning, Simon stared out at the wide flowing water... Not a lake. How had he gotten here? Bewildered, he looked around, rough bark biting into his palm where he gripped the limb of a tree.

Ah. He stood on a riverbank. The murmur of men's voices came down the water to him; the jungle wasn't far. Simon eased himself down to sit on the bank's soft dust. He wiped the back of a hand across his eyes, insides aching with more than hunger.

It was his duty to find a way home, to report what had happened in case Mara hadn't... No, he would *not* think that.

Shivering in the sunlight, Simon hugged his knees. Such a cold world this was! Three hundred miles, and the cold, and the terrible nights: how was he to cross that, find the St. Paul mission, when he knew so little of this place? A sob rose in his throat, choking him. He pressed his mouth against one knee to stifle it, biting the bony flesh there through the thick cloth, tasting dust.

The sparse tears that came didn't help, though after awhile the hush of the river calmed him some. He raised his head and watched it. He would have to ask the wanderers to help him. As much food as we shared with them, he thought bitterly, climbing to his feet, they should be glad to do what they can.

Both Chick and Arlie looked relieved to see him when he stepped out of the trees. All of the wanderers he knew sat around the fire now, along with two older ones he did not know. They were eating, passing around small loaves of bread from a pile of them heaped on a crumpled newspaper. He should ask them now, he told himself, trying to quell the hunger that had roared awake in him at the yeasty smell.

"There you are," Junkyard said to him, more cheerful than Simon had seen him. He handed up one of the breads. "Have a roll. Hot off the baker's truck!"

The bread felt very light in Simon's hand. He swallowed saliva as he sat. "Thanks you," he said faintly, tearing into it. Too soft, his mind told him, too small, but the taste was smooth as good beer, with a trace both of salt and sweet.

In three bites it was gone. Feeling weak, Simon eyed the remaining heap, but it was beyond the reach of his hand. Rounds of some meat were cooking on a flattened sheet of metal on the fire. He would have to wait for that too.

"I am…" He cleared his throat, still unable to look away from the food. "I am trouble to you, I think. Still I ask more, ask help to find St. Paul."

The older stranger looked up at that. "Sheesh, that's simple. St. Paul's on the main line to Chicago. Both the Goat Road and the NP'll take you there right enough."

Despair sank through Simon. Goat Road meant nothing to him, nor did the other one.

"I'll see you get there," Arlie offered, his voice husky.

They'd been right to cut his child's braid, Simon thought uneasily, not answering. Arlie had too eager a gleam in his eyes.

Karl stopped munching. "We can't go until Betts is better! I'm not gonna leave her behind," he said around a mouthful.

That was the pale-haired girl, Simon recalled. She had been sick. But how long did it take these people to heal from a disorder of the lungs with no iyar pukko to support their immune system? It might be days or even the whole of one of their weeks.

"'Course we won't," Chick said. He tossed another roll in Simon's lap.

Zeno's lip was curled. "Don't know about you, Chick, but I'm heading for Chi today, before that bad weather socks us. And in case you're wondering," he said, raising his voice and turning to eye Simon, "I don't plan on nursemaiding a crackbrained Wob half the way there; bet your life on that."

Simon digested this for a moment. "I understand," he said at last, hesitantly. "I will not be crackbrained."

The others laughed. Zeno's scowl deepened. "Forget about it!"

Face heating, Simon turned his attention back to the bread in his hand. He told himself not to worry. Others might help.

Deucey handled him a chunk of a yellow substance. It had a strong, sour smell. Wary, he tasted it.

"What is?" he murmured to Karl, on his left.

Karl eyed him. "Cheese. You know. The stuff they make from milk?"

Memory of past lessons nudged Simon. Milk stripped from a mother animal! Grimacing, he swallowed the bite; to spit it out would offend. He wasn't hungry enough to eat the rest of the unnatural stuff.

Nip reached across the fire, holding out his hand. Simon gave him a weak smile and dropped the chunk in his dirty palm, then wiped his own hand off on his pants leg. The smell did not go away.

Chick turned to him. He looked tired and a little pale beneath the warm brown of his skin. "How come you're so fired up about going to St. Paul anyways?"

Simon swallowed the last of his bread and opened his mouth to give the answer he'd come to earlier, of a comrade who would shelter him. Arlie, that newly cut hair sticking out in odd directions, spoke before he could, voice squeaking.

"They've got another one of them doors there. Betcha."

Speechless, Simon felt hair rise on the back of his neck.

Bad Eye looked up from one of the discarded sheets of newspaper. "Hey, Zeno. You got a achy joint telling you the weather's changing?"

Philippa stiffened, swallowing the last of her fried bologna with an effort. Trouble was coming; she could feel it.

"What are you saying?" Zeno scowled. "Achy joints are for old bums like you."

Bad Eye showed his teeth, uneven but solid. "Bad joints I got, only they don't tell me nothing but to take it easy. But see, I'm just asking on account of this weather report says different. This morning's paper, too. 'Continued fair to partly cloudy and unseasonably warm through Monday. Freeze possible tonight,'" he read.

Zeno's face darkened.

"Freeze possible, my Aunt Molly's drooping tits," the old man went on. "Guaranteed's more like. But see, I keep an eye on the weather reports. Makes a diff when you're working harvest, which is what we come up here to do."

"Sugar beets no damn good this year," the other guy rumbled. "Drouth and heat burned 'em up." It was the first time Philippa had heard him do more than grunt his thanks.

Zeno ignored him. "So? I hear different." He sounded bored. "You ought to know half those reports are wrong anyway."

Surprise eased the tension in Philippa's gut. For a wonder he'd believed her. "That one's dead wrong." Her voice came out rough. She cleared her throat before she went on. "Snowstorm coming in tonight, sure as shootin'."

Grinning, Bad Eye looked at her with his real eye. The glass one pointed off in a whole nother direction. "So you're the one with the achy joints! Young for it, ain'tcha, sonny?"

The last word warmed her, but you couldn't never tell when folks might turn mean. "Nossir," Philippa said cautiously. "I mean I ain't got achy joints. I can just tell about weather sometimes. Got it from my daddy, my Meemaw told me."

"Dog shit!" Zeno shot to his feet. "I'm not going to listen to this hyesse anymore!" He turned on his heel and strode off across the clearing.

Breathless, Philippa watched after him. Out of the corner of her eye she saw that Chick had scrambled to his feet as well, but he wasn't following his pal.

"Don't let it worry you," Bad Eye said confidentially, leaning towards her and spearing the last slice of bologna from the makeshift grill as he did so. "I run into old Zeno before. Got a hair trigger when it comes to his pride." He bit off a piece of the sausage and chewed it meditatively.

"Dog shit is right," Junkyard said, but he laughed.

She glanced at him. "We'll see come tonight."

Still grinning, Junkyard fished in his pocket. He considered the handful of things he pulled out, then held up a box of matches. "Tell you what. I'll bet this against that stub of pencil you got that it ain't gonna snow. Whaddya say?"

Philippa shrugged. "Deal." She wouldn't lose, but it didn't matter if she did. A body could find a pencil without much trouble. It was her penknife she missed.

Junkyard grinned wider, pocketing the matches.

Deucey was watching Chick. "Thought Zeno wanted you to go along to Chicago with him, Chick."

The Okie boy turned on him. "He ain't going nowhere! Just blowing off steam is all!"

Wiping his mouth, Bad Eye got to his feet. He nudged his friend, who stood as well. "We sure 'preciate the hospitality, but we got a freight to catch ourselves."

Junkyard looked up at them thoughtfully. "You guys headed to Chi too?"

Philippa saw Simon's head come up at the question.

Bad Eye grinned at Junkyard. "Wanna come?"

Junkyard glanced at Karl. "Naw. I'm sticking. West Madison's too close to home for me." But Simon's gaze followed the old man and his pal as they went back to their camp.

Zeno waited for him by the river. Silently Chick squatted down beside him, busying himself by rinsing out his cup.

"You're not coming."

Dread prickled down Chick's arms. "I want to be with you," he whispered, wondering if it was true anymore. He risked a look up at the broad set of Zeno's shoulders, the big, knotted hands, and his body assured him it was.

Zeno shrugged. "Then come."

"Let's stay awhile longer, Zeno. Chicago ain't going away. There's missions here in town if the weather does turn bad." Which it might. Enough uncanny things had happened that he was inclined to trust Arlie's instincts.

"You ought to know by now missions don't take girls," Zeno said, taunting, reading part of what he was thinking. "You plan on leaving that scrawny new girlfriend of yours to freeze?"

Chick swallowed. That was the heart of it, and Zeno wasn't going to listen anymore than he had before. He stood shakily, forgetting his can in the shallow water. "You know she ain't no such thing." But Zeno's eyes looked back at him, hard and shiny as flecks of obsidian. "Honest to Christ, Zeno! I just been helping the kid out! Don't mean nothing!"

"Yeah?" Zeno said softly. "Then give me one good reason why you want to stay."

On account of I never wanted to go to Chicago in the first place, Chick thought, but there wasn't no point in saying it out loud. He turned to look towards camp. He must have been shouting just now, because the other kids had all turned to stare. Arlie looked stricken.

Simon wasn't there though. He was off at Bad Eye's camp. The dumb Wob must be trying to talk them into taking him along. There'd be trouble from it.

"I-I like these guys," he stammered, though that wasn't really true; not all of them. Junkyard, for instance. But he liked being part of a gang. And, prickly as she could be, Arlie had come to rely on him just a little. There was something in that that was hard to walk away from.

"I don't. Gets old, hanging around a bunch of stupid kids." Zeno turned on his heel. "Come or not, as you like," he threw over his shoulder. Chick watched, torn, as the Greek grabbed down his coat from the branch where it'd been hanging, and headed for the gap in the trees that gave on the path to town.

"Beat it!" Across the clearing, Slick gave Simon a shove. Bad Eye finished kicking dirt over their fire, and the two of them followed Zeno down the trail, leaving Simon standing.

After a long moment Chick looked around for his can, found it no more than a speck on the rolling water, floating away.

"Goddamn buncha lousers," Junkyard said when Chick rejoined them. The Chicago kid tossed his cigarette butt down and ground it into the dirt with his toe. "Let 'em go. We don't need 'em."

15

Squatting in late afternoon sunlight in a sheltered spot along the riverbank, Philippa found that the threadbare scrap of bathrobe she'd used to replace the blood rag Mrs. Nestos had given her was still unmarked. She stared at the material, confused; unfolded it to make doubly sure. No bloodstains at all. She'd been wearing the cloth for hours.

It's stopped, she thought, though that didn't make sense, not after less than a day.

A wondering grin stretched across her face. She'd never heard tell that you could stop your monthlies by just deciding to be a boy. Maybe this was part of the same miracle that had healed where she'd cut herself, and her lungs and all. A miracle could change most anything. But wouldn't it be funny if the way her voice had been squeaking on and off today was on account of her voice changing, like guys' voices did!

That was plain foolishness. Sobering, she washed the day's mud and sweat from the parts of her she could reach without undressing too much.

Her clothes were another matter. Chick had set everybody he could get hold of—Deucey and Nip and Simon and her, and Junkyard until he got fed up and stomped off for town—to work cobbling together a better shelter out of whatever they could scrounge: branches, old signboards, and, in the case of the makeshift chimney, old bricks and stones and river mud. It would've been fun, only Chick had been touchy as an old snapping turtle ever since his pal left.

Philippa glanced at the sky. Too late to risk rinsing anything out, especially with the storm coming. The sky overhead was the same hard, clear blue, but there was a haze to the west. When she closed her eyes she could feel the heavy air swirling slow as a dream toward them. She'd just have to let the mud on her clothes finish drying and brush it off as best she could.

Sighing, she refolded the mostly clean rag and pinned it back in place. No use asking for trouble.

The shanty seemed hushed, even with the crackle of the fire and the guys breathing slow and regular. She'd claimed one wall of the dry-grass-filled crib that served as their bed. It was colder than being in the middle, but let her turn her back on the guys. Still, now that she wasn't sick and exhausted, the heat and smell of boys crowding close kept her from sleeping sound.

Karl snorted raggedly beside her. The raw scent of booze he put off didn't help at all. He'd staggered back from town a little before dark, and the only thing anybody'd been able to get out of him was that Betts wasn't doing so hot.

But from outside she heard no sounds at all, no rustling of dry leaves or cracking of twigs, no stir of wind. Philippa stilled and let the night into her mind. It wrapped around her, alive but peaceful, like a drowsing cat. She squirmed over on her back, careful not to poke anybody.

Above her the canvas roof of the hut sagged lower than she remembered it doing. Philippa smiled. Snow. Ordinary, quiet snow. The storm she'd felt had moved in.

"Started a while back," Chick said softly, startling her into sitting up. Exhaustion roughened his voice. "Couple hours, maybe." He sat cross-legged by their makeshift fireplace, a vague shape in the glow of the coals.

Philippa inched her way out of the nest of leaves and grass and went to sit across from him. "Don't you never sleep, Chick?" she whispered.

Rubbing both hands across his face, Chick shrugged. Mud dried to alligator scales streaked the backs of his hands. "Tried to. Can't. I'll wake somebody directly and give it another shot." He was mumbling.

"I can tend the fire," Philippa offered. She wouldn't mind sitting up alone for a spell. She liked being inside a storm like this, a natural storm, long as she was warm and dry and fed.

Chick stared down at the coals, red-eyed and blinking. After a moment he shook his head. Philippa let be. If he wouldn't go lie down, wasn't a thing she could do about it.

Aimlessly he poked at the fire, herding the coals together so they flared up, then raking them apart again. Eventually he spoke. "How long's this storm gonna last?"

Gratified, Philippa felt around in her sense of the storm like you'd probe with your tongue for a missing tooth. "Big storm," she said at last. "Slow moving. Through tomorrow, I reckon."

"Lotta snow, then."

She frowned. That didn't feel true. "Don't reckon so."

"Figure they're getting weather like this up east of here? Other side of Minnesota, say, or over to Wisconsin?" Chick asked.

Philippa glanced over at him. His mouth had pursed up tight and bitter. "Near as I can tell it's headed southeast, but slow, like I said. Don't know a thing more about it than that." He was thinking about Zeno. Seemed to her that pals split up all the time on the road. Still one or the other of them got bruised feelings about it on occasion. "Zeno can take care of hisself," she told him, meaning comfort. "He'll be OK."

Chick's face twisted up mean at that. "Reckon he will." He got to his feet and dropped his stick onto the coals. The business end of it had already started smoking. "Look, Arlie, you ain't got no idea what's what, so why don't you butt out?"

Stung, Philippa lashed back. "If it's so all-fired important to you, how come you didn't go with him?"

Chick swayed a little where he stood. She couldn't see his face clear for the shadows, though his shape—black hair and peacoat—stood out sharp against the rough, dimly-lit walls.

"Don't know. Thought I had something to do here," he said, the anger draining from his voice. "And maybe I do."

"Got tired of being that old wolf's liddle lambie, I was hoping," Junkyard growled from the bed.

Fists clenching, Chick froze in place. "You're blowing smoke, Junk," he said softly.

"No, I ain't. I seen him rubbing on you." Junkyard wriggled out from between Simon and Nip. "Yeesh."

"Maybe so," Chick answered, level-voiced. "But it happens you still don't know nothin' about it."

Junkyard faced him, his pale hair sticking out like a half-built bird's nest. "You don't need some old buzzard like that to get by, Chick," he said seriously. "I know how it goes. Yer hungry an' new to the road an' some guy comes along says he'll take care of you real swell. But it ain't good."

Understanding drifted slowly in on Philippa as she sat listening, as motionless as Chick and her face first cold, then hot, then cold again and stayed that way. How had she missed seeing this? Nobody could ride the rails for months like she'd done without learning about wolves, older hobos who had a yen for boys and who sometimes used force when persuasion didn't work. Back in late summer she'd been flopping with a bunch of other kids in a side-tracked boxcar when the whole crew'd piled out into the night after hearing a kid yell for help. They'd caught the man, too, and pounded and kicked him bloody before the bulls showed up and everybody scrammed. The whole thing had made her feel sick, the kid's cries and how the bum curled up on the ground trying to shield himself from their blows.

Nobody'd ever beat Hank up for what he'd done. But this felt different. This cut close to the bone in a whole nother way.

"Be fine without him," Chick whispered at last, and swallowed. "I know it."

Junkyard nodded, relaxing, content. Philippa kept her mouth shut. It was no business of hers to set him straight.

Chick looked down at her, waiting, eyes catching the firelight like deep water. She met his gaze, puzzling out the feelings, remembering him kneeling by her chair in that lady's kitchen.

She'd known he was taking care of her and just joshing her a little on the side, like you do with a pal.

Which was what she was asking for, wasn't it?

Yawning, Junkyard pushed aside the scrap of carpeting hung over the doorway, letting in a chill whisper of air. "Hey! It's snowing." He let the curtain drop and gave Philippa a long, considering stare that she had no time for.

Chick'd took care of her, and Zeno had been mad at him, and her, for it. And then Zeno run off to Chicago with a bunch of strangers. Philippa didn't like it, didn't like how she'd got tangled up in this mess between the two of them.

But Chick was waiting. She shrugged and gave him the bit of smile she could muster.

His shoulders eased.

"Barely freezing out there," Junkyard commented. "Be a sea of mud once the sun hits this stuff." He dug deep in a pocket. "Hey, Arlie."

She looked his way. He gave her a wicked grin and tossed her his matchbox.

Ice-cold water splashed on his face. Startled, still groggy, Chick sat up, wiping the drops away.

The low, dimly lit shanty seemed full to bursting with bodies, but so far as he could tell, nobody but maybe Simon had even noticed him rousing. Most everybody was clustered near the fire. Chick eyed Simon suspiciously, unlikely as it was that the Wob had that kind of devilment in him, to be flicking water at folks.

Simon, back to the splintery signboard that formed the back wall, stirred uncomfortably under Chick's glare. He'd been keeping his head down and his mouth shut since Zeno's pals had chased him off.

But Chick didn't want to think about Zeno or his pals. He scrubbed roughly at his forehead with the hand he wasn't leaning on. Hellfire, but his head was pounding. What the hell time was it, anyways? Getting on for dusk to judge by how dim it was.

But no. The drumming was outside his head, not in. Beyond their makeshift walls it was raining steady.

Chick looked up. There was a wispy layer of smoke between him and the old tarp that was their roof, but that didn't hide how it sagged swaybacked as a pregnant bitch dog. Another drop gathered and fell, though he wasn't under it this time.

"You's letting all the heat out, Karl." Deucey was shivering where he sat perched on the lashed-together framework that held in the dried grass of their bed.

Karl, leaning in the doorway, let the flowery carpet fall shut. "Cripes. Haven't seen this much rain all year. I should've flopped at Sally's," he muttered.

"Well, so why didn't you?" Junkyard asked, not looking up from the checkerboard drawn in the dirt floor.

"Thought you said there weren't no visiting hours at the hospital today, on account of it being Sunday," Arlie added from somewhere beyond Junkyard and Nip.

"Yeah. So what?" Karl mooched over to stare at the game, hands jammed in his pockets. "If I was in town I could at least ask the nurses how she's doing." The crossbeam they'd lashed the stolen tarp to drooped no more than a foot above his head.

Chick squinted at it, confused. Hadn't they set the branch higher than that? Karl wasn't near as tall as Deucey. And while it hadn't been as straight as he'd've liked, he thought he'd trimmed it off pretty smooth. From here it looked like there was a spiky piece coming off of it…

Understanding shot panic through him. He scrambled from the bed, edging past Deucey and grabbing the hatchet from where Arlie had left it leaning by the door.

"He got the collywobbles?" somebody asked wonderingly. Deucey, Philippa thought, frowning as she watched the soggy carpet flop shut behind Chick. She bit off her thread, then held the pants she'd been mending up to the firelight. A clumsy job, but they'd hold for a spell. And she had pockets again, even if she had nothing to put in them but Junkyard's matchbox. It was a lucky thing Deucey carried a needle and thread on him.

"Sick guys don't grab hatchets on their way out," Junkyard said, his attention diverted from his game.

Philippa hadn't got more than a quick peek at Chick's face, but it seemed to her he'd been more panicked than ailing. Reflexively she glanced up. The canvas was sagging again, heavy as the sodden clouds that hung overhead. Far as she could see it was no worse than last time, when Deucey had shanghaied Simon, as the next tallest guy, into helping him go out and bail it.

"He look there," Simon said, getting to his knees, his chin jutting out in what looked to her like the general direction of the fireplace. Which was about as lively as he'd been all day, other than shying away from her whenever she got close. The Wob was frowning. "Was worry," he added.

Philippa eyed the fireplace, but didn't see anything different about it. And the fire was going good, with a tidy pile of dry branches sitting ready to hand when it needed stoking.

Simon started to say something more, but Nip whooped just then, drowning him out. "Gotcha!" he crowed, scooping up bottle caps from the board. "Three in a row and you're out!"

Junkyard stared at the board in disbelief. "Hey! How'd you do that? Do it over, so's I can see."

"Lessons'll cost you!" Smirking, Nip set the board up again. "Who's next?"

Junkyard looked like he was considering taking a swipe at the younger boy.

"Kid's on the up-and-up," Deucey put in cautiously. "I seen it."

Nip turned to him. "So how about you, Deuce?"

Standing, Philippa grinned a little at the kid's cheek. She worked a union-suit-clad leg into the mended pants.

"Yeah," Deucey said consideringly. "I'll give it a whirl." He scooted closer to the checkerboard.

A stout forked branch pushed the door carpet aside, poking into the center of the small space. Philippa stumbled out of its way as Chick, dripping, dragged the butt end in behind him. Face grim, he jammed the fork under their roof beam and planted the far end in the middle of the checkerboard.

"Hey!" Nip cried, but Philippa had finally seen what'd sent Chick out into the rain: the crossbeam, obscured by the sagging canvas, had split halfway along its length and was set to break clean in two. She scrambled over to help him force it up.

The ladened roof tarp weighed a ton, even with Junkyard crowding in to help. "Take it slow!" Chick gasped as the water poured down the outside walls. "Don't bust it!" He had a point, she thought, panting, but she didn't see any way they could do it fast. Junkyard crowded in beside her, and then Simon.

Icy wet soaked through her socks. She spared a downward glance; saw water carving little streams in the dirt floor. Coming in through the doorway, she guessed, cursing as she strained to push the new post up. They could deal with that later.

The pushing got easier, and then the new post was in place, as upright as it was going to get, the beam still unbroken.

A loud, long hiss brought them all whirling around to face the fire—or where the fire had been. Steam billowed up from the blackened coals while sheets of mud ran down the bricks and stones of their fireplace.

"Cripes!" Karl said as the first brick fell.

A gust of wind through the ragged gap in the wall plastered Chick's wet pants legs to his shins. He stared open-mouthed at the hole, trying to make sense of it.

"Shoulda bailed first," Deucey said into the stunned silence.

Chick's numb hands clenched as another piece of brick slid free. He couldn't do anything right anymore. He'd thought he was being smart, using mud to slap a honest-to-John fireplace together. Then he'd gone and poured a ton of water on it when he hadn't even needed to. And still the rain fell, loud on the emptied tarp. Frustration bubbled up in his throat. Turning on Arlie, he yelled, "How long's this storm gonna keep up, huh?"

The kid gaped at him, making Chick feel like a louse. "Like I told you last night, Chick, it's big and moving slow. I don't figure it's near to over yet."

That wasn't what he needed to hear. If it'd stop they could clear out some of the mess and get a fire going again, at least. Chick watched her in angry misery. After a minute of this Arlie yelled back at him, voice squeaking in the middle. "Ain't my fault it's raining, Chick!"

Chick scowled at the muddy floor then, unforgiving, though whether of her or of himself he couldn't have said.

"Well, we can't stay here," Junkyard announced, pulling his knit cap down to his ears. "The sooner we hike our tails into town, the more likely Sally's or one of the other places is to have room for us."

Karl's face brightened at this suggestion.

Simon spoke, hesitant. "You know a people here? This Sally?"

Chick sighed.

"Salvaaashun Aaarmy," Nip said, drawing the words out. "A mission, see."

"You know what a mission is, right?" Deucey asked.

An odd, bitter look on his face, Simon nodded once in that abrupt way he had. "They bring you in. Feed you."

"Yeah, and preach ya damn ear off while they're at it," Junkyard said. "Swill not fit for rats to eat and a piece of floor for a bed. But there ain't no point in hanging around here."

Chick watched the others look around for what to take. He didn't bother. He'd leave the hatchet for whoever might need it.

But Arlie hadn't moved; hadn't said a thing.

Of course she hadn't. Missions didn't take girls, as Zeno'd been so kind as to remind him yesterday. Hadn't none of them stopped to remember that. Her chin came up when she saw him looking at her. "Be fine here," she said, sounding angry, but her eyes looked scared.

The others stared at her. After a moment Karl said hesitantly, "Maybe that lady would take you back for the night?"

Simon, his coat buttoned to his chin, looked baffled. Arlie only gave Karl a scornful glance, not bothering to answer.

Chick drew in a deep breath. "I don't see as we've got a problem." He looked at Arlie. He owed her this. "We got no skirts here, do we, brother?"

"Think the kid can pull that off, Chick?" Deucey asked, worried.

Chick waited. Arlie's mouth spread into a wide grin. "Naw. I don't see none," she said.

"No problem at all." Chick looked hard at the rest of them. "Long as everybody keeps their traps shut."

The corner of Junkyard's mouth quirked up. "Deal."

"Jiminy," Nip muttered, pulling the brim of his hat down over his eyes. Karl just shrugged.

At last Deucey nodded. "OK. Sure."

That left Simon. The guy didn't talk much, but he could put a real spoke in the wheel if he spouted off at the wrong moment. Chick turned on him. The Wob stared back, wide-eyed.

Chick blew out an impatient breath. "You gonna treat Arlie like a guy at the mission, just like the rest of us, right?"

Simon frowned uncertainly. "How else treat him?"

At that Junkyard chortled, setting everybody else off, even Arlie. "Yer a card!" He punched Simon approvingly on the shoulder. "Let's scram."

16

Simon breathed as shallowly as he could. The sweet-sick smell inside the mission's dim entry room, packed with unwashed bodies, made the bile rise in his throat.

"One at a time!" a man shouted from beside the inner doorway. They were all men, which made no sense. Did women not need shelter? "Try pushing past me and you'll be out on your ear!"

Outside on the street they'd stood single file, pressed close against the painted blocks for the little shelter the wall gave from the steady drizzle. Here they were wedged into a solid mass. Simon shuffled forward slowly as he got the chance, Nip and Karl in front of him and Deucey at his elbow. He couldn't see Arlie. Maybe he would lose the too-knowing boy in this crowd.

Deucey leaned to whisper in his ear. "See, all you got to tell 'em is your name and whereabouts you from. Tell 'em... Tell 'em Cincinnati. Don't say nothing more. They figure out you's a bohunk, and they're gonna stick you with scrubbing the johns for your supper."

Simon nodded his thanks as he puzzled this out, not wanting to open his mouth to answer. The air had a foul taste to it as well as the dreadful smell.

At least now he knew what he would be facing. And Deucey still believed he was from a land across the eastern ocean. Surely the others did as well, all but Arlie. He would be fine. He would find his way to St. Paul, and no Nightworlder who mattered would learn of the Ngorvislat in their midst.

Comforted, he pushed forward. When at last he reached the desk he answered confidently when the wizened man behind the desk asked his name.

The man raised his eyebrows behind the thick, framed lenses he wore on his face. "Simon what? I gotta have a last name too."

Oh yes! Two names, one belonging to one's birth group. The wanderers didn't often use them with each other, and so he'd forgotten. He couldn't afford such mistakes. Mind blank, Simon stuttered out the next answer he'd prepared: "S-saint Paul."

"Huh?" The man muttered under his breath, and then laughed out loud. "Sim-pole! Simon Simple! Son of a gun, your pappa must've hated you." He scratched the new name on his list as a familiar snicker from behind Simon told him Junkyard at least had been close enough to hear. "C'mon. Make it snappy," the man said. "Where you from?"

"Cincinnati," Simon said carefully, grateful again to Deucey as he took the small card that was his ticket. Let them laugh at whatever had amused them. He had passed this test.

"Pushing brooms," the man told him, and jerked a thumb over his shoulder toward the door. "See Henry."

"Arlen Calhoun," Philippa told the clerk, trying to sound bored. Trying, she realized, to sound as tough as Junkyard, who'd gone in just ahead of her. "From Fort Smith." Chick was at her back, ready to stick up for her if need be. The other guys had already all gone through.

The clerk glanced up. Her stomach clenched, but she held her face steady and met his gaze as he demanded her age.

"Fifteen come Friday week," she said defiantly. Chick poked her, warning her not to be a wise guy, she figured. But the birthday was real enough, even if she'd added a couple years on.

The clerk curled a scornful lip. "Pull the other one, son." He thrust the ticket at her. "One night and two meals. Downstairs. The kitchen."

Slipping the ticket in her newly repaired pocket, Philippa stepped out proudly into the main hall beyond the packed room. "Tim McCreery," she heard Chick tell the man, and had to suppress an unboyish giggle. The name didn't suit him at all.

Simon was some distance ahead, between her and the end of the hall where a yellow light bulb showed the head of the basement stairs. The Wob had stopped some mission stiff who'd come out of one of the little offices that opened onto the hall.

"You passed it already," the guy was saying, sounding bored. He pointed back up towards her. "First door you come to."

Simon turned eagerly to follow the guy's directions, and saw her. His face went stiff. The mission guy pushed past him and headed for the stairwell, but he didn't move.

Philippa set her jaw. She hadn't done a thing to him, and be damned to acting like she had. "What they got you doing?" she sang out.

Simon ignored the question and just waited, his eyes narrowed like a cat's that was getting ready to pounce. Nerves prickled between her shoulder blades.

"You follow me," he hissed when she got close enough.

Jumpy, and cranky on account of it, she said, "Ain't neither! You're between me and where I got to go." Somebody was coming up behind them: not Chick. The footsteps had a hitch in them, and the guy carried a powerful smell. She edged to one side to let him go around, which he did, mumbling.

Simon's eyes hadn't left her. "Not follow," he said through his teeth. "And not talk more of me, not in this place!"

Philippa felt her chin rise. "Aw, dry up!" But even as the retort popped out it came to her that he was scared some big shot would notice him. How come somebody from a world like his would worry about such things was a wonderment.

But then Simon was stuck here for now, just like the rest of them.

The mission's kitchen was brightly lit and filled with the steamy, raw odor of unseasoned beans cooking, overlaid with a strong hint of Lysol. Philippa's belly grumbled unhappily as she stepped down into the big room.

Karl sat glumly in a group of old guys all bent over baskets of potatoes. He jerked his head at the few paring knives left on a nearby table.

Philippa was pretty sure you was supposed to wait to be told what to do, not just jump in and pick your task. But nobody was paying attention. Be a boy, she told herself, and strolled over to the table with the knives. Most of the blades were honed down to almost nothing. Shrugging, she picked the one that fit her hand best. Stripping off her jacket and sweater, trusting the overalls would shield her, she settled in next to Karl on the bench. A couple of the old guys eyed her, and then glanced toward the boss cook, but they didn't say nothing.

Following Karl's lead she grabbed a potato from the bushel basket, swished it in the pail of dirty water by their feet, and started peeling. The potato was softer to the touch than it ought to be. She glanced at the cut-up ones in the huge pot in the center of the circle. Dirty grey ringed the cut surfaces close to the skin. Frost had got into them, which was likely why all these baskets of potatoes had ended up here at the mission.

Lots of baskets, she realized, totaling them up. "We got to peel all these?" she whispered to Karl.

He shrugged. "The more there are, the more there is to eat." He kept his head down, working doggedly and not saying much of anything. The older guys were more casual about their task, talking quietly among themselves about the roadwork the county had had them sweating at in the summer, and then of some gang of toughs that had taken to beating up drunks. Locals, all of them, as far as she could tell, even the gas hound with the shaking hands they called Paulie. It was a wonder that fellow didn't cut his thumb off. The potatoes he peeled mostly didn't make it as far as the pot.

Karl swiped hard at his sweaty forehead with the back of one arm. "You believe in prayer, Arlie?" There wasn't a hint of a joke in his voice. Philippa glanced at him in surprise, but he was staring off across the kitchen towards the row of sinks where a couple of unlucky stiffs were scrubbing crusted pots. She would've bet good money he didn't see them proper, either.

"I don't," he said, bitterness creeping into his tone. "Nor God, nor any of that guff the priests tried to sell us back home. Any God that'd let crap happen like it does would have to be just plain evil, the way I see it. Praying to something like that would just be asking for more trouble, don't you think?" He scrabbled in the bottom of the bushel basket for another potato.

Philippa's throat tightened, the past crowding in on her. Used to be Jesus and praying had been just part of things, like how the sun came up every morning. You could hide your head under the covers, but you knew the sun was there all along. Jesus had been like that, a strength you could lean on when you needed to, so that it was almost worth hurting sometimes, just to feel that comfort.

But then Meemaw had passed on, and it'd turned out most of the comfort had gone with her. Strength was still there to be found, but it was cold and vast and impersonal as the sky.

"I, I don't know about praying no more," she managed to answer, though her voice came out rough. "My Meemaw used to say prayer wasn't about always getting what you asked for. She said it was more for turning things over to Jesus, see, so's He could help you carry the burden of how things are."

Karl made a disgusted sound deep in his throat. "Baloney!" He hurled a chunk of potato at the pot. It hit the pot fair and square, but the thing was full enough it bounced right back out again. One of the local guys glowered at him and hollered out for another pot. "The thing is, Arlie, I need a damn miracle. Or at least Betts does." Karl hid his face in the crook of an elbow for a long moment.

Miracles. A different sort of memory ran warm through Philippa at the word. She glanced down at her left palm, slimed now with the potato juices. Shock sparked her nerves when she saw no sign even of a scar. Hand trembling, she wiped it off on her pants and checked again.

Nothing. She closed her hand as though to hold the wonder in. "Miracles happen, sometimes," she said, her voice near as raw as his had been.

His reddened eyes searched her face.

"You recollect yesterday morning," she said carefully, "when I said how my cut had healed up?"

Karl's mouth got a sour twist to it. Philippa hurried on. "Well, you saw the scar anyways, didn't you?"

He shrugged. "Yeah. So what?"

She held out her hand, spread wide. As he frowned down at it she balanced the knife on her thigh and stuck the other one out as well, for good measure. "It's clean gone."

Hope washed across his face, but it didn't stay. "So maybe you just heal fast." He busied himself with another potato. "And anyhow, it wasn't nothing but a little scar. Betts has pneumonia."

"My lungs and throat healed up too." Frustrated, Philippa took up her paring knife again. "It just ain't as easy to see."

"Yeah? And what did you do for it? Say hootchy-kootchy abracadabra, and poof! it was all better? Or pray, maybe?"

"No," she said, at a loss once again. If she'd prayed she didn't remember doing it. Seemed like it must have something to do with all the other strangenesses of the past few days, like the nature of things had somehow changed to make the miraculous ordinary. But she couldn't put her finger on it. "I got no earthly idea, Karl. I'd tell you straight out if I did."

Simon sat with his back pressed to the wall of the big, crowded room, belly aching with hunger. He hadn't managed to eat more than a bite of the stew, mingled beans and potatoes that had tasted to him like salted dirt. The bread had been so hard he'd managed only to gnaw at its edges, and dipping it as Deucey had shown him—"dunking," as he'd called it—made the stuff taste as foul as the stew.

This was a miserable world indeed, where those who claimed to be helping and instructing the unfortunate would, without shame, offer such *dakatl*, such garbage, as food.

He had to get back home.

Someone slid down the wall to sit too close beside him. Simon huddled into himself, ignoring the intrusion.

"I think they's gonna start giving out beds soon," the boy beside him said.

Arlie. Simon felt his skin twitch like a cow beset by flies. He'd done his best to stay away from the troublesome boy all evening.

"Not for the likes of us, a'course," Arlie went on companionably. "We get to bunk on our ears. Chick says we oughta claim our spot soon as the locals start lining up."

Simon found his voice. "You follow me again."

The boy was still for a moment; angry, Simon thought. That was good. Perhaps he'd go away.

"Ain't no call to be ugly about it," Arlie said at last, his voice strained. "I'm just trying to help, see, on account of you ain't ever stayed in such a place, just like me."

Simon put his head down on his knees.

"C'mon, Simon, I ain't done nothing to you! And I already said I'd help you get to St. Paul."

"You tell what you should not know!" Simon hissed, then tightened his lips to keep more from escaping. Anger and fear had betrayed him.

"I saw the door in the ice house my ownself, just before it blew," the boy said quietly. "Near scared me out of a year's growth. Mara told me other stuff."

Simon felt himself begin to shake: the Eye blazing up golden, as deadly as the jaguar they named it for. Mara stumbling into it (going home; surely she'd managed to cross safely?) Lukas screaming out his name. Sweat slicked Simon's skin.

Arlie swung around to crouch before him. "Hey, I'm sorry! I didn't go to stir stuff up." The boy put out a hand, but didn't touch.

And that was good, Simon thought, his teeth chattering as though he was cold. He would not be able to bear touch.

Then he saw the hand itself, focused on it for the first time —the hand and the wrist, circled by what could only be an iyar pukko, stripped of its covering though it was and white as bone, the color of death. Gaping, trying to understand how such a thing could be, Simon groped for his own iyar, and found it where it always was, where it had always been.

Mara's had gone with her into the slipgate; of course it had. Your iyar pukko was part of you, guardian of your health until you died.

As Lukas had.

"Thief!" he howled, launching himself at Arlie. "You steal from the dead!"

Stunned, Philippa sprawled backward, knocking into two guys who were standing in the way. And then Simon was on top of her, still yelling his foreign gabble, his weight pinning her down.

Black panic swallowed her. Frantic, she shoved at him with her right hand, the one he didn't already have hold of. She kicked and thrashed, but she had no leverage. Weak as a girl, and she couldn't get free; this was what happened to girls.

He was yelling, and she was too, and other folks as well. Lukas; the Wob was yelling something about Lukas and slamming her left hand over and over against the floor. But he wasn't even trying to pin her right one. Philippa groped for something to hit him with; caught what turned out to be somebody's ankle, which got promptly pulled away. Finding nothing else, she grabbed for Simon's ear and twisted hard, like her life depended on pulling it off.

Simon shrieked and knocked her hand away, catching her on the side of the head. But he pulled back at the same time, and she slithered free, kicking him in the gut as she went.

Staggering to her feet, Philippa crouched, ready for him to come at her again, her fists cocked, puny though they seemed to her. But Chick was there, and Junkyard and the other guys, not to mention a circle of avid men crowding around in their dark and ragged clothes; and then Chick had Simon by the collar, dragging him up, his own fist under Simon's nose.

Wet streaked Simon's dusty face. He was crying, and blood ran from a tear at the top of his ear. Still wary, Philippa straightened, breath easing in her chest.

Simon jerked his chin at her, bewildered outrage in his eyes. "That one," he wheezed, still breathless from her kick. "Arlie. He take Lukas' iyar! I see he wear it!"

Slowly Philippa brought her arm back up, the one he'd been banging on. The back of the hand and the wrist around the strap were purple, likely to bruise something fierce.

Or maybe not. Was yesterday's miracle a one-time thing?

"Is wrong!" Simon cried, seeing it, pulling against Chick's slackening hold. Chick stared at her wrist as well, his eyes narrowing. Then he met her gaze, the side of his mouth twitching up in a puzzled half-smile.

Simon's ear had stopped bleeding, the track of blood crusting over.

"I found it in the ashes," Philippa told them all. She looked around. "You guys was there. You know I never took nothing off Lukas, what was left of him." They looked back at her, frowning in puzzlement.

"Wasn't nothing left *to* take off him," Deucey said, and Junkyard's face screwed up sick, just for a moment, the memory of what he'd found showing bleak in his pale eyes.

"No fighting in God's house!" a man shouted, shouldering his way through the remaining circle of watchers. They shifted back, drifting away, out of the reach of trouble.

Chick's hand slid from Simon's collar to his shoulder. "No problem, Reverend. My pal here lost his brother in a fire a couple of days ago, see, and he's kinda jumpy on account of it."

"I didn't go to stir him up; honest I didn't," Philippa put in, trying to follow Chick's lead. The man—it was the preacher himself from the service they'd sat through after supper, his ill-cut suit coat buttoned tight across a pot belly—eyed the three of them suspiciously. Simon said nothing. Tears still leaked from his eyes.

The preacher stepped closer, a slick concern settling over his face. "So you've lost your brother, son?" Chick edged back.

Simon hesitated, then nodded. "Lukas. My fault," he whispered hoarsely.

"Wasn't neither," Philippa muttered, not sure if she should say anything, but not willing to let that stand. "The place went up so fast, and you wasn't there to do nothing about it." Chick took firm hold of her sleeve. As he pulled her away Simon's gaze flicked to her for a moment. She couldn't read his expression at all, other than the pain in it.

The preacher put a fatherly arm around him and leaned to speak in his ear. Simon stiffened, but didn't pull back.

"Let be," the Oklahoma boy told her quietly. "If the preacher thinks he's saving a soul, he'll forget about tossing us all out for fighting."

If Simon didn't bring him up short, Philippa thought, watching doubtfully.

"You were A-1, kid," Chick went on. "I wouldn't have stepped in at all, only I knew there'd be trouble to come."

Shame heated Philippa's cheeks. She shook her head. "If Simon'd been trying to pin me down proper, wouldn't have been a thing I coulda done. Only he was whaling away on just this one hand…" Her voice trailed off and they both looked down at the hand and wrist. The angry color was already fading.

Chick put out a careful finger and touched the pale knotwork of the bracelet. "What do you figure those things are? This one sure as heck ain't just some regular kind of strap. I saw how it fastened itself on you."

"Yeah, and looky here," Philippa said, trying to work a finger underneath it. "See how tight to my skin it is? But it don't *feel* tight." She took a deep breath. "It's something from that world they come from, like I been thinking it must be. Simon good as said it was."

"I'd say you was letting your imagination run away with you," Chick said at last. "Only I seen too many funny things lately." He studied her face. "You gonna have you another dandy bruise on that cheek. But I still say you did good with Simon. I'll give you some pointers if you want."

"No!" Simon cried, his voice breaking, bringing the two of them back around to stare at him. The Wob had pulled away from the preacher. "Is not the better world he has go to! This I know. This is why I cry!"

Trust the Wob to screw things up, Chick thought, sprinting over to sweeten the preacher up again. If he could. He might be better off just fading into the crowd.

But it was too late for that. He laid a hand on Simon's shoulder, hoping the Wob wouldn't bust him one for it. "Shh, Simon. You don't know he didn't go there."

Simon turned to him, confused. "Is you and the others tell me you find him burned dead. Here, in this—" He drew a ragged breath. "This dark world." The words sounded like a quote, and the preacher bridled, hearing them come back at him.

"Sure we did," Chick said hastily. "But that was his body. Don't you think his spirit might've cut loose and gone home?" Wherever the hell that might be.

His words had hooked the preacher back in, though Chick could see impatience in the slight curl to the man's lip. "That's right, son. Your brother's gone home to rest."

"Home," Simon said. Baffled pain filled his eyes. "I don't understand."

Chick turned to the preacher. "Reverend, you want to let me talk to him for awhile? He can be a little slow on the uptake."

The preacher looked relieved. "You do that. Ask any of our mission brothers if you need help."

Arlie and the guys came to stand by them as the preacher left. Chick felt their presence around him, a prickly sort of comfort. Simon looked forlorn, though, standing there in the middle with his brown-skinned hands dangling at his sides.

"Guy can't wait to go off and screw that dame that was punishing the ivories earlier," Junkyard said, watching the preacher thread his way through the throng in the general direction of the door.

Chick shot him a look. "Pipe down, Junkyard."

Junkyard snorted. "What, you didn't see how he was eating her up with his eyes while she wriggled around on that piano stool?" Nip sniggered, though nobody else did.

"Preacher man really don't care for our kind at all, does he?" Arlie said softly, arms crossed. The mottled red that had come up on her temple and cheekbone from Simon hitting her had faded some. Maybe it wouldn't bruise after all.

Simon turned to face him, his hands balling into fists, though not like he planned on hitting anyone with them. "You explain. Tell about a spirit going home."

Uncomfortable, Chick shrugged. "I was just mush-talking the preacher, is all."

The Wob looked frustrated, desperate for something more.

Deucey answered him, surprising Chick. He held up a arm; thumped it. "See, a body ain't nothing but meat and bone. Your spirit's what makes it live. You ever sit by somebody was dying? Felt the last breath leave 'em? That's the soul slipping free."

"Bull," Junkyard muttered. "When you're dead, you're dead."

Deucey turned to him. "Brother, believe whatever you care to. But as for me, I've felt souls go, my baby sister's and my brother Hosea's and my Momma's too. I can't say where they went, because the living ain't given to know that for sure. But somewhere, and why not home?"

Chick's throat felt suddenly thick. Chafed by the prick of feelings, he fought back the memory of his own dead, his own losses; of Zeno. Needing distraction, he checked on the others. Junkyard's arms were crossed like he was fed up with the whole thing, and Karl looked sullen and hurting. But Deucey's words had drained some of the raw pain out of Simon's face.

The Wob's mouth spread in what was too sad to be a smile. "One dies, my people say wind took him. Perhaps wind blow Lukas' breath all the long way home."

Arlie shivered. Chick saw that the kid's eyes were wet too, though her mouth had set stubborn. "And where's that, Simon?" she demanded. "Where's home?"

Simon's face went very still. "Czechoslovakia," he rasped— only the awkward way he said it, the name sounded to Chick like it started with a 'D'.

"Want me to go round up somebody speaks the lingo? Bet we got a few of 'em in this bunch." Arlie waved a hand at the crowd, most of whom had settled dispiritedly onto benches or the floor to wait. "Be old home week for you."

Chick considered hushing the kid, keeping her from winding Simon up again. He was weary of stepping in, though, and curious, to boot.

Simon cut his eyes at the men that filled the room. His handsome face had gone stony grey. "Always you are trouble," he whispered. The guys pressed close, sensing the shift in him, the weakness.

"Ain't neither." Arlie edged forward, and Chick drew breath, readying himself to grab her or Simon if it was needed. "It's you's the trouble, on account of you keep lying to us."

"Leave me alone, thief!" The Wob was beginning to panic. He looked for a way out, but he was surrounded, his back to the wall. "I cannot tell," he said at last.

"Mara did."

"She should have not! You do not understand. Is much dangerous."

Junkyard, head cocked and chin out, stepped up close to Simon. "Spill it! Where you from already?"

Simon's face twisted. "Ngorvisla," he spat. "Ntai."

In spite of his soured mood the back of Chick's neck prickled at the odd sung sound of the words. Hesitant, Deucey voiced the general confusion. "I ain't never heard of them."

"It's another world, like I been saying," Arlie told them. "Paradise. Ain't it, Simon?"

Nervous as a spooked horse, Simon glanced around again. "Is this world," he said, his voice low and strained. "Only different. Different history. Different *light*." He lingered over that last word like it was a holy thing.

"Not Czechoslovakia," Chick said, the only thing he was sure of. Same world; different history? What the hell did that mean?

Simon's hand flicked. "No," he breathed.

"Paradise?" Karl asked, the word coming out choked.

Simon didn't answer for a moment, homesickness gathering in his eyes. "Yes," he said then. "Yes."

Watching him, Chick was dubious. The hills of southern Oklahoma where he'd come up seemed like paradise to him, looking back, though from all he'd heard the drought that'd hit so hard here in the Dakotas was beginning to take a toll there as well. Any place you couldn't count on getting a decent living out of the ground from year to year made a doubtful Land of Canaan.

Aw, who cared? It was probably all bullshit.

But it seemed Karl was ready to buy the pony. "Can they fix sick people there?" the kid demanded, his hat bunched up in both hands. "Can you?" He jogged Chick's elbow as he pushed closer to Simon. "You claim that thing on Arlie's wrist belonged to your pal, and you got one too. Sounds like they had to come from this paradise of yours. And Arlie claims to have healed up right after putting that one on."

"Didn't do much for Lukas, then," Junkyard muttered, but Karl's reasoning had dropped into Chick's thoughts like a stone in a pond. Chick turned to stare at Arlie. Head down, the kid rubbed the wrist with the bracelet wonderingly. The reddened bruising was clean gone from her cheekbone and the back of her hand. And he'd seen how hard Simon had whacked her.

"Betts needs something, or she's gonna die in that hospital, see," Karl went on, relentless. "And you'd have froze and starved without us bringing you along. The least you could do is share one of those things with Betts."

"Is not 'those things'. Is iyar pukko." Simon's jaw had knotted up so tight it was a wonder he could talk at all. "Was part of Lukas, like hand or, or liver. As mine is part of me." He glared at Arlie.

"Ask thief to share with you."

17

Philippa stood, still dazed at what she'd learned, on the sidewalk underneath the mission's creaking sign. The brick pavement gleamed wetly in the glow from the street lamps. Rain still drizzled down, misty remnants that smelled of nothing much but raw cold. By morning the sky'd be blue clear out to the horizon, and every surface slick with ice.

It was funny how welcoming the cold felt. Inside the mission's slump block walls, with all those broke-down men pressed so close, she hadn't been able to feel the grand sweep of the storm moving out.

At least she wouldn't be breathing that mission stink for the rest of the night. Shivering, Philippa pulled her watch cap down over her ears, glad her clothes had had a chance to dry. Across the street a heap of rags that was probably a drunk lay in the doorway of the Goodwill, sleeping or something worse. The sight spurred her on. She called to Karl, "How far we got to go?"

He was already halfway down the street, but he turned back a moment to answer her. "Hospital's all the way over at the river. But we stay on Eighth and we'll run smack into it." A few eager strides further on he added over his shoulder, "Don't worry, Arlie. I'll get us there."

The hope in his voice twisted an uneasy knot in her stomach. "You know I'll do what I can for Betts, Karl," she told him as she came up beside him. "But it ain't like I got a notion in the world what I'm doing."

"It's gonna work. Fixed you up just fine, didn't it?"

Philippa flexed her wrist inside her pocket. She could hardly feel the bracelet against her skin. Simon hadn't said a word about how she was supposed to get the thing off. He hadn't even really said it could heal, but Karl had that much right. She was sure of it. But odds were this wouldn't be simple.

Karl wasn't gonna listen to any doubts on her part. "Well, yeah, it did," was all she said.

The hospital was a hulking big brick building with yellow light showing in the glass-paned doors at the top of the front steps. Karl lit out across the wide lawn with Philippa on his heels, sprinting for the back of the building. Her rubber chore boots flapped loose and rattling with every step, but the short dash didn't wind her at all.

There was nothing half so good as feeling fit once more.

Karl guided her into the deeper shadow of the building, to a flight of steps that led them down to a basement door. "Laundry," he whispered. "I prowled around some yesterday after the sister kicked me off the ward." Steady thumping came loud through the wood and glass of the door, punctuated by a long hiss. Through the window Philippa could see a shadowy hallway and a corner of the laundry room that opened off it. A woman in a too-big uniform stood with her back to them, feeding a sheet through a mangle.

Philippa shucked out of her clumsy boots; poked them up out of sight on top of the door coping. Steamy air sharp with the scent of scorched cotton drew her inside after Karl, who eased the door shut again before a breeze could rouse the laundry workers. His grip on her sleeve pulled her around to see the stairwell across the hall, its propped-wide door an open invitation.

Up she followed him, two steps at a time, their steps echoing off the white-plastered walls though they ran as lightly as they could. Past the first floor, and still they had the stairwell to themselves. Past the second; Philippa sucked harder for the air in her lungs, but the ascent felt like flying.

A door opened somewhere below, and confident words rumbled up the walnut staircase after them: "...fundamentally sound, I believe, Miss Fjelde. By this time next year the markets..."

A spurt of mingled fear and laughter propelled Philippa up the last few steps and through the door that Karl held for her.

The hall stretching before them was dim and polished and empty, though light spilled from a couple of doorways. From down the way a woman spoke with clipped assurance. Steps squeaked briskly across a floor, getting nearer by the sound of them.

Blue eyes wide, Karl yanked Philippa through the nearest doorway. Disinfectant and a hint of stale urine tainted the air in the big room.

"Markets, my hat," Karl muttered bitterly. He bent to whisper in Philippa's ear. "This here's the charity ward. Betts is one down from the end, see?" He pointed, but the lumpy shapes in the beds looked pretty much alike to Philippa in the gloom. "Pack 'em in like sardines, and we're supposed to be grateful," he hissed under his breath.

Karl was always grousing. Philippa knew what he meant, but she *was* grateful.

Out in the hallway the door to the stairwell sighed open no more than a few feet away. Philippa and Karl pressed further back into the deep shadow behind the room's door. Footsteps passed them, a deliberate tread accompanied by the clicking of someone in heels. Miss Fjelde more than likely, Philippa told herself, trying to calm her racing heartbeat.

"Oh, there you are, Doctor!" a woman's voice greeted the newcomers, her words echoing softly down the hall. "I'd've sworn I heard you come in already."

The man with the confident voice asked something, but Philippa couldn't make it out over the low moans of the patient in the bed across the aisle, calling over and over for a nurse.

"In here, Doctor. I've prepared…" The woman's words faded into incomprehensibility.

A couple of long minutes later, after risking a peek around the doorjamb, Karl breathed, "They went in one of the private rooms across the hall, I guess. This gonna take long?"

Philippa's stomach felt like moths had gotten at it. She tried to sound cool as she answered him. "No idea."

Karl looked nervous. "Well, I better not stay or we'll both get pinched," he said awkwardly. "Look, you can find her from here. I'll wait for you back down on Eighth Street." And he was gone, the stairwell door whispering shut behind him.

Philippa stood paralyzed. The walk down the double row of white-painted bedsteads all the way to the far end seemed an impossible distance. Suppose somebody was to come in? And which one was Betts, anyway?

Next one to the end, she told herself, and that's only two to choose from, left and right. Anyone comes, I'll hear 'em before they get here, and scoot under a bed.

But still she couldn't move.

A gaze caught hers as she stared down the length of the room. Narrowed eyes in a lined face watched her drowsily; a wrinkled old woman. The eyes blinked and blinked again. The woman rolled stiffly onto her side, away from Philippa. Released by this, Philippa stepped out into the room like she was walking on the lines of thin moonlight that had slipped in through the blinds, proof of the clearing sky outside. The moaning patient mumbled into silence, leaving only the wheeze and sigh of sleepers breathing, and the muffled squeak of her tennis shoes as she walked down the aisle to Betts.

Unable to sleep, Simon shifted on the mission's gritty floor. The wanderer lying too close beside him, a man with long, matted hair and few teeth, snarled something incomprehensible. Instantly Simon stilled, his heart pounding, fearing the wanderer would rise and go to complain of him. Questions would be asked that he had no answers for. His companions, hard pressed, might betray him. Or perhaps already a report had gone out to the hierarchy's enforcers, the cops, from someone who had overheard his confession, and they were even now outside.

Why had he not held out, held his silence? The first answer had doomed him, though he'd told himself the names of his people and his world would mean nothing to them. And they had not, but one answer led to others.

The air in the packed, fetid room pressed against his chest with the dull rhythm of so many people breathing. In. Out. In. Out. His lips felt strange, swollen and prickly.

"You sound like a goddamn steam engine," Junkyard grumbled next to his ear. A groping hand yanked Simon's cap from his head and dropped it over his face. "Breathe through that."

The act, the rough kindness, calmed Simon as much as the filter of wool cloth smelling of himself. But still he could not sleep here, could not lie unmoving. Cap in hand, he got quietly up and picked his way to the half-open door.

The corridor was colder, dimly lit by three widely spaced yellowish bulbs, and empty except for the man who sat slumped in a chair between the front door and the stairway to the upper floor. A guardian, a poor one to be sure, but he couldn't leave without being seen. And anyway he had nowhere else to go.

No stranger had heard his confession. No one was coming to seize him; that was only a night fear. Even Arlie would not betray him to the enforcers, in spite of Simon's childish assault. The boy was too intent on following him on his journey home, a danger, but a guarantee as well. Wearily Simon padded down the corridor, looking for another place to rest. All the doors were shut but the one he'd come out of. Reaching the lower stairwell and the corridor's end, he folded himself down on the top step, coat wrapped close, sagging against the wall.

For now he was safe enough. With care and luck, eventually he would find his way home. But after struggling for so long in the shadowed foulness of this world, without support from his bvariti, his comrades, to keep him centered, who would he be when he got there? Would the Dugri permit him to return?

Giving into tears was forbidden to men here, and disdained in women; so he had been taught, and experience had shown this to be true. Alone now, Simon huddled into himself and wept.

Just as she'd feared, it wouldn't come off.

Philippa tried again to work the bracelet down over her wrist, but it was like pulling at a fold of loose skin, like it was stuck to her. You could stretch it a little ways, but after that it hurt and still wasn't a bit closer to coming loose.

Betts needed it something fierce. The change in how the girl looked scared Philippa, her skin gone all greyish, flesh sunk away from the bones of her face. Fever lay on Betts like a drought of the body, and she didn't rouse even when Philippa wet a washrag with water from the glass on the bedside table and laid it across her forehead. Seemed the only thing between her and dying was whatever strength she had left to fight with.

That and the bracelet, if Philippa could only get it off. She squinted at it in the brief light of one of Junkyard's matches, picking at the complicated weave. Nearly as she could recollect, the strands had just sort of grown together around her wrist that night in the alley. How could you undo that short of taking a knife to it? A knife she didn't have, and anyways, that might spoil it.

There had to be a way. Simon wouldn't have sent her otherwise.

The rumbling of a cart was almost to the door before the sound roused Philippa. Quicker than thought she jackknifed under the bed and lay there rigid, heart thumping against her ribcage again as reddish light from a shielded flashlight leaked in around the edges of her cramped refuge.

After a minute or so a pair of black old-lady shoes padded right up to Betts' bed, the toes poking in a handsbreadth from Philippa's arm. Long, black skirts, too: one of the nuns who ran the place, rather than a nurse. The shoes shifted half a step, this way and that, as the sister worked. One shoe was coming undone, and Philippa's fingers found an itch to tie the laces together like the boys back at school used to do. She stifled a nervous giggle; clasped her hands against temptation.

What was the woman doing anyway, taking Betts' pulse? Giving her medicine? Whatever it was wouldn't help much. About the only thing you could do for pneumonia was to try to keep a body comfortable, and pray.

The nun muttered something under her breath, and moved on at last, though only to the next patient.

Minutes dragged by as the woman padded from bed to bed on her rounds. She paused at one bed a long while. Philippa heard her low murmur joined by someone else's broken whisper, and the faint click of beads.

Prayer beads. Papist idolatry, Meemaw would've called it, though Philippa's only objection now was how dreadful long they were taking. Sweating in the cocoon of her clothes, fretful and bone-weary, she let her fingers stray to the bracelet, feeling for the patterns she recalled.

If she rested the tips of her fingers very lightly on it, the surface seemed to fizz and pulse against her skin. She let her eyes fall shut as her fingers moved, and watched drowsily as faint colors chalked an image on the inside of her eyelids, like neon seen through frosted glass. Lines met and overlapped and twisted off again at odd angles, a dense, nonsensical weave of them, pulsing with energy like a tangle of telegraph wires.

Like the strands of the bracelet beneath her touch.

Philippa jerked her fingers away, and her eyes flew open. A suggestion of bedsprings sagged a few inches above her nose, which tickled from the dust. The reddish glow of the nun's flashlight pooled on the floor at the other end of the room. When Philippa touched the bracelet again it just felt bumpy, same as she was used to.

Had she dreamed all that, dozed off from being wore out from the long day? Likely enough, and yet it'd felt close to what she did when reading the weather, letting her mind run free and waiting to see what came. Which was near to dreaming, some ways, only it generally proved out true.

And if this turned out real too? Hope trickled through Philippa. She scooted up closer to the head of the bed, getting set for when the light came around again with the nun finishing her rounds. Then she took a deep breath and closed her eyes.

First thing she sensed once she'd wrestled herself to calmness was the earth's heat fleeing upward into the night. Philippa shivered inside her sweaty clothes. Determinedly she tried to draw her focus down to the tiny world of the bracelet.

Nothing. A rough, flexing surface that her fingers couldn't read at all. Philippa pressed harder, rubbing her fingertips sore.

Frustrated, she balled both hands into fists; tears stung the corners of her eyes. This wasn't getting her anywhere. Or Betts neither, lying dead to everything but her parched fever and the fight to breathe on the thin mattress above. Crying without making noise was something Philippa had got good at, but still it was hard when what you wanted was to howl and blubber and have somebody else make it all better.

There wasn't anybody else—hadn't been since Meemaw'd died.

Philippa wiped her nose on her sleeve, wishing she could blow it. Even in a ward full of sick people she wasn't going to risk drawing the nun's attention that way. She snuffled as quietly as she could manage and let her back sag against the hard boards of the floor, exhausted.

She'd been trying too hard, but how a body could set out to do something without trying to do it was a puzzle. She knew how to relax into sensing weather, but weather was as big as the world, while this stuff was tiny.

The notion of relaxing sounded awful good, whatever the reason. Philippa shut her eyes against the migrating shine of the flashlight. Once more a shiver took her. Being open like this she couldn't ignore the upwardly migrating heat outside the hospital's walls, or even the lesser flow of heat pulled from every surface, flesh or thing, in the ward.

One surface in the room was both, or nearly so. She wasn't looking for it; the dying flesh snagged her awareness, a peculiarity. Philippa shook harder, though the tremors seemed apart from her somehow.

The nun hadn't got to that bed yet. With an effort Philippa let the disturbing bit of knowledge go, stretching hard against the shuddering knots in all her muscles, her back, her calves, her hands.

Her hands; her fingertips. With a sense of completion, forgetting the black-skirted sister, the death, the chilling air, Philippa trailed the pads of two fingertips lightly along the knotted bracelet. Felt like miniature fireworks against her skin this time, and the pale colors beneath her eyelids sketched nothing but confusion. Slow, slow, she told herself.

And the sparkling strands came clear in that cave-like inner vision, dream-distant and still too thickly woven to make sense of how they linked together. Fascinated, she caught the trail of one, followed it through its minglings and twistings down into a new space, moist and solid and warm with the heat of a million dark fires, the boulders of ivory at its core shifting as she moved. Wristbones; her wrist.

The bracelet was pegged down in her own flesh.

A muffled gasp from somewhere outside her matched the shock and denial sweeping through her so exactly that she fled toward it. "Oh, Ellie," her lips whispered sorrowfully, and words she didn't know rolled *Requiscat in pace* from a tongue tasting the stale leftovers of whiskey-laced coffee Philippa hadn't drunk; not hers, not hers! Not hers, this smell of musky lavender, the lifting arm and sore-jointed fingers that felt for something on a light and bony burden. Panicked, Philippa jerked away once more, falling into the tight darkness beyond the nun's touch.

Smothered fires was her first thought, soft ash tainted with the smell of iron and old fat. An airless dread crept in to join the silence that weighed on her, muffling every sense. Then boulders creaked at the center of the narrow place like a paintless shutter wind-swung by a single hinge, and she knew them, wristbones again, but Jesus bless! not hers. Somebody else's wrist, the dead woman's laid gently down by that black-robed nun, and Philippa tore free and plunged shuddering back into herself again.

She lay curled into her body for what seemed a long while, clinging to each precious, easy breath, knowing she'd have to try again. Her exploration of the bracelet hadn't hardly started, and Betts' breathing rattled painfully above her. Betts' flesh would lie defeated like that dead woman's in a few hours, a day or two, when her strength gave out.

Reluctant to start again, Philippa stretched enough to unkink her arms. The left one felt cold and rubbery—numb from her lying on it, she figured. She worked on kneading life back into it, all down the forearm to the wrist…

The bracelet was gone. Philippa sucked in a breath. She felt more carefully. Her wrist was sure enough bare. Desperate, she groped the floor beneath her arm. Her fingers closed on the strap straight away. She balled it up in her fist, caught between bewilderment and triumph, ready to roll out from under the bed to finish what she'd come for.

A low murmur of voices stopped her cold. More light—a second flashlight—leaked under the edge of Betts' bed from somewheres close by: the bed across the aisle and down a few, where the dead lady was. A big pair of brogans had joined the nun's small black ones beneath a curtain drawn around the bed, by the wheels of a long cart.

Remembering that cold flesh brought a rush of bile into Philippa's throat. She swallowed. They'd be busy for a spell. She had time, if she was quick and mouse-quiet; if she wasn't too chicken to try. She slid away from the light, halfway out into the space between beds. Reaching up under the skimpy covers she felt around until she found Betts' hot, dry hand. Lucky for her Betts was lost deep in her fever, she thought, easing into a half-crouch, else the older girl would've yelled at the touch.

Her numb left hand wasn't good for much more yet than keeping the strap from slipping off Betts' wrist, but it wasn't like she had to tie anything. Philippa smoothed the free end up and over the one she'd pinned down. The bracelet stayed put when she let go. Trembling, Philippa breathed a prayer for it.

The curtain rang back along its rod. Startled, Philippa left Betts' hand dangling and dived for the deeper shadows under the bed, whacking her head on the enameled nightstand on the way and rattling the bedpan on its lower shelf.

"What was that?" a young guy's voice exclaimed softly. "We got rats in here?"

Philippa cussed silently under the bed, stiff with panic. The red light from the flashlights showed the cart near blocked the aisle, even if she could get past the nun and the orderly.

"There are no rats in this hospital, Nagy," the nun answered with icy authority.

But Nagy's shoes were already coming her way. Philippa bunched herself together, readying for a sprint, waiting, waiting. When the heavy shoes paused at the bed's shadowed side, Philippa slithered out on the other, into the reddish pool of light. She launched herself over the iron pipe of the next bed's footboard and past the white-hatted sister, gaping where she stood behind the cart with its long, sheeted burden. The orderly cursed and something heavy scraped a little way across the floor, Betts' bed when he ran into it, Philippa thought with a feather of her mind as she ran flat out, scrambling to manage the turn to the doorway.

Someone shouted at her in the corridor, but Philippa was already through the door to the stairwell. She pounded down the staircase until a startled orderly, a little guy this time, blocked her path on the first floor landing when Nagy yelled down to him to stop her. Swinging over the railing, she dropped to the next flight, taking the remaining steps three at a time as the tray the fellow'd been carrying spilled its contents down around her. Another step, the last, and her right foot came down on a vial, round and slick and crunching, sending the foot skidding off one way while the rest of her came down hard the other. But the open door to the basement was right in front of her, and Philippa scrabbled to her feet again, using the door frame to propel herself out of the sudden stinging odor of alcohol into the basement hallway.

And straight into a laundry worker, a big white woman with her arms piled with folded sheets. The woman snagged Philippa's jacket collar without quite losing her grip on her sweet-smelling burden. "Hold, boy! Why such a hurry?"

A loud series of thumps sounded from the stairwell, over a more distant but growing tattoo of footsteps that echoed down from the upper floors. The woman took a startled step toward the noise, dragging Philippa with her.

"Lemme go, lady!" Philippa pleaded, watching the outside door get further away. "I ain't took nothin', honest I ain't."

Tiredness lined the woman's face and reddened her eyes as she scowled down at Philippa. "*Ja*, is so? And what were you doing then? Come to sweep floors in the night like the good *nisse*?" But her gaze strayed back to the stairwell doorway before her question was done.

Philippa hesitated, considering a sob story about an ailing sister. But she didn't have time for that. Nagy's footsteps were getting closer, and the little guy was gonna pick himself up off the floor soon.

The long pause revived the woman's attention. She tightened her grip on the jacket collar, pulling Philippa up onto her toes.

Philippa looked up at her wide-eyed. "It was warm. I fell asleep," was what came out of her mouth. Lame, Philippa scolded herself, but the woman's sharp-eyed gaze softened, letting a sympathetic weariness creep in.

"Go," she said and released her hold.

Two flying steps and Philippa was fumbling open the outer door. She shot through it and pounded up the steps into the night, not daring to pause to grab her boots.

18

"Cripes, Arlie, what took you so long?" Karl's angelic features showed pinched and blotchy in the late moonlight. He was shivering, too, in that steady, bone-wracking way that said he'd been doing it a long while.

The night cold had gotten fierce, soaking through Philippa's clothes and stealing the core of warmth she still carried from the hospital. Her left wrist, bare now beneath her cuff, felt particularly exposed. Watching Karl shiver didn't help. She grabbed a fistful of his overcoat; tried to pull him to his feet. "C'mon, Karl. Gonna catch your death out here, and I ain't got no more bracelets. Reckon I'd have to let you die."

This brought Karl tottering lump-footed out of the doorway he'd taken shelter in. "You did it? She's gonna be OK?"

Philippa ducked her head. "Put it on her, sure enough. I had to scram, though, afore I could tell if it helped." Pride at what she'd done began to fill her.

Karl gave a whoop and whirled her around. As cramped up as he was from his icy vigil she was hard put to keep them both on their feet. Giddy, he staggered into the wall of the storefront, and Philippa slipped free of his enthusiastic hold.

He leaned against the bricks, oblivious to the tremors that still shivered through him. "Whooie! She's gonna be just fine now, I know it. You're top-notch, Arlie! A regular peach!" Karl punctuated this praise with a healthy slug to her upper arm. Philippa's grin stretched the cold-stiffened mask of her face, even as she rubbed at the ache.

A wild look coming into his eye, Karl cried, "Hey, c'mon!" and took off like a club-footed jackrabbit. Philippa stood staring a few seconds before she ran after. With her canvas-shod feet stiff but as yet unfrozen, she caught him up as he skidded on an icy patch into the empty cross street.

"Where we going?" she asked breathlessly. It was getting harder to pace him now as his longer legs stretched out.

"Nowhere!" he told her, whooping with laughter. He dodged into the alley, broadsiding a huddle of trashcans. Satisfyingly empty, they bounced when he hit them, rattling off the grimy brick walls and rolling across the gravel and iron-hard mud ruts. Philippa's grin returned: the kind of stuff boys did and girls never dared. She gave a sideways kick to the first of the fallen cans she passed. Encouraged by the racket she kicked her way through the rest, loosing a rebel yell that echoed up into the endless night sky.

Scowling in the sunlight, Chick spat on the small chunk of Arkansas stone he carried with him, and stroked the blade of his jackknife across the worn surface. "I ain't ready to give up, not yet."

Deucey shifted on the brick window-ledge of the empty storefront, his long face creased with worry. "I'm just thinking we oughta check at the jail, case they got themselves pinched."

Chick hunched his shoulders over his honing, not finding an answer. Arlie and Karl oughta have been here long since. It was past noon, even if all you had to go by was the sun.

A chill gust brought the smell of onions frying from the greasy spoon on the corner opposite. Three shopgirls on break strolled by, in cheap finery from Woolworth's. Deucey's soulful gaze tracked them on down the street.

"Dames like that wouldn't look twice at you," Chick told him.

"Didn't look once even. Put that durn pigsticker away," Deucey shot back. "Flatfoot's coming."

Feeling contrary, Chick tested the blade with his thumb. It'd do. He wiped it on his pants leg and snapped the knife shut.

Thing was, he thought as he watched the cop saunter up the sidewalk towards them, that whole goddamn rescue mission was more than likely a wild goose chase. Arlie had bought it hook, line, and sinker, and Karl too, of course, but Simon hadn't been meaning to be helpful. That weird bracelet had healed Arlie up, but he'd bet good money it wasn't made to be swapped around. Simon had as much as said so. And how was the stubborn kid gonna feel when she failed; if, God help them, Betts croaked?

"Let's check the hospital first," he said, easing to his feet. Deucey grunted, and followed him.

"Hey! Guys!"

Chick whirled.

Karl sprinted towards them, dodging the cop, waving an arm as he ran. "Thank goodness you're still here!" he panted as he came up to them, a grin splitting his face wide open, though his eyes looked bruised with tiredness.

Unimpressed, Chick scanned the busy street behind him. No Arlie. The cop was eyeing them now. "Where's the kid?" he snapped, taking Karl's arm to usher him on down the street.

Karl went with them without protest. "Sleeping. See, we carried the banner the rest of the night. The kid was beat, so I said I'd come. But listen! I went by the hospital and there Betts is, kind of pale, but sitting up eating soup! Arlie fixed her just like Simon said!" Out of breath as he still was, Karl was jigging with excitement.

"Now you're talking!" Deucey was beaming too, but a giddy confusion touched Chick's mind, shifting his thoughts around, bringing him to a halt.

"You're saying Betts has got that bracelet on?"

It was Karl's turn to look confused. "'Course she does. Doesn't think much of it either." He grinned again at the memory. "I had to tell her to leave it alone; it was making her better. She told me I was nuts."

Something tapped Chick's calf smartly. "Step along, boys. You're blocking the sidewalk."

Cold ran down the back of his neck, then hot. Fuming, he turned a wide-eyed look on the flatfoot. "Oh! Sorry, officer. We got kinda distracted." A shock of a different sort went through him when their eyes met. The man had a hound dog kind of face, but wasn't bad-looking for that.

The side of the cop's mouth curled up, just a little. "That's all right, bud. Just keep moving."

"Yessir," Deucey said meekly. The cop glanced at him and Karl, then back at Chick. He nodded at him and walked on.

When the cop was out of earshot Karl hissed, "Why was he looking at you like that?"

Chick shook himself. "Hell if I know," he lied, feeling easier than he had for days. Zeno wasn't the only guy out there. Not that a cop was worth the risk.

Deucey was looking at him funny.

Chick started walking. "Didja see him whack me in the leg?" he asked quickly, trying to summon up the outrage he'd felt.

"Heard it," Deucey said shortly, half a step behind him.

"I don't know," Chick went on, his eyes tracing the cracks in the sidewalk as they came to them. "Could be he thought he knew me from somewheres."

Philippa looked up from her small fire at the squeak of the loose board in the scrap yard fence. Chick's head poked in, cap first. After he'd wriggled through, Karl followed him.

She hugged herself tighter, though between the fire and the bright day she wasn't cold. She just didn't care to listen to Karl crowing about Betts when her wrist felt so bare. Worse yet would be hearing it hadn't worked at all.

Chick was sniffing the air, trying to home in on the fire. It was too small and the boards she'd pulled off the yard's sheds too old and bone-dry for smoke to show. Reluctantly she called out, "Over here!" Only good thing about the day, she thought morosely, watching them pick a way towards her, was that the rasp in her voice was gone.

Grinning broadly, Karl squatted by the fire, bouncing on his toes as he commenced rattling off about his visit. Chick settled comfortably on the running board of the stripped and rusting Hudson that kept off the worst of the chilly western breeze, and mostly kept his mouth shut as he shaved pale strips off a chunk of pine. He looked some better than he had yesterday.

She picked up from Karl's chatter that Betts' fever was down, and found herself glad for it. The rest of it rolled over her without sticking, other than a mention of soup. Hunger was part of what was making her feel low. Truth was, though, that without the bracelet she just felt different, duller somehow.

A red ball thundered by on the tracks beyond the decrepit wooden fence, shutting Karl up for a bit. Chick spoke as the pounding faded into the distance, before Karl got started again. "The others should be here directly," he told Philippa.

Karl nodded. "Deucey went to get 'em. I told him this was a fine place to jungle up until the riverbank dries."

"Long as nobody gets wise to us," Chick cautioned. Philippa glanced reflexively skyward to check again on her fire. She saw nothing more than the faint flicker of heat in the air. She wouldn't have had to even look to find it, she realized, letting her heavy eyes shut for a moment, feeling the dancing air flutter behind them.

That seemed new. Might be she could've sensed it before last night, but if so she hadn't known to try.

Karl poked the fire scornfully. "Heck, there's nobody within half a mile of here. The windows in the garage up front are all boarded up, with election posters plastered over 'em. Roosevelt and that old dog-face Hoover both, along with a bunch of local pols I never heard of."

Setting aside his whittling, Chick nudged Philippa's arm. He held out a apple in his long-fingered, chapped hand, and smiled encouragingly when Philippa took it. The apple was warm from his pocket, polished up bright like it'd just come off some grocer's stand. Which it likely had. Philippa summoned a weak grin for thanks, and bit down. Saliva flooded her mouth, the taste so sweet and tart it sent an extra shiver down her back.

Karl dropped his poking stick on the flames and turned to Philippa. "Say, Arlie, from what the lady in the next bed was saying, you got to Betts just in the nick of time," he told her earnestly. "Night nurse gave the black bottle to one of the other charity cases on the ward last night, and she wasn't as bad off as Betts."

The feel of that clotting, cooling flesh wrapped around Philippa once more. The apple rolled from her stiffening fingers. Only dimly did she hear Chick asking was it rotten? Rotten, she thought, grasping for a straw of understanding; not yet, but soon enough in the darkness under the smothering earth.

A hand gripped her arm, shaking her, turned her bound panic into a familiar nightmare. She struck out blind.

"Arlie!" Chick yelled in her ear, not letting go. She opened her eyes to see the two older boys staring at her in the bright afternoon. "What the hell's come over you?"

Sick disorientation soured into a flood of resentment. Philippa ignored Chick and turned on Karl instead—Karl, whose stupid talk had set this off. "Says you, Karl! That lady was dead afore the nurse reached her. I know! I was there."

Surprised, Karl held up both hands. "OK, Arlie, whatever you say!"

"We need to get you fed proper," Chick muttered, sounding disgusted. "Not to mention the rest of us."

Philippa got unsteadily to her feet. Her shins ached from the trashcans she'd kicked. If she still wore the bracelet they'd've healed up already. And even her ratty old rubber boots would've helped protect her legs. "Where's my boots, Karl? You forget to look for 'em?" Even through her irritation she was shamed by the shrewish whine in her voice.

"'Course I looked!" Karl sounded as much hurt as put out. "They weren't there anymore. Geez, Arlie! I'll get you some new ones, OK?"

Chick, standing now, pushed the apple into her hand. "Siddown and eat," he growled, frowning down at her. Head hanging, she stared at the apple, then brushed it off on her clothes and took another bite. Even with ash on it from where it'd rolled through the firebed the apple tasted swell. Philippa chewed it down to the core. The knot in her chest began to ease.

What Deucey had said could not be true, Simon told himself yet again, weary of the repetition but unable to stop himself. The tall youth had admitted he hadn't seen the iyar pukko on Betts' wrist. Tales passed from mouth to mouth were not reliable. Head down, Simon stepped absently from tie to tie, following the others through the alien day.

"Keep up, can't you?" the youngest wanderer called back to him. Startled, Simon looked up. The three of them waited further along the tracks.

"Hey, Deuce," Junkyard said, hands on hips, his mocking gaze still on Simon, "didja hear what Simon told the mission stiff his name was?"

Deucey waved a dismissive hand at Junkyard. "Aw, lay off the Wob. You told us that ten times already." Turning away, he led off again down the endless tracks.

Simon felt his face heat as he followed. He closed his lips firmly on an impulse to call after them that he hadn't said 'simple'—which only meant 'not difficult', did it not?—but 'Saint Paul'. But to answer such taunts only gave them more force. He'd learned that early, in the echoing corridors of Huagiyoh, his home warren, dug into the hills above the fertile Great North Bay of the western coast. Where he'd give much to be now, the hazing and the eternal smell of fish guts notwithstanding.

In some ways, though, his world and this one were alike.

After a few minutes more, Deucey slowed again and pointed. "I'm guessing that fence up yonder is where we're headed."

Glancing up, Simon stumbled over a tie, catching himself with one hand. The cinders left scratches on his palm, a couple oozing blood. Reflexively he touched a finger to the wet and wiped a faint smear on his forehead, singing under his breath the repeated line from the Four Atonements song: *Ohe, ako ngintob i-hibaatin fa.* Blood for our many failings...

He tightened the hand into a fist. The scratches stung, but they were nothing. His iyar pukko would smooth them from his skin.

That boy had not removed the stolen iyar; he could not have, and soon Simon would have the proof of it before them all.

"What is here?"

Philippa looked up to see Simon standing just inside the gap in the fence, staring at the jumble of wrecked and rusting cars. Seeing his confusion, she had a flash of just how strange this whole world must be to him. Maybe they didn't have cars where he came from. Maybe they flew everywhere, like angels.

Deucey turned to answer him. "Scrap yard, Wob! Also known as a junkyard, like what our pal here's called after." He slapped the back of Junk's grimy jacket. Junkyard scowled. "Place where old cars go to.die." Surveying the yard, Deucey added, "Give me some tools and a couple of days and I bet I could get one of these babies rolling."

"Yeah? And what'd you do with it then?" Junkyard scoffed, his hands stuffed deep in his pockets. Deucey ignored him and wandered off to examine the possibilities.

Nip's wizened face peered through the fence behind Simon. "Hey, get out of the way!" Roused from his amazement, Simon stepped past the wheel rims stacked along the fence. His gaze met Philippa's, and tightened.

She stood up straighter, recalling the wonder of what she'd done. But Simon didn't say a word of praise. He stalked over to her. "Show!" he demanded. When she just stared at him, not knowing what he was talking about, he grabbed her arm and skinned her sleeve back from the wrist.

"Hey, let go!" Philippa twisted free. "Jesus bless! What's wrong with you!" She rubbed the smarting skin, anger blooming.

Simon's face had gone bloodless under the brown, his gaze still fixed on the wrist. She shucked her left sleeve down.

"Figured I couldn't pull it off, huh, Simon?" she said, low-voiced so as to not drag the others in.

He backed up a step, weeds crackling under his boots. "How I am to know what you can do?" he whispered, his chin up, meeting her gaze squarely.

But he was scared of her. That new wonder quenched her flare of temper. Almost a man grown and more than a head taller than her, but that was wariness she saw in his eyes now, sure as God made rocks. Knowing it made her feel strange, like she'd got more solid overnight. She wasn't sure she liked it, but it was a sight better than the other way around.

"You giving Arlie grief again 'bout that thing?" Chick asked, appearing cat-footed and scowling at Philippa's side from a prowl around the yard. Junkyard's sharp gaze wandered to them, and stayed put.

Simon faced Chick with a kind of fierce relief. "I only ask to see," he claimed. "Is good he help Betts." Peaceful words, but the shift of his muscles said different.

Even Karl was watching now, alert to the prospect of a fight. "Was more like the other way around, Chick," Philippa said hastily. "Me giving him grief."

Chick transferred his glare to her. She stood still for it, and his expression eased. "Cut it out, then." He whacked her backhanded on the upper arm. Same place Karl'd hit. Philippa hid both her wince and a smile.

Simon turned and walked unsteadily away between the cars. Philippa's hand, which had strayed toward the bruise on her arm, settled for rubbing the bare wrist as she watched him.

"What's eatin' Simple?" Nip asked, coming to stand by her and Chick.

"Jealous," Karl opined from where he sat, a lazy edge of resentment in his voice. "Could've been him fixed Betts up, but he couldn't be bothered. Palmed it off on Arlie and then she did it up brown."

"*He*," Philippa insisted automatically.

"What?" Karl looked confused.

Chick stepped in. "You gotta remember to say 'he' not 'she', Karl, or you'll up and forget sometime when it's important."

Junkyard snorted, but Karl gave Philippa an apologetic grin. "Yeah. Guess I forgot."

Philippa nodded at him. She was glad for Chick's support, but her mind was elsewhere, working slowly through an idea. Simon hadn't been being lazy or big-headed like Karl thought. The Wob hadn't known how to help Betts, on account of the bracelets weren't supposed to come off. It was a hunch, but she'd bet good money she was right. What Simon *had* been doing was letting her take the fall. And then she hadn't failed—though she still was uneasy in her mind about just how she'd done it—and that scared him clear down to his marrowbones.

"Hey, Simon!" she yelled in the general direction the Wob had disappeared. "Soon's Betts is out of the hospital, we'uns'll get you down to St. Paul. Won't we, guys?" She eyed the others fiercely.

"What for?" Karl hissed.

Chick shrugged; gave her a lopsided smile. "Why not?"

Simon's untrusting face appeared above the crumpled top of a Model T. Philippa nodded to him, but kept most of her attention on Karl. "Maybe on account of it's the right thing to do? Betts needed help, and so does he."

Karl scowled. "It's not the same."

"No skin off yer nose, is it?" Junkyard challenged him, to Philippa's relief. "Unless Betts has got other plans for you." He grinned evilly at Karl. "Take you home to meet the family, say."

"You nuts?" Karl squinted up at Junkyard. "You should hear how her old man used to treat her!"

Sighing, Philippa slid down to sit on the running board across from him. "See, that's just it, Karl. Ain't none of us got homes, but Simon does, if he can only get back to it. I think that's worth helping with." Karl was listening to her now. And Deucey as well; he'd come up quiet as some wild creature while they'd been talking. Her line of argument swelled inside her with its rightness, shushing the nagging reminder in the back of her mind of what she hoped to gain for herself. "And if you're thinking he wouldn't help with Betts when he could've, I think maybe you're wrong. What I found out is those bracelets put roots right down into your arm."

This startled a squawk out of Nip. "That's disgusting!"

Philippa shrugged. "Likely that's part of how they can work on you. But my point is they don't come off like skinning out of your socks."

"Not come off unless you dead." Simon stood a few yards off, fists clenched. "Like Lukas. Or"—he brought one hand down like an ax on the other forearm—"cut arm off." Simon pointed at her with his chin. Her stomach went cold, but all he said was, "He do what is not possible."

Nobody said a thing for a long moment. Off in the distance a dog yapped monotonously. One way or the other death seemed to be part of things, Philippa thought, wondering with dread if somehow the dead woman had paid the price for getting the bracelet off.

Simon shifted restlessly. "You take me to St. Paul like he say?"

Karl glanced at the others and then at her. "Yeah," he said at last. "We take you."

19

*P*hilippa squirmed on the car seat, pushing at her new boots to take the pressure off the blister on her big toe. Karl had got a swell pair for her, not hardly worn at all, but in terrible need of breaking in. Before curling up to sleep she'd loosened the lengths of string that laced them, but still they chafed. And it was too cold to take them off.

Shivering, she sat up and peered out the dirt-smeared window at the jumble of cars. Truth was, it was too cold to sleep even if the boots'd been soft to her feet as glove leather. Crowding in with the guys in the peeling milk van Deucey'd found for them would've been warmer, but the sight and smell of the old mattress inside had made her head feel light and sick and cold. A rotting rubber or two lying around had made things worse.

Chick had cut his eyes at her, checking on how she was taking it, so she'd kept her trap shut, casually picking a wrecked Packard nearby to bed down in. Mice or rats had started on the seats but the car couldn't have been here long. It boasted glass all the way around, though the windshield was crazed with cracks.

Something clinked outside the window; not close. One of the boys up and moving around? But it sounded sneaky. Philippa took a corner of the ripped-up wool upholstery she'd wrapped herself in, spat on it, and wiped a clear place in the window grime. A dry wisp of cloud hid the moon, but she thought she could make out figures moving between the cars.

The cloud drifted on and she was sure of it—five of them at least, mostly big guys, Deucey's size or bigger. She hissed when she saw two more behind. Even-steven, she thought grimly; seven of us and seven of them, if more weren't coming. And creeping around that way showed they didn't mean a bit of good.

Chick'd been right to be worried. This must be some local gang's territory they'd trespassed on.

As she yanked her laces tight again Philippa looked around the inside of the car for a quiet way out, but there was no help for it: she'd picked the Packard for how well it sealed up against the night wind. She jerked on the handle and shouldered the heavy door open wide, the dented metal shrieking. "Chick!" she hollered. "Junk! Everybody out!"

A length of rusty metal rod lay among the other junk scattered on the ground beside the car, knobbed on either end. Philippa scooped it up as she launched herself toward the van. The rod was rough and icy to the touch, but satisfyingly heavy in her hand.

The intruders were too close. "Get that kid!" a barrel-shaped guy shouted. Two of his pals peeled off and came for her, vaulting car hoods in their haste. She kept on yelling as she ran. The door on the milk van crashed open, spilling Junkyard and Deucey out into the night, but she wasn't going to reach them before the two townies caught up with her.

One at a time seemed a better idea than both at once. Philippa zagged, charging straight for the smaller guy.

He gaped and stumbled to a halt, but his moment of confusion was brief. He bared his teeth, and moonlight flashed on something thin and bright in his hand. Philippa didn't have time to think about that, just whacked his hand hard aside with the rod as she dove into him. The townie grunted and went down with her on top pounding him with her left fist, bloodying his face, grateful for the trick Chick had showed her that afternoon of aiming deeper than surface skin. But the guy'd grabbed the rod with the hand she wasn't kneeling on, trying to wrestle it away from her, hissing rage between his teeth as they struggled.

The scaly surface of the rod scored her palm as he wrenched it free. Desperate, Philippa threw herself backwards, kicking him square in the nuts more for leverage than on purpose.

Howling, he hurled the rod at her. She got an arm up to block it, but one end rapped her hard above the ear. Crying, enraged at the pain, Philippa laid into him where he lay curled up clutching himself, kicking like fury.

A body blow knocked her breathless into the side of a truck cab. Before she got more than a glimpse of her new foe a fist slammed into her cheekbone. She flailed, trying to ward him off, to scramble away, and then he was gone, down in the tall, dry weeds with a dent in his head oozing blood and Chick standing over him with the tie rod, white-eyed and breathing hard.

"Hellfire," he gasped. "Had to get him off you." Philippa stared at him, shaking, unable to move.

"Watch out!" Deucey yelled. Chick whirled and caught the barrel-chested townie in the gut with the length of rod. The guy doubled over, wheezing, but he kept coming. Chick's second blow caught him across the back, knocking him to the ground. The guy started to push himself up, but by then Junkyard and Deucey had crowded around, steamed up and ready to take the townie down again. Junkyard kicked him in the side to emphasize the point.

The big townie struggled to his feet, swearing. "Goddamn road trash," he sobbed. "I saw what you did to Bailey! Swear to God you're gonna pay." Hatred blazed in his eyes as he backed away, though his chubby face was white as milk where blood and dirt didn't mark it. His eyes kept cutting to where his pal lay unmoving at Philippa's feet.

Junkyard followed him, teeth bared, his battered fists ready. Chick grabbed a handful of Junk's jacket to slow him. "Beat it, Jack," he screamed at the townie.

Junkyard turned to Chick in protest, but the townie had taken the advice and was sprinting for the fence. The first guy Philippa'd tangled with hobbled rapidly after him.

"We shouldn't have let 'em go." Junk yanked his jacket free, sounding disgusted. "They'll come back with reinforcements, see if they don't."

"Yeah, well, what was we gonna do with 'em, Junk, kill 'em all?" Chick demanded, his voice breaking high. "We can't stay here anyhow!"

Philippa slid down to sit on the truck's sagging running board. The townie's head was an awful mess, the white gleam of something that might be bone showing at the top of the wound among the lank strands of hair. Below that everything was black and slick with blood. She reached out an unwilling hand to touch the guy's shoulder.

Her movements brought the boys over. Junkyard swore when he saw the townie. "Ke-rist! I see what you mean, Chick."

Though his flesh was slack, life buzzed faintly beneath her touch. Was it breath she felt or something else? But that didn't matter. Philippa snatched her hand back. "He ain't dead!" she hissed.

"We are sure enough in a pickle this time, Chick," Deucey said solemnly, paying her no mind. He swiped at the trickle of blood that ran from the corner of his mouth. Simon turned away, his lean, bruised face twisted with a sick horror. Karl limped up to take his place, leaning on Nip's shoulder.

"Geez oh geez," Nip said, snuffling through a swollen nose. "Was it you killed him, Chick?" Karl just stared.

"He ain't dead!" Philippa yelled, kneeling by him. A long moment of silence followed her words.

"What do you mean, he ain't dead?" Deucey asked then. "A fellow gets a hole that size in his skull, he's dead all right."

Chick dropped to his knees across from her to feel for a pulse. Philippa didn't need a pulse to know the guy was alive, but she was glad somebody was listening.

"The kid's right." Chick fumbled with the buttons of his coat, then yanked it off, and his sweater and his outermost shirt too. Shivering, he wrapped the shirt gingerly around the townie's head to try and staunch the bleeding. Philippa hugged herself, feeling helpless. Even if she had the bracelet to put on him, she wasn't sure it could fix something this bad.

"Forget it," Junk told Chick, his Chicago-bred voice harsh. "Let's get the hell out of town. Maybe he ain't dead yet, but he can't live. And if he does, I feel sorry for the bastard." There was a gray tinge to his skin that Philippa thought was more than an effect of moonlight, and a queasy twist to his mouth.

"*Gri ngiten*! You are a, a…" Simon stammered angrily from behind them, searching for a name bad enough to serve. Everybody but Chick turned to stare at him. "Your heart has no center," he concluded at last, defeated.

"Shut ya trap, Simple," Junkyard told him without much force. "I'll deal with you later."

"We gotta try, Junk," Chick said.

Philippa nodded. "Me'n Simon'll take him to the hospital." She met Simon's eyes. Mouth tight, he returned her nod.

"And me," Chick said, determined.

"Not you," Deucey retorted. "Don't be dumber than your Mama raised you! Baby-face seen you sock him. The city bulls'll be looking for you special."

"And how in Christ's name you plan on getting him there?" Junkyard demanded. "It's miles to the hospital. Deuce's right about the cops, too, only it'll be all of us they'll be hunting. Betcha that fink's peaching to 'em already, while we stand around swooning like a bunch of skirts."

Karl cleared his throat. "Wheelbarrow in the shed up front. I saw it yesterday. We can put him in that. And I'll go too. Betts…" Karl's voice trailed off for a moment. "See, I won't leave her here. Damn nosy parker social workers'll ship her back to Indiana." Without waiting for an answer he limped off.

Junk looked around at them all, then shoved his fists deep in his pockets. "You guys've all gone soft in the head," he growled, frustrated.

The shallow wheelbarrow was battered and greasy from a life of hauling motors and junk around. Scowling, Chick laid a board across the handles to support the kid's legs. It wouldn't stay put. Guy was built broad and short like Junkyard, but still his legs dangled. Poor bastard didn't look more than fourteen, Chick thought, trying to ignore how bad he was shaking.

Damned wheelbarrow just wasn't big enough.

Chick cast about for more boards; found baling wire instead. He bound the length of board in place, yanking savagely on the wire to get it tight.

"Gonna be a mighty rough ride," Deucey said, watching him.

Chick stared up at him dumbly, then snatched his sweater off the ground where he'd dumped it, and tossed it to Arlie. Without needing to ask the kid slid it beneath the guy's head and shoulders, bunching it up to support his neck. Her hands came away streaked with shiny black. Under the makeshift shirt-bandage, the guy must still be bleeding.

"Hey, look! A pigsticker!" A little ways off Nip straightened up from poking around in the weeds. He waved an open jackknife with a blade long as his hand.

Arlie straightened from wiping her hands on a clump of grass. "Yeah," she said, her face set and her voice hard. "That guy I kicked in the nuts had it. Knocked it out of his hand with that—" She glanced at Chick uneasily. "—That rod."

The spit in Chick's mouth thickened. He hadn't had no choice but to do what he'd done. Numbly he watched Nip walk toward them. The scrawny boy held the knife out, handle first. "Guess it's yours then," he said. "Fair and square."

"Guess so." Arlie took it gingerly. From where he stood, a few feet away, Chick could see it plain on the kid's bloody palm. Its blade shone in the moonlight, thin with honing; deadly. After a moment Arlie snapped it shut and eased it into her pocket. "Thanks, Nip," she muttered.

Good, Chick thought distantly. Kid's got herself a knife again. But what might she do with it one day? What might he do with his?

They'd better get going if they were gonna do this kid any good, he told himself, but didn't move.

"We knocked out some boards in the front fence so you guys can get through," Junkyard announced loudly as he stalked up, dusting his hands off on his pants. Karl and Simon were close behind. Simon walked a little hunched over, like his ribs hurt. He'd been slow to fight, then awkward as a girl once he got going, and both had cost him.

Junk turned on Chick, scowling fiercely. "Ya coming with me'n Nip and Deuce to the rail yards, and no back lip."

Chick stared at him, still unable to move. Karl had grabbed the wheelbarrow handles and was wheeling it away, the guy's head rolling. Chick reached a hand out, a protest in his throat, but the Wob had run ahead to steady him.

Heavy cloth fell around his shoulders. "Put your coat on, Chick," Arlie said. "You're shivering."

20

*T*he old man who picked them up was drunk as a polecat. He stood on his touring car's brakes when he saw them, fishtailing across the empty road and half off onto the stiff mud of the roadside. Seeing that Simon and Karl had their hands full with the wheelbarrow, Philippa sprinted ahead to do the talking. Before she'd got more than a few steps, the old man slammed his car into reverse with a painful shriek of the gears, backing wildly in their general direction.

Cursing, Philippa stumbled to a halt, then turned and waved frantically at the guys, shouting, "Get him off the road!"

Karl had already seen the danger, and was trying to drag the wheelbarrow and its burden off into the weeds, but he had the front end. Simon, on the business end of things, had dropped the handles and was gaping like a moon-struck fool at the approaching car.

Shouldering him aside, Karl manhandled the wheelbarrow off the road. Philippa turned back to find the car's rear end wavering toward her no more than five feet away. She jumped clear with room to spare, landing on hands and knees.

The touring car whined to a stop beside her. The old man leaned out over the door. "Hey, what you *pojkar* doin' in da middle of da dern road?" he demanded. A reek of rotten fruit came off him, and his bloodshot eyes couldn't quite settle on a focus.

But they had to have a ride. "Gotta get, um, Bailey to the hospital," Philippa told him breathlessly, scrambling up. "A beam fell on him, and he's real bad. Give us a lift, mister?"

The drunk blinked at her suspiciously.

"Bailey's hurt bad, see." The kid's name came easier to her tongue this time. She jerked her thumb toward where Karl and Simon were carefully lifting the wheelbarrow back on the road. "All we got's that old wheelbarrow to haul him in, and we're scared he'll up and die on us, honest to Jesus, mister. Can you take us to the hospital? Please?"

The old man craned his head around to squint at them. "What da heck dey got in dere?" he mumbled. After a long moment he asked, "Somebody hurt, you saying?"

"Yeah, Bailey is." Philippa bit back her frustration. The guys came up with the wheelbarrow then, and she stepped back to give the old man room to see.

The drunken flush drained from his face as he stared at the kid. "*Gud i himmel*," the old man breathed. "Get him in," he ordered, sounding almost sober.

They hurried to obey, scooting the wheelbarrow up to get clearance to open the rear door. Simon took the town kid's head and shoulders and edged backwards into the car, with Philippa climbing in after to help drag the limp weight into place on the torn upholstery of the seat. Karl slammed the door shut as soon as they were clear, then turned and shoved the wheelbarrow off the road. He limped around and climbed up into the front just as the old man slammed the gearshift into first.

The car looked to be nothing but a rusty old flivver, but it had some horsepower under its hood. As it sped up Philippa grabbed for the door, dropping the horse blanket she'd found lying on the floorboards. The icy wind that sluiced in through the glass-less windows battered her face. Must be going fifty miles an hour, maybe even. The old man's whiskery face was tight with a sodden concentration, and the car roared pretty much in a straight line down the center of the rough pavement into town.

Better than swerving all over the place, Philippa told herself, heart pounding. Nobody else out driving this time of night anyways. Grand Forks was a dead-and-alive sort of place for all its size. Shakily she spread the dirty blanket over the kid while Simon eased Chick's sweater back under his head. Then she hunkered down in the space between the seats, and shut her eyes in a brief, involuntary prayer.

Simon cleared his throat, seeming unflustered by how fast the bare trees whipped by them. "Arlie. Eyes move, I think."

Philippa scooted closer through the rattling junk that littered the floorboards—farrier's tools, some of it, and empty cans and such. The back of the car stank of grease and stables. The bellows handle of a portable forge jabbed her knee. Angrily she swung it out of her way.

If the town kid had moved more than was due to the jouncing of the touring car's worn-out springs, she couldn't tell it in this light. He was paler under his freckles and the smears of blood, and his face had got puffy. His pug nose was running, the thin snot gleaming against his skin. Philippa had an impulse to wipe it for him.

Judging by the state of Simon's hands, the terrible wound was still leaking blood.

"Doctors will fix," Simon told her, raising his voice to be heard over the whine of the motor. "Soon we are there." He looked exhausted but the anguish that had ridden him back at the scrap yard wasn't so obvious.

Junkyard's raspy comment about feeling sorry for the kid if he did live came back to her. But that didn't bear thinking about now—that or the fellow with the dented head who'd used to show up regular for church back home in Mansfield, except for when he had one of what his momma called his fearsome headaches. Content at his chores was Clevis, but trying to follow anything the least bit difficult twisted up his face with a baffled woe.

Philippa set her teeth against memory. Living was flat-out better than not living. "I wish I had that bracelet to put on him," she said, the only thing she could think of to answer Simon's faith in doctors. "Now that Betts is better." It was as much her fault as Chick's the kid was lying here.

Simon flinched, and his hand closed over his left wrist, his own bracelet. Looking at it, he said, "Iyar pukko not... Not miracle. After doctors fix brain and bone, iyar heal him fast. If he has one. If he Ngorvisla like me." He paused, swallowing tightly. He met her gaze as she strained to hear him.

"Betts heals and I am glad. But is wrong she has Lukas' iyar —bad for her too, you understand? Is—was—iyar of boy. You must take off her." His hands clenched suddenly.

And give it back to you is what you ain't saying, Philippa thought sourly. But another wondering thought niggled at the back of her mind. A boy's iyar...

"Huh?" Karl peered over the back of the seat. "What're you talking a... Slow down!" he yelled, panicked as the touring car squealed hard into a left turn. Philippa skidded across the floorboards, piling head and shoulder into the side paneling. After an unsuccessful grab for the door Simon tumbled after her, landing heavily on her legs, his momentum shoving her face first into the seat cushion.

For a few frantic seconds Philippa fought to free herself both of the smothering upholstery and the weight that pinned her to the floorboards. Simon was shouting at her, but she kicked and scrabbled until she got her head free. Gulping in the cold, fume-tainted air, she squirmed around to see Simon face down amid the junk, pinned in his turn by the weight of the injured kid, who had slid, still unconscious, off the seat. Simon had his arms wrapped around his head and looked afraid to move.

Philippa squirmed her legs the rest of the way free and pushed herself up. In the front seat Karl was still cussing the old man, who was going fast as ever.

"Was dere dern job to hold him, ja?" the drunk shouted back. "I am driving!"

"Hold on, Simon," Philippa said, bending close to his ear to be sure he heard. "I'll get his head up and steady so's you can move." The injured boy was sprawled half on his side, the bandaged wound uppermost. His mouth hung slack. A touch to his chest assured Philippa he still lived. With a hand on the seat back for support against the jouncing of the car, she eased herself past the tangle of limbs and tools.

Careful this time not to kick anyone, she scraped clear a space to kneel. She worked an arm beneath the kid's broad shoulders, then reached for his head with her free hand.

The bandage was sticky wet. Philippa gritted her teeth against the feel of it, and the strain of lifting at that awkward angle. "Got him, Simon!" She braced her head against the door to help hold the weight.

Simon started to wriggle out from under the kid, increasing the pull on Philippa's arms. "Karl, give me a hand here!" she hollered.

Karl jackknifed over the back of the front seat, reaching past her to grab hold of the kid's jacket. Simon dragged his upper body free, grunting as though moving hurt.

The palm of Philippa's hand, the one cradling the town kid's head, started to prickle. She shifted the hand slightly, muttering a weary curse. "So what was you saying, Simon?"

But if he answered, she didn't hear it. Pain struck down into her palm like a ghostly nail being driven through it, piercing but gone as soon as she'd felt it. She yelped but didn't pull away as the kid's back arched like a stick bent to the breaking point over somebody's knee. A flailing arm knocked Karl the rest of the way off balance, and he began to slide headfirst toward them. As the kid twitched and jerked lesser shocks punished Philippa's hand—caused somehow by his fit? Still she kept her hand where it was, trying to cushion his head. A rank odor of piss joined the other smells.

Beside her Karl caught himself with a hand to the back seat, though the touring car was swerving wildly now. "What are you dam' pojkar doing?" the driver yelled at them, panicked.

"He's having a fit, mister," Karl yelled back, exasperated, his voice was muffled from him being upside down. "We'll take care of it. Keep your eyes on the goddamn road!"

The old man muttered, but the car steadied.

"See? He calms," Simon said, moving out of the corner he'd wedged himself in to avoid the townie's fierce, random kicks.

And it seemed to Philippa that Simon was right. The shocks to her hand had stopped, and although the kid's face was still contorted, he'd stilled. Except for his chest, which pumped fast and shallow, like that of a baby bird.

Karl, who'd managed to wriggle far enough back so he was again securely draped over the front seat, laid a hand on the kid's jacket front. "Why's he breathing like that?"

Philippa shook her head, baffled. "Maybe 'cause he's hurting?" There was so much she didn't know—why he was panting; why his nose was running so bad. She had begun to suspect the answers were there lying between her hands, but she didn't have a notion in the world how a body went about reading them.

The touring car rumbled around another corner, at near a reasonable speed this time. She tightened her grip, holding both herself and the kid's head steady. "Had we oughta get him back up on the seat?" she asked Simon. A glance through the far window showed her the unlighted brick storefronts of downtown Grand Forks; they were almost there. A few blocks away a siren shrieked and faded, sending a shiver down her spine. Ambulance? Cop car? Whatever it was was headed back the way they'd come.

The Wob flicked a hand, scowling. He bent, swaying a little, over the kid, gently tugging at his legs to straighten them. "Might fall more. No: again."

They ought to have figured on that when they put him in the car, Philippa thought. Simon was thinking the same way; she could see it in the set of his shoulders.

Something in the feel of the weight in her hands changed; paused. Philippa held very still, waiting for it to start up again, the flow that wasn't quite pulse or breath but that told her hands the boy was living. Seconds ticked by and it didn't. Refusing to believe, she groped after it with a corner of her mind, then recoiled, a taste of greasy ash bringing back last night's terror.

The touring car slowed as they swayed around one more corner. She met Karl's wide gaze. He took his hand from the kid's chest and, without a word, slid back into the front seat. Simon, unaware, went on fussing, tucking the horse blanket securely around the kid's body.

Body. Christ Jesus.

"St. Mike's," announced the old man, his brakes squealing as he brought them to a shuddering halt, killing the engine. "One of you kids run tell dem."

The seat springs squeaked and then the door hinges as Karl jumped down. "I gotta help them with the, the bandage," he said, his voice thick. He yanked the back door open. "He's bleeding again on account of being tossed on the floor. You'll have to go yourself, mister."

Philippa looked out, beyond Karl standing there white-faced and stubborn. The old man had pulled into the bricked drive that looped around to the emergency doors at the back of the main building, but he'd stopped just a little way in. The light above the front door spilled down the steps and made a pool of brightness on the leaf-scattered lawn.

The engine ticked as it cooled. "*Ohövlig pojke*," the old man said at last, to no one in particular. "Rude boy. I got eyes. You kids was fighting; I know how come he's bleeding." Fumbling, he got his door open, and stalked unsteadily toward the high front steps.

Simon stared at Karl, puzzled. "No more blood now."

Philippa had pulled back, letting the head rest on the floorboards. "That's right. He ain't bleeding at all no more," she told Simon flatly. "He's gone."

Unbelieving, Simon reached hastily for the kid's wrist.

"No time for that, Wob. We better scram before they come back." Karl nodded toward the hospital. "I'm getting Betts out of here if it's the last thing I do." He took a few angry, limping strides before Philippa's voice stopped him.

"Wait. We gotta take the guy with us." She felt cold down to her bones, and heavy. She didn't want to do this.

Karl turned to face her. "You crazy? He's dead!"

"Yeah, and the old man's drunk. He stinks of gin. They come out and find nobody in his rattletrap old car, they won't look no further."

Understanding tightened his face. "I'll get him out the other side, where it's not so obvious." He shut the door and hastened around the car.

"You fixing to help us?" Philippa asked Simon.

Simon wouldn't look at her. "Blood tells them," he said stiffly, still crouched over the blanket-wrapped form.

Philippa looked around; snatched at the sodden lump that was Chick's sweater. Sure enough, there was a darker patch beneath it on the seat cushion.

"Yes, I help," Simon said, low but definitely, like it was something he'd had to think over.

Philippa didn't pay him much mind. The stain on the seat they could cover up with the horse blanket—just strip it off the body and leave it here—but there was blood on that too.

She gave the woolen upholstery a yank but the raveled split that ran down much of the seat didn't reach far enough to do her any good. She slapped her pockets, feeling for the knife.

"Come *on*, Arlie!"

Philippa looked up. The dead kid was a long, awkward bundle draped over Simon's shoulder. She hadn't even noticed them pulling him out. Both the older boys looked nervous as cats.

"Get! I'll catch up." The wicked blade gleamed in her hand and Philippa swallowed, remembering again how close the edge had come to her. But it made quick work of the seat, starting a tear where she needed it. The wadding spilled out as she cut and ripped the bloody patch free. Scraping a handful of dirty straw out of the corner it'd lodged in, she sprinkled it over the hole and the rest of the upholstery to disguise its rawness. Scrubbing at the dark spot on the floorboards with a handful of the stuffing made no difference to the dirty floor, though the cotton waste came away stained.

The sound of a young man's voice brought her head up, though it wasn't close. "Go on in and sit down before you fall down, Gramps. We'll take care of it." A burly figure in a white jacket stood on the front steps with his back to her.

"Cripes," Karl hissed. "Shove in your clutch, Arlie!"

Philippa jumped. The boys were still waiting on her. Heart pounding, she spared one more glance around. An empty tin of motor oil lay by her hand. She upended it over the bloodstain on the floor, hoping for drips, and dived for the open door.

It was too late to make a run for it. Two orderlies carrying a stretcher were hurrying toward the car. She crouched on the far side with Karl and Simon in the bulky shadow of the tires, Karl mouthing panicky curses at her slowness. Beside her Simon crouched, teeth clenched, a hand on the fender to keep him and his burden balanced.

A door banged open and the touring car's springs jounced. One of the orderlies had got in. Philippa huddled back against the tire.

"Hell, there's nobody here!" Light from a flashlight spilled out the open door beside Karl. He hastily moved his foot aside. The guy speaking was the same one they'd heard before.

"Unless he went out the other side," the other fellow said.

Simon's breath whistled in and out, loud in Philippa's ears. She laid a hand lightly across his face to muffle the sound. He jerked his head back but didn't pull away. His warm breath tickled her palm, or maybe that was his life she was feeling. How was she supposed to tell the difference anymore?

"If he went out the other side, he don't need no stretcher," the first man retorted. "That old drunk's making a fool of us. Got Sister Joseph to drag us out of bed for nothing."

"Nobody up front either. Phew! Stinks in here." The door slammed shut again. "Yeah. Or some kid's made a fool out of him and it don't matter much to me which it is. Let's go in. It's colder than a damned icebox out here." Slumped against the tire, Philippa listened to them go.

21

Spread-legged, Simon leaned as much of the dead youth's weight against the wall as he could, breathing shallowly against the stench of cold urine that rose from the blanket-wrapped body. The pain of his bruises had eased, at least, as they began to heal.

This time he had tried not to give way to the weakness of fighting, he truly had, curling up on the ground to protect himself from the brutal kicks as his people had done during the Floods, the great nonviolent uprising that had washed the Haan overseers from Ngorvislat shores a century ago. It was only pain, after all. But then Deucey had come to pull the two youths off, and they'd both turned on him instead. If he'd thought, Simon could perhaps have tricked them, drawn them away...

He hadn't thought. They were hurting Deucey, who'd been kind to him. He'd picked himself up and savagely attacked them, and together he and Deucey had driven them off.

He shifted again under his burden, his hand patting the unresponsive flesh in an unconscious apology. He hadn't struck this boy down, but he might have. The days and nights passed on this world, but it was night that was claiming his spirit.

Arlie, silhouetted in the gap between the hedge and the hospital's wall, turned anxiously to peer at him. "Put him down," the boy hissed. "Ain't no telling how long it'll take Karl to get down here, even figuring he manages to sneak in."

Weary, the knot of grief and old guilt and—he had to admit it—fear hard in his chest, Simon didn't respond. He'd failed at so much. This task at least he would see done well.

At last the heavy door eased inward, and Karl stuck his head out. Relief spread across his face when he saw Arlie. "Come on," he whispered, letting the boy slip by him. "Keep your voice down. Simon with you?"

Simon stepped heavily from the shadows, the toes of the town youth's boots bumping his thigh.

"Criminy!" Karl, white-faced, stepping back but still blocking the entrance. "Don't bring him in here!"

Simon halted, outrage rising in him. "Yes, Karl!" he snarled. "Not to lay him like animal out in darkness!"

A hand tugged at Karl's shoulder. He gave way reluctantly.

"We'll find us somewheres decent to leave him off," Arlie whispered, sounding doubtful.

Simon grimaced. They would do more than that.

"Yeah, well, I sure don't plan on hauling him upstairs with us," Karl muttered, fastening the door behind them. "Get caught with him and we've good as tied a rope around our necks."

A confused image of short lengths of rope wrapped neatly under shirt collars trickled through Simon's mind as he turned ponderously on his heel, surveying the room. Perhaps Karl had meant the narrow scarves men here wore on formal occasions? But there'd been fear as well as anger in Karl's words. Perhaps it was like the harness a shamed person must wear back home, to teach them the consequences of acting as an animal.

An appropriate punishment for fighting. Swallowing, Simon pushed the thought away. That reckoning would come later.

The space was dim and grey and mostly bare, an antechamber of some sort. It smelled of chemicals as well; no fit place for even a brief *akra nt ako* ceremony. "Is holy space in hospital?" he demanded, breaking in on their bickering. There had, after all, been such a place at the mission, as unpleasant as it had been. Perhaps many buildings had them.

Karl glanced at him impatiently, then back to Arlie. "But what if I need help with her?"

The younger one stuck out his chin. "You won't. By now she'll be all fixed up."

Betts, Simon thought, stumbling under the weight of his burden. Well, he had warned them, though it meant again telling what they should not know. They would have to stand the consequences, whatever they might be. Babies died when given the uncleared *iyarit pukko* of the adult dead, a desperate experiment undertaken only under the pressure of a Haan embargo in the days following the Floods. Those given the *iyar* of a dead infant did well enough, though terrible gender distortions appeared later when the sex of the donor had not matched.

But he had other concerns now. They hadn't answered him. "I will find," he said, starting for the door.

Karl swore behind him, low and furious, and grabbed his elbow.

"Hold on! You can't just wander around thataway!" Arlie blocked his way, panic plain in his face.

Simon shut his eyes, wishing the whole ordeal was over. "Say where is then!"

"You are a number one saphead, you know that?" Karl's grip tightened. He pulled Simon the few remaining steps to the doorway. "Yeah, there's a chapel. Lucky it's down here in the basement. I guess it'll do to leave him in." He pointed down the corridor. "See? Turn left there. Chapel's on the right, couple of doors down. But for crissake don't let anyone see you!" He gave Simon a shove.

Drawing a strengthening breath, Simon set off down the corridor, trying for the funeral gait called *bu tlagin*, though his healing shoulder and ribs and back had begun to burn again now he knew he would soon be able to lay the dead one down.

Behind him Karl said something low to Arlie. Soft footsteps pattered up behind him. Arlie edged by, boots dangling from one hand. "I'll ride point," the boy whispered.

Simon sighed. That made no more sense to him than a lot of what they said.

Philippa had no trouble finding the chapel. The door had a brass cross hung on it, the kind with a tormented, half-naked Jesus. She eased the door open and stuck her head inside. Empty like Karl had said it'd be, and filled with a dim, flickering light. Candles in glass cups burned on the altar, and on a table off to the side. She opened the door wide, drawing Simon in before shutting it again behind them.

The place wasn't as garish as she'd feared, though there was an even larger Jesus-hung cross up front, and a blue-painted statue of Mary on the side table. The sweet candle smoke smelled like Christmas Eves spent leaning sleepily against Meemaw's comforting bulk at Holiness Baptist back home, for all the unseemly display.

"No drums," Simon said sadly, standing just inside the doorway. "No room for dance."

At his words a spurt of outrage shook Philippa, cold and hot at once. Dancing on somebody's grave; wasn't that how the saying went? Meemaw dead those two long years ago, laid out with her lips sunk away from her store teeth and her skin all waxy-looking in the pine board coffin. The congregation had sung and wept and praised Malvina Ivey to her rest, as was fitting. Though she'd found none of that inside herself that day of the funeral, neither tears or any kind of voice.

She'd always figured that was how come the preacher and Miz Harkins had packed her off to her sister's place so fast. They'd been glad to get such a hard-hearted child off their hands.

"Lay him out on one of them pews, and let's scram," she told him, unable to keep the harshness out of her voice.

Simon pushed past her down the aisle, still walking with that same funny slide to his steps. Grunting with the effort, he knelt down before the altar and eased the dead boy down onto the floor. Well, that'd do, she thought, but then he twisted round like a cat and shoved the nearest pew back hard enough that it squealed across the tiles and thudded into the pew behind it.

She took a step forward like she could stop him. "Cut that out, Simon! You want to bring the whole place down on our necks?"

His hawk's eyes rested on her, but not as though he really saw her. "By door is bowl of water. Bring me."

Philippa scowled. "We got no time for games!"

"Argue and we take longer. Bring me!"

In the face of his haughty manner her anger chilled to something more like fear. To keep him quiet she went back and lifted the china bowl from its fancy pedestal. Carrying it without spilling the water was hard, it being shallow and near full, but she did her best. Jesus knew why it was here in the first place. It was sure too small for foot-washing.

Simon had gone and unwrapped the blanket. Sprawled out on the tiles, the kid's body looked like a fright carving done in wax, without no trace of spirit left.

Pointing to the floor next to the boy's head, Simon said, "Put here. Where is knife?" He had a length of heavy green altar cloth in his hands.

"You nuts, Simon?" she said, bending to set the bowl down. "I ain't handing you no knife, crazy as you're acting."

He gave her a withering glare. "Is not crazy. You also have debt for his life."

A tide of grief and guilt drained through Philippa as she straightened; left her swaying on her feet. She tried to speak, to argue with him, but the heavy sense of obligation he'd tapped into tied her tongue.

Turning back to the body, Simon dipped the cloth in the bowl of water. With care he worked at cleaning the crust of blood from the face.

Throat thick, Philippa watched. The water turned brown as he rinsed the cloth. The stain brought out figures woven in it, a fancy border around a big crossed-out P, whatever that signified. Reluctantly she fumbled the knife out. "Whatcha gonna do?" she whispered, holding it out to him. Rip the cloth up, she figured, though what for she didn't want to guess.

He laid the knife beside the bowl, and didn't answer.

There wasn't enough water to wash the face clean, but Simon kept at it. When he had done the best he could he took up a littler cloth, ivory white with only the border green, and laid it out all neat on the dead boy's chest. He pried the knife open. "Give hand."

"Huh?" she said, confused, but Simon didn't ask twice. He grabbed her hand and held it. The blade flicked across her palm even as she tried to pull away.

Philippa yelped in shock as beads of blood sprang up along the cut. Simon forced her hand over the fresh cloth. "Squalling boy-child!" he hissed. "Hold! You dishonor blood giving!"

Afraid now of the knife, afraid he'd gone clean around the bend, Philippa obeyed though she had to fight herself to do it. Blood dribbled onto the cloth, bright, random red blotches against the white. They won't never get that out, a part of her mind told her, stupidly. When Simon released her, she backed hastily away from him, clutching her stinging hand.

Simon ignored her. Pushing his coat and shirt sleeves up above his bracelet, baring half his forearm, he held the arm out above the stained cloth. The knife slashed once, twice, again. His fierce expression didn't change, but for a tightness around his dark eyes. More red on the cloth, a wider pattern.

The click of the door latch brought her around. When Karl sidled inside Philippa let go the breath she hadn't known she'd held. Betts, thin but lively, slipped in behind him. Not looking up, Simon yanked down his sleeve over the cuts.

"What's taking you guys so long?" Frowning, Karl crossed himself and bobbed an absent kind of a bow before coming down the side aisle. "Don't you understand we gotta scram before the sisters get wise to us?"

Looking pale and anxious, Betts stayed back by the door. Her blond hair caught the light from the candle flames, like it'd been washed real good. Her old skirt was clean and mended. No coat, but she'd got herself a new-looking thick pink cardigan. Between hospital care and the bracelet Betts had done right well for herself. Philippa looked at the smear of blood on her clenched hand, fighting a spurt of resentment.

Simon's claim the bracelet was bad for girls had to be bunk, didn't it? Hadn't hurt her at all. In fact…

"That's a basin for holy water." Puzzled, Karl stood staring at the bowl of brown water beside the body. Then he scowled at Simon. "You used *holy water* to wash his face?!" He bent down and reached across the body to snatch up the bowl. Seeing what would happen, Philippa opened her mouth to warn him.

Fast as a snake striking, Simon nicked his outstretched hand with the blade. Karl, cursing, backhanded the Wob, and the knife went flying. Simon, not deterred, pinned both Karl's wrists and, as he had before, held the wounded hand above the cloth while Karl drove his shoulder into the Wob, trying to knock him down.

"Hey!" Betts, who couldn't see much on account of the pew backs being in the way, scrambled down the aisle to reach them.

Philippa dived for the knife. Regaining it, she snapped its blade shut without trying to clean it, and shoved it deep in her pocket. More goddamn blood; she was so sick of it. "Pipe down!" she hissed at Betts.

Simon let go of Karl and rolled away, dodging most of the kicks Karl aimed at him. "Calm, Karl! I do only what is needed."

"Needed! You cut me!" Karl stood over Simon, looking as shocked as he did angry.

Betts held determinedly onto the back of Karl's coat. "Let's just get the hell out of here," she pleaded, her voice cracking on the last word. Caught by that, Philippa studied her. The husky catch in the girl's throat was no more than a leftover from being sick, wasn't it? Just like hers had been.

It'd gone away after she'd took the bracelet off.

Simon got to his feet, face haggard but stern. "Little cut only, Karl. Little blood for akra nt ako, a debt cloth. See, show grief for his people, and, and give apology." He pulled his sleeve back. The deep, parallel cuts seeped but Philippa could see they were already closing. Betts and Karl stared. "Me also. And Arlie."

Philippa's mouth tightened. Easy for him to say. He had his bracelet, the iyar whatever he called it, to heal him up.

"You're nuts!" Betts let go of Karl and backed away.

"You don't do such?" A note of disbelief had crept into Simon's tone. "But meaning is clear. They see we do honor."

Spooky is how it looked to Philippa, and like to make the cops all the more hot to catch them. Her cut had begun to throb in time with her bruised temple. She scrambled to her feet. They had to get out of here. Betts felt the same way; she was already back by the door with her hand on the knob.

Karl, though, was too caught up in telling Simon just how unlikely it was that the kid's family and friends or anybody else would be fobbed off by what Simon had done. Sacrilege was his mildest word. "Go ahead and hold a bloody wake or whatever suits you for this guy," he told Simon, low and furious. "Hang around and let 'em catch you. Do whatever you want, go wherever you want to, but not with us, chump."

Simon stood flatfooted, dismay shaking loose the self-righteous set of his mouth. He cried, "You take me to St. Paul!"

St. Paul, where he'd find one of their slipgates to get him home, to the world Mara'd gone to. That land of milk and honey where, to judge by Simon, folks danced at funerals and sliced themselves up. But still she had to see it for herself. Mara would make things right somehow. For a whisper of a moment she felt again the dry brush of Mara's lips on her forehead.

Karl might listen to her, even riled as he was. He'd started for the door, muttering as he went, "I'm with you, Betts. C'mon, Arlie. Let's get out of here."

But Betts turned from the door, panic in her eyes. "Someone's coming!" she mouthed. They all froze, straining their ears. Heavy footsteps were coming down the hall.

Too late, Philippa thought hopelessly as she cowered behind the shelter of the pew, the body a lot too close behind her. Arguing like fools while a axe hung over their heads.

Hinges squeaked as the door swung wide. There was a full moment of silence. "I know you're in here, young man," a woman said, as no-nonsense as a schoolteacher. "I heard you halfway down the hall. Have you no sense of decency, making such a racket in front of God's own altar in the middle of the night?"

Nobody stirred.

"Shall I fetch one of the orderlies to dig you out?"

Simon pressed his hands briefly to his face, then unfolded himself from his crouch. "I am here." Philippa stifled a moan of fear.

"Better. But you're not alone, I wager."

Philippa heard a small squeak and a shuffling of feet, and her heart sank further. Betts, it had to be, fetched out from behind the door. Stay down, Karl, she thought furiously. Let the nun figure she'd caught two lovers fussing at each other. If she didn't notice the pew out of place or the sour stink rising off the dead boy, didn't come further into the room...

There was a note of satisfaction in the woman's voice. "Yes, I thought there'd be a young lady involved. Your name?"

"Mabel, Sister," Betts lied defiantly.

"I am Simon." His back poker-straight, heels thumping on the tiles, the Wob walked toward the door, out of Philippa's sight.

"Haven't I seen you before, Mabel?" The nun sounded puzzled.

Betts hardly missed a beat. "Could be, Sister. I've been in a lot lately visiting my Aunt Mae." She cleared her throat.

There was a pause while the nun considered this. "Well, never mind," she said at last. "You'd both better come along with me." From the faded sound of her voice the nun had turned to lead the way. A confusion of footsteps followed her until the door clicked shut, cutting off sound.

Karl huddled with his head buried in his arms. "She didn't have a thing to do with this," he moaned. "She'll be sent up and it's all my fault."

Philippa knelt beside him. "You figure that nun'll call the cops? Won't she just give 'em a talking to and kick 'em out?" If Simon didn't say something stupid, that is. He wouldn't mean to, but he was such a mooncalf sometimes.

Karl looked up at her hopelessly. "Even if she does, when they find the body, they'll be hot after her as well as..." His gaze wandered away from her face as a thought took him. "We'll move it somewhere else and tidy things up. Make it look like it was never in here."

Philippa shut her eyes, the knowledge that he was right settling like lead in her belly.

22

*Y*ellow light showed a false welcome at the train depot on DeMers; a patrol car was parked right out front. Karl and her had already seen two others on their skulk across town, plus the one that'd been parked in front of the hospital itself, which had near sent Karl around the bend with worry. She'd talked him down from that, pointing out that Simon had a good front, what with that coat of his that dirt didn't seem to stick to, and the cops wouldn't be looking for a guy and a girl anyways.

And they'd took care of the main trouble. Philippa shuddered, remembering the cold of the hospital's morgue and the dreadful job of stripping the body. They'd left him there laid out under a sheet, a notion Karl had been proud of as a hen was of an egg. Between that and his whining, she was about ready to bust him one.

A cop stalked out of the station, looking up and down the broad street. From somewhere off to the west a faint siren wailed, heading north.

"We'll hafta pick up the tracks further along," she whispered. Karl nodded stiffly. Limping from the pinching of her boots, she led the way back into the alley they'd just come out of. Fear gnawed at the edges of her stomach, but she didn't slacken her pace. Wouldn't catch her whining.

Up ahead a figure haloed by streetlight stepped into the far end of the alley. Quick as anything, Philippa and Karl squeezed down behind a battered wooden stand crowded with garbage cans. That close to the ground the stale reek of spilled fry grease cut through the nose-numbing effects of the cold.

"Think he saw us?" Karl mouthed. Philippa shrugged, though her heart was pounding like a blacksmith working hot iron. The man was coming on fast, not running, but striding and out of breath with it. He stumbled once or twice, and the second time they heard his muttered cussing.

At that Philippa's shoulders sagged with relief. She stood slowly up, and Karl with her.

The man flinched to a halt, staring, ready to run. He was a young guy, with a workman's cap and a baggy suit jacket that had the collar turned up as far as it would go. A three day's growth of whiskers showed on his hollow cheeks.

"What's doing, brother?" Karl called out just loud enough to reach him.

"Christamighty. You near give me a heart attack," the young man said, his breath smoking. "A raid's what's happening. Harness bulls is swarming all over the yards back there. If you boys was planning to beat the Goat Road tonight, I'd give it another think if I was you."

"What's got 'em riled up?" Philippa asked.

He hawked and spat to one side. "When do them bastards ever need a reason but pure snake meanness? Hell, I didn't stick around to find out. I'm gonna take a glim at the NP up yonder." He waved a hand in the general direction of the Northern Pacific tracks that ran parallel to the river. "You kids can tag along if you want," he added doubtfully.

Philippa looked at Karl, but he was keeping his mouth shut. "Naw. We got some pals we got to meet up with."

The man shrugged. "Jake with me. I don't need nobody riding my coattails." He jammed his cloth cap down lower on his head and hurried on past them. They watched, shivering, as he sprinted across the street. The cold soaked in worse when you weren't moving. Another siren screamed in the distance.

"Aw, geez, Arlie. Let's go back and wait on Betts to come out," Karl announced, a mulish set to his chin. "I don't trust that lousy Wob. He'll lead her straight into the bulls. Junk and Chick and those guys can fend for themselves."

Stunned, Philippa turned on Karl. "We promised we'd meet 'em!" After all the care Chick had taken of her she couldn't run out on him. He didn't even know the kid had died.

"So what if we did?" Karl shifted, restless to be going, nerves and misery gone to impatience like milk went to clabber. "Bet they're heading for the hospital right now to track us down. Anyway, I ain't taking chances with Betts."

Philippa opened her mouth to chew him out, but thought better of it. She couldn't be in two places at once, and she didn't dare lose track of Simon, or Betts, if it came to that, seeing as how she still had the bracelet. "Well, OK. You go on then," she told him. "But I'm still gonna try and find the guys."

He grabbed her sleeve. "Don't be a dope!"

"I got to risk it, Karl. Don't you see?" She met his worried scowl. "We'll meet y'uns. How about that warehouse this side of the NP tracks behind the hospital? The one's got that big sign for Chesterfields painted on it?"

"Wish you wouldn't do this," he said. She waited and at last he nodded. "OK. I remember it. We'll try."

She thought a moment more. "And if things get too hot around St. Mike's, then we meet up east, across the river, far side of the NP yards, OK? Seeing as it's a different state, the cops ain't likely to be so riled." How they'd manage to get across the river was another thing entirely, but that could wait.

A banshee shriek started up what seemed like no more than twenty feet from them. They both slammed back against the bricks, then slid down again into the shelter of the garbage stand. It took the siren fading off to the west before Philippa figured out it'd been from the patrol car in front of the depot, the other side of a block of three-story brick buildings. Heading for the Great Northern rail yards, likely enough, but no threat to them.

"Sheesh! That was too darn close. I'm getting out of here." Wide-eyed and drawn, Karl stood cautiously.

Philippa followed him up, looking at him in despair. "Just one thing more, Karl. Don't go losing Simon."

Karl's pale eyes went to ice. He opened his mouth to talk back. Philippa couldn't afford to give him the chance. "Listen to me, Karl! Sure he's trouble and he gives me the willies too sometimes. But that don't matter. Number one, we promised to help him. And if you lose him so do I."

"Well, show some sense and come with me then!"

"Hush," she told him. "Number two, you recollect why he's got to get to St. Paul?"

Karl nodded impatiently.

"Right. So we get him there, and we got ourselves a chance to cross with him. Land of milk and honey, Karl. What Mara and them was saying the night of the fire—food, shelter, clothes. They don't lack for any of it." A place of safety, she thought but didn't say.

"Bunk," Karl said, but Philippa knew she had him hooked.

"Don't think so. Remember the bracelet."

Karl paused, doubt coming into his face. "Yeah... But what was Simon was saying about it? That maybe it ain't good for her after all?"

Philippa shrugged, feeling the resentment well up again. "She's alive, ain't she? And she looked fine to me. Anyways, I'll take it off her right soon." Soon as she figured out how.

"You promise not to lose him, Karl?"

Wearily he spat in his palm and held it out to her.

Philippa looked down at it. That was how boys sealed deals. With a twisted smile she copied him; shook his proffered hand firmly, palm to palm.

Karl managed a nod. "Don't do anything stupid," he said, and turned to go. She watched after him, hugging herself once more, rubbing the cooling spit absently off on her sleeve.

A crash from the rail yards behind them made Chick startle.

"Ain't nothing but another freight making up," Deucey whispered at his elbow. They were all of them lying flat in the weedy shadows of a row of blimp-like natural gas tanks, watching the road for trouble.

"I know it," Chick snapped, and swallowed back the bile that had come up to burn his throat. "I'm just jumpy." They'd been lucky and spotted the raiding party sweeping through the rail yards in time, but now they were stuck here in some sort of city maintenance yard. A deserted factory to the north looked to be prime territory for holing up, but before they'd got a chance to lam across the road to it, a couple of cop cars had pulled onto the grounds. Neither had come back out, and a line of sheds blocked most of their view of the place. Maybe the cops had drove out the other side, but maybe not.

Chick buried his head in his arms, trying to loosen his clenched, aching jaw. He couldn't bear lying here much longer with nothing to do but shiver and worry and feel again the jolt along his arms as he'd hit that kid. And what about Arlie and them wheeling that poor bastard down the road? What with the city swarming with cops, they'd've been picked up straight off.

He ought to've gone with them. That way he'd have been there to take the fall.

"Come on, guys! Let's go!" Nip said, pushing himself up. "We can't stay here, and we ain't seen anybody for the longest time." The kid was stretched tighter than a slingshot ready to let fly.

Junkyard smacked the boy between the shoulder blades. "Keep down, runt! I'm telling you it's a trap. I can smell it."

"Shh," Deucey breathed at the same moment. "I saw…" But he didn't need to say more. What he'd seen was sprinting across the road towards them. Arlie, the stupid kid! Relief and rage and worry propelled Chick to his knees.

"Get 'em, boys!" a man roared off to the right, and shots spattered like a string of firecrackers. Chick threw himself down again, seeing Arlie go down as well, blind panic on her face though he didn't think she was hit. She rolled and scrabbled across the rough pavement for the shelter of the tanks.

"What the hell'd you do that for?" Junkyard snarled as Chick, shaking and cursing, dragged her into the shadows. "We're peached!"

"No, we ain't," Deucey said, breathless, peering through the welded pipe of the tank stand. "They got other fish to fry. See there?" He pointed down the way to where a handful of guys in heavy coats were thudding after two kids running flat-out. A third kid was down in the street, curled up, hugging one leg.

Shot when he hadn't done nothing but run. As he watched the uneven chase a humming built up in Chick's ears so he could hardly hear the others talking.

"I'm sorry," Arlie gasped, beginning to catch her breath. "I seen Nip pop up. Didn't have no notion at all those creeps was there. But Lord a'mercy!" Chick met her eyes for a moment. They showed almost as round as marbles, he thought absently, seeing hurt come into them as he looked away.

"You sure looked funny when those gats went off. Blam! Blam!" Nip's muffled giggles had an hysterical edge. White showed all the way around his eyes.

Junk cuffed him again. "Shut it, runt."

"Arlie! Is there places to hide over yonder?" Deucey demanded. The kid nodded dumbly.

"Well, then, let's scram while they ain't watching." Deucey grabbed Nip by the coat sleeve and dragged the younger boy after him. The two them pelted across the road, Nip's free arm flailing as he scrambled to keep up.

Arlie stayed put, her terrified gaze on the cops. Impatient, Chick poked her. Nobody was getting left behind on his watch. He snapped, "Scoot, Arlie!"

Reluctantly she crawled up by Junkyard, who was ready to go. Chick crouched behind them.

One of the men skidded to a stop and squeezed off a careful shot, but if it hit anybody, Chick didn't see. The cop holstered his pistol, scowling, and turned back just as Junkyard left the shadows.

Junk dropped flat in the dry grass. "God damn them bulls to hell," he said through clenched teeth as he wriggled backwards into shelter. His face was white and screwed up with hate.

The cop had stopped to check on the kid lying in the road. Two more of them reappeared from the cross-street. The shorter of the two frog-marched a stocky kid toward the broad gap between the sheds that they'd driven through however long ago it was. Seemed like hours. None of them looked over at the tanks, for whatever that might mean.

"Two down," Junkyard muttered. More cops reappeared. A couple of them dragged the hurt kid up and persuaded him along after his buddy. The humming in Chick's ears got louder.

"Looks like the other guy got clean," Arlie said under her breath, soft and almost like a prayer.

Junkyard snarled, "Clean dead. You wanna bet? Baby-Face must've spun 'em a real fine yarn," The Chicago kid didn't take his eyes off the cops. "You didn't say yet, Arlie. You think they found that townie boy? He did croak, right?"

Chick froze, cold and sick, wishing he couldn't hear at all.

Arlie didn't look at him. "Yeah. But it ain't likely. We, we left him in the morgue at St. Mike's. Laid him out all proper with a sheet on him." She was rubbing her hand on her sleeve, slow and rough like trying to rid them of something foul.

Hot tears stung the corners of Chick's aching eyes, before they chilled to ice and stung another way. This whole thing was wrong.

Junkyard had turned from his vigil to stare at Arlie, grinning in amazement. "You didn't! Arlie, that is A-1!"

"Karl's idea," she said, not smiling back.

The cops and all had disappeared back into the factory grounds. They were back where they started, with no way to tell if the cops were watching. Dully Chick searched the shadows across the way for Deucey and Nip, but saw no sign of them.

"Deuce'll wait for us, won't he?" Arlie asked nervously.

"Christ, you tell us," Junk said. "Karl and Betts and old Simple Simon are over there, ain't they?"

"That's just it. They ain't." Awkwardly Arlie filled them in.

Chick shut his eyes, hardly listening. They were all busting apart, and it was his fault.

Junkyard scowled, outraged, when Arlie told them about the Chesterfield sign. "Why didn't you say so right off?"

"I meant to," the kid mumbled.

"Wasn't time," Chick found himself saying, though he wished to hell she had. "Not with the shooting. No point in arguing about it now." He crept up next to Junkyard, slow as an old man.

A sound brought his head up: a thunk, and then another. "Hush!" he hissed, though nobody was talking. Another thunk and another. Car doors slamming shut.

"They're leaving!" Arlie said, looking hopeful.

An engine roared to life and then a second. The shiny black hood of a patrol car nosed out into the street. Chick squinted, trying to count how many were in it, but the streetlight glazed the windshield. When the car turned into the street he saw what might have been somebody in the passenger seat, and that was all. The back window was too small to see anybody through. And he didn't have any more luck with the second car.

"For all we know they could've left half those guys behind," Junkyard grumbled.

Stubbornness twisted itself tight down inside Chick. He whispered, "I ain't waiting no longer." He slithered backwards until he was right at the edge of the tank shadow. Picking up a piece of gravel, he whanged it off an old lard bucket that sat on the step up to the maintenance shop's front office. The bucket teetered for a few seconds on the edge of the step, then fell rattling off into the driveway, sand and cigarette butts spilling from it, loud as if somebody had kicked it. He waited.

Nobody came out to investigate.

"Scram!" Junk cried, and launched himself across the empty street. Chick watched as Arlie sprinted after him, diving like a rabbit into the darkness on the other side. Too fed-up and hurting to run, Chick took up a bigger rock and paced between two of the tanks out into the light of the street lamp. Winding up, he let fly at the sheds.

A hollow, satisfying boom echoed down the street. Chick stood a minute longer, his teeth bared. When there was no response he slouched across the street.

Arlie yanked him in, looking scared and angry. He shrugged her off.

"Nip and Deucey. They ain't here," Junkyard said, worried.

"Could be they figured we'd meet up at St. Mike's. It'd make sense," Philippa said when they'd finished a more thorough search of the grounds.

Junkyard just grunted, but he strode right alongside her when she led the way back into town, trying to be careful, trying to stay calm though it seemed like there was never any end to worries.

Chick lagged behind, head down and hands jammed in his pockets, not keeping a lookout at all. It had to be on purpose, Philippa decided unhappily, what with those long legs of his. Felt like she was dragging a burden heavy as a cotton sack behind her.

He caught up reluctantly when they reached the warehouse. They walked the whole length of it. Nobody was there but a hunting cat that vanished under the loading dock at the far end when it saw them. Just to be sure, Philippa bent to peer into the darkness. Nobody. Not even the cat anymore.

"Car!" Junkyard sang out, and all three of them piled in under the dock out of the reach of the headlamps. They hunkered down far back among the weeds and trash and watched as it cruised by much too slow. Whoever was riding shotgun was playing a powerful flashlight beam over the buildings as they passed.

"Shacks?" Philippa wondered. It wasn't a patrol car, but some new-model Buick that gleamed a rich brown in the reflected light. But railroad dicks generally patrolled on foot.

Junkyard shrugged. "Smart money's on not finding out."

"Upstanding citizens, just helping out the po-lice," Chick said bitterly under his breath.

Philippa let her head droop, wishing she could just curl up there, cold as it was, and sleep until morning. "Guess we got to head across the river on our own then." Christ Jesus let Karl have got Simon and Betts over there already.

"Fat lot of good that'll do Nip and Deucey," Junkyard snapped. When the car's red taillights disappear around a corner several blocks away, he duck-walked out to the dock's edge, pausing with a hand braced on the splintery beam to look back.

"Wait for me. I'm gonna go poke around a little; see if I can track them down before we go."

"Jesus bless," Philippa muttered. If they had to move she'd as lief get it over with. But he was right to check.

A freight rattled loudly by, heading north maybe to Canada. When the sound of it had faded Philippa at last ventured a question. "You mad at me, Chick?"

It took him awhile to answer, but more as if he was coming back from a long ways off than that he was fighting back a temper. "Huh? What for?"

"Well, that kid. It wouldn't've happened without me. I didn't mean to get you in dutch."

Chick shifted irritably and his voice took on an edge. "That's baloney. Just leave me be, Arlie."

Hurt and the general awfulness of the night knotted up tight in Philippa's throat. Wet gathered in the corners of her eyes and her nose stopped up; began to run. She turned her head away and rested it on her knees, trying not to sniffle. The tears turned icy on her skin. She wiped them away.

"Aw, quit bawling, will you?" Chick hissed.

Her breath caught in a sob, and then it was too late to keep them back. She wrapped her arms around her head and tried to muffle the sound of them.

"Hell and damn!" If there was pain in Chick's voice as well as anger, Philippa couldn't tell. He scrambled toward the open air, bumping his head on a crossbeam, cursing. Once out he strode away.

Panic cut short her tears. She yelled his name, not caring who heard. Chick broke into a sore-footed run and disappeared around the corner of a building.

By the time Junkyard showed up—not long—Philippa had got herself under control; had let the cold and night soak down inside her so as to steady up her spine.

Junk was breathless. "What happened? Where's Chick?"

"He run off." Philippa waved a hand toward the southwest and the downtown streets. "Got mad and left." Standing, she found herself lightheaded but calm as an icebound lake.

"Oh." Junkyard scowled at her. "Christ. Well, there's no help for it. After all that racket we gotta move." He led the way south, parallel to the NP tracks but hugging the buildings to keep out of the light.

"Don't guess you looked close at that Chesterfield sign," he said when they stopped to wait for a sedan and a bunch of folks hugging and loading baggage and the like to clear out from in front of the Northern Pacific depot.

Somebody's family, she guessed. A baby commenced wailing. "No," she said.

"I was looking at it when I head you yell. Somebody's scratched 'HOT' under it, real big, with a piece of coal. And then what looked like 'K-B-S-D-N.'"

Philippa nodded, gulping air. Wetness stung her eyes again, but that was surely just from the cold.

Junkyard waited a minute. The last of the sedan doors slammed shut. "Don't get all worked up about it," he said at last, much put out. He yanked his cap down lower on his forehead and turned his back on her. "Christ."

They hid out in a clump of junipers a good ways back from where the Northern Pacific tracks took the long curve before crossing the river to Minnesota. Uniformed cops with flashlights and clubs was making the rounds of the more usual places to wait.

"Damn Cossacks beating the bushes tonight," Junkyard muttered, but not like he was talking to her. He sat huddled up, smoking a cig he'd rolled, shielding the glow with his hand.

Philippa half dozed as she lay curled on the scratchy litter from the bushes. A red ball thundered past, slowing just enough to make the curve, and then a passenger heading the wrong way for them, puffing up to the depot. The cops rousted a couple of stiffs, marching them away with their hands on their heads.

It was while she was watching them that Junkyard poked her. He jerked a thumb back the way they'd come, where smoke billowed straight up into the night, pale against the starry black: a freight waiting on the passenger to go by. It wouldn't have time to build up a killing speed by the time it reached them.

Hopeful and scared, Philippa got ready, retying her bootlaces with stiff fingers. Then she curled up again to wait. Icy minutes crept by while the passenger train sat hissing at the station platform. A couple of shacks patrolled alongside it, checking the rods underneath.

And then its whistle screamed and the wheels started turning. Philippa sat up, settling her cap down snug over her ears. Soon enough all they could see of the passenger were the faint green lights on the tail end. A few minutes after that the freight's whistle blew, and they heard the puff and rattle of its approach. The cops and shacks were still out, swinging their flashlight beams here and there.

"Think they'll shoot?" she asked, and then was ashamed.

Junkyard spat. "Naw. Might hit the crew."

They stayed put until the engine and tender passed, then dashed for it. Somebody yelled and took out after them. Philippa ran faster, ignoring the pain from her boots, praying there'd be no switch to trip her up. A hundred other boes were running for the train too, swarming like locusts out of the dark.

A woman shrieked, in frustrated rage as much as fear, and men shouted. A gunshot tore through the other sounds, but only one, and no bullet whined past her ears. Ahead wildly jerking light from a flashlight showed up five boes going flat out —one beanpole tall, one little, three middling, and one of these last wore a skirt and pink sweater.

Relieved but too out of breath to yell after them, Philippa dodged under a bull's arm and pounded alongside the thundering train. Junkyard nailed the boxcar ahead of her. A ladder brushed her hand and she grabbed hold, snatching up her feet and hanging on for dear life, cut palm stinging as she banged hard against the side. Then she was flying, the cold, smoky wind pulling at her skin. She began to climb.

23

When the rails began singing, Chick was already halfway across the trestle, a pair of frustrated bulls shouting after him from the North Dakota side of the river. Likely figuring nobody'd be fool enough to try to cross that way, they'd been having a smoke down in the shelter of a clump of bushes, and hadn't spotted him until he was too far out to follow.

"Chumps," he'd muttered, his long strides spanning two ties at a time. Then unease soaked up through the thin soles of his boots with the beginning of the faint vibration. Chick stopped dead, twisting around to look over his shoulder, and there it was, glaring bright, a half-mile back and coming fast.

Panic slammed his legs into gear and he started running for the far side, stumbling over the ties now he couldn't take time to gauge his steps. He didn't dare glance behind, but the train whistle shrieked a warning and the hum grew to a heavy rumbling. Light from the train's headlamp spilled across the tracks ahead, and he knew he wasn't going to make it that way. He dived for the side, squeezing through a gap in the girders, wedging himself in as far to the outside as he dared. He hung on with clawed fingertips as the passenger train thundered past inches from his nose, shaking him so hard his grip began to slip.

And then it was gone, the smoke and rumbling fading. Knees weak, Chick slumped against a girder, his arms wrapped tight around it. What in the holy hell had he been thinking, coming across a trestle as long as this one? Trains had a straight shot at this bridge, with nothing to slow them, not like the NP crossing to the north a ways. But there'd been too many bulls swarming around that one, and stiffs hiding in every shadow, maybe some of whom he knew.

Tempting fate was what he'd been doing. Giving it a chance to kill him if it cared to. A shiver went through him, bone-deep, and he hugged the icy girder harder still.

He wasn't out of trouble yet. Leaning in a little, Chick looked down the tracks to the Minnesota side. Not far. He'd better hustle before another train came along. But hard as he tried he couldn't make himself loosen his hold, couldn't take the short step back down to the tracks. Cursing his cowardice and stupidity, he peered down over the edge into the darkness. Shadowy riverbank lay what seemed like a hundred feet below him.

"Can't be that far down," he told himself, his throat sour with sickness. Shakily he started working his way back along the outside of the girders toward the pier at the water's edge. Light from another train flashed in the corner of his eye as he dangled, kicking over the darkness for an endless moment before his feet found a crossbeam. Gasping, he let himself down to the top of the ladder-like framework built around the massive stone pier. Some kind of flood protection, he guessed, and thank Christ for it. Still he held on tight and waited while the second train pounded by fifteen feet above his head. Only when it was gone did he climb the rest of the way down.

"Holy Jesus, lad, we thought you was a goner," someone said behind him as his foot touched ground.

Chick whirled around, staggering at the uneven footing.

A big man stepped out of the shadow of the bridge, ragged and whiskered. There were other guys behind him in the darkness. "Candler Joe," the man said gravely, a wheeze to his deep voice. "Candy, they call me. Mutt and Hortie and me's jungled up a little ways down the riverbank from here. Why don't you come take a load off and tell us what chased you out on that trestle in the middle of the night?"

Gravel scraped as somebody sat hesitantly down beside her. Philippa opened her eyes, squinting against the morning sun. She'd been trying to catch some shuteye but, tired as she was, her mind wouldn't slow.

Simon settled back against the remains of the foundation wall that kept the breeze off them, then sat up again right quick as the cold of the concrete soaked through that fine coat of his. He hugged the coat closer, ground-in soot and dirt showing in the creases of his knuckles. Like hers, Philippa thought, pulling her hands from her pockets to look at them. Only his weren't cracked and sore from the cold. Bet his cuts were clean gone by now, too. Hers wasn't. Damn bracelet.

"Soon we go?" Simon's tone was low and even, but impatience seethed beneath it, barely held in check.

She jammed her hands back where they'd be warm. "When Chick comes," she snapped, a little too loud.

Simon's dark hawk's eyes fixed on her. "Yes. Where after?"

"So just how long are we gonna hang around waiting on that bozo anyway?" Betts demanded hoarsely, before Philippa had a chance to speak. Karl lay snoring with his head resting in the older girl's lap, and she looked fed up with it and lots else besides.

"Long as we need to!" Philippa shot back. "He'll show." She sat up. The breeze caught the bare back of her neck, and she shivered. No real weather behind it though, just the unsettled out-breath of the miles of raw fields, north and east and west, giving up the rain they'd so recently soaked up.

Junkyard, who'd been dozing, tipped up his cap to show one narrowed blue eye. "Maybe not, Arlie. Like I told you, I asked all the stiffs I came across, and nobody's glimmed him."

Dread and stubbornness kept Philippa from answering. Beside her Simon folded up, hugging his knees now, wound tighter than a clock spring.

"Guy probably just found himself another sweet daddy," Betts said peevishly, her face pale and pinched. She squirmed on the hard ground, and Karl's head slid to one side. Absently Betts cradled it closer. A dark spot showed on her skirt from him drooling. Last night on his way back to wait at the hospital he'd swiped a bottle off a dead-to-the-world drunk. He was still sleeping it off. It was a wonder he'd managed to nail that freight, but Jesus looked after drunks and fools.

"Chick ain't no goddamn fruiter!" Junkyard had rolled over to glare at Betts. "That old wolf just had him all turned around, see, and he was getting wise to it before this mess happened. So just shut up about it."

"All right, all right!" Impatient, Betts pushed her wind-tangled hair back with one hand, the Wob bracelet peeping from the cuff of her sweater. "Whatever you say, Junk! But we can't afford to sit here for days waiting on the guy, even with a state line between us and the Dakota cops."

She'd've been dead by now, Philippa reminded herself, eyeing the wrist, trying for the charity Meemaw had put so much stock in. Betts would've been cold and limp and empty like that townie boy when they'd left him laid out in the morgue. Alive and loud-mouthed was a sight better than that.

Soon as she could concentrate on it, though, she ought to try to get the bracelet back. See if she could figure out just what Simon had meant about it being bad for girls—assuming he hadn't just been talking through his hat.

Truth be told, though, Betts didn't look as fixed-up as Philippa had figured she would by now.

Nip shifted uneasily where he sat on the wall. "Maybe he got pinched, Arlie. Maybe that's why he ain't shown up." A helpless fear hung around the kid like the smell of sickness, and had ever since last night's fight.

But she was scared too, even if she did feel years older than him. That was as much the cause of the gnawing in her middle as being hungry. A lot easier to think about the bracelet. Philippa drew a harsh breath. "If he did then I got to go back. I got to speak up for him."

She didn't want to say that. She sure didn't want to do it—

give up a chance at Mara's paradise and go to jail instead? Or worse, get sent back to the farm, and Hank.

That thought made her dizzy. She'd run away again. She'd take a pitchfork to Hank if she had to. But whatever it took she'd pay her debts, no matter what Simon might say of her.

"Speak for who?" Deucey asked from the far side of the wall. Startled, Philippa craned her head back to look up at him.

"Where you been?" Junkyard asked.

"Pennying up." Deucey held up a crumpled paper sack, dark in spots with grease. "Ain't much. Toppings and a couple of baloney butts." He handed over the sack and Junkyard, muttering happily, set to divvying up the food. Watching, Philippa swallowed back the spit that flooded her mouth. Even Simon loosened up enough to show interest, though Betts waved off the chunk of baloney Junkyard tried to hand her.

Deucey vaulted the wall, a rolled-up newspaper tucked under his free arm. He took a seat on a more broke-down stretch of wall. "Speak up for who, Arlie?"

She tore her eyes from the food. "Chick," she said after a moment, the fear returning. "If he got himself pinched. You didn't see no sign of him?"

"Naw," he said. "Not hide nor hair. But I don't figure it was him they got." He held out the newspaper.

Her hands gone shaky, Philippa took it—today's Grand Forks Herald. When she had it opened out he bent over and poked a finger at a piece near the bottom of the front page.

"Attack On Local Youths," she read out, and felt the others still to listen. A curl of breeze caught the pages, flapping them as she went on.

It had been a gang of vagrants, the Herald claimed, with robbery the likely motive. One boy was missing, reported dead by his companions. The authorities were searching for his body. Police and deputized citizens had made a number of arrests during the night at the rail yards, including two who'd been identified as members of the gang, one of them injured while resisting arrest.

"Dirty rotten liars," Nip said without much force. A desolate relief settled over Philippa as the kid took the paper from her and laid it out on the ground to go through it himself.

"That was those two poor bastards we saw 'em catch, betcha." Junkyard rapped the page with a greasy hand. He sighed. "Chick just ain't coming."

He didn't say a thing about how it was her fault, how if she'd been able to take care of herself in the first place, or at least hadn't gone and sniveled like a girl, Chick would likely be here now. Philippa hung her head, hearing the words anyway, heavy in the silence that fell over them.

Deucey took the chunk of baloney Nip handed on to him. "There's a freight headed southeast that's making up right now," he told them, his mouth full.

Betts roused Karl, who groaned when he sat up, holding his head. The stale crumbs of meat and bread Philippa had eaten worked uneasily in her gut. She couldn't think of any good argument for staying.

Simon unfolded himself and stood, tense as a cat ready to pounce. "Where?"

Junkyard glanced at Philippa, then wiped his mouth off on his sleeve. "St. Paul, right, Deucey?" he growled. "So give it a rest, will you, Simple?"

Hastily swallowing the last bite of his fried egg sandwich, Chick snatched up the croker sack and hurried after the older men. "You sure that driver fellow knows what he's talking about?"

The four of them—Chick, Candler Joe, Mutt, and Hortie—had spent the last hour unloading flour and canned goods and the like off a flatbed truck. The breakfast sandwiches, cooked up by the grocer's wife, had been their pay, along with a few half-full sacks of battered foodstuffs. Only one sandwich apiece when Chick could've eaten five without noticing, not to mention that he was pretty sure the sack he'd been handed held nothing but undersized potatoes. Still the aftertaste of yolk and bacon grease lingered rich in his mouth.

The men had been planning to flip a freight going south, which had sounded swell to Chick, but after talking to the truck driver Hortie and Candy were all fired up about heading to International Falls or some such godforsaken town up on the border. Seemed some big company was hiring mill hands. Mutt hadn't said yea or nay, but so far as Chick could tell he hardly ever said anything at all.

"The guy swore his brother-in-law got took on just yesterday," Hortie told Chick over his shoulder. "Called all that way to give him the news!"

Getting to International Falls meant, first of all, hiking north across most of East Grand Forks to the NP tracks. The Goat Road didn't go up that way. Not much chance of running into anybody, even so. After the trouble across the river there were bound to be swarms of stiffs there fixing to beat their way out of town, but given his druthers Chick wouldn't have gone anywhere near those yards.

Candy slowed to let him catch up. "Worth a try, ain't it, lad?" he rumbled, his blue eyes kind, and maybe more than that. A touch of warmth bloomed in Chick's belly, reluctant as he was to feel it. "Roof over our heads for the winter," the big man was saying. "Food in our bellies." One eye closed in a lazy wink. "Good pals for company."

That's family; that's home. The words whispered in Chick's memory, making him shiver. He'd said something like that not long ago, but when?

The night of the fire. Chick stumbled on a pothole, smoke and flames and screaming filling his mind until someone's strong hand—Candy's—caught him by the elbow.

"You OK?"

Chick blinked, grief like a rock inside him. "Sure. Yeah, Candy, I'm jake." So many dead, and now one of them at his own hand. "I was just remembering stuff."

Candy let go of him gently enough, though his face hardened. "Better give that up, lad. The past don't buy no groceries." He lengthened his stride, head down, the slight wheeze in his breathing growing harsher as he pulled ahead.

Chick watched the big man, wanting to reach out to him in return. Bad lungs and bad memories: another old doughboy, it could be, though Christ knew there was plenty of things other than mustard gas could wreck a guy's lungs.

Soldiers got used to being killers. But in wartime they called you a hero, whatever a guy might think of it himself.

When they got to it, they found the rail yard itself was off-limits, patrolled by hard-eyed men with brake clubs and a few rifles. Eastward along the right-of-way was crowded with knots of men eager for a train slow enough to flip.

"Get outta town before dark," a man told them, shrugging, "and nobody'll bother you. Anyway, that's what they're saying."

"You'd think they'd let guys on before the drag gets moving if they was so hot to be rid of us," Hortie grumbled under his breath as they went on. The freight they wanted wouldn't be along until early afternoon, so there was no point in waiting with the crowd.

Candy slapped him on the back, grinning, his ghosts banished. "Ain't the way the game is played, friend Hortie."

Chick kept his eyes peeled but he saw no sign of Arlie and the others. They must not have waited long, he decided at last, a sense of self-righteous betrayal overtaking his wariness.

"Somebody hunting you?" Candy asked quietly, laying a hand on Chick's shoulder as they picked their way past a lost-looking family. "Or you hunting them?"

Not looking at him, Chick shrugged under the weight of his grip, comforting and confining at once. "Nobody that matters."

"Glad to hear it."

They fetched up at a small fire some folks had risked starting. A No. 10 can steamed in the middle of the coals, smelling a bit like coffee. Squatting on his heels, Mutt handed out a squashed loaf of bread from his sack to muttered thanks.

Restless, Chick took out his jackknife and the carving of an old man he'd started that morning by the river. A careless stroke took off half the nose, and he tossed it on the fire. Disgusted, he left his sack in Candy's care and wandered up the tracks, looking for coal that might've fallen from a tender, but eyeing the folks he passed as well. On his first go-round he found a few bits. He dropped them by the pinched-face woman tending the flames when he got back.

Candy nodded to him but said nothing. Chick felt the man's gaze following him as he walked on, hunched into his jacket. This time he had a harder time keeping his eyes on the ground. If there was any coal left to find he didn't see it. A few guys gave him the fish-eye as he went by, like they thought he might be a heavyfoot come to spy.

"No luck?" Candy called as Chick neared the fire again, empty-handed. Uncertainty wrinkled the corners of the man's eyes.

Chick shrugged. "Nothing," he yelled back over the growing rumble of another train. He didn't bother looking around to see it. There'd be plenty more before theirs came along.

Ahead three men paused in crossing the tracks to stare at the approaching freight, then scattered as the whistle blew three angry blasts. The engine and tender thudded by Chick, the engineer scowling from the side window at having to slow.

Up ahead by the fire Candy patted the bare dirt beside him in invitation. Chick's legs ached, but he couldn't rest yet.

"Chick!" The shriek came from behind him, almost lost in the racket of the train. He whirled around.

Arlie was crouched in the open door of a boxcar, mouth still open and her face as naked of defenses as a new-hatched bird. Deucey's head popped out above hers. The piebald boy squinted at him doubtfully.

Chick gaped while the boxcar gained on him and the raw look on Arlie's face closed in on itself. Giving up on him.

Then he was running alongside the train, trying to build up speed to match it, and thank Christ those guys on the tracks had kept that engineer from balling the jack. He passed the campfire, snatching his croker sack from Candy's outstretched hand, catching a glimpse of the man's wry mouth as he took it. But hands were reaching for him from the boxcar. He slung the sack inside and grabbed for them, feeling the hard slap of flesh as somebody took hold, pulling him along, pulling him up. His foot snagged, and suddenly he was down and dragging, boots bouncing off the tie ends as he tried desperately to kick high enough to find the step.

A hand seized the waistband of his pants, and then he was

up, lying on his belly on the gritty floorboards. He lay there gasping like a beached fish for a long moment, eyes stinging and a laugh bubbling up inside.

At last he rolled over to see Arlie and Junkyard and Deucey staring down at him. He grinned. "Hell, that's hard on shoe leather!"

Part Three

24

Philippa steadied herself with one hand on the boxcar wall, fighting a fierce urge to knock the lopsided grin off Chick's face. Kick him hard in the ribs, maybe. Sometimes he leaned just a little too hard on that charm of his.

The grin faded some. "Am I glad you guys yelled," Chick said, a trace of pleading in his eyes.

She couldn't find any words to answer him with. After a long, wary moment a young guy with bad teeth who sat nearby spoke up instead. "That was a close call, brother!"

Junkyard reached down to pull Chick up off the scored planks of the floor. "I half wore out my shoes looking for you, Chick. I oughta paste you good."

Chick settled himself Indian-fashion. Though he'd cleaned up a little since the fight, he still looked haunted. Philippa's spurt of anger died away. But even when Junkyard and Deucey dropped down to sit by Chick, and Nip scooted closer, she kept her place by the open door. Simon stayed put as well, watching sleepily from the stretch of wall they'd claimed. Karl sat there too, his head in his hands, paying attention to nothing and nobody. Beside him but not touching, Betts lay curled up tight like her belly was hurting.

Chick's gaze had strayed to Philippa, but soon slipped down to stare far across the brown fields. "Met up with some boes under a bridge," he told them. "Just sort of stuck with 'em. I looked for y'all when we hit the yards, but didn't see nothing."

He stopped for a moment, his head hung low. "Figured y'all might be better off without me anyways."

Junkyard whacked the side of his head, hard. "Chump." Deucey's narrowed eyes and silence echoed Junk's opinion.

"But how'd you get across the river?" Nip asked. "Cops had the place sewn up."

Chick shrugged like it didn't matter. "Walked across the GN trestle."

At that Philippa gave up her post by the door and stalked toward him, swaying with the car's motion. "You did what!" she found herself yelling. "Jesus bless, Chick, you oughtn't to be let out without a leash."

Chick met her gaze head-on, the weary grief in his eyes and around his mouth changing not a whit. "Guess I wasn't thinking."

Guess maybe getting killed was exactly what he was after, she thought, smoldering. Whether he'd own it or not.

Well, and maybe she couldn't entirely blame him for that. When the anger drained away, her legs folded up beneath her like being riled had been the only thing holding her up. "Well, leastways you're here now," she said, sitting down hard. "But try not to do anything that dumb again, huh, Chick?"

A ghost of a smile twitched the side of his mouth, though it didn't touch his eyes. He nodded.

Junkyard snorted. "Christ. We can always hope."

Chick looked restlessly around the crowded boxcar, looking for the others, Philippa guessed. He blinked when he saw Betts sit up, pushing her hair back from her face. "Geez, Arlie, she looks a lot better than the last time I seen her." Philippa warmed at the praise, though Betts still looked peaked to her.

Junkyard had twisted around to leer at the fretful girl. "Yeah, don't that dame knock yer eye out? I'd like to have a go at her some time."

The crude words knocked all the feeling from Philippa's body but a dull crawling tingle under her skin. The pounding of the boxcar roared in her ears. For a second another face took the place of Junkyard's, too familiar and years older, with eyes that told a body they were nothing but a thing to be used.

"Lay off," Deucey said, his harsh words a lifeline though he wasn't looking Philippa's way. "Betts is Karl's girl."

"Oooh, Deucey!" Junkyard turned on him. "Don't tell me you're sweet on her too!" He whistled a mocking snatch of tune and lay back, arms crossed under his head. Deucey didn't answer.

It was just nightmares haunting her, Philippa told herself, watching them distantly. Old nightmares. And hateful as Junkyard had been, he hadn't held back on account of a girl listening in.

But she *was* a girl. She could fool folks most all the time into thinking she wasn't, particularly if the gang stuck by her. But she'd be thirteen in a couple weeks, getting older every day and her body changing to be more like Betts' was.

Unless maybe the bracelet—the iyar of a boy—could change her. Stop her monthlies. Change her voice. Maybe even stop her breasts from growing. The hope, unlikely as it was, brought feeling back to her limbs and breath into her starving lungs. Experimentally she flexed stiff hands. For Betts' own sake as well as her own, she'd have to try to take the thing back soon.

She looked around at all the weary faces. Not here, though. Not...

A gust of stale air swirled in through the open door. Shocked, she coughed out the breath she'd taken. The stuff smelt dead as the air in one of them Egyptian tombs might've done. Dread prickling down her spine, Philippa turned wide-eyed to the door just as a burly guy, muttering a curse on engine smoke, heaved the door closed and plunged the boxcar into twilight. She opened her mouth to protest being shut in with the bad air, but then from one breath to the next it was gone. Tense, she waited.

For awhile nobody said much but the card players grousing about how they couldn't hardly see their hands. After a bit the kid with the bad teeth spoke into the rattling quiet. "How'd the rest of you fellows get across?"

"Nailed a freight with must've been a couple hundred other guys," Junkyard said, yawning. "Couldn't stop us all."

"You know they had a roadblock on the DeMers bridge until eight this morning? And even after that they was keeping an eye on it. I stowed away in the back of a truck is how I got across." He sounded kind of forlorn.

"Wasn't so much to that roadblock. They shook us down and told us to git," said a raspy voice a little further off. "Glad to see us go, they was." Though her eyes had got used to the dimness, Philippa didn't look his way. Her nerves still strained to catch any new whiff of bad air.

"It was young guys like me they was looking for," retorted Bad Teeth. "They pinched a couple of my pals is how I know. Right after the raid on the Great Northern yards. Shot at us, and I mean _at_ us. Brothers, I tell you I flew!"

Paying attention now, Philippa pushed herself upright with a hand to either side. Beside her Chick had stiffened.

Junkyard sat up too, slow and easy. His face didn't change at all, but for a watchful look that came into his eyes. "Either of your pals get hit? Story in the Herald says a guy they pinched last night near the yards was 'injured resisting arrest.' Says he and another guy they hauled in was members of a gang that jumped some local kids. Killed one of 'em." He pulled the folded front section of the newspaper out of his pocket. Betts had the rest of it layered under her sweater for warmth.

"Killed somebody?" squeaked Bad Teeth, paling. He held out his hand and Junkyard dropped the paper in it. "Don't know nothing about that."

None of them said a thing while he was bent close over the small print, straining to read in the poor light. Up near the front a man threw down a hand of cards and cackled, "Three queens! Pay up, Charley."

"'Identified as gang members!'" Bad Teeth read out in disbelief. "Well, if it's Porky and Notion they're talking about, they're lying fit to beat the band, the lousy bastards. Probably killed that kid themselves."

Deucey cleared his throat uneasily. "Blame us for everything. Nothing new in that."

"Maybe it ain't your pals they's talking about," Philippa offered, though from what they'd seen the night before, it was almost sure to be. Made her sick to think of it.

"Oh Christ, I hope not." Bad Teeth tossed the paper on the floor and put his head in his hands.

Chick reached out to snag the front page. Scooting close to the streak of light that came in from where the door wasn't quite pulled to, he began to read.

"Hey, Arlie. You asleep?" Chick said into the darkness, just loud enough to be heard over the steady clicking of the iron wheels on the tracks beneath them.

The kid jerked beside him. After a moment she answered, stuttering a little with the cold. "N-naw. Too hungry."

Chick felt for the mouth of the croker sack under his cheek, and dug out a potato. They weren't none of them much bigger than a pocket watch, and a little soft besides, but food was food. "Chew on one of these," he told her, cautiously feeling for her arm, not wanting to spook her. Cold as it was, she'd curled up on her own.

Sure enough, he could feel her shivering. Arlie's hand found his, closed it tight around the potato and pushed it back toward him. "No thanks. C-can't stomach 'em raw."

Chick stowed it back in the sack. He listened for awhile to the other sounds, the snoring and some guy near the back of the car whose endless hacking coughs made him cringe, and underneath it all the train. At last he spoke out of his wandering thoughts. "You dead set on going to that place Simon and them come from?"

Arlie's breath caught. "Yeah. I got to, Chick!" she told him fiercely. "I just got to."

He frowned, baffled. Even if things were better there, what little he'd picked up from Simon about it didn't make it sound like any kind of home he'd want. "How come?" he asked. Of course, the kid was convinced that Mara had gone back there. That could be part of it. It'd been clear as daylight Arlie'd fallen for the bossy girl in a big way, even if she was maybe too young to know what was what.

It was a long moment before she answered him, and even then the words were halting. "There you can say no, and nobody'll push you. Mara said so." Chick frowned, not understanding. Arlie shifted restlessly, something—an elbow maybe—brushing his arm. "And anyways, there ain't no place here for us, Chick. Nobody wants us, any of us. Lessen they want to hurt us, or for us to take the blame for stuff," she added bitterly.

A lump settled in his throat, making it hard to breathe. Unsteadily Chick asked, "You figure those guys they pinched is gonna fry for what we done?" If they did, that'd be three guys he'd good as killed, not just one. That fear had been eating at him for hours.

"Jesus bless, Chick, I hope not!" She added, "I can't see Baby-face fingering any of 'em for the killing itself. He saw us clear enough, and it's us he wants, don't you figure?"

Maybe. And maybe not. "I been thinking about going back," he whispered, an answer of a sort. That pal of theirs had gone back, or at least Chick guessed he had. He'd dropped off the train without a word the first time they'd stopped for water.

"Yeah," Arlie breathed after a bit. "Me too. Can't get myself to do it. Guess that makes me yellow."

Deucey, huddled up next to Chick, spoke into his ear. "Can't hang nobody without they got a body. And when they do find it, it's gonna be pretty clear those kids couldn't've had nothing to do with putting it there. For whatever that's worth."

"What I say," growled Junkyard from the far side of Deucey, "is that it was pure and simple self-defense, and I'm sick to death of all this mooning around and jawing it over."

Hell, thought Chick, his face heating, is everybody listening?

Junkyard wasn't done. "See, it ain't us lying about what happened, and us going back won't stop those mugs from lying. So we just stay the hell out of North Dakota. It's simple. Shut up and go the hell to sleep."

Nobody said anything after that. Chick lay awake awhile longer thinking about it, but the knot inside him had eased.

The train wailed its warning once again, a mournful sound like that of the ceremonial *kuakuatl*, the conch shell trumpet. Simon broke into a run, clutching his capful of ash-baked potatoes to his chest. Bare branches whipped his face and hands as he burst through a thicket, but he did not slow.

"Leave the damn fire, Deuce, Arlie!" Karl yelled behind him. "You guys want to get left?"

Simon ran faster, grateful for the daylight. He would not be left; he could not bear that. Ahead of him wanderers swarmed into the open boxcars while the train workers, greatly outnumbered, ignored them.

Couplings clanged with the strain being put on them, and the big metal wheels started slowly to turn. Gasping, Simon scrambled up the embankment, finding Chick and Betts by his side. Chick vaulted into the waist-high opening and turned to pull the young woman up. Simon gave her a boost. Then, less sure of himself, he used the step, grabbing with one hand for the doorpost. Holding the cap made him awkward, though, and his leg got tangled in his coat when he raised it to climb inside.

"C'mon, Simple!" Junkyard cried from behind him, "Quit blocking the door!" Hands launched Simon upwards. He landed badly, on a knee and both elbows, spilling the potatoes across the floor.

Desperate, Simon kicked himself forward, arms out to corral as many as he could. Several rolled past his reach. Whooping, a couple of old men piled onto them. A third man grabbed for ones within the circle of his arms. Hissing in sudden, blinding rage, Simon caught the man's hand, twisting it under.

"Mitts off!" Junkyard roared, and suddenly they were all gathered around Simon, his own band of wanderers. Power filled him, sweet and just. So easy to press a little further, snap the wrist bones, teach this one at least not to steal from them.

"OK, OK, I give!" The man squealed as Simon's hands tightened. "Lemme go! I won't do it no more!" he babbled.

Stunned by what he had almost done, Simon let go. The man scuttled back out of reach, rubbing the wrist. "Can't blame a stiff for trying," he mumbled, his hungry eyes downcast. The first two men were crouched at the back of the swaying boxcar, stuffing potato into their mouths as fast as they could manage. Everyone watched, even those who had food of their own.

"Sheesh," Nip said, dragging a sleeve across his mouth.

"Close call," Chick agreed. He held up his coarse brown bag. "I got most of the rest of em' here, all I could find in the ashes."

Arlie laid a couple more before Simon's nose. "Deuce and me found these ones when we was smothering the fire."

"They ain't getting any doner." Betts took the bag from Chick and shakily poured its contents out to join Simon's cache. The young woman had eaten nothing yesterday. It had worried him, though the responsibility for her disordered system wasn't his.

"Let's divvy them up," she said. "I'm starving."

Getting to his knees, Simon found one more smashed into the gritty floorboards. He stared at it, feeling a baffled shame.

"Yeah," Karl told him cheerfully, biting into the first of his share. "It's a sad day when a guy finds himself fighting over spuds." He looked at his potato. "Especially undercooked ones."

Simon looked at him, then got up, leaving both the smashed potato and the small heap that was his portion. He would fast. He often went without food in the Five Empty Days that preceded each turning of the year. Hunger would remind him to curb his temper. Legs wide to keep himself from falling, he picked two of the potatoes from his pile. "You share," he told them, motioning to the rest. "I do not eat."

He turned away from their wide-mouthed surprise. When he knelt before the man whose wrist he'd almost broken, the man tried to scoot away from him until Simon held out the potatoes.

Cross-legged in the open boxcar door beside Betts, who was mending Karl's jacket, Philippa chewed cold potato. She still had a few left. Simon's fit of virtue that morning had taken the edge off her appetite, but she was just as glad to have them now.

The freight rattled southeast through early afternoon at what she judged to be a steady thirty miles an hour. Not much to see, nothing but farm towns, bare fields out to the edge of a clear blue sky, and lately the occasional glitter of water from wide stretches of mud-choked marsh. The sun felt good though.

Betts tugged a needle through the edges of a torn seam, Lukas' iyar whatever showing bone-white under the grimy pink of her sweater cuff. "See, kid, it ain't like I don't appreciate you sneaking in the hospital to tie this charm bracelet on me. Karl swears it saved my life." The corner of her mouth curled in a skeptical smile. "But you mind showing me how to get it off?"

Nettled, Philippa took a moment to bridle her tongue. "So how you feeling? Yesterday looked like your gut was giving you hell."

Betts' smile died. "Cramps. Bad ones." Her hands tightened on the cloth. "Seems I lost a baby," she whispered hoarsely.

Philippa's mouth went dry. "When? At the hospital?"

Betts flicked a glance at her. "When I woke from the fever breaking. Monday, I guess it was." Her voice hardened. "Hey, don't look like that, kid. What do I need with a lousy baby?"

"Guess so," Philippa mumbled. Numb, she leaned sideways to let Simon edge past. He stuck his head out, peering into the wind and smoke of the freight's passage.

Eyeing him suspiciously, Betts bent close to Philippa's ear. "Don't say nothing to Karl, OK?" she rasped.

Wide-eyed, Philippa nodded. "Cross my…"

A sudden side gust rocked the car. Stale-tasting air, with something nose-prickling, like scorched pepper. Frozen, Philippa watched the twisting dust trail the gust raised across the barren field. Same as yesterday—here and gone again. Something bad wrong with these cats-paws of wind.

Hanging tight to the doorpost, Simon squatted down by her. "Arlie. I have question."

Hastily bundling her mending, Betts got up. Philippa caught her as she rose. "I won't say nothing." The girl gave her hand a squeeze before she slipped free.

Simon looked after Betts. His brown skin seemed stretched tight as a drum over the bones of his face. "She is OK?"

Philippa shifted uneasily. "Getting better." Simon opened his mouth, fixing to lecture her, so she hurried on. "And 'fore you say nothing, I plan to take it off her, soon's I get me a chance. So what's your question?" When he looked down his nose, she snapped, "Can't do it with all these people about, can I?"

After a look over his shoulder, he gave a reluctant nod. After a bit he said, "We in St. Paul tonight, yes? I hear so."

"Late. If we're lucky."

Simon nodded again. "This is good. But I ask, is possible to pass in darkness and not know?"

His question startled a bark of laughter from Philippa. "Pass St. Paul? Heck, Simon, it's ten times the size of Grand Forks!" Karl and Betts and some of the others turned to look at her.

Simon looked offended. "I do not know!"

That worried her. "Look, Simon, you know where this place of yours is, don't you?"

He looked at her, his hawk's face wary. "In a warehouse, by the lake."

Her stomach clenched. Maybe he just didn't want anybody else to know? "OK, you don't got to tell me if you don't want to. But they's hundreds of warehouses in St. Paul, and I wouldn't be a bit surprised if they's a few lakes as well, being as this is Minnesota. You got some way of finding the right one, ain't you?"

He looked away, his face impassive. "This is not a worry for you."

"Not a worry?" she yelled, scrambling to her feet. "You been begging for days for us'ns to get you to St. Paul, and it's all for nothing?"

"Hey, what's he saying, Arlie?" Karl demanded, getting to his knees. "Has he been blowing smoke?"

"No smoke, Karl," Simon insisted. "No smoke. You take me there and I thanks you. But you can not follow. *She* can," he said, nodding at Betts, who looked wary. "If we say yes. She has the iyar pukko. Without you can not cross."

Chick was listening; Deucey and Betts were too. Even the old guy with the straggly mustache who was playing checkers with Nip was listening in a baffled kind of way.

"What the hell's the Wob talking about me for?" Betts asked, voice rising as confusion turned to anger. She turned to Karl. "I ain't going nowhere with him. He's crazy as a bedbug!"

Karl shushed her. "Tell you about it later," he said, but it was Philippa he was watching, wanting her to fix things.

Thoughts rattled around Philippa's brain like dice in a cup. She scrubbed at her temples with both hands. For certain she'd have to stop dragging her feet about getting the bracelet back. But if she managed it, that still wouldn't do a thing for Karl or anybody else.

"I'll figure it out, OK, Karl?" she whispered. "I'll figure something out."

The boxcar shuddered once more, sending a couple of guys staggering. Philippa grabbed for the doorpost, panic sweeping her mind clear of everything else. It'd been another gust of that wind, though only her nerves told her that. No smell because the air itself hadn't touched them. She shut her eyes, reaching out. Nothing. The gust had dissolved just like the others. She reached out further.

There. A strange prickle almost like heat lightning, directly to the east. It wasn't very strong. She raised her head and looked around, though with the door on that side sealed shut there wasn't anything to see. Might not be even if it was open.

Philippa pushed off the wall, picking her way to the far side of the boxcar. She laid her palms against the door like it'd make a sounding board for something that wasn't sound at all, and leaned there, head down, waiting. Somebody said something to her, asked a question, but she brushed the words away.

Nothing. She drew a breath, let it go.

A prickle. Maybe. She stilled again, and shock ripped through her palms, her mind, the ocean of air above and around them. Philippa snatched her hands away but it did no good. A poisonous heat spiraled out, howling, from a growing tear in her mind. Panting, she fell to her knees.

No, not in her mind, but out there, out east, growing and whirling. A tear in the world. A tear like the one that night in the ice house.

Hands gripped her shoulders and shook her. "Arlie! What's wrong?" Chick.

She blinked, and the wounded air was gone. The rattle of the train, the babble of voices, felt like silence. The day had gone unsteady though, even here.

"A wind's coming, I think. A bad one." Philippa knew it was worse than that, but the whirlwind was what mattered now.

Out in the fields that slid by, weed stalks barely stirred and blackbirds pecked among the stubble. Off in the distance was the line of a river as it curved back around to meet the tracks.

"Looks OK to me," Junkyard said, but not as though he didn't believe her. Betts looked doubtful, but Nip stowed the pulp magazine he'd won playing checkers inside his jacket.

"Kid get spells like this often?" a guy sitting just forward of the door asked.

"Weather witch," Chick told him flatly. "A good one." Karl nodded confirmation.

On her knees now, Philippa searched the passing fields for any forerunners of the wind. Her spine ached and crawled from trying to read the chaos.

A light breeze curled across the fields, and a flock of the blackbirds scattered at the bending of the weeds. "Feel that?" Philippa said. "Smell it?" She glanced around at her friends and the skeptical faces beyond them. "Kinda stale?"

The doubting guy grunted and settled back against the wall. "It's just smoke from the engine."

"Dunno," said somebody from the back of the boxcar. "That don't smell like coal smoke to me."

"Don't smell nothing. Don't see nothing," the doubting guy said. He cocked his head to one side. "I hear another train coming. But this stretch is all double track."

Now that the fellow had pointed it out Philippa could hear it rumbling to meet them. Something odd about the sound, though, a whine that set her teeth on edge.

Chick went white. "Hellfire! Ain't y'all never heard a twister?"

The tawny colors of weeds and stubble and dirt dimmed, though the sky above was just as sweet and blue. Dust billowed up from the field and Philippa's nerves broke. "Jump!" she shrieked, struggling again to her feet. "It's behind us. Hit the ditch!"

"We're going too fast!" Junkyard yelled back, hanging onto the door frame and looking out, but Chick didn't hesitate. He edged over the side, finding the step with one foot, then leaped clear. Junkyard's lips tightened. He turned to Nip long enough to say, "Don't forget, runt—tuck your head and roll!" and then he followed.

Metal screamed on metal as the brakes caught. The boxcar slammed into the one ahead and then was hit in its turn by the one behind it, knocking Philippa into somebody; she never figured out who.

The other boes were up and crowding close, getting in the way, but Philippa had no time to listen to them, to read their faces. "Out!" she cried, herding Karl and Betts and Simon across the bucking floor to the door where Deucey was levering his lanky body over the edge, with Nip poised to go.

Deucey leaped, and Nip behind him, both gone.

Simon looked at Philippa.

"Tuck and roll," she told him, praying he understood. She slid her legs over the side, groping for the step. Clinging with one hand to the door frame, she looked down at the blur of cinders. Jesus bless, but she was going to die! She sprang for the weeds, her right foot striking the ground and pushing off, but already her balance was gone. Tucking, she tumbled forward, the world spinning and thrashing her from every side.

She came to rest on her back, sucking for breath, the sky right above an ugly yellow-brown edged with wide blue, and swinging so sickeningly that she shut her eyes against it. The squeal of the freight faded, though the roaring didn't. Flat on your back in a ditch wasn't the worst place to meet a twister, she thought, and tried to move.

Shooting pain surprised a cry from her. She lay back, then tried again, teeth clamped shut. Panting, she rolled on her side.

"Karl!" Betts' scream tore through even the wind. Without knowing how she'd done it, Philippa found herself unsteadily on her feet, squinting downslope along the line of track as wind battered her. A roaring column of whirling grey and brown dragged her gaze upward from the figures she'd barely had time to see. Huge, tall as heaven, the twister blundered across the path of the freight as the line of cars squealed and shuddered to a halt on the trestle halfway across the river.

25

Nothing more than eyes and mind, Philippa was pinned fast by the weight of what she saw: the wide, spinning, tortured fury of the storm; the tumbling of tiny boxcars and girders as the twister's skirt struck freight and bridge; and deep inside at the heart of the storm, the black tear in the world that drove it.

Without form, and void; and darkness was upon the face of the deep... The verse, recalled from some long-ago church school competition, echoed in her mind. The void itself—that's what was beyond the tear. Philippa felt she could reach out and touch the impossible, lightless edges of that gap, could easily fall in. She let the wind push her down, knees resting on the harsh comfort of the earth. Grabbing the coarse weeds to hold herself down, she shut her eyes as she couldn't shut her mind.

"Arlie!" Hands gripped her bruised shoulders and shook her. "Come help!"

Crying out at the pain, she wrenched herself away both from hands and vision.

"Look at me, Arlie!" Deucey hollered.

It was the edge of panic in his usually steady voice that brought her around; that, and a vague memory of Betts screaming Karl's name. She blinked at him, still dizzy.

He looked terrible, pale and beat-up. One coat sleeve was ripped half off, and scrapes on his arm and hands oozed blood. "Junk can't see nothing, and Chick's hurting so bad he can't hardly breathe. I think Nip's arm is broke. I can't… I gotta… Arlie, ain't there nothing you can do?"

She stared back up the tracks the way he must've come, but saw no sign of Chick or anybody. There was only the top of the slope and the dry grasses whipping in the wind. She looked back at him. "With what?" Her voice cracked. "I ain't no doctor."

"Just help me get 'em together in one place, at least?"

Philippa heard him, but she was tangled up in trying to answer her own question. Three of them hurt, and Betts had her bracelet. She turned to look for the older girl, back towards the twister, or to where it had been. That was, she saw with numb relief, now heading away to the southwest. It was…

"Arlie!" Deucey yelled in her ear. "Snap out of it!"

She pointed. "The twister. It's dying." The heart had gone out of it; the tear had sealed. Knowing that steadied her.

Deucey grabbed her sleeve and tried to pull her around.

"Simon's coming," she said, meeting his gaze at last.

Simon was, in fact, running up towards them with a spraddled, driven gait that said he was about blown but wouldn't stop on that account. A long way behind him she picked out Betts in her shell-pink sweater, crouching beside a long shape in the grass. Between, all along the tracks, folks were picking themselves up, stiffs who'd jumped from the cars, or train crew.

Simon stumbled as he reached them. Recovering, he panted, "Betts says you come, Arlie. Karl is bad."

Philippa stared slack-mouthed from Simon to Deucey and back again, trying to think what to do. Betts' bracelet—how long would it take her to figure out getting it off? And who ought to get it then? Her head felt like it was stuffed with grey goose down, soft, muffling every thought. She heard Deucey ask something about moving Karl. Someone a good ways off was shrieking, not words. Just raw pain.

Simon was shaking his head. There was a yellowing bruise high up on his cheekbone where she didn't recollect there being any before. New and already healing. He had one of their precious bracelets too. She clutched at the thought.

"I have not see," Simon was saying, "but she say, 'neck looks funny.'"

With his words the world snapped back into focus. Philippa swallowed bile. "Can them bracelets fix a broken neck?"

Simon froze, looking spooked. He drew a breath, then answered like the words was being pulled out of him. "With other help, maybe. If soon."

Not much hope, but, cripes, she had to try. And at least Betts was right there handy. "OK, OK, no use dithering." She pointed downslope. Her mind was racing now. "I'll go see if I can get Betts' bracelet off to help him. You guys go…"

At the brow of the hill Chick appeared, hunched over and grey. He shambled weakly down to them, looking dazed.

Deucey and Simon, with their longer legs, got to him first. As she limped after them Philippa found one ankle stiff and hurtful, wrenched in her fall. She could manage on it, though, and the pain helped ground her.

Deucey slipped an arm around Chick, to help prop him up.

"Nip's leading Junk," Chick mumbled. "I come on 'cause, 'cause I…" He appeared to forget what he was saying. Beads of sweat stood out on his pale skin.

Simon scowled, gesturing. "Put down!" he said to Deucey. "Will fall."

"Won't," Chick wheezed, trying to straighten. "Busted some ribs, is all. Where's Arlie?"

Puzzled, Philippa stepped closer. "Right here in front of you, Chick."

Looking relieved, he struggled to focus on her. "You bailed out OK then?"

"Sure, Chick. You think you could make it a little further if these guys was to help you? Betts says Karl's real bad off, and wants me down there."

He nodded, but his pinched, sweaty face showed a different story. Simon was right. Chick was going to fall over any moment, even with help, but still she had to go to Karl if he was to have any chance at all. Maybe they could get one of the other stiffs to help carry Chick?

In any case she wanted Simon close. She might have to try to talk him into letting her borrow his bracelet too—supposing she could get 'em off in the first place.

Christ Jesus. Wasn't no choice about that now. "Deuce, would you go back for Junk and Nip?"

Deucey looked surprised and not best pleased, but he let Simon take over supporting Chick. As Philippa turned to limp away she caught sight of Junkyard's face, blood-streaked and stony with fear, as he and Nip mounted the other side of the low hill. Junk couldn't have found the way by himself. His wide-open eyes begged for light and didn't look to be finding any.

She sucked in a shocked breath. "Holy Jesus! Give 'em some help, Deuce. I'll come back if they can't make it all the way, I swear!" And Philippa hobbled the best she could down the hill.

Hadn't been any point in hurrying for Karl's sake. His neck was broke, right enough, and the spark fading from his flesh when Philippa touched him.

Betts must've read the look on her face, because the older girl sat back on her heels and, wrapping her arms tight around her middle, began to rock and cuss quiet and steady. Her pale eyes blazed with the effort not to cry.

Philippa recalled the betrayed look Karl'd got night before last when he realized the townie kid was dead. Now it was him. Glancing around, she spotted his hat lying nearby. She went and got it and knocked the dirt off against her leg. Her overalls, she saw in dull surprise, were ripped all the way from above her knee to the ankle, sagging open to the wind.

Didn't matter. Straightening Karl out a little, she laid the hat over his face, like he was sleeping. She didn't feel much of anything but an aching sort of protest she didn't have words for. Or time for, come to that.

"Betts."

The older girl didn't stop either her rocking or her muttered curses. Philippa took hold of her arm. "Betts, I got to get that bracelet off you now. Chick and Junkyard's both bad hurt, and putting one of them things on 'em is the only thing I know to do to fix 'em."

Betts didn't look at her.

Driving footsteps scrunching the cinders brought Philippa's head around—Deucey again, running. She looked beyond him for the others, and found what looked to be them about a hundred yards off, still further upslope than anybody else.

"Chick's fainted dead away," Deucey gasped as he slid to a stop beside them. "Can't rouse him…" He fell silent when he saw Karl with his face covered.

Philippa wanted to reach out and snatch the bracelet off Betts, but it didn't work that way. That much she was sure of.

"Gimme your hand, Betts," she said, trying to sound like she had a right to boss the older girl around.

"Go away."

Philippa held herself back from screaming at Betts. "Wish I could," she said as calmly as she could manage. "But Junk's been knocked blind and Chick… Chick had death in his face when I seen him." And that was true, Philippa realized as she said it. "You want other folks to die too?" She glanced up at Deucey to see if he'd help her if it came to that.

Deucey nodded, his lips tight and not quite crying.

A shudder of grief went through Betts. She thrust out her left hand and covered her face with the other.

Taking a deep breath, Philippa took the skinned-up hand in hers and pushed up the filthy sleeve of the cardigan. Unsure of the next step, she hesitated. Deucey had knelt down next to Betts and put his arm around her. Betts' shoulders began to shake with sobs, but she left her hand where it was.

Chick had to have this, Philippa told herself grimly. Refusing to think further than that, she stretched out on the rough ground, her trembling hands circling the bracelet on Betts' wrist. She shut her eyes. What had she done that night lying in the dust under the hospital bed?

She'd started out by tracing the workings of the bracelet.

Going down inside was easier this time, near as easy as walking through a door. The fizzing, rainbow twists of the pathways inside the strap felt familiar, and she found a strand that went down into the wrist with no trouble. She was braced for the shock of the dark fires that burned in the moist flesh, but not for the wave of desolate pain that rolled over her, drowning thought and feeling. Gasping, she held on. It's Betts, she screamed silently, not me! But her Meemaw lay cold on the saggy bed they shared, responding no more to being shook than a chunk of hard old clay. Had left her behind, alone, and all the church ladies' hugs and tears and lemon cakes couldn't change it.

Light crashed in on her, and the worst of the hurt went away. Above was a sky scudded with grey and white clouds, wide as the world. Deucey still held Betts, stroking her tangled hair while the girl cried, not as hard now. And though she couldn't see him, Karl still lay dead no more than a foot from her head.

Death, Philippa thought in weary bitterness, tears cooling on her cheeks. That night in the hospital had had death in it too, but this time it cut deeper.

Betts had moved her hand, but not out of reach. It felt cold and fragile as Philippa doggedly took it up again.

As she shut her eyes she realized there'd been death that first time too, after the ice house fire. A charred lump and this strap was all that was left of Lukas. Her eyes snapped back open. The bracelet came off because Lukas was dead. Simon had said so. That was the only time they were *supposed* to come off.

And her whole arm had been numb after the bracelet had dropped away from her wrist that night at the hospital, almost like the life was gone from it.

Philippa drew a ragged breath, seeing her way, but scared at what she had to do. If she wasn't careful, she might do Betts an injury. Though her hand had been just fine, afterwards. Forcing the circling thoughts away, she let go, let herself sink down one more time into the bracelet, and Betts' flesh.

Grief rolled towards her like a flood. She stood beneath the wave and became what she had to do, the job and nothing else, and grief and hurt powdered to dust around her. Made her feel thin, a ghost made of leather or maybe hammered out of sheet metal. But that was all right. Here she was a tool.

And the feeling was familiar anyway.

Cooling the wrist was like sifting dirt on a fire to damp it down, and easy enough to start with. She didn't know how cool it'd have to be to fool the bracelet, so she went slow. As the warmth bled off she realized it hadn't been truly pitch dark inside, because it got darker, a kind of reddish glow dying down.

And then the bracelet—or maybe it was Betts' own defenses —fought back, pumping in heat and building up the glow around her until the not-quite-light shone dark as garnets in a candle flame. Philippa struggled to choke it down, but couldn't.

Exhausted, she stopped fighting. This couldn't've been how it happened before. Then she'd got herself almost trapped in that woman's just-dead body, and without a thought for what was happening in her own flesh.

That was what the job called for. If reaching out for Karl's body was like pushing her way through thick mud, she told herself that had nothing to do with fear or with anybody's grief.

The truth of the matter was he was already in her mind, or at least the Karl-shaped thing that was left lying sprawled out under the sky was. She'd gotten too good a look for it to be otherwise. She found a lifeless hand and sank down inside. Wet ashes and old grease settled into her mouth and nose and eyes, smothering her. She fought to stay put as thinking got harder and harder to do.

She was snatched out into daylight, a cry echoing in her ears, Betts' panicked yell. Philippa blinked once again at the sky, her lungs pumping as she hungrily sucked in air. Her hands felt thick and numb and empty.

"You did it!" said Deucey. Philippa, wondering, tried to look but hardly had the strength to lift her head.

"But my hand," Betts cried. "It's gone all numb and stiff."

Spurred by fear, Philippa rolled to her side. "Lemme see." For the moment her own hands were next thing to useless. "Hold it up to my face, OK?"

With Deucey's urging, Betts pressed the back of her hand against Philippa's cheek. Sighing as she felt the spark in it,

Philippa told her to keep the hand warm and to try wiggling her fingers. "It's kinda like it fell asleep, see. Mine did too," she explained. "It'll be fine."

She pushed herself to her knees and tried to pick up the strap with fingers that felt about as handy as a bunch of wieners. Gingerly Deucey scooped it up and poked it down inside her pocket.

"How long's it been?" she asked.

Deucey glanced back up the hill. Simon stood there in his shirtsleeves, looking anxiously in their direction. "Dunno. Maybe ten, fifteen minutes? You need us to come help?" he asked as she stood.

Betts pulled away from him, her numb hand rustling among the tatters of newspaper under her sweater as she held it close. "Go if you want. I ain't leaving him. I can't, not... not yet."

Her words trailed away and Philippa thought wearily, yeah, what are we going to do with him? Leave him to the folks who'd be swarming over the wreck any minute now? They'd stick him in a morgue like the one at St. Mike's, and then in a pauper's grave with neither stone nor name. She swiped the back of a hand across wet eyes; salt stung her scraped-up skin.

All that would have to wait. And in the meantime, Betts was right. Somebody ought to sit with him.

"No," she told them. "You guys stay."

Deucey got a thoughtful look, and held out his hand. "Borrow me your pencil, then, if you would."

26

*R*estless with the need to be of use, Simon strode down to meet Arlie, fists shoved deep in his pockets. Their weak sun had come out of hiding and the wind had stilled, but without his coat he was cold through.

No matter. Here he was always cold. Laying the coat over Chick had been right.

Arlie awkwardly dodged around two men tending a bloody gash on the forehead of a third. "Hey, got a rag to bandage this guy with?" one yelled as he passed. Arlie called over his shoulder, "No time! Sorry!" He panted, limping, up to Simon.

"Karl?" Simon asked, though with small hope. Arlie was *haat ifobetla*, uncanny, but a broken neck was surely beyond his powers. It was not the boy, after all, who had cured the young woman's lung sickness. Lukas' stolen iyar pukko had done that. At the thought his stomach roiled with a familiar unease.

When Arlie wagged his head wearily in that negating gesture, Simon felt nothing, a gap where feeling ought to be. He had judged Karl weak-spirited, a complainer, but more was due one's companions.

"How's Chick?"

Arlie's anxiety anchored him in the moment's need. "Bad," Simon told him, turning to lead him back. "Hurt inside him, I think. Come. Hurry." He couldn't bear to ask if the boy had managed his unnatural feat once more.

The slope was steeper here, and for a time Arlie said nothing. His limp was getting worse, and pain lined his face. "Lean to me," Simon offered, his hand out ready to catch the younger boy around the waist.

Arlie hesitated, a hitch between one step and the next that put him out of reach. "Don't need help."

"Forget pride," Simon said impatiently. "Hurry is needed."

"I said no!" Arlie glared at him as though he had given serious offense.

Shutting his mouth tightly, Simon strode ahead. These people were touchy about foolish things, but arguing took time.

Arlie struggled to catch up with him. After a moment the boy asked, his tone placating, "Junkyard still can't see?"

"Still," Simon answered, biting the word off. "Head was… was banged. And shoulder out of place, but we make right."

Arlie nodded, hobbling on a couple of steps farther. "I got the strap off Betts. But that's only one, see."

Simon felt his jaw go tight. A prickle ran down all his skin.

Arlie drew a deep breath and blew it out. "See, I got to have your bracelet for Junkyard, Simon. Just for a bit."

Speechless for a moment, Simon stumbled to a halt. "Is not 'bracelet'!" he managed to say at last. "Is my iyar pukko, and I am not dead for you to take from me!"

Arlie swung around to face him, the bruised face gone pale with rage. "Look at you, walking around all healed up already! You don't need the blamed thing, but Junk's gonna end up spending the rest of his life peddling pencils on a street corner. And all you got to say is 'it's mine!'"

An unreasonable shame touched Simon, though he did not know why selling pencils was worse than other commerce; a prestige issue he didn't understand, perhaps. Trying to keep his voice even, to neither shout or plead, he answered, "Is selfish to say, 'this hand is mine?' Maybe you ask I give one eye, say I don't need two?" He clasped his right hand around his wrist, his iyar. "Is part of me, like eye, like liver."

The boy bared his teeth. "Them things come off, like eyes and stuff don't. Twice now I proved it! You Wobs is supposed to be so big on everybody sharing," he spat. "Appears to me it only goes one way with you, chump. Why don't you go preach to some other fools? Let them help you get to St. Paul!" He spun on his good leg, torn pants leg flapping, and stalked off.

Sweating and shaken, Simon trembled as he watched the boy go. St. Paul and his own people were not that far now, he told himself. He didn't need these troublesome wanderers.

The thought comforted him not at all.

Doggedly Philippa drove herself the last hundred yards up the slope, knowing Simon wasn't following. Looked like she'd put paid to her notion of getting to Mara's world. And as for putting the iyar on herself, to see what would happen, that was for a time when folks wasn't dying. She swallowed past the painful knot in her throat.

Surely Mara would've helped if she'd been here. Wouldn't she? But might-be-maybes cut no mustard. If Philippa hadn't gone and lost her temper she could've worked on Simon some more, eased him into it. More than likely if he'd worn the thing his whole life he was just scared to let loose of it, even for a little while, and scared as well to admit it. Boys were like that; it was one thing she didn't plan on learning. A body could be scared and brave all at the same time.

She risked a glance up when she was almost there. Chick was lying flat out with something tan tucked around him. Simon's coat. Philippa swallowed once more. Junkyard lay beyond, an arm draped close over his eyes and mouth screwed up tight. Nip sat between them, small and huddled around his arm.

Seeing her, Nip got awkwardly to his feet, a spark of hope in his black eyes. "You got it?" he breathed.

She nodded, tight-lipped. Brave was what she'd have to be now, because she was sure enough scared. Chick wasn't moving at all, and what in Jesus' name could she do about Junkyard?

Fumbling the strap from her pocket, Philippa dropped down by Chick's side. His face was pale and waxy, ghostlike next to his black hair. She could hardly breathe for fear she'd been too long.

"He's breathing," Nip told her, seeing her worry. "I just checked him." Deucey or maybe Simon had splinted the kid's arm with a bunch of sturdy weed stalks, and safety-pinned that sleeve to his jacket to make him a sling. She could see from Nip's pinched face that the arm hurt like blazes, though.

A touch to Chick's forehead reassured her, but not much. She rousted one of his hands out from under Simon's coat and yanked up on the sleeve. The wrist and hand looked to be nothing but bones under skin pale as skim milk. Philippa wrapped the strap around and held it in place a minute, praying for it to hold, to do its magic. Seemed like it shifted weirdly under her hands. Hastily she let go.

It stayed put, and she let go as well of the breath she'd been holding. After that wasn't nothing to do but let it work. She could see no sign in his face that anything was changing, and couldn't bear to sit still and watch.

"He gonna be OK?" Nip asked in a small voice.

"Jesus willing." She tucked the limp hand back under the coat and smoothed it down.

Nip watched her. "Where'd Simple go? I thought he was coming back with you."

Reluctantly she looked back downslope. At first she couldn't spot Simon at all. Her gut knotted at the thought that he'd done what she'd told him, gone off coatless on his own. Away east across the pasture where a highway ran parallel to the tracks, a handful of men had flagged down some cars and a farm truck —catching rides out of here, or getting help? None of them was Simon, though.

And there he was, halfway down the tracks to Betts and Deucey, on his knees holding some guy's shoulders while another fellow, a brakeman to judge by his cap, bent over the guy's leg. Philippa pointed him out to Nip. "See? He's helping other folks."

Then the sweep of the tracks drew her eyes down to the river and the shattered trestle, where boxcars were tumbled together like a heap of old chimney bricks. Philippa stood gaping, thinking she ought to have known how bad it'd be. But somehow that time of watching the twister belonged to a different world.

How many folks hadn't jumped? How many were down there, drowning in the wreckage?

She made herself turn her back. Her work, such as it was, was here. She surveyed Junkyard, who hadn't moved but to ease his shoulder.

"How's he doing?" she asked Nip.

"I can talk just fine for myself, thanks," Junkyard said through gritted teeth.

"Glad to hear it, Junk," she said with a twisted smile for his tone. Pure Junkyard. Funny how his testiness could grow on a body. "Other folks I been seeing ain't so lucky."

After a moment he asked, "Karl?"

"Dead." Saying it hurt, but there was no point in prettifying a thing for Junk. He wouldn't appreciate it.

Junkyard grunted. "I guessed he might be."

With a cry, Nip pushed himself to his feet. "No!" He stared downslope to where Betts sat huddled up in her pink sweater with Deucey close beside, and the body hardly showing in the weeds. "That ain't fair!"

And wasn't that the truth. "You want to go pay your respects," she told him, "I'll take care of things here."

Nip looked for permission to Junkyard, who somehow knew it. "Beat it, brat."

Philippa waited until he'd started down the tracks. "Simon said you hurt your shoulder, too."

"Dislocated. Deuce put it back for me right off. Hurts like hell when I move it, but it'll be jake." Junkyard grimaced. "My head feels like I got kicked by a horse, but I guess that'll get better too."

"And your eyes?" she asked.

"They don't hurt." His mouth wobbled like he was fighting back tears. After a minute he ground out, "Can't see nothing but stuff like fireworks out of the left one. Blurry stuff and the same goddamn fireworks in the other."

She puzzled over the fireworks, but she didn't need to understand. "Can I look at 'em?"

"What does it matter?" he asked roughly. "Nothing you can do about it. Chick needs that damn bracelet worse than I do."

Philippa looked over at Chick. Was there a little more color in his face? She saw his chest rise and fall beneath the coat, and that *was* better. "Simon's got one." Her jaw set. "I already tried talking him out of it."

"Simple?" He laughed, but there wasn't a trace of funny in it. "Good luck. Is that why he took off?" He took his arm away from his face, though, and opened his eyes.

They stared blankly in her general direction. "Not even a black eye or nothing," she said, wondering. "They look just like regular." She shivered at her lie. What they looked like was eyes that saw straight into hell.

"Yeah. So I hear," Junkyard said, bitter. He covered them again.

A loud snick behind them made her whirl around. A jowly-faced man in travel-wrinkled blue serge stood on the tracks, just lowering a cheap box camera. He had the look of a drummer; must've come over from the highway, which was lined with vehicles now. "Hey, kid," the salesman said, and pointed at Chick, "Is that guy dead?"

Fury lit a white-hot blaze behind her eyes. "No, he ain't, you goddamn sneak! Beat it or I'll bust your lousy camera!" She bent to grope for throwing stones among the cinders.

He backed off, holding out both hands, stumbling on the ties. Made a better target of his Brownie, she saw as she straightened with a palm-sized rock. "No offense!" he was saying, looking not nearly scared enough to suit her. And he wasn't going away. "I'll give you a nickel for the shot, OK?"

Junkyard had sat up painfully; was groping his way to his knees. "Camera? What's he doing?" he said, frustration raw on his face.

She let fly.

The guy jerked his hands up to protect his face so the rock hit his elbow instead, but he squealed and dropped the Brownie. "OK, OK, I'm going!" he cried, bending to snatch it back up again. Turning, he ran smack into Simon, who grabbed hold of the man's lapels. Philippa was relieved as all get-out to see him.

The drummer paled. "Hey, look, fellow, I wasn't doing anything."

"What he do, Arlie?" Simon asked without turning his fierce hawk's gaze from the man.

"He was snapping pictures of us like we was carnival freaks or something!" She hated how her voice squeaked: like a little kid, or worse, like a girl.

"I'll kill him!" Junkyard howled. He stumbled to his feet, blind eyes hunting frantically for an enemy to hit.

Worry crowded out some of Philippa's anger. She moved closer, though she didn't care to lay hands on Junkyard unless she had to. His baffled rage made her want to cry. She forced herself to something resembling calm. "Just get that camera," she told Simon, who frowned. She added, "The box he's holding." As she said it, a reason for what'd been an instinctive demand came to her: what if the rat was to sell his picture of Chick and them to the papers?

The man didn't fight when Simon plucked it from his hand. "Sorry, Jack," he said to Simon, his heavy face puckered up like he expected to get hit. "I didn't mean no harm, honest."

"Drop it on the ground and stomp it good," Philippa said, as Deucey panted to a halt beside them, the birthmarks on his face an angry red from exertion. "That'll fix it. Them things ain't much more'n heavy cardboard."

"What's going on?" Deucey asked her, his voice low. Philippa was too busy to answer.

"Arlie? Arlie, just lead me to him!" Junkyard begged. "I'll teach the lousy bastard to gawk at us!"

Nip, cradling his bad arm and as out of breath as Deucey, slipped up beside him, scowling with worry. He let go of the arm to pull on Junkyard's sleeve. "Sit down!" he pleaded. "Simple's taking care of it. You're gonna hurt yourself!"

His face twisted with shame, Junkyard yanked away from Nip. He made it a couple of steps before his foot caught on a bunch of weeds. He fell, windmilling in panic, to land heavily on his knees with something that might've been a sob.

The muscles in Simon's jaw bunched at this. He tightened his grip on the guy's coat, hauling him up on his toes. "People are hurt. People are dead! Why do you not go help?" he demanded. Holding the guy off with one hand, he dropped the Brownie; brought his boot down hard. The black box crumpled sideways.

The drummer looked ready to cry, but he didn't answer. Simon gave the guy a shove. Looking hunted, the man edged away for ten feet or so, and then turned and ran down into the field, which was busy now with people hurrying back and forth hauling equipment. A siren hiccuped into silence as an ambulance pulled up out on the road. It wasn't the first one she'd heard, Philippa realized. She just hadn't been paying attention.

Hearing angry thuds and the labored rasp of Junkyard's breath behind her as he pounded dirt with his good fist tensed up Philippa's back with worry. Nip was trying to calm him. Simon had knelt down by him as well, she saw when she ventured a glance back, but Junkyard started up cussing until Simon backed off. She dropped any notion she'd had about lending a hand. Hard as it was, Junkyard was going to have to settle his ownself down.

A khaki tent was going up close to the river. A line of folks were laid out in the tromped-down grass near the billowing canvas, with guys in white coats moving among them. Betts was down there too, looked like talking to somebody. Philippa squinted in puzzlement.

It was Betts, all right. It was hard to mistake that sweater. Philippa scanned for Karl's body along the line of track, and couldn't find it. "Deucey?" she said uncertainly.

Deucey had squatted down next to Chick. "He's got him a little more color," he said, muffled hope in his voice.

Hastily Philippa joined him. Chick felt warmer to the touch and not so clammy, though he showed no sign of rousing. A fragile relief filled her lungs along with the breath she drew in. "Deuce," she said again, her gaze on the steady rise and fall of Chick's chest. "Did somebody move Karl?"

"Yes. I see them do," Simon, crouched nearby, answered her. "They come here soon, I think."

A falling-away feeling in her chest brought the sting of tears to her eyes. Philippa blinked them back.

Simon leaned toward them, resting his weight on one hand. "Arlie. I…"

But Deucey was talking too, a finger resting on the back of her hand, claiming her attention. "See, Betts and me, we pinned us a scrap of newspaper to his shirt with his name wrote on it, and the town Betts said he said he come from," Deucey was saying, soft enough she had to strain to it. "My grandpa told me the Kentucky volunteers did that back in the old war when he was little. Oh, yeah." He groped in his pocket. "Here's your pencil back." He held the stub out to her.

She took it numbly, thinking at least Karl wouldn't be nameless. The crunch of cinders brought her head up. It seemed Simon hadn't just been guessing about them coming here as well.

"What've we got here?" the man asked them, an old colored guy in a white smock with a stethoscope stuck in his pocket. The fellow carried a clipboard with a cross marked in red on the back of it, and he sounded all business. The knees of his trousers were rusty with what looked like blood as well as dirt.

Deucey spoke. "Busted ribs, we think. Trouble breathing, and then he just keeled over."

"Let me take a look," the Red Cross man said, moving Philippa out of the way. He pulled up Chick's eyelids and felt his skull, and then along his ribcage and belly. "Christ," he said under his breath, scrambling to his feet. He cupped big hands around his mouth and shouted down the line for a litter. It took a couple of tries, but finally a fat guy waved acknowledgment.

"You fellows up to carrying him down to the docs?" the colored guy asked Simon and Deucey. "We're short-handed."

"Yes," said Simon stoutly, getting to his feet.

Deucey glanced at Philippa. "Yeah, I guess so," he said uncertainly, while she tried to get her weary brain to figure out what them taking Chick away might mean, particularly if he was getting better on his own now. Could you tell a doctor or an aide, or whatever this guy was, you didn't need him?

The man turned to Nip. "OK, what about you? Broken arm?"

Nip was still trying to persuade Junkyard to lie down, cussing under his breath at him, and looking near tears. Junkyard's mouth was a tight slash across his face. "Yeah," Nip said, not looking at the guy. "Deuce and Simple there set it."

"OK. You want somebody to give a look, go down to the staging area by those trees and wait." The guy was already looking Junkyard over. He squatted down next to him and touched him lightly on the shoulder—his good shoulder, Philippa saw. "How about you, fellow? Can't see? Is that new?"

Junkyard jerked away. "Hell, no," he growled. "I'm a blinky on the bum, whadda you think?"

The Red Cross guy looked again to Deucey. Deucey laid all it out for him while he scribbled notes on his clipboard. Philippa saw his face tighten at the mention of the fireworks.

Junkyard objected when the guy wanted to take a closer look. "I got a bump here," he said loudly, and gingerly touched the back of his head. "And a humdinger of a headache. And I ain't having nobody poking at me, see?"

The man's face didn't change. He scribbled something else down. "You want a doc to look at your head or that shoulder, get your pals to help you down there and wait until the team gets to you. Otherwise I suggest you take it real easy for awhile. Now, is there anybody further up the line?" When they shook their heads, he tucked his clipboard under his arm and stood. He beckoned Simon and Deucey to fall in with him as he started back down the tracks. Simon looked to Deucey, who shrugged. They trailed him.

Philippa followed, her thoughts spinning. She had to know more to figure out what they ought to do.

When they were a few yards down the tracks, the fellow stopped. "Look, when the litter comes, don't waste any time getting the black-haired kid down there," he said quietly to the boys. "And when they ask *why* he's there, you tell them one word: spleen. Get me?" When Simon nodded, he said, "Good. They'll do their best for him from there."

Philippa swallowed. 'Do their best' in that soft tone of voice meant the guy didn't expect Chick to make it; he thought it was too late for him.

But already he was some better. "What do they do for spleens?" she asked Deucey as the guy walked off.

"Take 'em out is what I've heard," Deucey said, looking sick around the mouth. Simon frowned.

If Chick was already healing, cutting him that way wasn't needful. Philippa didn't know what spleens did, but it stood to reason they had a purpose.

There was still Junkyard. She ran a few painful yards on her swollen ankle to catch up with the man. "Hey! What about Junk's eyes? Can't they help him at all?"

The colored man sighed as he stopped again to look at her. Simon and Deucey stopped as well to listen. "Not much chance of that, son," the guy said. "Keep him flat on his back for a few weeks, and he might get a little of his sight back. He don't need to be in a hospital for that, and we're gonna be short of beds. Now if he starts throwing up or wants to sleep all the time, or anything like that, get him to a doctor. But otherwise…" He shrugged.

She let him go, her balled fists shoved deep in her pockets. It was about what she figured, but still it made her angry. How'd they expect a road kid like him to stay flat on his back for that long, and so late in the fall, too? She watched him stride away, and then eyed the guy with a flapping coat who was sprinting up the tracks towards them, the poles of a litter sticking out from under his arm. So far as she could see the docs didn't have any answers for them at all.

"I guess blind is blind," Deucey said from behind her. He sounded defeated, and that made her angry at him as well.

"No, it ain't. Not necessarily." Philippa turned to stare at Simon, challenging him.

He covered his face with his hands. "Yes," he whispered. "I come for this, but so much happen. But give back if sickness takes me? What is nothing to you may kill me."

Watching how he fought back his fear, Philippa's sense of victory turned to vinegar on her tongue. "Yes," she told him, squinting up at him in the afternoon sun. "Swear to Jesus I will." She thought of spitting into her hand to seal the bargain as Karl had done that last night in Grand Forks; thought of Karl's hand, lifeless.

She swallowed against bile and squeezed shut her eyes. Once again she'd have to go down into that smothering darkness.

27

Simon rested his head on the roof of the cab as one by one the others climbed down from the high truck bed. Bed—that was yet another of the odd double meanings in their language, he thought dazedly, too tired and chilled to move. A bed was what you slept on, but it seemed now the word also meant a platform on which things were carried. Things such as thirty or more battered wanderers packed in together hour after hour as the truck rattled along and the chill wind tore at their faces.

"Getting us out of their hair," Deucey had explained that morning as they'd waited on the trucks. "See, a little burg like this 'un ain't set up to handle so many of us. With the tracks out they got to haul us someplace to be shet of us. It's pure fool's luck the Twin Cities is closer than anyplace else."

That meant St. Paul. Simon had asked, just to be sure. Deucey's dialect could be as hard to follow as was Arlie's. From what people on the train had said yesterday about how long it would take to reach the city, he guessed the truck might have brought them half of the remaining distance. But perhaps they were closer. The truck moved more quickly and much more steadily on its black road than the slow freight had on its tracks. The driver had stopped only once before, to urinate in the high grass along the road.

Around him the wanderers called to one another, a note of relief underlying the slushy babble of voices. Simon wrapped his arms around his head to shut them out.

Before the dark came down again he would reach the city, yet he found nothing inside himself but weariness. The first meaning of bed was all he longed for now. His whole body buzzed and his neck ached and a dull burning filled his head, making it hard to follow one thought with another. And his left wrist felt naked, with his last shield against this world stripped away.

That was it, he remembered, his thoughts clearing in a flood of fear. Without his iyar pukko, St. Paul was only another alien city. He could not enter the Eye without it; could not return home. The dugrilat of the St. Paul mission might locate him through tracing his or Lukas' iyarit, even on the wrong wrists, but when they found the unnatural thing he'd agreed to...

Arlie had sworn to return it. He would get it back and find his people. They would not need to know what he'd done.

"Hey you, lazy bum!" the driver yelled, thumping the metal side of the cab. "Make it snappy. I ain't got all day!"

Simon raised his head, blinking away the road grit, slow to understand it was him the man was shouting at.

"C'mon, Simon!" Arlie called, peering up through the wood slats that made a fence around the bed. Still pale, Chick leaned heavily on the younger boy's shoulder. Behind them stood Junkyard, scowling, Nip hanging onto one sleeve with his good hand, ready to guide the blindfolded youth if need be. The blindfold had seemed to keep Junkyard calmer on the journey. Arlie had insisted that he lie down the whole way, as well, in spite of complaints from the others.

A few steps away Betts stood waiting, shoulders slumped, the blanket she'd been given last night rolled up under her arm. The others also carried their blankets, all of them ready to leave. And most of the wanderers were already strung out along the road, walking away with that rolling, long-distance gait they had.

Simon flushed. "Ah, we are here?" he found himself asking, feeling stupid and clumsy as he made his way to the back of the truck, one hand on the top board to steady himself. "So soon?"

"Christ, Simple," Junkyard muttered. "Guy begs us to get him here, and all he can say now is 'so soon?'" Head bent, he fumbled with the thick cloth knotted around his eyes. "I'm sick of this damn thing," he said as though he thought someone would argue. After a moment he gave up on the knot and yanked the blindfold off. With a hiss he slammed his arm across his eyes.

Poised with one foot reaching for the ground, Simon paused, unable in that moment to move. Then, despairing, he let himself down to stand in the pitted roadway. His sacrifice had been for nothing. Shakily he looked around for the city.

Arlie had said St. Paul was much larger than Grand Forks, but fields of dead grass stretched out beyond the curb where the truck was parked, with but few buildings. An odd one off to his right brought his head around in uneasy disbelief. It was huge, with a cascading roof like those built by the cursed Haan across the western ocean of his own world. But those walls were massive, a shield against the sky for a people too arrogant to burrow sensibly into the earth, whereas this building seemed only a shell set with many windows. Warily he eyed it, but of course no shaved-head *dzinsit* came from it, trailed by parasol-carrying slaves.

His mouth tightened in a bitter smile. That was one fear he need not have. The tyrants of his people's past were, in this world and this land, a powerless minority, few enough that he had yet to see one. He turned away, rubbing his aching neck.

Ah, he thought then, sucking in an awed breath. Those must be the cities. Beyond the row of trees lining the road rose two jagged clumps of immense, square-built towers reaching to the sky.

The truck pulled away, leaving a cloud of smoke behind it. Simon barely noticed. His mouth was hanging open. He shut it, not wanting to look more foolish than he already had. "*Qodi?*" he asked in wonder, turning to Arlie. "Why make so tall?" but the boy didn't seem to hear him. He was watching Junkyard wipe the back of a hand across his eyes, Simon's black *iyar pukko* showing at the cuff of one coat-sleeve.

There'd be no luck in this place, Philippa found herself thinking. Something about it got under her skin, scraping her nerves like chalk squealing on a blackboard. "No good, huh?" she asked Junkyard, worry making her voice harsh.

Junkyard sniffled. "Damn sun's too bright," he rasped. "That's all." He swiped at his eyes again, then let the hand fall. Blinking away the wet in his pale eyes, he squinted at her, a shaky smile beginning to crease the corners of his mouth. Hope she was afraid to feel began to warm her belly.

"It worked." Junkyard's smile spread into joy. "Damn if it didn't! Right eye's still kinda hazy, like there's spiderwebs in the way? But I can see!" He drew a breath and blew it out again. "Christ, but you guys don't know how good this dump looks to me."

Nip whooped. Loosing Junkyard's sleeve, he threw excited punches at the older boy's gut with his good arm. Good-naturedly Junkyard fended him off.

"Glad to hear it," Chick said from above Philippa's head, his voice weak. "'Bout time we had us some luck." His weight shifted on her shoulder, and he stepped away, stumbling over the curb. Though she caught hold of the back of his jacket, that didn't help hold him up. Turning in surprise when Chick jostled him, Simon grabbed awkwardly at both his arms.

"Got to sit down," Chick whispered, righting himself. "Just till we figure out where we're heading," he added. "I can walk."

Philippa flushed. Chick was healing, but he ought to be in bed somewhere, getting took care of. She'd made sure he wouldn't have that. But the docs would have cut him open if she'd let him be carried down to the tents by the river yesterday.

Betts tossed her blanket onto the curb and piled Deucey's on top, Deucey having gone off to ask directions. "Here," Betts snapped, dragging Chick to the heap by one sleeve. "You're about to take Arlie and Simple down with you."

Wordlessly Chick lowered himself to sit on the blankets. Philippa rubbed the shoulder he'd been leaning on, trying not to be obvious about it.

Absently Simon shrugged his coat straight on his shoulders, the pinched look wiped from his windburned face by Junkyard's news. "My people feed you, give you beds." Seeing his new hope, Philippa felt a clutch of fear she hadn't expected. He'd want her to get his iyar whatever-it-was back to him now.

"And where might that be?" Betts demanded of Simon.

He looked down his nose at her, but cheerfully. "In a warehouse here, by a big lake."

"One-Note Charley," Junkyard jeered, another sign he was feeling better. "I've heard that tune before. You got some idea which way we ought to head?"

The direction came to Philippa clear as if somebody'd whispered it in her ear. Southeast, some ways beyond the row of skyscrapers that must be downtown St. Paul. She shuddered. That way lay the center of where that chalk-scraping feeling came from. Of course there was nothing to say that had a thing to do with Simon's slipgate—nothing but the feeling in her gut.

Simon was pivoting on one heel, frowning like he did when he was thinking hard, but managing to look lost all the same. After a long minute he faced them, floundering. "With a picture of city, I find them," he said at last. "A…" He struggled a moment for a word. "A map."

Junkyard and Betts both looked scorn at him.

"Libraries have maps," Nip offered.

"We'll find us one. Tomorrow," Philippa said, jumping into the gap. "Bound to be too late today."

Simon turned on her. "Give me my iyar pukko," he demanded, not loud. The sudden desperation in his narrowed black eyes made it half a plea.

Philippa swallowed. Could she do it at all without somebody newly dead at hand to guide her? When she'd taken Simon's bracelet off him yesterday, Karl's body hadn't been close by no more. She wasn't sure if she'd reached out to where it lay with the others in the temporary morgue under the trees by the river, or whether it'd been memory gave her the key. In that inside place she went to it was hard to tell regular distances and all.

But Junkyard still had some haze in one eye. Best if he kept the bracelet on a little longer. She started to tell Simon so. A shrill whistle brought them all around. Deucey, standing with three older guys, waved them over.

Chick rubbed his face, glad the others had trooped off to hear what Deucey had to say—something about a boarded-up movie house they could jungle up in, and a downtown soup line. He really did feel lots better. His chest didn't hurt at all, not even a bruise anymore. It was just that he was lightheaded, like there wasn't enough blood in him to reach that far.

"Up and at 'em, Chick," Arlie said some little time later, standing before him, a hand out to help him up. "Looks like you get a chance to show us how good you can walk."

He managed a crooked grin. "Leave you chumps in the dust." He took the kid's hand and heaved himself up.

Simon had followed her. Voice low and fierce, he said, "Junkyard sees. He does not need my iyar pukko."

Standing still was worst of all. "Lay off the kid," Chick growled, wanting to push past and get walking. Arlie stepped aside for him, a thump on his arm to let him know she'd handle it herself. That brought a grin in spite of how his head felt.

"We ain't got time just now, Simon," Arlie said as Chick came up beside her. "Ain't but a couple of hours till dark."

Simon's handsome face shut down. He turned away to join Deucey where he waited with their guides. The kid took a few steps after him. "See, I ain't welshing on our deal. I said I'd get it back to you, and I will. Tonight, OK? But we got to get settled first."

Simon didn't turn around.

"Damn bellyacher," Chick muttered. Walking was better, though he wasn't sure how long he'd hold up.

Arlie sighed. "I don't know, Chick. He swears he'll get sick and die without that bracelet. But the thing is, I ain't exactly sure I can do it here."

Chick stiffened, afraid to ask what that might mean about the one on his wrist. Everybody told him he'd have been dead without the damned thing. It wasn't that he doubted them, but wearing it made him feel half a prisoner.

The kid had got a few steps ahead. Chick pushed to catch up, though his balance went wobbly for a moment.

"You ain't feeling sick, is you?" she called after Simon.

Simon turned, just for a moment. "To you does not matter," he answered fiercely.

As they followed the older men into the city Chick's stride lengthened and steadied. Pumping that blood higher, he told himself in congratulation. The kid dropped back to walk at his elbow. Ahead of them but off to the side, a little more in the street than was sensible given the traffic, Simon walked with his head down.

After a long spell Chick raised his voice to ask, "When you get the bracelet back, is that gonna help you find this warehouse of yours?"

Simon looked like he wanted to object again to it being called a bracelet, but all he said was, "No. They find me."

Philippa huddled deeper into the blanket around her shoulders as another gust swirled past. A little after dark the fitful, icy breeze had come up, the first exploring fingers of what felt like a push of dirty weather rumbling out of the west. Ordinary, but no more pleasant for that.

The flames of their small campfire had blazed up. Coughing, Deucey ducked his head to avoid the worst of the smoke. The span of the bridge overhead made a roof of a sort, but it and the broad river gave the wild air a channel to sweep down onto them. Other folks had already claimed the choice spots where heaps of stones or a bush or two gave some shelter. Still, this was a sight better than the rat hole that derelict movie house had proved to be. Cleaner, at least, in spite of the trash, not to mention farther from the center of that nerve-scraping feeling, though nobody else had seemed to notice it at all.

"How come the smoke always blows my way?" Nip, sitting cross-legged next to Deucey, grumbled.

"Warmest side of the fire," Chick pointed out cheerfully. He'd livened up considerable since their supper of bread and thin tomato soup and a soggy packet of liver they'd sliced up and seared over the flames. Junkyard claimed to have snatched it off a counter under both the grocer's and the customer's noses, the dope.

Hunched over like a molting hawk, Simon watched her from across the flames. He kept rubbing his neck like it hurt him. Getting sick maybe, but he wouldn't say. She turned away, uneasy even with the comforting ballast of food in her belly.

Deucey cleared his throat. The sound echoed off the concrete span. "See, I was thinking now we's settled a little, we oughta do something to say goodbye to Karl." His right hand fumbled at the inside pocket of his corduroy jacket a moment before extracting a pint flask and holding it up. King George Whiskey, aged in Kentucky, or so the label claimed, though given the ingenuity of bootleggers Philippa took leave to doubt it.

Betts' breath hissed in at the sight. "Damn the fool all to hell. Yeah, he'd like that." A sheen of tears gleamed in her eyes. She reached. Solemnly Deucey handed it across to her.

The flask was three-quarters full. Philippa, the corners of her mouth twisting in a desolate smile, wondered where in the world Deucey had come by it. He wasn't the sort to roll a drunk.

With shaking hands Betts screwed off the cap and downed a healthy swallow, then passed it on. Nobody said a thing as it went around, but Philippa could see they were all thinking of Karl, same as her.

Even Simon. His fever-sharp gaze broke, and he hid his face for a moment behind clenched hands. When Chick nudged him, handing on the hooch, he drank jerkily. Wheezing, his eyes wet and jaw bunched, he held the bottle out to Nip.

When it came to her Philippa took a careful swig, and managed not to spit it out. The stuff burned her throat near as bad as breathing that fire had, or so it seemed for the second or so it took to go down. But that was OK; it was for Karl, a little hurt to ease a bigger one.

Junkyard was last in the circle. He took two quick slugs and then passed the bottle, with a good inch left in it, back to Betts. He looked at Philippa. "Guess I'm ready." Simon's gaze fastened on the two of them hungrily.

Upending the flask, Betts drained it, then stared down at the empty in her hand. "Dead soldier," she said, with a choked laugh that was hard to tell from a sob. Without looking she hurled the bottle into the fire, where it cracked against a stone. Deucey pulled her against his shoulder, wetness gleaming in his eyes as well. She turned into him, burying her face.

Head swimming just a bit from the alcohol, throat tight, Philippa stretched out on her back on the stony ground next to Junkyard. Like a grease monkey sliding under a car to get at the works, she reflected with a touch of bitterness. Gingerly she took up Junkyard's broad hand. She wriggled, trying to escape the fist-sized stones under the grass and weeds that were trying to burrow holes in her spine. It was going to be a lumpy night's sleep when it came to that.

Christ Jesus let this work.

But it wasn't hard. Maybe the booze helped. Shut eyes and a few slow, deep breaths pared her wandering mind down to the single focus. The strands of the strap's neon maze filled her mind, and then she was down inside the damp heat of Junkyard's wrist. It took her a couple of tries, but when she reached out for Karl's hand with no thought for time or miles, it was there as she remembered it, ash-black and smothering inside and just beginning to cool, his death fresh inside her mind.

Thought cooled too as she anchored herself there in the airless dark. Something was wrenched away, something she'd set herself to... to do what with? But the light was gone; night, and sleep (was it sleep? A tiny voice yammered panic in her ear) pulled her down gentle as a flow of honey.

A blow to her middle shattered her drowsiness. Air sharp with woodsmoke and river stink rushed into her lungs in reaction. Starving, she forced it out again and dragged in another scant lungful with muscles stiff as taffy.

"Jiminy, you didn't have to hit the kid!" somebody was saying and a deeper voice answered, "Worked, didn't it? Hand me that blanket." Wool scratched her face as she was rolled about, her limbs stiff as winter logs.

Confused, she tried to open her eyes. She'd been trying to... trying to... She couldn't remember. Had she fallen in the river? She was so cold. A slit of wavering light appeared as she pried one eyelid up. About then shivers took hold and shook her so hard her bones and teeth rattled like dice in a cup.

"Blankets ain't enough. I'm gonna put the bracelet on."

Chick's voice? She tried to see. The shrill "No!" that followed was Simon's; she was sure of that much.

Sense came to her slowly. If they put Simon's iyar on her, she'd only have to take it off again. She tried to speak but couldn't force the words between her chattering teeth. Very slowly and jerkily she shook her head. She got her eyes open enough to see Chick's dark-winged face above her, and the understanding that sparked there.

But oh, she was so cold.

"Unwrap her then," Betts ordered.

"Him!" said Chick.

"I don' give a good goddamn for that game you guys're playin'," Betts retorted, her words slurring just a little. "Somebody's gotta get next to …him, then, if you insist. Warm him up. And I'm the one to do it."

Memory rose up: the sway and smoke of a train, and Betts burning with fever. "Come lay next to her, Arlie." Karl's voice, coaxing. Dead or living, he was part of her now.

"Too bad we killed that whiskey," said Deucey as he helped pull back the blankets. "Would've helped."

"Wouldn't neither!" Nip answered. "Alky's why stewbums freeze to death."

"We'll do a sandwich," Chick said.

Warmth soaked in slowly, from both front and back. Much too slow, and the press of bodies, the rank smell of other folks' sweat, and smoky hair against her face, made Philippa want to run and flail and scream, to somehow tear her self out of this unsafe body. She couldn't run, and they were trying to help; she knew they were. She held herself in, and shook all the harder.

"Ssh," said Chick in her ear. "Relax. You're making it worse." He rubbed her arm while Betts worked on her hands.

Making it worse. Philippa held on, hoping no one would see the wet that leaked from the corners of her eyes.

Chick shushed her again, and after a spell Deucey, sitting close, began to sing soft and slow.

"I am a poor, wayfaring stranger…"

The familiar tune helped some, a calming distraction. Deucey's voice was rough around the edges, but tuneful. "In that bright land to which I go," he sang, building strength as he went, and Chick was humming along under his breath, the droning bass part she'd heard all her life at singings.

Betts shuddered into sobs. Without thinking about it, Philippa tightened her arm around the older girl. Somebody crying was no threat to her.

Deucey faltered at Betts' tears, but he picked the song up again and sang it through. A voice from a nearby fire joined in at the second verse.

And then other voices, not so nearly in tune, started up a dirty version, some of which Philippa'd heard before. The cracked tune echoed off the concrete archway. 'When The Work's All Done This Fall' answered it, and another song she'd never heard a name for.

Listening, warmer now and holding Betts as the girl's sobbing eased, Philippa fell asleep.

Somewhere in the night she woke, alone in her blanket, thank Jesus, to a rhythmic gasping from somewhere close by. Two voices, blended high and low. The cold that sat in her bones turned to leaden fear. Philippa pulled the blanket tighter around her head as understanding trickled in.

Nothing to do with her if they chose to do it ten feet from other folks, she told herself, trying to shut her ears. Jesus wept, but she was tired of the fear eating at her. Passing as a boy was safer, sure, and it helped with other stuff as well. Truth was she liked being a boy—but that didn't do a thing for the fear when it came.

Chick was better, she told herself dazedly, finding comfort in the thought, and then couldn't recollect just what that had to do with anything.

A muffled cry turned, after some moments of rustling silence, to sobs, and a low voice whispering comfort. Betts and, and… Deucey.

Philippa shuddered, curling in on herself, trying to be glad for them.

28

*T*he first grey light of day roused Simon. He rolled over inside the thin cocoon of his blanket, grunting at the stiffness of his muscles, held tight all night against the cold.

But that terrible ache and thirst and weariness was gone. Contented for the moment, Simon wrapped his other hand around the slight ridge his iyar pukko made on his wrist, enjoying the comfort of its rough texture.

He'd had to put it on himself. Junkyard had held onto it all the time they'd worked to bring Arlie around, but finally had tossed it to him.

There were songs for putting on an iyar pukko, and jokes and small rituals of well-wishing that went with it, but he was no newly weaned baby receiving a silk-insulated and unset one. This was his, patterned with the rhythms of his own body, and his skin had felt raw without it. He'd done as these Night-worlders, these *ihaaztbinit kahgomadri*, did, simply wrapping it around his wrist where it belonged. It had stayed put, had set its *gaadzet*, its rootlets, into him, become part of him again.

Elsewhere in the jungle a few wanderers moved about, tending fires, talking in low voices, but no one at their camp stirred. A truck rumbled across the bridge. Simon sat up in sudden doubt, eyeing the bridge's dim underside.

Finding someone by the signature produced by their iyar pukko was not a certain thing in a place as complex as a Night World city. The mission's monitor could show no more than direction and an estimate of distance. Iyarit pukko had, after all, never been meant for such a function.

Whoever was sent to find him might have already passed overhead, not knowing to look below the bridge. Simon cast aside the blanket and scrambled to his feet.

One of the muffled shapes by the dead fire groaned and opened a groggy eye to peer at him. "What's got you up at this hour?" Deucey's voice, raspy with sleep. Betts' pale head was tucked beneath his stubbled chin.

Caught off guard, Simon nodded upward towards the span. "Ah, I go wait for my people. Perhaps they go by and not see."

"Mmm," Deucey said, his eye sagging shut again. "Better you than me."

Face flushed as though he had been caught in a lie, Simon stood for a long, frozen moment, studying his companions. Junkyard and Nip were spooned together, the bulk of their shared blankets over the younger boy. Junkyard snored gently, his face turned to the concrete sky. A couple of feet away Chick slept alone, a flattened cardboard box over his feet and legs. Arlie also slept alone, what was visible of the broad child's face creased with blind worry. Cardboard lay beneath him as well as on top, which must have been Chick's doing, though Simon did not remember it from the night. Why they did not sleep curled together, those two, sharing their warmth as the others did, was another of the many things he did not understand.

Simon sighed. He'd promised them all shelter and food, and truly they were owed at least that, however crude and incomprehensible he found them. But how much easier it would be to leave them behind—Arlie in particular, with his uncanny abilities and open desire to break yet another taboo by crossing after Simon to Ntai.

Mingled grief and despair tightened Simon's throat. It was Mara who had begun that one thread of all this dreadful tangle, telling the boy of their world. But his own weakness had made things far worse.

Other than wrapping his arms more tightly about Betts, Deucey hadn't moved again. Deucey at least trusted him. He wondered if any of the others would have. Simon turned away, leaving his blanket on the stony ground.

Though he had never met her, Simon recognized the dugrila cadet at his first glimpse of her in the seeming endless stream of women and men hurrying across the bridge to their daily work. She wore a long, one-button Nightworlder coat of a design he'd seen repeated many times in the mission storerooms of Ebvili, but it was her face that identified her, the warm brown skin and proud nose, and the round-eyed uncertainty written across it.

Those eyes widened even more when he stopped her with a hand on her arm, and greeted her in their tongue. "You are not Lukas!" she stammered.

Grief weighed Simon down at that name. "No," he said, as steadily as he was able. "Lukas died when the slipgate failed, and perhaps Mara also. I am Simon."

"Ohe, please excuse my surprise, bvarit! I am Lena." Pride in her provisional honor name eased her agitation somewhat. "And Mara is well."

Thanks be to Diyo, he thought, sighing as that familiar fear lifted from him. A hurrying, red-faced man muttered a curse as he dodged around them. Standing together, they blocked much of the sidewalk. Simon drew Lena to the metal railing.

She frowned in confusion. "But surely you are mistaken about Lukas." She was no more than fifteen. Nausea gathered at the base of Simon's throat. He knew before she spoke what she would say, and cursed himself that he had not foreseen it.

"The monitor picked him up here, with you, bvarit. Only something went wrong with your signature, an interruption. We thought you had died."

He shut his eyes a brief moment. "As you see, I live," he said curtly. "Lukas does not. The monitor was wrong." If he went below the bridge now and summoned his companions of this last week, if he led them to the mission as he'd promised, what would he be leading them to? Even if Arlie held his silence it would not be possible to hide that Chick now wore Lukas' *iyar pukko*.

Recalling his own outrage when he first learned Arlie wore it, Simon's nausea thickened. He took Lena's arm again, steering her back the way she'd come. "I will explain to your *idbvarit*." But even that he would put off as long as he dared.

29

*T*he jungle looked like hell, Philippa thought, scratching sleepily at an itchy scalp. Cans and bottles and other trash were scattered everywhere between huddled sleepers and the remains of last night's fires.

Chick had got their own fire going again, heating river water in the can they'd used for the soup, not that there was a thing to put in it now. Maybe she could borrow some, use that little bar of soap the Red Cross had handed out to wash her hair. That was one of the swell things about a boy's haircut; it dried lickety-split.

But only if the day got warmer. Cloud shadows raced sunlight across the choppy surface of the Mississippi, and the breeze was cold, carrying the taste of distant snow. Not here; not yet, but it was going to be a raw sort of day. She pulled the blanket tighter around her shoulders.

"You OK?" Chick asked.

Philippa nodded. She was achy, and the cold had settled in her bones, but she supposed that beat whatever'd happened last night. She wrinkled her nose, trying to remember.

"You quit breathing on us," Chick told her without her asking. The breeze had brought a healthy flush to his cheeks and the tips of his ears. "That bracelet fell off slick as a whistle, but you didn't come out of it."

That's right, she thought, breathless again at the scraps of memory that came back to her with his reminders. She'd been taking Junkyard's bracelet off him. And had found the dead hand she needed, Karl's hand if that was possible. And then… she didn't know. Something had gone wrong.

Chick fed cardboard to the small blaze, scrap by scrap. Traffic rumbled by far above their heads. "Thought we'd lost you, for a fact." Absently he rubbed the strap on his own wrist.

Yeah, Philippa thought, eyeing it fearfully. He was well enough for her to take it off him today, looked like. Maybe she'd been careless last night, her head spinning from the booze, and had gone down too far into that dead place. Or maybe it was just a matter of luck and hers was running out.

Either way she had to try. If Simon hadn't been lying to her, she'd need Chick's iyar to cross over. Not to mention the changes it might make inside her, a whispery hope she pushed aside for now.

But what about Chick and the rest of them? How'd she get them across? She looked at her pals, her gaze wincing away from Betts and Deucey, who were tangled together in their blankets. On her side of the fire Junkyard looked to be rousing, though Nip slept like the dead, a fold of his jacket over his head.

And nobody else, not within the circle of their camp. Alarm prickled her nerves. Her brain must still be half-froze for her not to have noticed before.

"Where's Simon?"

Chick jerked his thumb upward. "Heard him say he was going up top so his Wob pals could find him. Awhile back now."

Philippa scrambled stiffly to her feet, tripping some on her blanket. No tan coat was visible where the slope of the riverbank met the bridge's coping, though he might be up on the bridge itself. Still not taking her eyes off the spot, she asked, "He's got his bracelet then?"

"Sure." Chick squinted up at her. "Wasn't he supposed to get it back? We figured you meant him to have it."

She looked at him then. "Well, yeah. He needed it. I think he was fixing to get sick. But if they come for him and we ain't around, we can't follow 'em."

Chick hunched his shoulders; looked away. "I don't want to go," he said at last.

"You don't want to follow him?" Philippa scowled, worry making her impatient.

He shrugged. "I don't care about that. I just don't want to go across to that place. You know." The slanting light brought out the high angle of his cheekbones as he worked something out in his head. "You maybe remember Deucey singing last night?"

Philippa thought a moment. She'd been so cold... "'Wayfaring Stranger'? Yeah. What about it?"

"I've always been of two minds about that song, even back in my church days. Got a fine tune, see, but the words ain't right. My home's here, Arlie. I know it deep in my gut. I just ain't found the exact place yet. And that being the case, there's no call for me to go running off to some other folks' world."

Sour disappointment choked Philippa until she pushed it away. For now it was just as well he didn't, she told herself, what with only one bracelet between them. Once she had it back— her thoughts stumbled again on that, but she kept going—once she had it back she'd go across; get the lay of the land; find Mara. Then she could come back to fetch anybody as wanted to go.

She needed to get moving. Finding the water in the big can not much more than lukewarm, Philippa tipped some into her hand.

"Hey!" Chick said as drops sizzled in the low flames. "Don't you go putting out my fire."

She bared her teeth at him, mock-ferocious, then splashed the quickly cooling water on her face, running her wet fingers through the short fuzz of her hair to comb it. A lick and a promise Meemaw would have called it, but it was the best she had time for.

She stood. "I'm going up to look for him."

Chick just nodded.

Simon wasn't there. Philippa told herself she'd known he wouldn't be, but if that was true, how come she felt so betrayed? A kid hawking papers claimed he'd seen a guy like she'd described meet some black-haired girl. The two had headed east across the bridge.

Slowly Philippa turned that way, but the itch in her mind, faint here on the Minneapolis side of the river, kept her turning until she faced southeast again. She bared her teeth for the second time that day. It was a gamble, following that feeling, but it was the only bet she knew to make.

"Thanks!" she told the newsie, and hightailed it back down to the others.

Getting everybody up and moving seemed to take forever. "I know where they're headed," she'd insisted. "I can take us right there. See, it's got a door or something, like the ice house did? I feel it, plain as plain, only this'un don't feel near so bad."

Junkyard and Nip were all for it, and Chick kept his trap shut. They set about breaking camp, dousing the remains of the fire and rolling up their blankets. Deucey seemed amenable as well, but he kept stopping in the middle of what he was doing to watch Betts, even when she wasn't doing anything more interesting than working the tangles out of her hair.

But mostly what she did was argue. "Why in Christ's name would anybody with a lick of sense want to go near such a place? In case it's slipped your mind, that fire in the ice house killed three people, and came damn close to killing the rest of us."

Two, Philippa told herself, it killed two, but didn't say it out loud. One argument at a time.

Junkyard, ready to go, stood arms crossed at Philippa's shoulder as she went through the whole thing again, about how the bracelet that'd saved Betts' life, not to mention Chick's and hers, had come from this other world where nobody ever went hungry. Simon was from there too, and he was heading back now he thought he'd given them the slip. But he owed them plenty. They had a chance to go with him if they caught up in time.

She didn't feel quite right saying that last, but it popped out of her mouth before she thought.

Betts had heard most of it before, and wasn't buying any. "Simple said you had to have a bracelet just to get across."

"Assuming he wasn't blowing smoke to scare us off," Deucey spoke up, surprising Philippa.

"Yeah," she said, relieved at his suggestion. "We don't know 'til we try. And if need be, one of us'ns can go across and get bracelets for the rest, see. Only thing we can do."

Betts raised an eyebrow at Chick. Philippa headed that question off before it got asked. "I'll take it off Chick when we get there. He don't need it no more, and he don't want to cross." Gravely Chick nodded at her.

"I'll go," Nip said eagerly. He was still messing with his blanket.

Junkyard laid a heavy hand on the kid's shoulder. "Arlie's the best one to do it if it comes to that, brat. We'll get our turn."

Betts snorted. "And what'll we be doing in the meantime? Waiting 'til the snow flies in sunny Minnesota and you come take us to Canaan? Not me, buster." She tied a bit of string around her blanket to make a handle. "I'm gonna go promote me some breakfast." She looked at Deucey, her free hand on her hip and head tipped quizzically. "You coming?"

Philippa's shoulders sagged. Deucey wasn't likely to hold out against what Betts wanted. The notion of them all splitting up this way hurt.

But she couldn't stand around jawing any longer. "I'm going after 'em. Anybody else who's a mind to can come along." She shouldered her own blanket and headed out, Junkyard trailing. She picked her way between the two nearest camps, eyes on her feet; the riprap was treacherous. Stones crunched off to the side, hasty footsteps, and Chick swung in beside her. Grateful, she gave him a mock punch in the arm.

He smiled a little, though it had a sad twist to it. "Attaboy."

"Hey, guys, wait up!" yelled Nip. "I'm coming!"

They turned. Nip had given up trying to roll his blanket with only one arm, and had just balled it up. A corner dragged along behind as he hurried to join them.

"Don't run!" Philippa called back, alarmed. The dope'd take a tumble and not be able to catch himself.

Deucey stood back by the dead fire, turning his cap in his big hands. Betts watched him, her back stubborn. Deucey glanced up, his gaze catching on Philippa's. He raised a finger: Wait.

Hope crowding into her throat, Philippa paused where the path began to climb. Give him and Betts space to work out what they were going to do, she thought, a little dizzy. More time passing, but she wouldn't think about that.

Gentle heat met Simon when Lena pushed open the door to the warehouse's inner room. He sagged against the doorpost as warmth soaked into his skin, his muscles, his bones. Tears pricked his eyelids.

"Bvarit Simon!" a smooth voice said, vaguely familiar. "Welcome! But where is Lukas?"

Looking up, Simon met the man's hard eyes in dismay. Widtrob! No, not Widtrob any more. He'd gotten an honor name when he crossed to his first mission, back when Simon had still been Faahu, a *huali* cadet new to the Dugri academy at Ebvili, no more than two years past the shearing of his child's braid. "Hiram?" Simon ventured.

Hiram bared his teeth in a grin. "You haven't forgotten me."

Never, Simon thought, a knot of the old resentment in his belly. Arrogant Witrob had been, and arrogant Hiram still was, if the way he stood there, head cocked and arms akimbo, was any clue. "I remember." As he spoke it came to him that Hiram was almost certainly idbvarit here, instructor to the cadets who crowded around. Sweat broke out on his skin, the winter clothes suddenly stifling. How could the Mission Council ever have chosen the worst bully of his company? Simon held his hands out, bowing formally though his teeth were clenched. "May I enter?"

Hiram left him so, turning instead to the cadets. "What is wrong here?"

Simon straightened, disbelieving, a drop of sweat running down the side of his face.

"*Qi* should remove the cap, idbvarit," an eager voice answered, a boy who wore his shirt and trousers like a costume. Widtrob had always had his followers. An older boy added, "*Tlet-kahgomadri* don't bow."

"That's right. They hold hands."

Lena at least didn't join the chorus of answers.

"*Shake* hands," Hiram corrected, smiling with his big white teeth. "But only when being introduced, and not always then. And you must remember to use their gendered pronouns—'he' should remove the cap."

Rage took Simon into a place beyond the heat. He grasped the bill of his cap between thumb and forefinger and tipped it smartly forward and down. "You guys mind?" he asked sarcastically. Junkyard's words in his mouth; Junkyard's crude manners. Without invitation he stepped forward, onto the wide, pale-green line that had been painted just beyond the threshold, and then past it, into the bright, windowless room. Desolation swept through him between one step and the next. The line was only paint on a wooden floor, a symbol, and not the cool water of the *atlbaqib* that washed the rest of the world from your feet as you entered home.

This was not home, and all the more so because Hiram was in charge. Simon drew a raw breath. But it would lead him there, given a little more time.

"Much better, Simon! A good demonstration." Hiram's smile had grown wider still. "'To grow gills, live underwater', yes?"

It was not a comfortable proverb. Those who grew gills suffocated in the dry air. Simon bared his teeth back at Hiram, and pulled off his coat, turning to hang it on one of the hooks near the door. "I would appreciate something to eat, idbvarit. I have had a hard journey."

They brought him a bowl of mulligan stew and a wedge of the local maize bread. Getting new dugrilat used to eating as the Nightworlders did was part of training. But the food was hot and good, and at least the training regime did not require sitting on hard wooden chairs at a high table. He could be grateful that those were rarely found in the jungles of the wanderers.

Cross-legged on his cushion, Simon finished the second bowl brought to him by the boy in the awkward clothes. No one asked questions of him as he ate, of course, which gave him time to think. By the time he'd put the bowl to one side and wiped his mouth, he hoped he was ready.

Hiram bent forward, intent. "Now tell us your tale, Simon. First, news of Lukas! Lena says you swear he is long dead, though our sensors show otherwise." Scorn colored his words.

Startled, Simon met his hard gaze. "Not long dead! Eight days, if my count is right; no more than that." Of course, given the much faster passage of time back home on Ntai, that might be as much as two *biyot* there, forty days or more.

Which was still not so long. Simon drew breath, putting the odd comment aside and settling his nerves again to what he must say, and what he must not, for the sake of his companions of the last week. "Lukas died when the slip tore open, bvariti. We were trying to shut it down, he and I, one of us on each anchor." Simon shifted, looking down in grief at his hands. He held his voice steady. "One of the wanderers shouted that the building was on fire, and I was distracted. Only for a moment, but that was enough." He looked around at them all, Hiram's scowl, the faces of the cadets—so much younger than he they seemed, though he was but three years older. "The Void swallowed me, as it had Mara, but spat me back out again in this world. What killed Lukas I do not know, but our wanderers found his burnt body in the ashes of the fire, and buried him after their fashion."

"So they told you." Casually Hiram had slipped down to the floor, so that his cushion was at his back, but his arms were stubbornly crossed.

"Yes."

Hiram nodded to a cadet kneeling by what looked to be a console radio, the grille open to reveal a slate with the sheen that showed it was awake and functioning. "Solly?"

Simon braced himself.

The youth cleared his throat. "Ah, one iyar pukko within range." He glanced up. "I mean of course other than ours, here in this chamber."

Simon turned to him, sighing. "Yes. And it identifies the bearer as Lukas. I do not dispute it. But I know Lukas is dead."

Hiram sat up, opening his mouth to speak. Simon cut him off. "It would be irresponsible of me to say more on this until I stand before the Mission Council."

Coldly Hiram considered him. Simon met his gaze squarely. He would not dare push things now.

"However, one thing has changed from when I checked earlier, idbvarit," the cadet said uncertainly. "The iyar pukko is much closer. No more than ten li—ah, three miles?"

Simon stiffened. Arlie; it had to be the uncanny boy's doing, somehow tracking him back here. He would have to tell Hiram something; convince him to clear the place, to take them all back across to Ntai until Arlie and the others were gone.

Watching his unease, Hiram smiled.

30

*P*hilippa sank down to sit on a stump, ankle stuck straight out in front of her. The truck ride yesterday had rested it, but walking all the way across St. Paul had made it sore again. Then she'd gone and wrenched it good at the edge of this damn marsh. "That'un there," she said tiredly, pointing. At least there wasn't any doubt in her mind which of the warehouses it was. The feel of the place had her strung tighter than a barbwire fence in midwinter. "That's it. But we shoulda stayed with the tracks."

Following the line of her arm, Nip whimpered. The others stared.

"Christ," Junkyard swore. "That's just dandy."

The dilapidated two-story building stood no more than a hundred yards off, not far from the lake edge and at the end of a row of similar warehouses along a half-mile long spur that led back to the CMSP&P tracks. It was just too bad for them that there was a good-sized creek between them and it. If it'd been summer, Philippa thought, measuring the width with her eye, they could've forded it OK. This late in an October day and as dog-tired as everybody was, if she was to try leading them into the water nobody would follow, except maybe Chick, and that to haul her back out again.

"Well," said Chick after a long silence, "guess there ain't nothing for it but to work our way back up to the tracks." He was livelier than the rest of them, thanks to the bracelet. If she had it back, her ankle would be healed already. Though if healing was the only issue, Nip needed it worse.

She had to get it back. But not right yet.

It was another minute before Philippa forced herself up to lead the way along the creek bank back toward the main tracks. Likely the most sensible thing was to go way back around the woods that edged the creek, but she didn't have the heart for it. Low water had left a muddy shelf where the tangle of brush mostly didn't crowd right down to the edge. With luck they could make their way along that.

Within a first ten steps enough mud had stuck to Philippa's boots so it felt like she had a brick tied to the bottom of each one, which didn't help her ankle one little bit. The others were as bogged down as her. They kept going, though, heads hanging, trusting her to get them through.

After a few minutes of slogging and ducking branches Chick said thoughtfully, "Lot of dead wood in along here."

Philippa stopped to look back at him, waiting to hear what he'd come up with. She was too tired to ask. Betts piled into her, and scowled. "You change your mind again, huh, Arlie?"

Chick pointed up to where the midpoint of a long-dead birch lay caught in the dry, rustling branches of a willow. "Think that'll reach across the creek?" Philippa's gaze followed the line of his arm, and seeing that, Betts looked too.

"Gonna make a racket, coming down," Deucey warned, but a smile twisted the corner of his mouth.

The loose, peeling bark made the footing tricky, but they'd all got across. Deucey'd slipped and got one foot soaked. He leaned now against one of the sparsely growing trees on the south bank, wringing out his holey sock. "So what now, Arlie? We just walk in on 'em? Say howdy and when does this drag pull out?"

Philippa squinted at the warehouse consideringly. Nobody had come out when the tree crashed down. She'd kind of hoped they would. Maybe they were on the far side of the building and just hadn't heard. Simon and that pal of his must've got here by now—unless they'd already gone across home.

Lord a'mercy, she thought. If they wasn't there, their slipgate was.

"More or less," she answered. "But on the Q-T, see. We don't want 'em to get the wind up if we can help it." She picked up her blanket roll. "We got a right to be here. Simon owes us."

"You got that right," Junkyard growled.

"Jiminy," Nip said, "I sure could use something to eat."

Philippa's stomach clenched at the reminder. They hadn't had a thing to eat all day. Her fault for pushing so hard.

Betts got a puzzled look on her face. "Listen. Ain't that drums?"

The wail of Lena's conch trumpet shuddered through Simon, tugging at the barrier he'd built around himself since he and Mara and Lukas had first crossed through the Jaguar's Eye. He let himself fall to his knees, the wooden floor warm on his bare skin, vibrating with the trip-rhythms of the two drums.

He hadn't asked for the purification ritual of *akra gro kaagin* before they escorted him home, as Hiram had claimed. However, arguing about it would have taken too much time. He had to convince them his heart was cleansed and then get them all safely across before Arlie and the others came. The wanderers would find no one here, and Hiram would not be confronted by abomination.

The boy with the lefthand drum thumped out the beginning of the heart call, weaving into the other drumbeat's steady syncopation. The familiar pattern sounded in the center of Simon's chest, spilling out fear and grief and despair. He fought against it; he had no time in which to truly lose himself, but his own hands patted out the sequence on the floor. The conch wailed once more, and a cry tore from Simon's throat, pulling him down into the darkness of himself.

After unmeasured time the drums faltered into silence. The smell of dust and salt was thick in Simon's nostrils. He was face down on the boards, his cheeks wet and his throat raw.

This wasn't how the pattern ended, Simon thought, bewildered, beginning to shiver in a sudden draft.

"Christ! You guys murdering somebody in here?"

Philippa stumbled as Chick pushed past to stand by Junkyard, who'd flung the door open in the first place.

"Don't pay him no mind," Chick said loudly into the suddenly dead-quiet room, his cap off. She'd bet he had it bunched up in his hands in his best back-porch manner. Trying to mend Junkyard maybe getting them off on the wrong foot, though it had sounded near as bad as a pig slaughtering as they'd come in from the cavern of the main warehouse into the outer office.

No drums, Simon had said regretfully over the body of that townie kid, back in the hospital chapel in Grand Forks. Maybe he and his pals had been holding a Wob-style wake for Lukas. She craned her head to one side to peer over Junkyard's shoulder, him not being quite as tall as Chick was.

"'Scuse us for interrupting," Chick went on politely, though his back was tense. "But Simon there said you fellows would front us a meal if we was to show up?"

Heat rolled out of the place like August sun beating down on pavement. Sweat blurred her eyes. Philippa pulled her own cap off and wiped her forehead on her jacket sleeve.

The light in the room was mild and shadowless, the walls a clean white. And everybody in it, boy and girl, was as bare nekkid and wide-mouthed as new-hatched birds. Blinking in startlement, she didn't see Simon at all at first, until he rolled half-over on the floor to squint up at them. His black eyes were swole up from what looked to be a champion bout of crying, but it was dread that shaped his face now.

A young man stepped between them and Simon, heavy-shouldered and red-faced with outrage. "Wait outside!" he snapped, slamming the door. Junkyard and Chick stumbled back.

Philippa looked at the others.

"Geez," said Nip.

Junkyard scowled. "Some kind of welcome that was. They gonna give us the slip again while we sit out here like dopes?"

Philippa shook her head, face still hot. "Ain't no way out of there but this door here. Well, not unless they got them a trapdoor in the floor or something. That gate thing ain't in there."

"Sheesh." Deucey turned away and mooched over to the wall of pebbled glass that divided this office space from the main warehouse. "Maybe we shouldn't oughta have busted in on them like that." He slid down to sit with his hands dangling between his knees. Betts didn't say a thing, though her face was as flushed as Philippa's felt.

Could be Deucey was right, but what was done was done, Philippa thought, feeling irritated with him and knowing she wasn't being fair. She paced the length of the room, unable to settle even to rest her ankle. The dead center of the discord that had led her here was out in the main room, no more than fifty feet off. When they'd come through there she'd spotted what looked like an old freight elevator in one corner, with junk piled around it. Had to be it.

Junkyard couldn't seem to stand still either. Betts started nosing around in some boxes stacked up at the far end of the room, which maybe Deucey could say something to her about while he was worrying about making the Wobs mad.

Chick stopped Philippa, arm stuck out to show his wrist. He said quietly, "Ain't a bad time to take this thing off, Arlie."

She stared at the bracelet, and then looked up at him. "You're right, Chick." She drew a steadying breath. Don't think about it, she told herself. Just do it. "Sit down."

They sat in the corner by the inner door. The floor was swept clean but for the mud they'd tracked in themselves. She eyed the drying clumps—yet another thing to rile the Wobs. At last, forcing herself to go on, Philippa took up Chick's wrist. "If it comes off but I don't wake, put it on me right away, OK?"

Junkyard turned to stare. "Christ, Arlie, you damn near croaked last time."

"Got to do it," she said, not looking away from Chick.

"Cross my heart," Chick told her, sketching the cross on his coat front.

Nip scooted closer, his face hopeful. "Can I have it this time, Arlie? This darn arm…"

Behind him the door opened. She and Chick both froze like they'd been caught doing something they oughtn't.

The man who'd been so mad came out first, dressed, thank Jesus, and more-or-less regular if you didn't count the dull red color of his coat. He looked around at them with the kind of stuck-up smile she'd seen too many times to trust, then nodded to the enameled stockpot the tall girl right behind him carried. She was dressed too. "This is only what is left of our meal. We will cook more." He spoke mostly to Betts and Junkyard, who happened to be standing right in front of him. Other Wobs crowded out in his wake, one boy with a tray of bowls. Simon came last, looking like he was sleepwalking in a bad dream.

Chick's arm slipped in her grasp as he rolled to his knees. "Thank you kindly! We're awful sorry for busting in on y'all."

Red Coat turned to him, that polite smile fixed on his face. His eyes, though, were cold and black. "Not important," the man said, smooth as butter, as Chick slipped his arm free and stood. "We were startled, that is…" Red Coat broke off to stare at Chick's exposed wrist, and the iyar thing on it. The smile dropped away, became nothing more than teeth. "Simon," he said softly, not taking his eyes off Chick, "I see what you would not tell!"

Philippa's breath caught in her throat. She ought to've seen trouble like this coming after how nutsy Simon had gone when he first found out she had the thing on. And he was a reasonable enough guy in his way, not like this Red Coat. Shaky, she pulled herself up to stand by Chick, who was looking alarmed, getting set to run or fight if he had to. Though Jesus knew where they could run to in this place.

Chick glanced at the iyar. "This what's bothering you? Heck, mister, I don't even want the thing."

Philippa swallowed. She couldn't bear the thought of handing it over, not after all they'd gone through just to get here. But Jesus knew what the Wobs might do to Chick if she didn't. Chop his arm off, maybe. "See, it ain't no problem. I was just getting…"

Simon cut her off, loudly. "Hiram, this is business for the Mission Council! There is more than you see!" He stepped forward past the bunch of shocked-looking young Wobs, back straight as a rifle barrel.

Red Coat—Hiram—did turn and look at Simon then. "Do you swear it?" he asked flatly.

"I do." Simon's face looked carved from stone. He was fixing to take a fall, though whether it was for them, or what it was about at all, Philippa couldn't be sure.

Hiram's smile came back, though it was faint. Moving easy as a cat, he looked to her and Chick again, and then around at the others: Junkyard with his fists bunched and Deucey's hand gripping his shoulder; Betts beside them, crowding Nip so he was stuck behind her. "Do not be worried. Please go in where it is warm. Eat and do not follow. You understand we must discuss this in private." He motioned his guys toward the main warehouse.

Out to where the gate was that'd take them home.

Maybe it'd be the smart thing to do, but she couldn't just let them go. Red Coat—Hiram—had already reached the door. Philippa found herself following, talking loudly. "See, what he ain't saying is they don't want us to see 'em get on that freight elevator out there. Ain't gonna take 'em upstairs. It's gonna take 'em clean to Canaan, on account of that's their door home. And what he don't know is I spiked it afore we come in."

Simon turned a white-eyed look on her. She winked at him, feeling the lie pour strength into her.

Hiram didn't turn around. "Simon! What have you told them!"

There was dead silence for a heartbeat or two. "Very little," Simon said at last, bitterly.

Hiram put a hand in his coat pocket. He's got a gun, Philippa thought, going numb, but he didn't pull one out.

"Oh? But it is not important now." After a still moment Hiram went on out, his people following uneasily.

A shrill hum built inside her, echoing up her spine to the back of her skull, though nobody else reacted. To drown it out she hurried to the door; shouted after them. "I'll put your door right if you take us across with you, those as wants to go, anyways. That's all we're asking."

Hiram glanced back at her. His lip curled and she saw her bluff go bad. "Foolish child. Simon at least should have told you that is not possible."

Then he looked at Simon, his hand still working in his pocket. "Lead us. The honor is yours."

Simon went grey beneath the brown of his skin; he'd believed her threat. "Yes," he whispered and walked away, chin up and shaking, straight for the elevator...

Straight for a line of golden light that blinked into being a foot above the elevator platform, that opened like a clothes chest, like an eye with a pupil of sun, like a door into heaven—like all these things and none of them. A light that tied your eyes in knots looking at it.

A babble of voices behind her, but right then for Philippa there was nothing but Simon, black and hesitant against the heart of the light, and then gone.

At a word from Hiram the other Wobs hurried to follow Simon; one by one they disappeared the same way. Hiram bowed, grinning, and waved his free hand toward the office behind them. "You are welcome to stay." Then he walked into the light.

Philippa howled and flung herself after him, but darkness—why hadn't she seen before how it held the gate's light like an eye socket cradles an eye, or a hand holds a ball?—was closing its mouth, down, down, until only the blazing line was left to let her through, so she shut her own eyes and dived.

31

Chick blinked. Just like that, Arlie was gone. The lighted doorway was gone; the Wobs were gone, and there wasn't a thing in that back corner but the dim shape of the freight elevator with its makeshift gate hanging from one hinge. Bile soured the back of his tongue and salt stung his eyes, though he'd known the kid was set on going.

But this! It made his brain feel like a car going down the road with a flat tire.

"Geez," Nip said, reverence in the word this time. He pushed past Chick, drawn to the elevator. Junkyard grabbed his collar long enough to caution him to watch what he stuck his nose into.

Betts crossed her arms and leaned against one of the wooden uprights that framed the glass wall. "Thought Simple told us you had to have that thing on to go through." Her face was pale enough to make the circles under her eyes stand out like bruises.

"Aw, he was feeding us a line of bull," Junkyard said.

Feeling hollow, Chick trailed Nip over to the corner, flexing his hand as he went, muscles straining against the strap. "Dunno about that," he said over his shoulder. "Guy's a piss-poor liar. Mostly he just clammed up, if you'll recall." He hated how the

Wob bracelet felt so tight against his skin, and the notion it was doing things inside of him. And now the hell of it was he was stuck with the thing until Arlie came back, when she'd been the one needed it.

If she came back.

Aside from the elevator there was nothing in the corner but dust, some broken crates, and a few spiderwebbed pieces of machinery. Chick frowned. One was a battered arc welder, own brother to the one he'd seen back in the ice house however long ago it'd been. He looked around, trying to see in the failing light from the high, dirty windows.

Wedged between the elevator and the wall was the squat shape of a second welder.

"Betcha Arlie got across just fine," Junkyard said stubbornly.

Hope so, Chick thought uneasily as he squatted by the first welder. There wasn't any way to know. "Maybe. Arlie don't much abide by the rules," he answered, more for himself than Junkyard. Cautiously he poked the metal with a fingertip, then snatched it back. "Hell, this thing's hotter'n a pistol!" He stuck the finger in his mouth.

Nip, who'd been standing on the elevator platform staring hopefully up into the space above, came to join him. "Can't be hot. It hasn't got a cord to it, or a generator or nothing." He hunkered down in front of the welder and peered at the dial, adding to Chick's frayed nerves.

Deucey shivered. "We're all crazy, ain't we? This is just a whatchamacallit, a mass, a mass…"

"Hallucination," Nip said happily. "Come look at this."

"Yeah, and me seeing anything at all's nothing but a damn pipe dream," rasped Junkyard as he wandered over to join them. "We ain't imagining any of it.

"Huh," he said, puzzled. "Looks kind of like the old Lincoln in my uncle's shop, only the numbers don't make sense."

It was buzzing too, very faintly. Chick bent closer to be sure, close enough that the heat from it warmed his cheek.

No. The sound came from the Wob bracelet. He could feel it as well now, faint but deep in his bones. Annoyed, he rubbed the wrist. Goddamn thing.

Funny that the Wobs went off without trying to get it back.

One step; two, and Simon's questing foot found solid floor. Blue light danced in the corners of his eyes from the activation charge that whirled around the slipgate pillars.

This time the Void had not swallowed him. Arlie's claim had been only bluff. Relief loosened Simon's joints, and his first full step back into the Hall of Crossings, into his own world, was an awkward one. Hungrily he breathed in air that smelled faintly of someone's cup of kaklotl, of spices and the scent of sweet resin that permeated clothing hung in the Ebvili drying closets. Simon gazed around. The great domed hall was nearly empty of people. It must be sleeptime, and the food he smelled some unlucky technician's supper.

"Simon?" The voice was no more than a stunned whisper.

He turned. Vaitnu, who'd had such difficulties opening the slipgate those long days ago, stared at him.

"After so long, it is you!" She half-rose from her cushion, then hastily sat again at her console. "Step forward, Simon, out of the way. Come stand by me. Someone else is coming through." Her hands danced over the slate. She spared him an eager glance. "Is it Lukas? Mara will be so relieved to hear of your return!"

"No," he answered, slowly shrugging out of his coat, "not Lukas." The grief and guilt choked his words, but beneath it joy still welled up at her welcome, at the sight and smells of the familiar warren. Disgraced or even dishonored he might soon find himself, but this was his own place.

"Ah, no, Simon, is it so? But one of you back is better than none, which is what we thought we had after—how long has it been? More than half a year?"

The coat dangling by one sleeve, Simon gaped at her. Nine biyot? How was that possible?

Not looking at him, Vaitnu chattered on. "And here qi is! One of Hiram's nurselings, to escort you home? Uncommonly thoughtful of Hiram." Lena stepped out of the blaze of the Eye, looking relieved and uncertain and very young.

Her reappearance shook Simon from his distraction. Even given the time differential between the worlds, Hiram would be here soon. Perhaps he should have gone on, straight to the Council antechamber to call for emergency audience without Hiram present to act as his accuser. He could go even yet.

No, he thought, straightening his back. He would endure Hiram. And too much hurry was as bad as too little. Boldness was the key with the senior dugrilat who oversaw the Mission, unlike those of the Great Council.

"Did they tell you that the catastrophic tear at your ice house mission destroyed all our calibrations for the entire system? It took us..." Vaitnu paused, frowning. "What is this now? More are crossing?"

Lena glanced at Simon, an anxious, birdlike motion. Solly appeared out of the light, scowling.

"Yes," Simon said. "All of them."

Made it! Philippa crowed, giddy with the relief of not finding herself skidding face-first across the freight elevator platform. For a fact she wasn't in the warehouse anymore. It was funny, though: she thought she'd spoken right out loud, but maybe not because she hadn't heard a thing.

Couldn't see anything, either. Dummy, she told herself, you shut your eyes.

Opening them didn't seem to make any difference, if she did open them. Pitch black was a daytime color next to this lack of anything at all to see.

Philippa swallowed, or thought she did. OK, so maybe there was a place in between her world and Mara's, like the gap between boxcars. Leaping from boxcar to boxcar was scary too, but sometimes you had to do it. It didn't take but a second and then you were grabbing for the catwalk, hanging on, safe again. Trying for patience, she waited.

Nothing. Nothing but the thoughts trickling through her mind. At last she called out softly; called 'hello?' or thought she had. But she didn't hear the word or anything. Or, for that matter, feel her tongue touch her teeth, or her lips moving.

Scared, she tried to speak again, concentrating on it real hard, but if she moved mouth or made a sound, she couldn't tell.

Couldn't feel herself breathing either. She wasn't smothering, though; no, she wasn't, she told herself as a bodiless panic rose and gnawed at the edge of her thoughts. She wasn't cold, wasn't drowsy, not like last night under the bridge, taking Simon's bracelet off Junkyard.

Was it last night? Without even the in and out of breathing she couldn't be sure of anything about time, except that the moment she was in kept going on and on in utter darkness.

Memory turned in her like a knife, brought up the shriek of that woman who'd slipped one sticky-hot night last July when she'd tried to jump the gap between cars. Just like that she was gone, and nobody'd seen what happened to her. Not that anybody needed to. You fell that way and you died quick and ugly.

Darkness. Fallen into darkness; the words echoed in Philippa's mind and she couldn't get past them. Darkness deeper than being inside a dead hand. Deep as that light-eating tear at the center of the twister, fallen into *that*.

Howling.

Darkness.

Simon drew a harsh breath before he told her more. "Hiram is evacuating the training mission, Vaitnu—temporarily I hope. I need to speak to the Mission Council as soon as it can be arranged."

The technician, whose hands had stilled at the word 'evacuating', pulled herself together. "Yes, I suppose you will!" she said mildly. "I will alert them."

Two more cadets had come through, much too close together for safety. Vaitnu was too busy to rebuke them. Uncertainly they went to stand by Lena and Solly, stripping off their over-warm clothing. Simon watched them whisper among themselves.

Lena spoke up at last, pushed by the others. "That ihaaztbin —the one with the black hair—was that truly a…"

"Council business, Lena!" Simon snapped, going cold. He bent to speak in the technician's ear. "Your pardon, Vaitnu, but the senior dugrilat must hear about all this first."

She glanced at him, a faint smile twisting her mouth. "I will hear of it soon enough, bvarit." More loudly she said, "Step aside, Frank! Hiram has yet to come through."

It was the last of the cadets, Simon saw, the boy who had played the lefthand drum. Now for Hiram. He forced his hands to unclench.

Vaitnu gasped. "Simon! This at least you should have warned me of!" Her hands were moving in a blur. "All of you, get out of here. Go wait in the atrium," she cried angrily, the blood drained from her face. "You also, Simon! Hiram has triggered the sealing of the slipgate!"

Chick woke, groggy and warm, rolled in the luxury of two blankets. Had he heard something? He listened, still reluctant to open his eyes.

Nothing but the wind outside and Deucey's fitful snores, and after a week of sleeping next to the guy Chick was used to that. He'd prodded the corner of the blankets into a more comfortable pillow and settled down to doze again when his wrist flared in pain.

Yelping, Chick sat bolt upright and gripped the wrist. What the hell was the blamed thing doing to him?

"S'wrong?" Nip muttered.

"Nothing," Chick told him, feeling sullen. "Go back to sleep." He sat hugging his knees, his head beginning to sag, until the burst of pain came again like needles stabbing into the joint, there and gone again, but leaving an ache behind.

"Hell!" Chick disentangled himself from the blankets and dragged on his boots. Stumbling, he let himself out into the shadowy cave of the warehouse.

He hadn't got two steps before he saw it: one of the welders glowing red like a horseshoe ready for quenching. It had a funny kind of shimmer to it that made his tired eyes want to cross. The breath knocked from his lungs, Chick eased his way toward it, like the thing might run away if it saw him. Stupid, but he couldn't make himself go faster. A little closer and a blurry red glow from the second one showed him where it stood wedged against the boards of the wall.

That was bad. He could feel the heat beating off the closer one, and it was a good ten feet away. Drag them out into the middle of the warehouse, he told himself, his thoughts beginning to race. Better yet, pitch them outside in the gravel. But he couldn't even get close to them, much less grab hold.

He had to have help. Chick turned back to the office where the others slept, and the bracelet jabbed him again. He sucked his teeth and kept going.

"Junk?" he called softly, standing in the doorway, and then thought, the hell with it. "Hey, guys, wake up!"

He grabbed for his peacoat and the blankets, wadding them up in a ball which he stuffed into the top of one of the food boxes, his brain a step behind his hands. Right; they'd best get everything out first and then try and deal with the welders.

"Where's the fire?" Junkyard asked grumpily, sitting up.

Chick hoisted the box. "Here, if we ain't lucky! Get everybody up and out, Junk. Them welder things is glowing like a stovepipe afire, and the walls might catch."

"Huh?" Junk crawled to the door, still tangled up in his bedding. He stuck his head through for a look. "Christ! Is that thing as hot as it looks?"

"Yep. Deuce! Betts! Get your kicks on and get moving!" Chick pushed past Junkyard and made for the nearest double door, gasping when his wrist seized up again, but not slowing. He knocked the bar up out of the way and elbowed one of the doors open. An icy wind blew it the rest of the way back, banging it against the wall. Chick screwed up his face as the wind cut into him. He should grab his coat out of the box and pull it on, he told himself as he scrambled down off the dock.

But he didn't. He just raced back in for the other box, and to make sure they were all up and moving.

Uncomprehending, Simon blinked. "Sealing the slipgate?"

"Oh, yes." Vaitnu gestured at the console slate. "See there?"

Pulsing yellow ringed the display. Simon couldn't get his mind to settle on the interweaving of meanings that raced through the mandala, though his heart was beginning to pound in time with them. "But why?"

"I," she said, biting off the words, "am only the technician."

A technician who would have to stay at the console throughout the long, tense process. Simon brought to mind all he could remember. It was safe, he'd been taught, or as safe as any process could be that focused such massive amounts of energy to weld shut a hole in the world. But the protocol called for everyone but the one necessary technician to leave the area. If a strict harmony could not be held, particularly at the climax, a flare might scour the shielded Hall clean.

Breathless, Simon knelt beside her. "I swear to you I didn't know Hiram planned such a thing!"

"That is not a great deal of comfort." She drew a shuddering breath and let it out again. "But it is some. Go speak to the Council, Simon.

"Ah," she drawled in angry mockery. "Here is the idbvarit at last."

Hiram stepped easily from the blazing Jaguar's Eye, untying the belt of his coat, casting it and his hat aside. "That difficulty you brought down on us is solved, Simon," he cried in triumph, then looked puzzled. "Where are my cadets?"

Philippa drifted inside her mind, tangling now and again with stray memories. Some of them she clung to: the fortifying sourness of a mess of greens simmered up with a ham bone after a cold Saturday of chores and play; breath puffing in the stinging air as she split kindling for Meemaw, proud she was big enough to do it; the high voices of the Holts's littler ones next door playing catch-me-can and the brash crows cawing, shiny black in the sun. One day or many, all run together, and Meemaw still alive, swatting at her for sassing back.

Alive! Philippa pretended as hard as she could, but once you got that far it was too late. Meemaw dead, and what came after, tumbled over her, and she would've curled up and covered her head if that had meant anything here.

Here, where emptiness chewed at the edges of what little she had left. Here in the Void.

Philippa fled back into memory, digging for summer or the chalk-dust smell and drone of schoolrooms; found bits of them but they slipped away, tallied rather than tasted, and left her only the chaff. A bedraggled kitten played to death by dogs; hot shame at a recitation forgot halfway through in front of God and everybody; Meemaw shriveling up after the mill closed.

Corinne and Hank coming to fetch her in a borrowed DeSoto after the funeral.

Feeling Hank's black gaze on her and knowing enough to be scared, to keep her distance, only she'd failed time and again. His talk and his touch burning like ice, like acid, memory pulling her down again into then and she couldn't move or barely even breathe. Like here.

But she'd got away from him; she had! And if she was stuck now, at least being here didn't hurt that way.

She had a gang that'd fight for her, older kids who asked her to do things they never could. Read the weather; take off the Wobs' bracelets. And how had she done that?

By reaching out somehow with her mind.

Clinging to that, Philippa groped outward, the only direction there was, looking for something; for anything at all.

Chick dragged the thick end of the branch Deucey had found across the dock. Junkyard ran ahead to hold open the doors against the knife-like wind. Finding something long enough to reach the welders with all the heat they were putting off had taken awhile.

"Devil take me!" Junk howled, stumbling back from the open doorway. Shimmering yellow light spilled across the concrete dock around his feet. Gaping, Chick dropped the branch and joined him.

It was like staring into the sun.

Jerking his hand back from the doorpost, Junkyard swore again. "Whole damn building's shaking. Let's get the hell out of here, Chick."

And he was right. The concrete beneath Chick's feet trembled like the hum off a radio set. They bolted for the edge of the dock and leapt for the ground, just as Deucey came barreling around the corner yelling, "Out! Get out!"

Away seemed the best idea, and they found themselves hotfooting it for the lake, fighting the wind for headway. A growing rumble chased them, felt as much as heard. Whole thing's coming down, Chick thought, panicked, as the ground danced beneath his feet and the rumble behind them built to a deafening roar of breaking wood and glass and metal.

A whump of stale air knocked them sprawling into the teeth of the night's wind, a few yards from the water's edge. Chick found himself staring dazedly at the cold gleam of ice stretching out to the dark line of trees at the lake's far side. Whole thing froze solid, he thought stupidly. Same as the one by the ice house.

"Betts!" cried Deucey hoarsely, rolling over.

"Nip and her'll be jake," Junkyard said, picking himself slowly up. "They were pretty far back to start with." He turned to look behind them. "See? That next warehouse's still standing."

Standing, yeah. But its few windows were busted, and some of the siding looked to have fallen away. He pushed himself to his knees, shaking, not trusting the earth to hold him. There'd be no point in waiting now. Arlie couldn't cross back here, and Lord only knew where other doors might be, if there were any. Supposing he ever wanted to see one of them again, which he didn't.

Might as well get used to the damn bracelet.

Fingering it, Chick clambered to his feet. The ground held still beneath him as he straightened, and the wind was dying down. "Hell," he said, and spat wearily in the sand. "Wanna fetch Betts and Nip, Deucey? We'd best scram before the cops get here. Can't you see 'em pinning this mess on us?"

New grief had flooded Simon as he drew the curtain closed behind him, curling him into a knot on the cool tile of the floor. While the Mission Council assembled he had a little time to himself here in his own chamber. Time to prepare, but at first he couldn't think of that.

They might still escape the destruction of the slipgate, his band of rough wanderers—if they chose to leave the shelter of the warehouse with the darkness coming down and nowhere else to go. "Ah, bvariti," he hissed into his balled fists, "I betrayed you with my promises."

He would have betrayed them in any case. He was honor-bound to tell what he knew. If Hiram had not destroyed the slipgate, most likely a team would be preparing to cross, intent on clouding the ihaaztbinit's memories and reclaiming Lukas' iyar pukko. With luck Simon might have convinced them to let Arlie take it off Chick, as an alternative to the quick amputation that was the only method his people had, thanks to the arrogant Haanit control of the technology.

And all that was only what had to be done to protect their mission. Hiram, though, had chosen in his spite to simply 'solve' the difficulty. Vaitnu too might have died of it.

The rage that rolled through Simon then brought him up off the floor. Shaking, he washed his face at the ever-flowing basin at the foot of his bed.

If he spoke against Hiram as his first act, rather than taking responsibility for his own actions, the Council's judgment might well go against him. Simon stood a long moment, gulping in steadying breaths. Then, eyes still stinging from the tears, he dressed himself in his festival vest and kilt and went to pay what debts he could.

Anything different, Philippa told herself. Find anything that stands out against this nothingness. And tried not to try too hard. After all, she had all the time in the... all the time she needed.

Hard not to run from that notion, so she threw her mind outward instead, searching, like feeling for a stickaburr buried in the wool of your socks.

She found her own body first, the moist bands of limp muscle, the stacked boulders of her wrist bones. Going there made some sense, Philippa guessed, even if it didn't do her any good now. The reddish light of the tiny fires in her flesh seemed bright to her, though the whole of it felt somehow stale.

Learning the trick took her awhile, but finally, her brain feeling like it was split in half, she got the boulders to rumble gently against each other.

She could move. She just couldn't feel it in the usual way. There was comfort in that, in having a body she'd often wished she didn't, but it didn't get her out of here.

Think weather, not wrists, Philippa told herself; that was more likely to be the size of what she wanted.

Time passed, or didn't.

Panic began to chew at her again. Pretend, she whispered soundlessly. Pretend you know the something different is out there and it's just a matter of finding it. Make it up if you have to. The Wobs had ways through. Mara had got across, she was sure, and she'd seen Simon and them cross with her own eyes. That was what she needed, even if she had to come at it another way.

And there it was! singing threads of warmth spinning from what seemed nowhere. She reached for one. It stung her hand like nettles. Never mind that! Philippa told herself, and seized hold. Dizziness took her by the throat, hurled her out somewhere beyond the realm of sense, but she did not let go.

Without warning the thread spun itself into a sun of thrumming, blazing gold that swallowed her whole. Brain drowning in light and sound, Philippa threw herself onward with a desperate strength.

And the sun spat her tumbling out onto a bank of rank green grass. Dazed, she lay staring up at lashing branches outlined against a ruddy gold sky. Yellow fruit like apples rained down around her. Dust devil, she began to think, but the branches calmed before the thought was done. A fine exhaustion pressed her into the welcoming earth, slowing the workings of her brain.

Was it sunset? Dawn? She squinted upward, lazily considering the color of the sky, but there wasn't any shadow to this light. It came from everywhere, soaking into her bones like the song of a thousand wild voices, utterly alien and beguiling.

She was drowning this time in warmth and the sweet-sour smell of growing things and the scratchiness of cool grass against the skin of her palms; yeah, drowning like a fish in water.

Mara's world.

Canaan.

Sighing, weary and content, Philippa let go and shut her eyes.

GLOSSARIES

Philippa's World:

black bottle: (n) poison reputedly given to poor hospital patients
blow smoke: (v) exaggerate
bo; boes: (n) hobo; hoboes
bohunk: (n) Bohemian; Eastern European
boil-up: (n) wash
brakie: (n) brakeman
bull: (n) policeman or detective; nonsense or lies
buys no groceries: (v) makes no money
carry the banner: (v) walk the streets all night
catwalk: (n) running board along the tops of boxcars
Christers: (n) Christians
cloudy-headed: (adj) foolish; not in touch with reality
croker sack: (n) burlap bag
dehorn: (n) alcohol intended for use as antifreeze, or derived from Sterno and other sources
dust-up: (n) fight
flip: (v) board a moving train
frill; frail: (n) woman or girl
front: (n) appearance
fruiter: (n) homosexual
grab iron: (n) steel bar attached to side of boxcar or engine as handhold
harness bull: (n) uniformed officer
hyesse: (interj) shit [Greek-American slang]
jackroller: (n) tramp who robs other tramps
jake: (adj) excellent; all right; fine; okay; hunky-dory
jocker: (n) road kid's teacher; sometimes relationship is sexual
jungle: (n) hobo camp
kicker: (n) foot
lamb: (n) boy sexually involved with older man
lam: (v) leave quickly; strike
main stem: (n) hobo district of town
makings: (n) papers and tobacco
misery: (n) weak or foul-tasting coffee

moniker: (n) road name

nail: (v) board a moving train

nipio: (n) infant; young boy [Greek]

peach: (v) tell on; betray

penny-up: (v) a mixture of buying and begging, seeing what can be gotten for a penny or two

put on the low needle: (v) talk softly

road kid: (n) young tramp

scoffing: (n) food; meal

shack: (n) railroad detective or brakeman

sky pilot: (n) preacher

stew bum: (n) bum wasted by alcohol

tender: (n) vehicle directly behind train engine for carrying fuel and water

tooling ringers: (v) ringing doorbells

toppings: (n) stale buns and bread and doughnuts begged or bought very cheaply from bakeries

Wobs: (n) Wobblies, members of IWW; any labor activist

wolf: (n) older hobo who preys sexually on younger ones

yuns: (pronoun) you-all

Simon's World:

akra gro kaagin: (n) cleansing ritual for one who needs to unburden him- or herself

akra nt ako: (n) literally 'singing down the blood' or blood sacrifice; a set of mourning rituals of which the blood-stained atonement cloth is only the first and most general

anchor: (n) one of a pair of devices which control the opening and closing of a slipgate [English translation]

atlbaqib: (n) small stream of water that separates the work side (see **navl si**) from the home side (see **draas**) of a warren or Ngorvisla communal dwelling

biyo: (n) a month of 20 days; pl. **biyot**

bu tlagin: (n) a ritual gait suitable for funerals

bvarit: (n) comrade (navl si work neuter); pl. **bvariti**

dakatl: (n) waste; garbage

draas: (n) home; the highly gender-specific 'left-hand' side of a Ngorvisla communal dwelling

dugri: (n) mission

dugrila: (n) missioner: pl. **dugrilat**

dzinsi: (n) a Haan official; transliteration of the Haan *jinshi*; roughly meaning 'benevolent minister' (used ironically)

gaadze: (n) literally 'little root'; one of the tiny filaments that penetrate the flesh of the wearer of an iyar pukko, anchoring it and giving a pathway for the device to interact with the body

qodt: (adv) why

gri ngiten!: (interj) Damn barbarian! (literally, one whose thoughts or heart has no center)

Haan; Haanit: (n) people of the former ruling country; they still are the most technologically advanced country. The Ngorvislat despise and fear them

haat ifobetla: (n) literally 'opener of the wind's gate', i.e. a witch

haatzo: (n) literally 'wind-taken', i.e. dead

hand-servant: (n) Haan body-slave [English translation]

huali: (n) rabbit; first year cadet at Ebvili, the mission headquarters

idbvarit: (n) literally 'comrade boss'; work coordinator; pl. **idbvariti**

ihaaztbin: (n) one without roots; wanderer. The term used for Night World hoboes; pl. **ihaaztbinit**

iyar pukko: (n) literally 'guardian of balance'; supplemental immune system worn on the wrist; what Arlie and the kids call 'bracelet'; pl. **iyarit pukko**

Jaguar's Eye: (n) common nickname for a slipgate [English translation]

kuakuatl: (n) ceremonial conch trumpet

Kahgomadri: (n) literally 'Night World'; Ngorvislat name for Arlie's world

kaklotl: (n) a bitter, spiced chocolate drink, more common than coffee, although they have that too

li: (n) a Haan linear unit of measurement adopted by the Ngorvislat, equivalent to about a third of a mile

Nahui ako-ngintobit: (n) the Four Atonements song; part of the akra nt ako ritual

navl si: (n) work; the gender-neutral 'right-hand' side of their way of life

ngiten: (n) uncivilized person; literally one who does not share

Ngorvislat: (n) 'Cultivators'; the political movement that overthrew the Haanit a century ago; the country Simon and Mara come from; what Arlie and the kids call Wobs. A single individual is **Ngorvisla**

Nir nev: (n) 'Big Slip'; the blazing hole in the fabric of their sky that banished night and started all the trouble about 4000 years ago; God

Night World: (n) see **Kahgomadri**

Ntai: (n) what they call their own world

Ohe, ako-ngintob libaatin fa: repeated line from the Four Atonements passage in the akra nt ako. Translates roughly as 'blood given for our failings'

Passage: (n) a coming-of-age ceremony where a child's braids are cut [English translation]

qi: (pronoun) neuter pronoun used in navl si

slipgate: (n) a constructed gate between worlds [English translation]

tlet-kahgomadri: (n) literally, Night People, or Night World People

ACKNOWLEDGMENTS

Grateful thanks are due to:

The participants of the 1999 Rio Hondo Workshop, way back at the disastrous beginning of the tale, for picking up the pieces. In particular: Sage Walker and Walter Jon Williams, plus Karen Joy Fowler, Nina Kiriki Hoffman, Ellen Klages, Mark J. McGarry, Maureen McHugh, Sean Stewart, Ray Vukcevich, and Cynthia Ward.

Also to the members of the Very Small Array, Plotbusters, and Critical Mass critique groups, among these: Daniel Abraham, Terry Boren, Doug Clark, Yvonne Coats, Debbie Daughetee, Terry England, Emily Mah, John Miller, Laura Mixon Gould, Pati Nagle, Pari Noskin Taichert, Joan Spicci Saberhagen, Melinda Snodgrass, Steve and Jan Stirling, Nancy Varian, Jerry Weinberg, and of course both Sage and Walter again.

Then there are the good friends who have, in various ways, offered support and insight: Jane Lindskold, Jim Moore, Jo Rebeka, Karen Sunde, and Landra White.

Without Thomas Minehan's 1934 classic *Boy and Girl Tramps of America* to steal from, this would be a poorer tale. As well, without "Sweet Prospect" (#65 in *The Sacred Harp*), and the singers who have kept all these songs alive, my story would be lacking a key portion of its soul.

And finally, memory and time being what they are, I may have forgotten a few names here. To you, both apologies and thanks.

A Singing in the Bones

Book Two
of
Away Yonder

*D*reams like smoke held her down, stifled her, tore flesh from off her aching bones, over and over, until she found a way out, and woke.

Philippa lay still, heart pounding, mouth dry. Liquid trickled somewhere nearby like water overflowing the basin of a spring, but it was a smell that had roused her, or at least it claimed her attention now; a rich smell somewhere between cocoa and coffee. There were other smells beneath that one, sweet and musty, but they weren't as strong and she didn't have anything to tie them to. The cocoa-coffee one made her hungry more than thirsty; made her feel real, and not quite as scared.

Somewheres beyond the room she was in folks were talking, their voices echoing like they were in a cave. Maybe the smell and the voices went together, but she couldn't make out a word of what they were saying.

Well, of course not. She'd crossed over to the Wobs' world, and she didn't know their lingo. Philippa dragged open her eyes, fighting a weariness that made any movement a struggle.

An eggshell, she thought, blinking in wonder at the ceiling. I'm inside a godawful big egg! She wasn't, of course. Looking around a little showed her that. The ceiling was domed and had a creamy eggshell shine to it, but the windowless walls were more or less straight and square. Only more or less, though, and that was funny in itself. Niches were cut into the walls here and there. A big one half-sheltered the bed she was lying in.

The light was cool and shadowless. She couldn't see where it came from unless it was the whole smooth surface of the dome. Behind the light somehow was a faint buzzing that she felt inside her bones rather than heard—not the sound of the golden sky, but more like you got when a radio was warming up. Put together, the light and strange-shaped room and the echoes and the hum gave her a floaty sort of feeling she could've done without, weak as she was.

One of the voices came clear, snapping off some kind of order, sounded like. A voice she knew: Mara, laying down the law. A shiver ran down Philippa's backbone that was only half anticipation. The soft slap of footsteps sounded; drew closer. Somebody—maybe Mara—was heading her way.

The wonderful smell got stronger. Philippa watched the filmy blue curtain that billowed in the doorway, her empty stomach in a knot, hungry, nervous. But when Mara pushed the curtain aside she was smiling.

At that Philippa's own mouth stretched wide, though tears stung the corners of her eyes. She'd made it here, and to prove it Mara herself was standing right in front of her, with welcome on her face.

An older-looking Mara, hollows at her temples and beneath her cheekbones that hadn't been there before. They made her look more grown-up. She looked taller too, but that was likely on account of the bed being low to the ground.

"Awake?" Mara asked. She carried a small wicker tray with a shallow bowl on it, and a cup with two handles. Beneath the tray her belly curved out like a circus balloon.

Pregnant! Six months along if Philippa was any judge of things. Philippa tried to swallow.

How long had it been?

She must've said it. Mara beamed, not understanding. She glanced down at herself. "Is, ah, jake, yes? Am..." she thought a moment "...twenty-seven of your weeks from start." She bent to set the tray on a table Philippa hadn't noticed before. "Excuse my bad speech. Long time since, since I spoke..."

"How long!" Philippa croaked again, unable to wait for Mara to figure out the words, hoping for an answer that'd do her some good this time.

Mara thought again. "Two years? More?"

The room—the eggshell ceiling, the bunched curtain, Mara's face—floated away from her and the buzzing got louder. No, it was a hum; a faint echo of the wild chorus she'd heard from the sky. It was far away, and many feet of smothering earth lay between her and it.

"No, no!" A warm hand squeezed Philippa's cold one, and Philippa grabbed hold as though the life that burned inside it would keep her from drowning. "Time pass here and your home not, not same," Mara said hesitantly, squatting next to the bed. She pursed her lips. "See, at ice house twenty days. Come back here, gone half year maybe."

Philippa watched her talk, trying to follow the words, but they had shapes that wouldn't quite fit her thoughts. Bits of some story from a schoolbook niggled at her but even that wouldn't come clear. Something about thunder rumbling in the mountains?

Thunder in her bones was more like it. Fretful, scared, she shifted against the hum that was almost an ache.

Mara slipped a hand beneath Philippa's head. "Drink. Is *kaklotl*—like coffee," she said, lifting her and holding the cup from the tray to her mouth.

Philippa had time to see that the cup was full of thick brown foam before she took a sip. Soft on the tongue; gritty between the teeth. And bitter. Much too bitter, she thought at first, when she was expecting sweet, but she swallowed it down just the same. It was sort of like chewing a piece of the unsweetened chocolate Meemaw had used to buy to bake with, something Philippa had only tried once, and not just because she'd got swatted for it.

But it was no more bitter than coffee. Her mouth felt hot even with the stuff swallowed, though her head cleared some. She took another sip.

"Good," Mara said. "Make you fat." Her smile was getting strained, but she held Philippa up until she'd had all she could handle.

Rip Van Winkle. That was it; a funny-sad story about a ne'er-do-well who got a snootful of dwarf-brewed beer one night, and had woke to find twenty years gone by at home.

Philippa's head sagged back onto the hard, skinny pillow. This was her, a kid from a little town in the Arkansas hills, not some guy in a fairy tale. Yeah, with a ceiling overhead looked like something out of the Arabian Nights. "So a day here might be a week back home?" she ventured, the dread in her throat bitterer than the chocolate drink.

Mara made a rolling motion with her hands. "No! Other way."

Nightmare receded a little. "A week here is a day there," Philippa whispered. She brought up a hand to rub her aching head. A skeleton's hand, the bones of the wrist wrapped round by one of their bracelets.

Mara said yes, and some other things. Philippa let the words flow on past her.

How long did it take to starve so thin? How did you figure time stuck in the between place? Her being gone even a couple of weeks was too long. She'd promised to come back for everybody. Well, Junkyard and Nip, anyway, and the others if she could talk them into it. Like Chick. She didn't want to leave him behind.

Wetness ran down her cheeks to pool in her ears. She sniffled, trying to stop crying but that just seemed to make it worse, and Mara was watching her, looking worried and put out all at the same time. Philippa turned her head away, and gave in to the sobbing.

"Tell," Mara said, rubbing her shoulder in awkward comfort.

"See, I got to go back to get the others and bring 'em here. I promised." She drew a hiccuping breath. "But how'm I gonna find 'em?"

Mara jerked away, her eyes gone cold and her mouth straight as a board. She stood, towering over Philippa. "No! *Nir nev* bring you, OK. You are give to us, and welcome. We teach you and you stay. But we bring no one back."

Philippa shrank back, her insides curling up in the face of Mara's anger. "Sorry," she whispered, the promise she'd made swamped with cold fear. She didn't know any of the rules here, didn't know how to talk, or who this Nir nev might be, or anything at all. And she didn't want Mara mad at her.

Mara took a deep breath. "OK. You could not know. And I am bad to yell."

She would have to learn as quick as ever she could, Philippa told herself, swallowing to get the mingled taste of bile and the bitter drink out of her mouth. And then she'd see what was possible.

"See, I bring corn soup also." Coaxing, Mara bent to hold the bowl where she could see and smell it.

The stuff smelled OK but looked like a soupy grey mush. Philippa shook her head. The ache in her belly might've been hunger, but she couldn't face eating. The kaklotl hadn't quenched her thirst. In fact her mouth still burned a little from it. "Water?"

Mara nodded, reaching across her for another cup Philippa hadn't noticed, one that sat in one of the half-dome wall niches. Seemed like everything here was domes, the ceiling, the arch of the doorframe and the one that held her bed, and now this. And all of it looking like it was made somehow out of bone china—unlike the cups and the bowl, which were thick and painted up bright as Christmas.

"Water always here," Mara said, shifting the cup a little on the shelf. Clear liquid poured out of a little spigot to fill it.

Handy, Philippa thought as a hedge against the sudden prickling that ran down her nerves. She could feel the path the water took through its run of pipes just as plain as if she could see it, a silky flow behind the wall that vanished away once the cup was full and the water shut itself off.

Licking her lips she asked, "How do I work it?"

Mara looked surprised. "Put below the spout. Cup fills."

Philippa held the cup herself this time as she drank, though her hands shook. She sipped the water carefully in case it might be the water that was different instead of her.

Tasted like well water, cold and just a little earthy. When her mouth was clear she nodded.

"Sleep again." Mara gave her hair an affectionate pat as she took the cup away, putting it back off to the side of the spout. She turned away and bustled around tidying things. Philippa traced the twisted patterns of the bracelet on her bony wrist—a cheerful yellow with green snaked through it, not ashy grey like Lukas' burned one was, or black like Simon wore.

Was Simon here too, and those other Wobs from St. Paul? Philippa decided not to ask. She didn't want Simon to come visiting, not after he'd backstabbed them so bad. What she wanted was Chick and the guys. "When do I start this learning?" she asked, grief like a knot in her throat.

Mara turned around, looking pleased with her. "Good! I will arrange."

With the bracelet on—the *iyar pukko*, she reminded herself to call it, the way Simon'd insisted on—she'd heal up quick, and she'd learn as fast as they would teach her. But all of that would take more time. She was miles behind already and the race hardly yet begun. How long would Chick and them wait for her?

When Mara had gone, taking the tray with her and with a funny little bow like somebody in a moving picture, Philippa gathered her strength and nudged the cup over under the spout. She shut her eyes and traced the path of the water through the red-shot darkness behind her eyes all the way back to where the pipe ran down beneath the floor before the flow shut off. And then she reached further, found the constant trickling water that sounded in the space beyond the head of her bed, and followed it back to the same source.

It was all so strange.

About the Author

Texas-born and Southern-bred, Sally Gwylan has made New Mexico her home since high school. Her first professional sale--the novelette on which this story is based--was to **Asimov's Science Fiction.** She now lives in a small handmade house some miles west of Albuquerque. The world being full of a number of wonderful things, she sings, gardens, builds, and studies history when she is not writing.

Made in the USA
Charleston, SC
06 November 2012